sailor

sailor

Tom Epperson

A Tom Doherty Associates Book

New York

I'd like to extend my thanks for their help to Jay Bullock, who taught me about qigong, and to my wife Stefani, who is always there for me.

SAILOR

A Forge Book
Published by Tom Doherty Associates, LLC
175 Fifth Avenue
New York, NY 10010

www.tor-forge.com

Forge® is a registered trademark of Tom Doherty Associates, LLC.

Library of Congress Cataloging-in-Publication Data

Epperson, Tom.
  Sailor / Tom Epperson.—1st ed.
    p. cm.
  "A Tom Doherty Associates book."
  ISBN 978-0-7653-2892-2 (hardcover)
  ISBN 978-1-4299-9860-4 (e-book)
  1. Organized crime—Fiction.   2. Los Angeles (Calif.)—Fiction.   I. Title.
  PS3605.P59S25 2012
  813'.6—dc23   2011047593

First Edition: March 2012

Printed in the United States of America

0 9 8 7 6 5 4 3 2 1

To crows and coyotes, and other survivors

The hand of the Lord was upon me, and carried me out in the spirit of the Lord, and set me down in the midst of the valley, which was full of bones, and caused me to pass by them roundabout: and behold there were very many in the open valley; and lo, they were very dry. And he said to me, Son of man, can these bones live? And I answered, O Lord God, Thou knowest.

Ezekiel 37: 1–3

.

The blood-dimmed tide is loosed.

Yeats, "The Second Coming"

the first week

Tuesday

"You're gonna be rich someday," she said to the sailor.

"You see that in the cards?"

"Yes. I see a glittering treasure."

"What else do you see?"

She stared at the cards. Said nothing.

"Ma'am? What else do you see?"

She was young. Maybe twenty-five. A big nose but otherwise pretty. But then it was like she was turning into an old hag in front of his eyes. And then she became dust and blew away.

He wasn't in the tent anymore. Was outside somewhere in the dark. A storm was coming up. Lightning flashes, thuds of thunder. He felt lonely and scared like a little kid. He was afraid he was about to cry, then he actually did cry. More than just cry. He wept.

He woke. Eyes dry despite the dream. He heard the rhythmic swish of the waves like the boundless breathing of the dreamless sea and then sat up. Gazed out from Point Mugu. Fog shrouded the ocean. Seeming to meld with the gray water. It was dawn. It was chilly. He breathed with the waves slowly and deliberately, in through the nose and out through the mouth. His breath condensing. Adding his breaths to the greater gray.

He got out of his Ultralite sleeping bag and walked off a bit and peed. His pee steaming. He was facing the gigantic mound of Mugu Rock. On the other side was the Pacific Coast Highway and on the other side of the highway another gigantic mound of rock that made the first mound look little. He had passed this way many years ago and been so struck by its sublime and ancient beauty he had vowed to come back some day and spend the night. To sleep in the rocky embrace of Point Mugu and see what dreams it brought him.

He took a bottle of water out of his rucksack and drank and then a box of raisins. On it the pretty Italian gal in the sunbonnet. He remembered her from when he was a kid and now he was grown yet here she still was. An ageless pagan raisin goddess. He walked over to the edge of the cliff and sat down. The beach was about thirty feet below. Configurations of rock rose up to nearly eye level. There was a bridge of rock that looked like it would be fun to walk across.

He opened the box of raisins. A sea bird cried and gyred.

Gray sat there chewing and watched the water.

Deiter the Cheater, under the flapping pennants, amid the blazing windshields, looked across the highway. Buster's was a yellow-brick building with neon beer signs in the window. He could see her moving around inside.

"Thinking about pussy?"

Portly Wesley Beason was walking up.

"How'd you know?"

"You just had that thinking-about-pussy look on your face."

"I'm gonna go get some lunch. Want anything?"

"Pie."

"A whole pie or just a piece?"

"Do I look like I could eat a whole pie? Don't answer that. Just a piece."

"What kind?"

"Any kind. As long as it's banana cream."

Deiter waited for a break in the traffic then walked across the highway. In his Zegna cream and gray-striped suit. He had high cheekbones and dark eyes that harked back to the Indian in him.

He took his usual table next to the window. She brought him over a glass of iced tea and a menu.

"What's good today?"

"The turkey loaf's been popular."

"I'll have that then."

"I wish all my customers were as easy as you."

"I'm just an easygoing guy."

He drank his iced tea and looked out the window at the DEITER "THE CHEATER" CHEATS FOR LESS sign and the big trucks passing on the highway. He sighed at the thought he'd be forty in a month and wondered what life was all about. He perked up when she came back with the turkey loaf.

"I been sitting here trying to figure it out."

"Figure what out?"

"The mystery of you."

She laughed a little. "What mystery?"

"I think there's a damn big mystery. Just showing up here like you been dropped outa the sky."

"I've told you. I came here to make a fresh start. People do it every day. There's nothing mysterious about it."

"But why here?"

"Why not here?"

"So what did you do? Throw a dart at a map of the United States and it landed on Brady, Oklahoma?"

"Maybe. You want some more iced tea?"

"Please."

He watched her tightly blue-jeaned hips sway away across the room. Her black hair falling on her shoulders. She came back with a pitcher and sluiced tea into his glass.

"Bet you get asked out about a dozen times a day."

"Yeah. By *you*."

"I figure we're in the same fix. You left your husband and my wife left me. And both of us are lonely."

"I hear you've had a lot of wives."

"Four. Is that a lot? Listen. Why don't we drive up to Tulsa to-night? Have dinner in a real restaurant."

He was used to getting a quick and definite no but instead she said nothing. He sat up a little straighter in his chair. Getting the feeling he got when he was about to sell a car. *What can I do to make you my customer?* is what he always asked.

"You like seafood?"

"Sure."

"White River Fish Market! Best seafood in the state!"

"It's too late to get a babysitter."

"Bring your boy along. I love kids. I got five or six of 'em myself."

"Nah. I don't think so."

"Come on, Gina. He who hesitates is lost."

Gina smiled. "Okay."

He grinned. "Yeah?"

"But it's a school night. We don't have time to go to Tulsa. Why don't you just come to my place? I'll cook you dinner."

"And I'll eat it."

"Seven all right?"

"You better believe it's all right."

Wesley was sitting behind his desk doing paperwork. He cocked his head and gave Deiter a critical look as he walked in.

"Where's my pie?"

"Oh shit."

"Damn it, Rusty. I was looking forward to that pie."

"I'll go right back over there and get you a piece."

"No. Forget it. I don't want it now."

"Well don't sulk."

"I'll sulk if I want to."

"I got a date."

"Who with?"

"Angelina Jolie. Who do you think? Gina."

"You're shitting me."

"Tonight. Dinner. Her place. Candlelight. Wine. Soft romantic music."

"How come you're the lucky one?"

"She musta heard about my twelve-inch pecker."

She washed her hair with Bumble and Bumble shampoo. Put on some L'Oréal HiP lip gloss and Dior mascara. Plunged into her closet and came out with clothes unworn for years. But Luke was hanging around not looking like he liked it.

"Whatsamatter?"

"Do you have to do this?"

"Do what? I'm just having a friend over for dinner."

"It's a date. I can tell."

"What do you know about dates? You're ten years old for chrissake."

"He's called Deiter the Cheater."

"He sells used cars, it's a joke. Do you think if he really was a cheater he'd call himself the Cheater?"

"I don't know."

"Well he wouldn't." She sat down on the side of her bed and pulled him over. He stood there uncomfortably in her arms. "Look. You and me, we've gone through a lot together. I swear to God it's gonna get better but right now we just have to make the best of it. I want you to be a normal kid as much as you can and for one night I'd just kinda like to feel normal too. Okay, so maybe this is kinda like a date. But he doesn't represent any kind of threat to you and me. Nothing'll ever be as important to me as you. You know that, right?"

Luke nodded. She brushed some hair away from his forehead then gave it a kiss. He turned away. Went to his room to play Halo. His favorite video game.

An autumnal cold front was moving through and the temperature dropped and it began to rain. Gina sipped red wine as she worked in the kitchen and she heard the rain and it made her sad.

Fleetingly she had a sense of being outside herself and looking at her whole life. Seeing simultaneously Gina as a sad young woman and a sad little girl and a sad old lady. All three listening to the eternal rain. The doorbell rang right at seven.

Deiter came in smelling of cologne and bearing wine and flowers and with rain glittering in his hair. Maybe he was a little old for her but he really was nice-looking. Hard to tell what was under a suit but he seemed to have a lean fit body. To go along with a ton of cornball charm.

He was appropriately effusive over her appearance. Luke was summoned and introduced. Deiter gave him a gift: a Harry Potter flashlight.

"Thanks."

"You like Harry Potter?"

"I like the movies. I haven't ever read any of the books."

"Yeah, I'm not much of a reader either. Probably hadn't read a book cover to cover since *Bootlegger's Boy.* And that was twenty years ago."

"What's *Bootlegger's Boy?*" said Gina.

"Barry Switzer wrote it about his life. He was the Oklahoma football coach."

"I didn't say I didn't like to read," said Luke then he turned to his mother. "Could I go back to my room?"

"Okay. But we'll be eating dinner soon."

They watched him leave.

"Well that went over like a lead balloon."

"He liked it. I could tell. He's just shy."

"I can relate."

"You can?"

"Sure. All this blinding self-confidence and charisma you see when you look at me? It's just an act."

"No kidding."

"Nope. Inside I'm just a bashful country boy."

She got him wine and sat him down in front of some smoked mozzarella and toasted bread and went back in the kitchen. The sauce was simmering and the water for the pasta was beginning to boil. The door opened and he came in.

"That sauce smells amazing."

"Thanks."

"Secret family recipe?"

"No, it's just the usual. Garlic, onions, basil, parsley." She started cutting up a tomato for the salad. "Sorry, I'm running late. I meant to have everything ready before you got here."

"Hey I'm not in the least bit of a hurry. So how you liking life at the Osage Creek Apartments?"

"It's okay."

"I lived here once for a brief while. When I was between marriages."

"How come you've been married so many times?"

"Guess I just like getting married."

He set his glass of wine down on the counter and leaned back on it and folded his arms on his chest and crossed his ankles.

"I been thinking. Maybe you oughta cross the highway and sell cars for me."

"You serious?"

"I think you'd be good at it. You're a good talker, you're likeable, you got a good sense of humor. And it's like my mother says—if you want the right man for a job hire a woman."

"Thanks. But I think I'll stick to waitressing."

"That's what you've always done? Waitress?"

"Uh-huh."

"What line of work was your husband in?"

"He was a businessman."

"What kind of business?"

"He had his finger in a lot of different pies."

"Kind of an entrepreneur type?"

"You could say that."

"Peterson's your married name I'll bet."

"Why would you bet that?"

" 'Cause you don't seem like a Peterson."

"What do I seem like?"

"Oh I don't know. Something more—exotic."

She laughed. "Oh yeah, I'm real exotic all right."

"You're exotic to me."

"So how'd you get in the used-car business?"

"Inherited it from my daddy. He was Deiter the Cheater the First."

"You like it?"

"It's okay. Sometimes it gets kinda old."

He walked over to her and put his hands on her waist. She looked over her shoulder and he kissed her.

"You're about the prettiest thing to hit this town in fifty years."

"Who came here fifty years ago?"

"I don't know. Maybe some movie star had a flat tire. On her way back to Hollywood."

The doorbell rang. Gina frowned. "Who could that be?"

"Probably somebody selling something. I'll go run 'em off."

He walked across the living room with the taste of her on his lips and an extra bit of bounce in his step. The doorbell rang again. He opened the door.

The apartment was on the second floor at the top of a flight of stairs. A little winded from the walk up, a massively fat man stood outside under the glare of a yellow light. Twice as fat as Wesley. Dark curly hair wet with rain. Heavy black wool coat with rain on the shoulders. Red sweater and black pants. Hands stuck in the pockets of his coat. Looking about as much like a Buddhist monk as like a salesman.

"What can I do for you?"

"Is Gina here?"

"Who wants to know?"

"I'm Toddo. Her cousin. From back east."

"Oh her cousin!" he said as he opened the screen door and ushered him in. "She didn't tell me you were coming."

The man looked around the room. Deiter grinning at him.

"From back east are you?"

"Yeah."

The man pointed past Deiter looking mildly puzzled. "What's that?"

Deiter looked around. Saw nothing notable. Just a wall with a picture of a fox hunt on it. Horses and hounds and riders in red jackets and white pants. The first bullet didn't kill him or even make him unconscious. He went down like a puppet whose strings had been cut then found himself looking at a bug's-eye view of the carpet. Then the man shot twice more into Deiter's brain.

He looked over and saw the boy standing at the threshold of a hallway.

"Hey Luke. Where's your mom?"

Luke didn't move his head but without even meaning to he cut his eyes toward the kitchen. The man walked toward it. It had a swinging door and he pushed it open with his left hand. His right hand holding the silenced Ruger Mark II .22. A cascading mass of boiling water smacked him in the face. He screamed and fired blindly but not without purpose, his shots spaced regularly across the room. Gina heard the rounds ripping the air, one just to her left and then with a loud clang one hitting the pot and nearly knocking it out of her hands and one about an inch from her right ear. She swung the pot and hit him in the side of the head. He stopped screaming and dropped to his knees, his scalded head steaming. He started to raise the gun and she hit him again harder even than the first time. He dropped the gun and pitched forward and fell on it and didn't move.

She dropped the pot and yelled for Luke and then he was there. A little wisp of a boy. Terror seeming to diminish him even more.

"Are you all right?"

He nodded staring at the man. "Who is that?"

"I got no idea. What happened to Rusty?"

"I think he's dead, Mom."

"Oh god."

The man was breathing heavily as though slumbering deeply. Blood leaked out on the floor through his curly hair. She grabbed the knife off the counter. Prepared to start stabbing him if he stirred.

"Help me."

She wanted to get the gun that was buried under the three or four hundred pounds of Toddo. But moving him was like trying to turn over a water bed. They strained and gasped.

"Mom, what should we do? Should we call 911?"

She saw the white top of a piece of paper sticking out of his coat pocket. She pulled it out and unfolded it. It was a MapQuest print-out giving directions from the Tulsa airport to her apartment. A phone number had been written on it. A number that she recognized.

"Shit!"

"Mom, what's wrong? What is it?'

"We gotta get outa here. Now!"

She looked once at Deiter on the living room floor and didn't look at him again. They had practiced this like a fire drill. Grabbing prepacked suitcases and their laptops. The goal to get out the door in under a minute. They clattered down the flight of stairs and fled into rain and night.

Gray, his rucksack on his back, walked down Alejo Avenue. It was the main drag of the town. There wasn't much to it. Some small businesses like a shoe repair store, a pet supplies store, a Pilates place, a liquor store and bait shop, a grocery store. A Mexican restaurant, an Italian restaurant, a coffee shop, bars named the Prince o' Whales and the Harbor Room. Some two- and three-story apartment buildings. To the south, hills covered with big houses rose up steeply. To the north was a flat expanse of grassy wetlands that had somehow escaped the bulldozers of the developers. Straight ahead the street ended at sand dunes and the sea.

It was only about eight in the evening but already King Beach seemed to be getting ready to pack it in. Just a few other people on the sidewalks and an occasional car passing by. It seemed oddly

untouristy and untrendy for a Southern California beach town. He
heard a rumbling then suddenly a jetliner roared above the hills
angling toward the sky. Taking off from LAX. Seeming nearly close
enough for him to hit it with a rock.

A young guy was walking rapidly toward him talking on a cell
phone. He was wearing a hooded sweatshirt that had KALASHNIKOV
across the front. On his forehead was a tattoo of a swastika with
wings. A dog on a leash was walking beside him. Half malamute
and half god knew what. It was just about the most pitiful dog Gray
had ever seen. Only the ragged remnants of chewed-off-looking
ears. His right eye scarred and sightless. Patchy brown and white
fur stretched too tight over his sturdy frame. Wearing a punishment collar lined with inverted spikes. The guy never looked at
Gray as they passed each other but the dog did. Gray looked over
his shoulder and saw the dog looking back over *his* shoulder.

A big wooden sea horse painted yellow was poised above the
entrance of a blue stucco building. He lingered and looked in. Life
was going on in there. The bar was crowded. A blond waitress carried a towering platter of orange king crab legs to a table. Gray
went in as behind him another jetliner blasted into the sky.

The decor was nets, tridents, seashells, and mounted fish. He sat
down at the bar and ordered a draft beer. An old man next to him
who didn't seem to be able to move his neck turned his whole body
to take a look at him.

"Isn't it amazing?"

"Isn't what amazing?"

"How Sam Snead could never win the Open."

Gray had no idea who Sam Snead was but nodded anyway. He'd
dropped his rucksack on the floor by his stool. The old man looked
down at it.

"Traveling?"

"I guess so."

"To or from?"

"Well that's a good question."

The old man laughed as if Gray had given the only correct

answer to some ancient mystic riddle. He stuck his hand out and Gray shook it.

"I'm Norman."

"Gray."

"It's a sad night, Gray. A very sad night."

"Why?"

"Mr. Jones is dead."

"Sorry to hear that." He slurped up some beery foam. "Who was he?"

"My cat."

"How did he die?"

"Natural causes. Kidney failure. But it was basically old age. He was even older than me in cat years. I've found twenty-seven rubber bands over the last week."

"Where did you find them?"

"Here and there. Mostly just lying on the ground. It's amazing how many rubber bands you see if you're looking for them. So maybe you're wondering why I bother to pick them up?"

"Yes sir. I was wondering that."

"Don't call me sir. Do you know what entropy is?"

"Something to do with physics?"

"That's right. Entropy is the movement of all the matter and energy in the universe from a state of order to a state of disorder. It's like a popsicle dropped on a sidewalk by a careless child on a hot summer day. Pretty soon it's gonna be a sticky little puddle of nothing. The universe is like that popsicle. It's melting and there's not a damn thing we can do about it. It's a process that can't be stopped. *However.* It can be slowed down."

"Is that where picking up rubber bands comes in?"

"My god, Gray. You're way ahead of me. I'll keep picking up rubber bands until I have maybe a couple of thousand. Then I'll donate them to a school or something. The rubber bands will again be performing rubber band functions instead of just being trash on the street. In a small way, for a short while, entropy will be reversed."

"Tell you what, Norman. I'll start keeping my eye out for rubber bands."

"I'll tell *you* what. I'll buy you a drink if you drink to Mr. Jones."

"You got a deal."

The Honda Accord sped west on Interstate 40. Through the empty endless Texas night. Amarillo up ahead. Not that they were going to Amarillo. They were headed west merely because it was the opposite of east. Away from that malignant place out of which had issued the fat man in the red sweater.

Luke had always cried a lot for a boy and had been crying tonight but now was quiet. She glanced over at him. His face was turned away. She couldn't tell if his eyes were open. Maybe he had slipped into the exhausted sleep of the desperate and lost.

The radio station she had been listening to was fading out and she looked for another. But she couldn't seem to find anything but twangy country music and crazy preachers shouting about damnation. So she turned the radio off.

It was quiet except for the monotonous sounds of the car. She felt as isolated as if she and Luke were in some sealed capsule hurtling through the icy darkness of the farthest reaches of the Milky Way.

She looked at the digital clock on the dashboard. It said it was midnight.

Wednesday

Toddo Palmentola thought he was having a bizarre nightmare about cows then realized he wasn't asleep. Six or seven of them were standing around his car. He had never been this close to cows in his life. One was only a couple of feet away. She made a belching noise and swung her head abruptly toward him like she was about to put it right into the window and bite him and in a panic he grabbed his pistol off the passenger seat and jabbed the long silencer at her.

"Get the fuck outa here!"

She plodded off, tail swinging. Green-brown shit tumbling out of her butt. The Ford Taurus was near a tree about twenty feet from a dirt road. As far as he could see in any direction were rolling grassy hills and scattered trees. The sun had just come up and the cows cast stretched-out shadows as they chewed on the glittering grass.

The water bottle was empty but he unscrewed the cap anyway. Lifted it to his lips. A drop or two came out. Then he flung the bottle at another cow that was getting too close. It bounced off her flank but she didn't seem to notice.

He saw a red pickup truck off in the distance. It disappeared in a dip in the road then topped a hill and came down slowly. Splashing through a puddle left by last night's rain. Then it stopped. The cows began walking toward it, their nostrils puffing steam. He saw a man in a baseball cap in the cab. He was looking Toddo's way.

Then he got out. The truck door chunked shut. He was burly, flannel-shirted, work-booted. He came toward Toddo. When he got a better look at him he seemed taken aback by his swollen terrible head. The splashes of drying blood.

"Jesus Christ, mister. What happened to you?"

Toddo croaked through blistered lips: "Accident. Water heater. It blew up."

"Good lord. What are you doing out here?"

"I got lost. I was looking for a hospital. You got any water? I'm dying of fucking thirst."

"I got water in the truck. I'll go get it." He peered past Toddo and saw the gun lying on the seat. Then he looked back at Toddo. "I'll get that water. Be right back."

He walked toward his truck. Glanced back over his shoulder. Toddo didn't like the glance or the way he was walking. He picked the gun up and shot the man twice in the back. He went down near his truck. He didn't move for a moment then lurched up and half crawled half stumbled as Toddo shot repeatedly at him. His cap fell off revealing a bristling flattop and a bullet struck the sole of his boot then he disappeared behind the truck.

"Fuck!" Toddo said.

He hastily ejected the old clip and popped in a new one. He saw the driver's-side door of the truck opening but didn't see the man. He opened the Taurus's door and grunted and wheezed as he pulled and pushed himself up and out. He lumbered over the grass. Stepping right in a ploppy pile of manure. The cows had moved off and were watching from a distance. He kept his eyes on the truck and his gun pointed at it but there was still no sign of the man. He saw reflected in the curving glass of the passenger window a crimson-faced monster approaching with a gun. He looked down through the window and saw the man sprawled on his stomach across the seat pulling a gun out of the glove compartment. A big long-barreled cowboy kind of a gun. Toddo shot through the window just as there was a tremendous *BLAM* and the window disintegrated. A lump of lead broke his clavicle then issued in a spray of blood from the fat and muscle between his neck and shoulder. He staggered backwards and sat down heavily. He cursed and wheezed and pointed his gun at the window waiting for the man to appear. He waited for a full minute then struggled to his feet. He made a wide circle around the truck. The driver's door was open. The work boots hanging out. One leaking blood.

He was still holding the six-shooter. One eye half open in the sly squint of death. Toddo leaned in just in case and put a bullet in his head. The corpse gave a long leisurely burbling fart.

He sat down under the tree, his back against the trunk. It was an oak tree and was half full of leaves. The sun slanted in and bathed him in a beautiful crystalline light. Like he was some holy person who'd been sitting there for quite some time and was about to attain enlightenment.

His cell phone rang. In his car. On the passenger seat. TerHorst probably. But it seemed as likely that the tree would uproot itself and walk over to the car and pick the phone up as that he himself would do that. The phone fell silent.

The cows were drifting back. Gathering around the truck. One looking in through the shattered window.

A leaf spun down out of the tree and landed near one of his shit-covered Gucci loafers. He had never thought much about death but wondered if he was about to die. In this place. In Oklahoma, under a tree. The world began to tilt and Toddo felt a vertiginous swirling. He thought he was a kid and his father had taken him to the Copacabana. Bobby Darin was singing "Mack the Knife." His wife was in the audience. Sandra Dee. Nobody had ever been cuter than Sandra Dee. What a gargantuan crush little Toddo had on her. Gidget. Right there in the flesh. Drinking a martini.

He heard a car and looked up the road and saw a navy-blue SUV. It pulled up behind the truck. It sat there awhile engine idling. Then the engine was switched off and terHorst got out. Holding a nine-millimeter. He took a look in the truck then came toward Toddo. Sunglasses, shaved head, and thick dark moustache. Tan suit and gold ostrich-skin cowboy boots. He put his gun away as he looked down at Toddo. He seemed amused at the situation.

"Man, Toddo, you're a mess."

"Where the fuck you been? Gimme some fucking water."

"That little old gal kicked your ass."

"I'm fucking bleeding to death. You gotta get me to a doctor."

"Okay." He took a Hav-A-Tampa cigar out of his pocket, removed its cellophane wrapper, lit it with a purple plastic lighter. "Did you know that Jesus Christ is coming back to earth again?"

"No."

"Well he is. Who's the fella in the truck?"

"I don't know. The farmer in the fucking dell."

TerHorst laughed. He took a look around. "This is probably his property. Nice spread. So that's not your real name is it?"

"Huh?"

"Toddo. That's not your real name."

He shook his head. The world was tilting this way and that. TerHorst was tilting. Amid luminous billowing clouds of smoke.

"What's your real name?"

"Salvatore."

"You know something? You're the first Salvatore I've ever met."

"Who gives a fuck? Gimme some water. Get me to a doctor."

"The first Toddo too for that matter."

He took the nine-millimeter back out and shot Toddo in the head. Then he went through his pockets. He found twenty-two hundred-dollar bills in his wallet. He tossed the wallet down on his stomach and put the money in his pocket. Then he found the MapQuest printout that had his cell phone number on it.

"Shit."

If he was looking at his number then maybe Gina had looked at it too.

He went to the truck and poked around in the back and found a two-and-a–half-gallon can of gasoline. He doused Toddo with it then held the lighter to his pants cuff. He went up in a satisfying *whump* of blue flame. Thin white smoke rose up through the tree. Dried-out leaves fluttered in the updraft.

He went to his Land Cruiser and got a screwdriver out of the glove compartment. Then he went to the car and took off the license plates. Humming "Help Me, Rhonda" by the Beach Boys as he did so. The cigar clamped between his teeth. Then he stood there staring at the car as he took off his tie. He had seen this done in a movie once and had wanted to do it ever since but didn't know if it would work. He unscrewed the gas cap and stuffed in the tie leaving some of the skinny end hanging out. He lit the tie with his lighter and walked off a ways and smoked his cigar and waited. It worked. A boom and a burning as the cows went galloping off in terror. As the extra ammo in Toddo's pocket began to go off like firecrackers.

He got in the Land Cruiser and tossed the license plates in the back. He turned around and headed back toward the highway. Behind him black smoke boiling up out of the apocalyptic pasture. He'd gone a mile or so when he saw a strange sight: a huge teenage boy pulling a green and yellow John Deere tractor. He was wearing a harness and was hooked up to the tractor with a chain and leaning forward nearly to the point of falling and swinging his thick arms as he dragged the tractor up a slight rising in the road. Now he stood up and took a towel off the tractor. Wiped his face with it as he watched the Land Cruiser come.

TerHorst stopped and lowered his window.

"Howdy!"

"Howdy," the boy said breathing heavily. He was wearing red sweatpants and a gray T-shirt that said BRADY BOBCATS in red letters and he had a brace on his right knee. The shirt was soaked with sweat and steam streamed up off his head.

"I don't mean to ask a stupid question. But how come you're pulling a tractor?"

He gave a bashful smile. "Aw I do this every morning before school. I'm rehabbing my knee."

"What happened to it?"

"Blew out my ACL. Playing basketball last summer. I went up for a rebound and came down wrong."

"You play football?"

"Yes sir. But I'm gonna be out the whole season. My senior year."

"Man, that's tough."

"When it happened I was so disappointed I thought I couldn't hardly stand it. But Daddy told me winners don't give up, they get up. So now I'm getting myself ready to play in college."

"Offensive line?"

"Yes sir."

"So what do you go? About six four? Two eighty?"

The boy smiled again. "That's about exactly right."

"I'm good at that. Guessing heights and weights."

"I'm gonna get up to about three hundred. And I need to get faster too. Before I got hurt I was running a five-three-forty. I wanna get that down to five-two, maybe even five-one-five."

"Sounds like you're a determined young man."

"Daddy says I need to just concentrate on getting a little better every day. He says you chop down a tree by taking one swing at a time."

"Where do you wanna go to college?"

"Well Oklahoma State was real interested before I got hurt. Now they kinda seem to be backing off. But there's a coach at Arkansas that calls me every week."

"My daughter went to Arkansas."

"Did she like it?"

"Loved it. It's a big-time party school. And she loves to party."

"I'm not much into that."

"But they got a great football program. Woo pig sooie, right?"

The boy laughed. Then he looked down the road in the direction terHorst had come from.

"Looks like something's on fire."

TerHorst looked in his outside mirror. Saw the dark smeary cloud of smoke. He took out his gun and as he raised it the boy must have seen it out of the corner of his eye, turning his head and ducking a little. The bullet skipped off his skull. Blood spurting as it took some hair and scalp with it. The boy lunged at terHorst and maybe he would have been able to wrest the gun away and get his big hands around his neck and kill terHorst and save himself and go on to Arkansas and become an All American had not the harness jerked him back. TerHorst shot him in the forehead.

He leaned out the window and took a look. The boy lay there in his harness like some old draft horse that had finally given out. TerHorst shot him several more times. And then drove on.

They had driven till about one a.m. then her head had snapped up and she had found the car half off the road heading into the grassy median. She had taken the next exit and they had checked into a motel. They'd left at seven and now were moving at a steady seventy on the interstate as the sun climbed behind them. As behind them the man was murdered and the boy was shot down.

"Where are we *going*?"

"Quit asking me that."

"But *where*, Mom?"

"Someplace safe."

"I'm hungry," he said a little later. So was she. Dinner last night never having happened. They stopped at a McDonald's. She had an Egg McMuffin, he a Southern Style Chicken Biscuit. She was still wearing the black blouse and black pants she had picked out so carefully for her date. She felt overdressed. For McDonald's. For running away. She poured nondairy creamer in her coffee. She noticed Luke looking out the window at a girl in the parking lot. She was reaching back into her car to get something and her shirt hiked up revealing above her low-slung jeans pink thong underwear and a blue tattoo. Gina wondered if he was getting interested in girls. Hopefully not in that kind of girl.

Her cell phone rang. She took it out of her purse and looked at the caller ID. It was terHorst. She put the phone away. It continuing to ring rather plaintively in her purse.

"Who is it?"

"Nobody. Wrong number."

"How do you know it's the wrong number without answering it?"

She gave him a look. "Eat your biscuit."

In the restroom she sat on the toilet peeing and weeping with her stupid Dolce & Gabbana pants around her knees. The world seemed a wide dangerous wasteland in which she and her son were doomed to wander. She remembered seeing something on TV about a woman who'd been kidnapped by a psychopath and the police had been able to track her down and save her because of signals her cell phone was giving off. She washed her face at the sink. She thought about leaving her phone there. Someone—say the girl in the pink thong underwear—would find it and take it with her and they would be tracking her and not Gina, they might follow her to Mexico or Canada while Gina and Luke made their escape clean as a whistle. But then she thought about what they would probably do to the girl in the pink thong underwear if they ever caught up with her. She took the battery out of her phone and dropped both in the trash.

Half an hour later they left Texas and crossed into New Mexico. Their Honda Accord was green but it was represented on the map on terHorst's computer screen by a blue car with a red circle around it. "Land of Enchantment!" terHorst said. The computer showed the Accord's speed and its latitude and longitude with its position being updated every five seconds. As he watched the little blue car twitching along the interstate he felt a surge of power and let loose with a joyous gust of laughter. It made him think of the scene in *The Shining* where Jack Nicholson looked down on the model of the hedge maze and saw the tee-tiny figures of his wife and son moving in it. Gina and Luke were like little ants and he felt as big as a mountain. They were frantic and futile and he was calm and purposeful. He could just cruise down the highway smoking

Hav-A-Tampas and listening to *The Eagles' Greatest Hits* and would catch up with them before too long. No more than twenty-four hours. They would be stopping to sleep at some point and he certainly wouldn't.

His cell rang. It was McGrath. In Oklahoma City. His best friend and boss.

"You heard about what's going on in Brady?" said McGrath.

"I sure have."

"You think they got her? And the kid?"

"Nope. They would've just killed her, not kidnapped her. I think she's flown the coop."

"But she hasn't called you?"

"No."

"Why not?"

"She's probably just scared. Doesn't know who to trust anymore. Can you blame her?"

"Jesus Christ, Frank. This has never happened before. We've never lost anybody."

"And we still haven't. I'll find her."

"I can't figure out what the hell happened. There's a dead used-car dealer in the living room and signs of a struggle in the kitchen and now I just heard three more bodies have turned up outside of town."

"Who are they?"

"A farmer and his son and another body they haven't ID'd yet. Somebody set it on fire. And set fire to a car. It's nuts."

"How do you know they're connected to the one in town?"

"I don't. But Brady ain't Detroit. People aren't ordinarily being killed there left and right."

"You talk to anybody down there yet? The chief of police? The sheriff?"

"No, I wanted to talk to you first."

"You know, nobody knows about her except us."

"Well sure. Exactly. That's why they need to know who and what they're dealing with."

"What for? I'm on top of it. I'll deal with it."

"Frank, it wouldn't be right not to tell 'em—"

"You think it'd be right if we got fucking fired over this? It was our job to protect her and we didn't."

A silence on the other end and then: "Where are you?"

"On the 44. Headed west. Her and I have gotten pretty close. I know how she thinks. I think I know where she might be going."

"I don't know how long I can keep a lid on it."

"Just give me a few days. I'll find her and we'll relocate her and the boy. Everything'll be hunky-dory again in no time."

"How do you think they found her?"

"Who knows? Maybe Luke called his granddad to wish him happy birthday."

More silence from McGrath. TerHorst watched the little blue car give a twitch forward. They'd be passing soon through Tucumcari. *Tucumcari.* That was in some song. By the Eagles?

"What about all those dead people in Brady?" McGrath finally said.

"Let the dead bury the dead."

He drifted up out of some abyssal depth. Opening his eyes to a pastel-y room filled with sunlight. For a moment he didn't know where he was then it came to him: the Sea Breeze Motel.

He got up and shaved and showered and toweled himself dry and the bathroom shook a little as a plane took off. He came out and, still naked, faced the window and began a standing meditation. He imagined a golden ball in his lower abdomen filling up each time he took a breath. He was seeking that place inside himself where there was no Gray but Gray was ubiquitous. Gray was around every corner and was following him when he looked around and another plane departed and Gray was dancing on its wings and he gave up and got dressed and went out.

A housekeeping cart was standing near the open door of the next room. A small nut-brown woman appeared. She smiled at him.

Her face plain but the smile lovely. Even with a tooth or two missing.

"Good morning," he said.

"Good morning."

"Es un lindo dia, no es cierto?"

"Si, muy lindo. Quiere que le limpie el cuarto?"

"No se preocupe. Todavia esta limpio."

"Okay."

"Es Guatemalteco?"

"Si, como lo supo?"

"Reconoci su acento."

The motel was at the west end of town just short of the dunes. It was light blue and light pink and pleasantly shabby. The dunes blocked off any view of the sea. It didn't seem like very many people were staying there. A black crow and a white gull faced off over a cellophane bag that still had a few potato chips in it. In search of breakfast he walked toward the ascending sun.

They drove through the piney mountains around Flagstaff but didn't see them: she because she was looking only at her past and future, he because he was engrossed in a handheld video game. But after a while he said: "It's not fair."

"What?"

"We keep moving. I can't make friends."

"I know, it sucks. You think I like it?"

"But it's different for you. You get to decide what to do and I just get dragged along."

"It's called being a kid. Get used to it."

"But none of this is my fault."

"You saying it's *my* fault?"

"Well if you hadn't married him then none of this would be happening."

"Okay. But if I hadn't married him then *you* wouldn't even be here."

"What's so great about being here if things are gonna be horrible all the time?"

"Things aren't always horrible. Today's horrible. But tomorrow might be great."

Not bothering to respond to that he went back to his video game.

TerHorst had gotten laid once in Flagstaff. By the bartender at the bar in the motel he was staying at. Mexican gal. Couldn't remember her name. Skinny but with big tits and a bushy bush. Exactly like he liked them. That had been over twenty years ago. She was probably some fat Mexican mama now. Depressing what life did to people.

His cell rang. It was Pat the Cat from Staten Island.

"Where is she?"

"A little west of Flagstaff."

"And you're . . . ?"

"A little east of Albuquerque."

A dog began to bark in Staten Island. "Shut up, Smitty!" ter-Horst heard.

"So when you sending a replacement out for Toddo?"

"I'm working on it."

"Poor Toddo. He was quite a guy. And such a sense of humor. He'll be missed."

"That schmuck. He couldn't've fucked up things any worse if he'd tried."

"There's something we need to talk about."

"What?"

"My deal."

"What about it?"

"We need to renegotiate. I'm having to do a lot more work than I thought I would."

"You're getting too much already."

"Let me put it this way. I'm your only link to Gina and Luke. I've got you over a barrel. It's my way or adios."

"Fuck you. You cocksucker."

"Okay. So long."

He hit the off button. Puffed on his Hav-A-Tampa. The cell rang again.

"Hello."

"You're forgetting who you're dealing with."

"Now that couldn't be further from the truth. I have the greatest respect for you, Mr. Cicala. You're a legend in your own time. A role model for young scumbags everywhere."

"What do you want?"

"The mortgage payment. The whole thing."

"I'll give you half."

"Okeydoke. Talk to you soon."

Half an hour later he saw there was a problem. The blue car had ceased to move but the computer showed it to still be traveling sixty-nine miles an hour. It stayed stuck for several minutes then abruptly the car vanished along with the whole map. This text came up: APPLICATION MOBILETRACKER IS NOT RESPONDING. PROCESS TERMINATED.

He had found out about the SpyTown MobileTracker on the Internet. Now after cussing for a good twenty seconds he called up tech support. A cheerful fellow with a thick foreign accent answered. He claimed his name was Ted. Ted told him it was possible that solar flares were to blame but ninety percent of performance problems and operational outages were caused by faulty installation. Usually an improper placement of the GPS antennas.

"Okay, Ted. So what do we do?"

"Why don't you simply check the antennas to see if you installed them properly?"

"Tell me something."

"Yes sir?"

"How am I supposed to check the antennas to see if they're installed properly if I can't find the fucking car because the antennas probably weren't installed properly?"

"Hm. I see what you're saying. But there's another possibility."

"I'm all ears."

"The power supply could have been detached by another party."

"So somebody figures out it's there and pulls the plug."

"Precisely."

"Well thanks a lot. You've been a big help. And I'm saying that in all insincerity."

Ted sounded pleased.

"You're quite welcome, sir."

He didn't want to contemplate the consequences if it didn't start to work again. He resisted the impulse to give his computer a good whack. He started to drive faster as though that would do any good. Indigestion began to burn in his chest and he pulled off at the next gas station and filled up and bought some Tums. Paying for it all with one of Toddo's hundred-dollar bills. He crunched up several tablets as he cruised west and then it was back! The little blue car ticking along I-40. Nearing Ash Fork, Arizona. He sighed and said: "Hallelujah."

They crossed the Colorado River into California. The sun was close to setting and she had to lower her visor against it. Needlelike peaks shined to the north.

They plunged into the Mojave Desert and the night. He fell asleep. His mouth was open and he was breathing heavily. Like there was a shortage of oxygen in the car. She looked at the pairs of red lights she was following and the approaching pairs of white lights on the other side of the interstate and felt a part of some giant system of coming and going she didn't understand. It was hard to believe there were actual people in any of those cars. Even in this car. The Honda Accord. More like two weary phantoms at the point of fading from life altogether.

Luke raised up and looked around in a panicked way.

"Why can't we stop? Why are we still going? Where are we going?"

He had sat on the dunes and watched the sun go down and night envelop the world. He was used to being alone for long stretches but tonight for some reason he felt the need to be in the company of people.

He went to the Sea Horse. He was hungry and took a table and looked at the menu. There wasn't much on it he could eat. He finally settled on a Mediterranean salad.

It wasn't as crowded as it had been last night. He ate and ordered a second beer but drank only about half of it. The waitress tried to flirt. Her name was January and she was a pretty blonde but he didn't flirt back. He was feeling oddly out of sorts. He hardly ever got sick but wondered if he was getting sick now. He kept an eye on the bar. Looking for the old man. Norman. But he never showed up.

He paid and left. Walked back toward the motel.

He saw a rubber band on the sidewalk. Bent down and picked it up and put it in his pocket.

They checked into a motel on the outskirts of Barstow. A Burger King was in walking distance and they ate silently and went back to the motel and Luke went straight to bed but Gina showered. Luxuriating in the spray of hot water against her flesh. Imagining it dissolving her. Turning her into steam. When she came out of the bathroom all she could see of him was his dark hair against the pillow. She took a semi-auto pistol out of her purse. A Glock. Got into her bed and slipped it under her pillow and turned on the TV and turned off the light. She flipped through the channels. She settled on a reality show about a bunch of pretty young city girls vying for the affection of a hunky young farmer in Missouri. They wore tight little shorts and had spirited competitions where they shucked corn and shoveled manure and chased chickens and put them in cages so they could be taken to market as the handsome young farmer looked on. Trying to judge which of the city girls would make the best wife.

TerHorst was still worried about the MobileTracker. It had gone on the blink a couple of more times. But it was working now. The little blue car had remained motionless for an hour and a half. They must have stopped for the night. Which meant he would catch them in about four hours.

He turned on the radio and listened to a preacher named the Reverend Billy. Reverend Billy said he was broadcasting from a trailer in the middle of the desert and the End of Days was nigh and there were only sixty-six people in the whole world that weren't going to hell and he was one of them. He said certain animals would also be raptured into heaven including his dog Mike. He said hundreds of angels were swarming around his trailer tonight and he could hear the muffled beating of their wrathful wings and then a dog began to howl and he said that was Mike howling because he was terrified of the angels.

TerHorst was disappointed when the Reverend Billy's signal evaporated into the ether. He believed in hell and heaven and wondered if he might be one of the sixty-six. He thought about Gina. Pictured her lying in bed in whatever motel she was at. Her boobs loose under a camisole. Her tiny panties. He had always wanted to nail her and now was his last chance.

His cell rang. It was Cicala again. He let his voice mail pick it up.

He'd had a lot of time to think as he'd driven hour after hour and a plan had begun to open up like some beautiful blossom. He wouldn't wait for Cicala to send someone else. He'd take care of Gina himself. Luke too. Cicala wanted Luke back but that was just tough. Gina hadn't called him or answered any of his calls which must mean she'd figured out it was he that had led Toddo to her and Luke. And he had to assume Luke knew what she knew, therefore he couldn't let either live. And why take half the diamonds when he could take them all? Cicala would be pissed and might authorize a hit but they'd have to find him first.

He winced a little and rubbed his chest. The Tums didn't seem to have helped his heartburn much.

The sailor wandered along the shore of a vast lake. It was night and a big moon was out. There were stands of reeds in the shallows and they were all dry and dead and rattled like bones as a breeze blew through them. And the shore was covered with fish bones that gave off a ghostly phosphorescent glow. That crunched under his feet. He understood the lake was utterly dead. Not a minnow or a tadpole or a dab of algae existed in it. He also understood he had to cross the lake because behind him in the desert someone was looking for him. Someone he was helpless against.

He walked out through the rattling reeds. The bottom was mucky and sucked at his feet and the water was as warm as blood. A sheet of moonlight lay on the lake and he sloshed through it. The water up to his knees and then his thighs. Then the light began to dim. The moon was disappearing. An eclipse was eating it up. Then the water was up to his shoulders and the last curved sliver of the moon was gone and his feet weren't touching the bottom anymore. He was treading water and looked around and couldn't see a thing. Lake, sky, and desert having merged into a single overwhelming darkness.

In the shabby motel at the edge of the sea, his eyeballs jerking furiously under the lids, Gray dreamed.

Thursday

Gina awoke. Her heart beating fast. She had had a bad dream. They had found her and Luke. They had burst through the door. They were holding guns that were flashing and banging—

She looked over and saw Luke in the next bed asleep then found under her pillow the cool hardness of the Glock.

She turned on the lamp and got out of bed and shook his shoulder.

"Luke! Wake up!"

He could barely get his eyes open. Looking up at her as at a tormenter.

"What's the matter?"

"Get up. Get dressed. We're leaving."

He looked at the clock on the night table.

"Mom—it's the middle of the night—"

"Come on!"

When he glanced at the map and saw the little blue car was moving again he wasn't really surprised. He'd chased a lot of people in his life and they would often behave erratically. Which didn't necessarily mean irrationally. If you were unpredictable you were harder to catch.

He was only a few miles behind now. If they had been on a perfectly flat and straight road with no other cars in between he'd be able to see their taillights. He flew past the motel they had slept at and the Burger King they had eaten at. When he caught up with them he would hang back and wait. Smoke a cigar and watch. Next time they pulled off he would be right behind them. By the time they saw him it would be too late. As if he were some big jungle predator. On noiseless paws. But he hoped it would all come down soon because he was getting very tired and felt like hell. Nauseous. Food poisoning maybe. That taco plate in Winslow.

And then the map and blue car froze again. Flickered and disappeared. APPLICATION MOBILETRACKER IS NOT RESPONDING. PROCESS TERMINATED. He hollered and laid on the horn for about ten seconds. Presumably MobileTracker would return but in case it didn't he needed to get a visual on them fast. He pushed the gas.

Luke sat for a while in mute misery as the lights of Barstow slipped away. Then he looked at his mother.

"I have to go to the bathroom."

"Oh Luke. Why didn't you go before we left?"

He winced. Put his hands on his stomach. "It's bad, Mom."

"Okay. Hold on."

Soon she saw a gas station lit up in the cold dark. Turned on her blinker and glided off I-15. Two minutes later the Land Cruiser zoomed past. He was going nearly a hundred now. He weaved in and out of what traffic there was. He thought he saw the Honda once but it turned out an old man was driving. As he came up even with his car the old man looked over at him. TerHorst was not one to let his imagination run away with him but it was like he was being looked at by the Grim Reaper. A skull with eyeballs in it.

Cop lights flashed in his rearview. He cussed and hit his blinker and moved into the right lane and began to brake and eased onto the shoulder. The California Highway Patrol car behind him all the way.

He lowered his window as the patrolman walked up. Shined his flashlight at him.

"Could I see your driver's license and registration, sir?"

TerHorst showed him his ID and badge. "On the job."

He was young and handsome with smooth olive skin. His name was Martinez.

"Shit. Sorry about that, marshal. Did I screw things up for you?"

He shrugged. "It's okay. You're on the job too."

Sweat gleamed and trickled on his face and his breaths came quick and shallow. He couldn't believe that this was happening to him.

"You okay, sir?" said Martinez.

"Mind if I get out?"

"No. Of course not."

He pushed the door open and took a few stumbling steps toward the back of his SUV then bent over and puked in the flashing blue and red lights. Cars whipped by and he was buffeted by their windy wakes. He stood up and wiped his mouth with the back of his hand.

"Is there anything I can do for you?" Martinez said but he didn't answer. He was looking at a cluster of trucks. As they thundered by he saw in the middle of them the green Honda. Luke was looking him right in the eye. Though terHorst was in the process of having another heart attack he couldn't help but laugh.

"Mom, Mom, that was Frank!" said Luke twisting around and looking back at the dwindling red and blue lights.

She was holding on tensely to the steering wheel. Concentrating on her driving. She'd gotten trapped somehow among these roaring snorting trucks and was trying to extricate herself.

"What?"

"Frank! Marshal Frank! He's back there, Mom! He was pulled over by the cops!"

She looked in her rearview but couldn't see anything.

"It couldn't be Frank. What would he be doing here? In California?"

"It *was* him, Mom."

"What did he look like?"

"He was bald, he had a moustache. He looked like Frank!"

"Lots of bald-headed guys with moustaches in the world. So how you feeling?"

"Better I guess." Sullen. Seeing he wasn't going to be believed. She reached over and pushed his hair away from his eyes.

"You need a haircut."

"No I don't."

She stroked his hair. His precious hair. Nothing else could be loved so much as every last atom of him.

"Go to sleep. It'll be morning soon. Things'll be better. You'll see."

They hit LA about an hour before sunrise. They had a lot of company on the 10 from commuters coming in from the desert. They passed near the tall buildings of downtown but comparing them to New York were unimpressed. They followed the Santa Monica Freeway all the way to the end. Went through a curving tunnel and found themselves on the Pacific Coast Highway. The ocean glowed dimly in the dawn. Soon Luke fell back asleep and she was alone with her thoughts. Up to now she had had no plan. Except to run in a hell-bent way for her and Luke's lives. If there had been a bridge extending west over the ocean to Hawaii she'd probably have been on it. But it was as if the change of direction had broken the momentum of flight. Heading up the coast of California she wondered what she ought to do. She didn't know much about geography but knew Washington and Oregon were up there and then Canada and Alaska. San Francisco was up there. She'd always wanted to go to San Francisco. Or they could hole up here in Los Angeles for a while. Hide themselves away in the huge city. She saw a sign that said Sunset Boulevard and on a whim turned right and left the coast.

Luke woke up to palm trees and big houses.

"Where are we?"

"Beverly Hills. Where the movie stars live! Maybe we'll see one. Jogging or something."

But none were seen and they continued east. They entered Hollywood and parked on Hollywood Boulevard and walked around. Like they were just a couple of tourists from a land called Hell. He complained he recognized hardly any of the names written in cement in front of the Chinese Theater or who had stars on the pink and black Walk of Fame but then she pointed out Godzilla's star and he agreed that was cool. Nothing was open yet but quite a few people were about. An old black man who looked either asleep or dead was slumped in a wheelchair holding an empty Styrofoam cup. A jowly white man walked a pit bull that had a flabby tumorous growth hanging off its shoulder. A cluster of people stood in the cold waiting for a bus. As Gina and Luke waited on a corner for a light to change they saw a demented-looking man hobbling toward them. His clothes filthy. His hair and beard so long and unkempt his head looked like a big ball of hair with eyes and nose and mouth barely visible in it. He was looking at her and muttering to himself. She was prepared to go in her purse for the Glock but then the light changed and they crossed the street. She looked back and saw he wasn't following but was staring after her. His mouth in his tangled beard opening and closing like a fish's.

"Look, Mom, McDonald's!" said Luke with the enthusiasm of a kid in a TV commercial. It was a relief to move out of the cold grungy morning into the restaurant's light and warmth. It had just opened and they were among the first customers. He got the Deluxe Breakfast and she the Hotcakes with Sausages. Photographs of movie stars hung on the walls and they sat down in a booth near the front under the photo of Leonardo DiCaprio. Luke was facing the street and seemed to be looking at something and she looked around and saw the deranged man lurching past the window at high speed as though running from or in pursuit of someone.

"I hate it here," said Luke. "I wanna go home."

"Right now I'm your home. And you're mine."

"What are we going to do?"

"Just let me worry about that."

"But you don't ever tell me what you're doing."

"I'm doing the same thing now I've been doing for years. I'm just trying to keep us both alive."

"Maybe we need help, Mom. Maybe we should tell someone."

"Like who?"

"The FBI?"

"Tell the fucking feds? Who do you think's after us, Luke? Them and our own fucking family!"

He was silent. Eating a piece of bacon.

"Look. We'll just take it a day at a time. Live off the grid. No cell phones, no credit cards. No way for anyone to track us down. We'll use cash for everything. We got plenty of cash."

"And diamonds."

"What?"

He drank some orange juice.

"Luke?"

"You think I don't know things 'cause I'm a kid. But I know a lot. And I know about the diamonds."

"Okay, so I got diamonds. We're lucky I got diamonds. Any time we need the money I can sell one off. We can go on for a long time 'cause of the diamonds."

"Where'd you get them?"

"Your father. He gave them to me."

"And where did he get them?"

"I guess he bought them."

"He stole them."

"Okay, so he stole them. He's a criminal. That's what he does."

"But you shouldn't keep them, Mom. You should give them back."

"Give them back? To who? They don't have *names* on them. I got no idea where they came from."

"But if you keep them aren't you a criminal too?"

She felt her face get hot. She threw her plastic fork down on her pancakes.

"Everything I do's for you! It's all for you, Luke! And now you're calling me a *criminal*? You're acting like you're too good to sit at the table with your own *mother*? Where do you think our cash came from? You think I earned it being a waitress at that crummy joint? It came from *him*, Luke. The criminal. He's paying for your breakfast. He's paying for your clothes. And if you can't live with that you oughta quit eating right this fucking second and take off all your clothes and walk out that door naked! Live on the street! With the crazy guy! I'm sure he'd love the company!"

He had tears in his eyes and was frightened, and feeling like she was falling into a bottomless canyon of remorse she got up and went around the table and sat down and put her arms around him.

"I'm sorry, honey! Oh I'm sorry!"

She held his head to her chest.

"Everything'll be okay, baby. Don't you worry."

She heard him sniffling and felt tears wetting her shirt. She was looking out the window. Across the street a motorcycle cop had pulled a guy over and was standing by the car looking at his driver's license. Behind the car the lights on the motorcycle flashing blue and red.

Gray walked through Gordon's Market carrying a plastic basket. Into which he put a loaf of whole wheat bread, cheddar cheese, toothpaste, two tomatoes, five bananas, a purple onion, and a quart of skim milk. When he came out he saw a car with a flat tire. Its trunk open. A young woman and a skinny boy puzzling over an instruction manual.

"Need some help?"

Gina looked at Gray.

"No thanks."

But Luke seemed exasperated. "Mom—"

"I used to work in a gas station," said Gray. "I've changed about a million tires. I can do it for you in a jiffy."

"Come on, Mom. He can do it in a jiffy."

She looked him over. A mild-looking young man in a black wool cap holding a bag of groceries.

"Okay. Thanks."

Gray set down his bag and went to work. He noted the license plate.

"Oklahoma huh?"

"Yeah."

"Out here visiting?"

"Uh-huh."

He felt a tense vibe coming off them. They watched in silence as he loosened the lugs and jacked up the car.

"Mom? Can I go get a Coke?"

"Okay. Get me one too. And come straight back."

"You want a Coke?" he said shyly to Gray.

"No, I'm good, thanks."

Luke started into the store but then looked back as an American Airlines jet exploded out of the hills. His eyes got wide.

"Pretty cool huh?" Gray shouted over the roar.

"Yeah!"

He watched the plane wing out over the ocean then he went in Gordon's. Gray twirled off the lugs with the wheel brace. Dropping them in the wheel cover. Another plane took off.

"Geez!" shouted Gina. "What a place for a town! How do people stand it?"

"You get used to it I guess. It's actually a real nice place. Kind of calm and peaceful. Except for the planes."

"Do you live here?"

"Nope. Just visiting. Like you."

They heard a honk. A red '65 Chrysler 300 convertible had pulled up. The driver wearing a baseball cap that said OLD DUDE.

"How are you, Gray?"

"Hey Norman."

He turned his shoulders and stiff neck toward them and gave Gina the once-over. "Aren't you going to introduce me to your friend?"

"I would if I knew her name."

"Gina."

"Gina. What a wonderful name. I'm Norman."

"Nice to meet you, Norman."

"Do you believe in love at first sight?"

"No."

"Me neither. Long way from Oklahoma."

"Yeah."

"Well see you later."

He cruised off in his Chrysler down Alejo Avenue. On the back bumper an aging RON PAUL FOR PRESIDENT sticker.

Gray put on the spare and hand-tightened the lugs. Luke came out with two Cokes and a package of Ritz Bits Peanut Butter Chocolately Blast crackers.

"You're not eating those," said Gina.

"Why not? I'm hungry."

"We've been eating too much junk. We need a decent meal," and then to Gray: "Any good places to eat around here?"

"The Sea Horse if you like seafood. I've heard Domenico's is good if you like Italian."

She and Luke drank their Cokes as they watched Gray finish up and snap the wheel cover back on.

"You *are* a good tire changer," she said.

"Glad I'm good at something."

He put the flat and jack and brace in the trunk and shut it. When he turned around she was digging in her big purse and then she thrust a twenty at him.

"Thanks for the help."

"No, I don't want that."

"Please, take it—"

"Mom," Luke said looking mortified, "he doesn't *want* it. He did it just because he's nice."

She put the twenty away. "I didn't mean to offend you."

"You didn't."

"Where I come from everyone always expects to be tipped for everything."

"In Oklahoma, you mean?"

She looked at him but didn't say anything. Another plane blasted off.

"You need to get the flat fixed soon. That's just a temporary tire."

She nodded.

"Where's the Italian place?"

He pointed over their shoulders. "Just down the street. See it?"

"Yeah. Well. Thanks again."

"Sure. Have a nice visit."

"Come on, Luke."

"Bye, Luke."

"Bye."

He picked up his bag. Watched the boy and woman walking away. Then he went in the other direction toward the motel.

His room had a little fridge for the milk and cheese. He made himself a sandwich and as he ate it and drank a glass of milk he wondered what would have happened if he had offered to buy them lunch. The woman would have said no and the boy would have said, "Oh come on, Mom." Maybe the boy would have won. In which case he'd be sitting now at Domenico's gazing across the table at her beautiful face instead of having this lonesome lunch in his room. Ah well. The road not taken.

He took a tattered paperback out of his ruck and flopped on the bed. The book was *Journey to the West*. A Chinese novel from the sixteenth century. It was about the Monkey King and his epic journey to India in search of a Buddhist holy book. The Monkey King had been born out of a rock. He was mischievous and rebellious. He was a great fighter who was in constant conflict with various gods and demons. He could cover 180,000 miles in a single somersault. He had mastered the seventy-two transformations and could turn himself into anything he wished: a man, a bird, a tree, a horse, a pebble, a bug.

Gray read for a while then dozed off. He dreamed his bed floated right out of the motel then floated west out over the ocean then he woke up. An hour had passed. He went in the bathroom and splashed water on his face. He decided to take a run on the bike path on the beach. He put on shorts and sneaks and went out.

The green Honda from Oklahoma was parked in front of a room three doors down from his. He looked at the room as he walked by. The curtains were pulled shut. He wondered what their story was. He remembered his impression of them as they had stood on the sidewalk in front of the market. They might as well both have been holding up big signs that said: We're in some kind of trouble.

It was nearly night. He watched the lights of the cars on the Verrazano Bridge. Watched Brooklyn begin to glitter on the other side of New York Bay.

Smitty whimpered. He didn't like the cold.

"We'll go in soon, boy."

But not yet. Because he liked to stand in the cold on his balcony and see the night come on. Sipping scotch. Pat the Cat. Atop of Todt Hill.

"Mr. Cicala?"

It was Latreece. His wife's nurse. From Jamaica. About five feet tall and three feet wide. Her skin so black he could hardly see her.

"Yeah? What is it?"

"Your wife?"

"What about her?"

"She be asking for you, sir."

"How the hell is that possible?"

"With her eyes. She be asking with her eyes."

As he came in her room he saw she was smiling at him. But she was always smiling. The right corner of her mouth sagging a little along with the whole rest of her right side. Half her brain had been turned to mush by a hemorrhagic stroke. He walked up to her wheelchair and took her left hand and patted it.

"How you doing, baby?"

He got a warm look from her hazel eyes. But everyone and -thing got that same look: Latreece and the maid and birds in the garden and obnoxious TV commercials and her own withered reflection in the mirror and even Smitty whom she had disliked intensely for his uncouth ways before the stroke.

"Latreece said you wanted me."

It would have been nice if she had squeezed his hand in response but she never did anything like that. Just the smile and look. Which in some ways was an improvement. She had not been handling old age well. She had possessed beauty in her day and couldn't accept its loss. She had turned into an ill-tempered and bitter old bitch who hardly ever smiled at or looked sweetly upon him. But he missed talking to her. You weren't supposed to talk about business with your wife but it was the biggest secret of his life that he had talked about it with her all the time. She had been cunning, shrewd, and ruthless. She had understood people at a glance. She had said: Trust this one. Send that one away. As a test of loyalty have that one cut this one's throat.

The doctors told him research was showing the brain was very plastic and one part was capable of taking over for another and he should just keep talking to her like she was the old Millie Cicala.

"TerHorst. That cocksucker. He won't call me back. I don't know what the fuck's going on. Maybe something's gone wrong. Maybe he's trying to fuck me."

Millie smiled at him.

"That guy we sent. Palmentola. He's dead. Did I tell you already? I can't remember shit anymore. I think he did it. TerHorst. Easier killing him than taking care of the fat bastard. There's nothing worse than a dirty cop. Don't get me wrong. They're a necessary evil. I don't know where I'd be without 'em. But they're the scum of the earth. Loyal to nothing but their own scumbag selves. But as soon as we get Luke back he's a dead man. He wants diamonds? I'll stuff 'em down his fucking throat. I'll choke him to death with diamonds."

Millie smiled at Smitty who had shuffled in with Pat.

"You were right about that cunt. She had everybody fooled. But not you."

Millie had hated Gina for the reasons everyone else had loved her: her looks and her laugh and her generosity and her sparkle. He kissed her on the forehead and accompanied by Smitty went down the wide staircase. Made with marble imported from Italy. He called up Bobby Lamonica and told him to make arrangements for the two of them to go to Lewisburg tomorrow. Then he walked through the cavernous kitchen. Smitty's claws clicked on the marble floor. He tapped on the door of the maid's room.

She was twenty-six. From Venezuela. A heart-shaped face and huge dark eyes. Like the eyes of some creature that lived in the trees of a jungle and came out only at night. Looked up at the moon through the black branches and waited for its prey to pass.

"What you want, Mr. Pat?"

"You know what I want."

She smiled and opened the door wider. He went in. She closed the door softly. Smitty stared at it a moment then plopped down in front of it. He was an English bulldog with bad digestion and a brindled coat. A gift to Pat from Joey and Gina. Soon he was asleep. Snoring as loudly as a man.

She Googled: "murder in brady oklahoma." Watched a bunch of articles in the Oklahoma press pop up about the killing of Rusty Deiter in her living room and about three more homicides outside of town: Ricky Vickers, a forty-three-year-old farmer, his seventeen-year-old son Eric and an unidentified man who'd been set on fire. Sheriff John Marr said he couldn't remember so many killings in Creek County in a single day and he didn't know yet if the one in town had anything to do with the ones on the Vickers farm. He described the unidentified victim as "extremely obese" and she knew it was the man who had come to kill her and wondered how he had ever wound up on fire in a cow pasture. She read about how she and Luke had disappeared in a mystifying way along with their car and were being looked for all over the state. "We don't know if they've been kidnapped or they're victims or witnesses or what," said Brady Police Chief William "Big Bill" Holder. "We just know we're really concerned about their safety." Chief Holder went on to say that Mrs. Peterson and her son hadn't lived in Brady long and not much was known about them. "She was a waitress over at Buster's and was well liked by the customers and her fellow employees. But evidently she kind of kept to herself." When asked if she was a suspect in the killing of the used-car dealer the chief replied: "Let's just say she's a person of interest. The investigation is wide open."

She became aware that Luke had come up behind her and was reading over her shoulder.

"Extremely obese, Mom. I'll bet they're talking about that guy!"

"Probably."

"They set him on fire. They burned him up!"

Then he read some more.

"Mom, what does it mean that you're a person of interest?"

"It means they think I killed him."

"But that fat guy did it. I saw him do it."

"I know. You poor baby."

"We gotta tell 'em the truth. See, there's a number. For the police department. We should call it."

"No."

"Why not?"

"Just 'cause you're innocent doesn't mean they're not gonna put you in prison."

"But I'll tell them what I saw. They'll believe me."

"Oh honey, you're just a kid. They're gonna think you're lying to protect me. And even if they did believe you that still doesn't solve our problem. Your father and your grandfather. That's our problem."

"But we can't hide from them forever."

"But we have to. We have to hide from them forever."

She got up and went to the window and pulled back the curtains and looked out. As if the Cicalas or their minions might be approaching their motel room at this very moment. Fog was moving in from the ocean. Tumbling over the dunes into the parking lot. She watched the fog and was filled with horror at the thought of all the death in Brady. Its citizens being murdered because of her brief presence in the town. Like she was a thing that was not itself evil but that created conditions in which evil might flourish.

"You know the best thing I ever ate?" said Norman.

"What?"

"Kringle."

"What the hell's kringle?"

"A Danish pastry. I had it in Racine, Wisconsin. A blueberry kringle. Mm-mm. It's been fifty years but I can still taste it."

Gray and Norman were sitting at the bar at the Sea Horse sharing a basket of fried mozzarella balls.

"What's the best thing *you* ever ate?"

Gray didn't answer. He was looking toward the front entrance. Norman moved his whole torso and looked that way.

"Oh. Her again."

Gina and Luke were standing there waiting to be seated. Now January greeted them and led them to a booth.

"My god," Norman said. "Is she pretty."

January handed them menus.

"Would you like something to drink?"

"A Coke," said Luke. "Lots of ice."

"A vodka tonic," said Gina. "Lots of vodka."

January laughed. "Okay."

They perused the menus.

"What looks good, Luke?"

"I want . . . the Pirateburger."

"All that is is a hamburger. This is a seafood place. Don't you want some seafood?"

"No."

January came back with the Coke and the cocktail.

"Those two gentlemen at the bar?"

Gina looked. Saw Gray and Norman.

"Your drinks are on them."

"Tell them thanks but—"

"Mom, that's the guy that changed our tire."

"I know."

They were looking at her expectantly. They seemed unthreatening. She smiled at them and mouthed thank you. They both looked pleased.

January took their orders and left. Gina took a sip of her vodka tonic. She wasn't much of a drinker but she thought she might get a little drunk tonight.

"Mom? Can I go say hi?"

"But we don't even know him."

"Yes we do. Sort of. Maybe we can all eat together?"

"Don't you wanna just have a nice quiet dinner with me?"

"But I always eat with you."

"Is that so terrible?"

"Come on, Mom. Can't we just do something different?"

She saw the yearning in his eyes. For something different from the nightmare of the last forty-eight hours and the nightmare of the last couple of years and the larger nightmare he was born into. Nightmares nestled one within another like Chinese boxes.

"We'd have to ask his friend too."

"Okay."

"Go ahead. Go ask him."

"You want *me* to?"

"It was your idea."

He sucked up some soda through his straw like it was a fortifying shot of liquor then walked over to the bar. She couldn't hear what he was saying but Gray and Norman immediately grabbed their drinks and the basket of mozzarella and came her way. She scooted over and Norman sat down by her while Luke and Gray slid in on the other side of the booth.

"Well Gina," said Norman, "looks like fate has brought us back together."

"Looks like it. Thanks for the drink."

"It was my idea. Gray just went along with it."

She looked at Gray. "Is that true?"

"Afraid so. Norman's the brains behind the operation."

"Luke," said Norman, "have some mozzarella balls."

"Okay."

"So you decided to stay," said Gray to Gina. "In King Beach."

"For tonight anyway."

"Where are you staying?" said Norman.

"The Sea Breeze Motel."

Norman's face darkened. "I see."

"Is there something wrong with it?"

"Well, since you asked. It's a known haunt of some very shady characters."

She looked concerned. "It is?"

"Relax," said Gray. "That's just Norman's way of saying that I'm staying there too."

January came back. "Everybody okay?"

"I could use another beer," said Gray.

"And I think young master Luke would like some more mozzarella," said Norman.

Luke nodded vigorously.

"Okay," said January and started to go.

"January?" said Norman. "There's really no reason for you to be jealous of Gina. Our relationship is strictly platonic. So far."

"That's good to know."

"Gonna be in California long?" said Gray to Gina.

"I'm not sure yet."

"Vacationing?" said Norman.

"Yeah."

"But what about school, Luke?" said Norman. "Aren't you missing school?"

He was taken off guard by the question. He looked at his mother.

"I homeschool him."

Luke nodded. "Yeah."

"Just for now. Till we find the right school."

Gray and Norman exchanged a look. They clearly were making this up.

"So Norman, you live in King Beach?" she said.

"No, I have a condo in Marina del Rey. That's one town north. Used to be a nice place but now it's being ruined by over-development like everything else. So I like to hang out here. In King Beach. It'll never be overdeveloped because of the airplane noise."

"I haven't heard any planes tonight."

"The fog. It shut down the airport. I used to live here. When I was first married. We had a little yellow bungalow on Vista del Mar. God we were happy. We just didn't realize it. That's how it goes," and then to Luke: "You know King Beach is haunted?"

"Really?"

"By the ghosts of little girls. A couple dozen of them."

"Why little girls?" said Gina.

"There was an orphanage for girls here. In 1923 it burned down. Lots of the girls died in the fire. But some people say they hear them sometimes running down the street talking and laughing like little girls do. They're harmless. They just want to play. Sometimes over at the park people see swings moving back and forth but no-body's sitting in them."

"Maybe it's the wind," said Luke.

"Maybe. But a friend of mine told me he was walking through the park about sundown and there wasn't a soul in it and then he saw the seesaw going up and down up and down. He watched it for about five minutes. That wasn't the wind."

"I'm not so sure I believe in ghosts," said Luke.

"I'm not so sure I do either. But I'm not so sure I don't."

Gina looked across the table at Gray. "What about you?"

"I try and keep an open mind."

He seemed to be the quiet type. And soft-spoken. Gina liked that. She'd been around so many loud men in her life.

"So what do you do?" she said.

"I'm a sailor."

"A sailor?"

He nodded.

"You mean like on yachts and stuff?"

He shook his head.

"I was in the navy. I haven't been out long."

"You were on a ship?" said Luke.

"Yeah."

"What was its name?"

"The *Thomaston*."

"Was it a battleship?"

"No. A landing ship."

"What does a landing ship do?"

"It supports amphibious operations. Landing craft are launched from it."

"So you *used* to be a sailor," Gina said. "You're not anymore."

"No. I'm still a sailor."

"He's a tough nut to crack, Gina," said Norman. "I've tried. Personally I've concluded he's a dangerous desperado on the run from the law."

She had another drink. January brought the food. Grilled red snapper for her. Norman did most of the talking as she and Luke ate. Gray drank his beer and listened. Every so often he looked at her. He had interesting eyes. Blue-gray. Calm. And sort of sad. What did he mean that he both was a sailor and wasn't one?

She had kind of tuned Norman out but then realized he'd just said something to her.

"Pardon me?"

"He asked you where you grew up, Mom."

"Obviously not Oklahoma. New York, right? Maybe New Jersey?"

"We moved around a lot. I grew up in different places."

"She's a tough nut to crack," Norman said to Gray.

———

They walked through the fog back to the motel. They had Alejo Avenue all to themselves.

"What's wrong with Norman's neck?" said Luke.

"He said he broke it a few years ago in a motorcycle accident," said Gray. "He went off a curve on the Pacific Coast Highway going eighty miles an hour."

"Norman on a motorcycle," said Gina. "That's a scary thought."

"Could be he made it up. I get the feeling he's got an active imagination."

"You mean you're not really a desperado on the run?"

He shook his head.

"But if you were you wouldn't tell me."

"Nope. That'd be against the desperado code."

The fog seemed to muffle their footsteps and their voices. They could have been the only people alive in a world gone to fog. They saw up ahead the pink blur of the neon sign that said SEA BREEZE MOTEL.

Possibly because of the vodka tonics she dropped her purse when she went in it for the room key. It landed on the concrete with a clunk. Gray picked it up and handed it back.

"What you got in here? Bricks?"

She could have answered: No. A semiautomatic pistol. And a bag of stolen diamonds. But instead she said nothing.

"Well if you need anything I'm just three doors down. Room eighteen."

"What would I need?"

He shrugged. He knows, she thought. He knows we're in deep shit.

"Okay," said Gina. "Thanks."

"Good night."

"Good night."

"Good night, Luke."

"Good night."

That night Luke dreamed about the two dozen little dead girls. He could see them coming out of the fog. Advancing on the motel. They had white skin and black sunken eyes. They spotted him standing at the window and turned in unison like a flock of birds and headed his way. They didn't look harmless. They beat on the window with their fists and the glass shattered and they began to climb in. He ran out the front door and across the dunes. Right behind him the ghosts of the little girls running just as fast as he was. And then the dream changed. He was in some dark neighborhood on Long Island. The ghosts were still after him but he seemed to have escaped them. But then he heard whispering all around and realized the ghosts were there but invisible, at which point he woke up.

His mother was asleep in the other bed. He got up and went to the window. The fog had lifted and the parking lot was empty.

Friday

Unlike Jamie he didn't give a fuck about the ducks. A flock of several dozen lived outside the prison hanging out at a pond at the minimum-security camp and a nearby stream. Five of them had got in the habit of winging over the walls around one thirty every day and landing on the edge of the softball outfield where Jamie would be waiting with a bag of bread. He'd make weird ducklike noises in his throat and they'd quack back at him, waddling toward him side by side and spaced out evenly like they were in some kind of military formation. They were mallards: three green-headed drakes and two drab brown hens.

It was a gray rotten day with a wind that cut into you. He watched Jamie chuckle as he threw out the bread and the ducks rushed to it.

"What's the fucking point?"

"Huh?"

"If you were fattening up them ducks to eat 'em there'd be a fucking point. But they eat up all your bread and take a crap and fly away. So what's the point?"

He laughed again. "'Cause it's fun, Joey. It's a lotta fun."

He had a flat ruddy face and white-blond hair. A fatless ripped body with sinews and veins popping out all over. A wife and kids in Boston got five hundred bucks a week for his services as Joey's bodyguard. He was inside for the usual drug stuff but supposedly had killed a couple of guys outside and had beat to death a guy in USP Atlanta with a tube sock filled with combination locks.

"You know what foie gras is?" Joey said.

"No."

"I'll get some for you. It's fucking delicious."

"I'ma kill you! I'ma cut yo dick off!"

It was an insane inmate named Little Willie. A black guy maybe an inch over five feet tall. Joey had never said a word to him but he seemed to have developed some kind of fixation on Joey. He was standing about twenty feet away glaring wildly at him.

"You hear me, motherfucker? I'ma cut yo fucking dick off!"

What made the threat somewhat credible was that Little Willie had been in California at a camp in Lompoc where they raised cattle and he had worked in the slaughterhouse and used his knife to do just such a thing to another inmate.

Jamie moved on him menacingly.

"You're scaring the ducks, asshole."

Little Willie skittered away. A guard named Glaspers yelled: "Hey Joey! Your father's here!"

He sat at a table in the visiting room with his father and Bobby Lamonica. As soon as he had walked in and seen their faces he had known the news was bad. Palmentola dead. Gina alive. Luke still with Gina. And terHorst. Where the fuck was terHorst?

"He's getting grabby," Cicala said. "He kept wanting a bigger and bigger piece of those fucking diamonds."

"What are you saying?" said Joey. "He's already clipped Gina and took off with the rocks? Then where the fuck's my son?"

"Keep your voice down. Where do you think we are?"

"I know where the fuck I am. I'm where that bitch sent me!"

"Joey, if you don't calm down I'm getting up and walking outa here. I mean it."

"Okay. Okay. I'm calm."

"Joey, it's gonna be okay," said Bobby. "Luke's fine. Ain't nobody gonna hurt a kid like him."

"It's all on her. For putting him in this position. Why didn't she just walk in our house with a fucking hand grenade and pull the pin and blow us all up? Why'd she do this to us? We were a fucking happy family!"

"I know how you feel," said his father. "But the past is the past. We gotta deal with what's going on right now. And the first thing we gotta do is find terHorst. 'Cause we find *him* then we find *them*."

"Yeah and how we gonna do that?"

"I'm putting all our best guys on this."

"All our best guys are in the fucking can. Like *me*. 'Cause of *her*."

"As your father and his grandfather I swear to you. We're getting him back."

"What good does swearing do? I could swear I'm flying to the fucking moon tomorrow. So what? I ain't flying to the moon."

"There's a book you need to read. By Norman Vincent Peale. *The Power of Positive Thinking*. I haven't got to the position I have in life by thinking negative."

"Yeah. Great. Read a book. I'll put it on my fucking reading list."

The fluorescent lights made a barely audible buzzing. Bobby was working his way through a bag of Cheez Doodles. A young inmate and his wife or girlfriend at a table in the corner were admonished by a guard to keep their hands off each other.

"You haven't asked about your mother. Don't you care how she's doing?"

"'Course I care. How's she doing?"

"The same. One step above a vegetable."

"You're always pissed when I don't ask about her then you always say she's the same. A vegetable. What kinda shit is that?"

"You were just a kid, you probably don't remember. But she went off on this trip to Europe one time. By herself."

"You're right, I don't remember. So what?"

"She read some kinda women's lib shit in a magazine when she was sitting in the beauty parlor getting her hair done. She comes home and tells me she needs to go find herself. She thinks she's gonna find herself in Europe. So she packs up all her suitcases and calls a taxi and goes. And that's what it's like now. Like she's packed up all her suitcases and left. She's left but she's still there. Smiling at me all the fucking time."

"I'm sorry, Pop. Maybe she'll get better and not be a vegetable no more."

He went back out on the yard. Jamie was waiting for him. He was dumber than shit but always did exactly as he was told. Little Willie was there too. Eyes wide showing their whites as if Joey were a figure that provoked horror in him.

A tall white bird with long legs and a long curving neck walked very slowly along the edge of the lagoon. Peering intently into the water. Then it began to move even slower.

"It sees something," said Luke.

Suddenly the neck straightened out and the bird speared its head into the water and silver flashed in its orange beak and then the little fish was making its way down the inside of the long neck.

They walked on. Gina thinking that didn't seem like such a bad life. Fishing solitarily in a beautiful green lagoon.

The lagoon was part of the park. There were also a baseball field, a playground, a picnic area, and a wide expanse of grass with a single tree sticking out of it. Somebody was moving around the tree in a graceful nearly dancelike fashion. They got closer and saw it was Gray.

"What's he doing?" said Luke.

"Some kind of martial arts thing I guess."

They walked up to within about fifty feet of Gray and stood and watched. If he noticed they were there he gave no sign. He glided clockwise round the tree in its dappled shade then turned and went the other way. His arms flowing from one position to another. In perfect silence and his face serene.

Two young men and a dog were walking by. The dog was the

mangled malamute Gray had seen on his first night in King Beach. Holding his leash was the guy with the winged swastika on his forehead. His friend had CRAZY WHITE BOY tattooed on his neck and was wearing a cammie T-shirt. Their shaved heads shined in the sun. They were known in their world as Quex and Stitch.

They watched Gray with obvious amusement then began to mockingly imitate him, walking in circles with blank looks on their faces and then Quex yelled: "What kinda faggot kung fu shit is that anyway?"

Gray kept going round the tree.

"Hey!" Stitch yelled. "Pussy-ass bitch! We're talking to you!"

Still no response from Gray. The dog stood looking from Gray to the two guys and back to Gray. Gina could hear him whimper faintly. Then Quex dropped his leash and cupped his hands around his mouth and yelled at Gray: *"What makes the green grass grow?"* Then he and Stitch both yelled: *"Blood blood blood blood!"*

"Let's go," Gina said.

She grabbed Luke's hand and they began to walk away. Quex yelled again: *"What makes the green grass grow?"* then he and Stitch stomped their steel-toed boots into the grass and yelled: *"Blood blood blood blood!"*

Luke looked back over his shoulder.

"But Mom, shouldn't we help him?"

"He doesn't need help. And it's none of our business."

Quex and Stitch were stomping their boots faster and faster.

"What makes the green grass grow?"

"Blood blood blood blood!"

"What makes the green grass grow?"

"Blood blood blood blood!"

"What makes the green grass grow?"

The dog was growing agitated. Barking into the air at nothing. But Gray could have been blind, deaf, and dumb as far as the skinheads and the dog were concerned. He continued his tranquil circuit and countercircuit around the tree. And Gina and Luke were relieved when behind them the yelling and stomping stopped and

Quex picked up the leash of his scarred dog. He and Stitch bumped knuckles and laughed and left. As Gray went round the tree.

A scavenging gull flapped into the air. Getting out of the way of the green Honda that was leaving the motel parking lot.

"Do you think Gray was scared?" said Luke.

She shrugged. "He didn't seem to be."

"Then how come he let those guys talk to him like that?"

"'Cause he was smart. Those guys were garbage. What's the point of getting in a fight with garbage?"

"But Dad always said don't take any shit off anybody."

"Yeah and what's your dad doing now? Making office furniture in the pen. And don't say shit."

"*You* say it."

"It's that adult-kid thing again. I can say it but you can't. And don't say it's not fair."

"It's not fair."

She looked at him then laughed and he laughed too. First time she'd heard him laugh in a while. They were headed to a shopping center in Marina del Rey. Since they had left nearly everything in Brady they needed nearly everything: socks, shirts, jeans, underwear, cosmetics, toothpaste, some groceries for the little fridge, a bottle or two of good red wine. They went east on Alejo then turned left on Lincoln and then terHorst watched the little blue car with the red circle around it turn left onto Fiji and then twitch north on Admiralty Way.

He was lying in bed in a little backless nightgown in Barstow Community Hospital. He was sharing a room with an old man with congestive heart failure who sounded like he was dying. Groaning and coughing unceasingly. Wet horrible phlegmy coughs that turned terHorst's stomach. He had barely slept last night because of the old man and had cussed him out to no avail and had been haranguing the nurses to get him a new room or a new roommate but hadn't got anywhere so far.

He watched with interest the blue car approaching the intersection of Admiralty and Mindanao. This was the first time she'd left King Beach since she'd arrived yesterday. Was she on the move again or just running some errand?

Officer Martinez came in.

"Hey Frank, how you feeling?"

"Better, amigo. Terrible but better."

"Well that's good. You look better."

"I need to get outa this shitting place. They're trying to kill me."

"Who is?"

"My doctor."

"Why?"

" 'Cause I'm a Christian."

"What difference does that make?"

"His first name's Mohammed. His last name's some kinda towelhead gobbledygook I couldn't pronounce on a bet. Need I say more?"

"What does he wanna do?"

"Cut my chest open and fuck around with my heart. I'm not letting him. I've been doing some research on the Internet. Lots of alternatives to surgery these days. Holistic things. Diet, exercise, vitamins. Did you bring it?"

"Yeah."

The highway patrolman glanced around to make sure the coast was clear then brought a Milky Way out of his pocket. TerHorst ripped the wrapper off then began to munch it up happily.

"If a nurse comes in here and tries to stop me just shoot her, okay?"

"No problem."

"Oh Jesus. Oh lord," said the old man.

"Don't let Dr. Goatfucker hear you talking about Jesus," said terHorst. "He'll mercy-kill your old ass."

Martinez looked at the laptop. Saw playing cards against a green background. A game of solitaire in progress.

"Who's winning?"

"Me," said terHorst. "I always win."

"What's your biggest regret?"

"Hm. Biggest regret," said Gray. He and Norman were eating a basket of fried zucchini strips at the bar at the Sea Horse. "That's a tough one. Have to get back to you on that."

"Want to know *my* biggest regret?"

"Sure."

"I didn't do nearly enough fucking. I didn't do one percent of the fucking I should have."

"Why not?"

"I was married most of the time. I let morality get in the way. What a damn fool. Nothing beats fucking. Speaking of which. What's happening with you and Gina?"

"Nothing."

"She hasn't left has she?"

"No. I saw her and Luke out at the park today."

"And how did that go?"

"I just saw her. I didn't talk to her."

"For god's sake, son. Get on the stick!"

Gray shrugged. "I'm not sure she's really into me."

Norman shook his head in disgust. Dipped a zucchini strip in the ranch dressing.

"*A.* She's clearly into you. Last night she was looking at you with stars in those gorgeous eyes. *B.* Even if she wasn't into you it would be your job as a virile big-dicked American male to *make* her into you. I shouldn't have to be explaining all this."

"I don't really wanna be involved with anybody. I like being alone."

"It is not good for the man to be alone. Look at me. The only thing more pathetic than an old man living alone with his cat is an old man living alone without his cat. To Mr. Jones."

They lifted their drinks.

"To Mr. Jones."

Norman scratched his chin. "Wonder what the deal is with her. Gina."

"She's on the run. From something."

"Yeah but what?"

"Crazy boyfriend or husband?"

"Could be. Or maybe from the law."

"Wait a second. I thought *I* was the one that was on the run from the law."

"Well you both could be. In fact I would say that's probable."

"What do you think she did?"

"Maybe she was working in a bank and stole money. Like Janet Leigh in *Psycho*."

"Hm. And now she's ended up in this cheap motel."

"By George! That's right! Which raises the question: Who's Norman Bates in this scenario?"

"I don't know, *Norman*. Who do you think?"

Norman laughed.

"I got an idea. I'll play Cupid. I'll take you and Gina and Luke out to a nice lunch tomorrow. There's this place in Santa Monica I think you'd love."

Gray was silent.

"What do you say?"

"Maybe I shouldn't get in too deep with her. If she's got all these problems."

"Oh come on, Gray. Young men are supposed to get in horrible trouble because of pussy. That's what they're born for."

She sat atop a dune just beyond the motel. The sea breeze riffling a clump of grass. She sipped wine from a glass tumbler and watched the red sun's dwindling. About a fifth of it was still above the horizon.

"No drinking on the beach, ma'am. It's very illegal."

She looked around and saw Gray.

"You're not gonna make a citizen's arrest are you?"

"I have to. It's my duty."

"I got a better idea."

"What?"

"Join me."

"Okay."

He sat down beside her on the packed sand. She had a bottle of red wine in a paper bag. She pulled the cork out and replenished the tumbler.

"I've only got one glass."

"Fine by me."

He took the glass from her and drank and handed it back.

"Where's Luke?"

She looked over her shoulder. Down at the motel. "In our room. Watching TV. I think we both kinda needed a break from each other."

"Yeah?"

"Yeah, you know how it is when you're on a trip with somebody. You can start driving each other a little nuts. I mean what kid wants to be with his mother twenty-four hours a day?"

"He's a nice kid."

"Sometimes I think he's too nice. Not tough enough."

"I got a feeling he's plenty tough."

"Really?"

"Uh-huh."

She drank more wine and thought about Luke.

"I know one thing. He deserves a hell of a lot better life than what I've given him."

"Where's his dad?"

"He's not in the picture."

"You're divorced?"

She nodded.

"He a bad guy? Luke's dad?"

"You could say that."

"Was he mean to Luke?"

"Yeah."

"Is that why you left him?"

She looked at him and smiled a little. How had he gotten so close to the truth so fast?

"Sorry," he said. "Don't mean to be nosy."

"I saw you in the park today."

He nodded.

"Those guys were real assholes huh?"

He shrugged. "I try not to judge."

"Gimme a break. What are you, some kinda hippie that loves everybody?"

He took the glass from her and drank. "Live and let live. That's what I try and do."

"Luke asked me if you were scared."

"What did you tell him?"

"I said you didn't look scared."

"There wasn't anything to be scared of. Those guys to me weren't anything different from anything else in the park. They were just some sounds. Some swirls of color."

"You make it sound like they weren't even real."

"Maybe they weren't. Maybe none of us are."

"Maybe if I drink some more you'll start making sense."

She drank straight from the bottle. She was beginning to feel a pleasant warm glow inside like the sun was settling into her own heart. Some gulls flew down the coast. On their graceful unhurried way to wherever they spent the night. The low long bulk of an oil tanker was moving as imperceptibly as the sun.

"So I guess you must really love it," she said.

"What?"

"*That*." Indicating with a sweep of her hand everything in front of them.

"Yeah."

"Is that why you became a sailor? 'Cause you love the sea?"

"I guess I loved the idea of the sea. I never saw it till I was seventeen."

"Where are you from?"

"Iowa. About as far from the ocean as you can get."

"So what did you do on the—what was it called? The *Thompson?*"

"The *Thomaston*. I worked in the engine room."

"You probably didn't see much of the ocean down there."

"I didn't mind. I liked it there. It was like the heart of the ship. It was like the ship would die if we didn't keep it going."

"How come you left the navy?"

"Just felt like it was time."

"What have you been doing since then?"

"Nothing much. Kinda drifting."

"You can't drift forever."

"Why not?"

"I can tell you're real ambitious."

"Maybe I am ambitious. In my own way."

"What way is that?"

He didn't answer. She looked back again at the motel. He had noticed she couldn't seem to go more than twenty or thirty seconds without doing so.

Just south a plane took off. They watched it soar out over the ocean.

"You gonna be around much longer?" he said. "You and Luke?"

"I don't know. It's kinda day to day."

"What are you guys up to?"

"We're just—kinda drifting."

One giant wing dipped and the plane began to circle back for a trip east.

"Norman wants to take us all out to lunch tomorrow. You interested?"

"Maybe. Where?"

"This place in Santa Monica. He says the food's great."

"I could use some great food."

The sun was nearly gone now. She took another pull from the bottle. It had been so long since she had gone to bed with anyone, she had been all set to do so with Rusty Deiter but that hadn't worked out and now she was with this strange gentle guy with eyes the color of the gray-blue sea. She glanced at his lips wanting him to kiss her and he seemed to be thinking about it then turned away. They regarded together the vast vista of water and sky. Both feeling miniscule like grains of sand. *It's like we're sitting at the end of the world*, she thought and he thought: *It's like the edge of the earth*. The sun shrank from the slenderest sliver to the tiniest dab. And then winked out.

Red rats were running up and down the curtain. "Go away!" he whispered. He had fought in the Korean War and now thought he was a prisoner of the Red Chinese. They were trying to break him. Brainwash him. He didn't know how much longer he could hold out. He was really afraid of the red rats. And now a rat dropped from the ceiling and landed plop on the foot of the bed. He called out in a quavery voice: *"Go awa-a-ay! Go awa-a-ay!"*

Suddenly the curtain was ripped back and terHorst was standing there.

He coughed dismally. Pointing a shaking finger at the rat on his bed. "Kill it. Kill it."

TerHorst looked and saw nothing.

The old man watched terHorst come toward him in the half darkness holding a pillow with both hands. He lifted his withered arms to try to fend him off but then the pillow slammed down on his face. He grabbed terHorst's forearms and tried to push him away but the force he exerted was so slight terHorst hardly felt anything and then he was falling into a dark pit, it was deep, deep and he fell, fell but he knew the rats were at the bottom waiting.

All struggle ceased in less than a minute but terHorst kept pressing down. He knew the old man was just unconscious. It took several minutes to suffocate somebody. The room was never warm enough, he had complained to the nurses about it but as usual they'd ignored him and now he could feel the cool air on his bare back and ass. He was weak because of the heart attack and his arms were getting tired but there was nothing to do but lean over the bed and push the pillow. It was a dull way to kill a man.

She sought sleep but the dead people in Brady demanded to be heard. She was assailed by images of assassins fanning out across the country. Showing pictures of her and Luke to sharp-eyed strangers. Searching for that one mistake she'd made that would lead them to room 21 of the Sea Breeze Motel. She imagined them swarming ninjalike across the parking lot. Her gun was under the pillow but what was she supposed to do? Break out a window and blaze away like some invincible heroine in a Hollywood movie? She was just a regular girl. A waitress from Long Island who had fallen in love with the wrong customer. She'd been lucky with that fat guy but there was no reason to suppose her luck would continue.

Some red-eye flight roared up then rumbled off.

She got up and went in the bathroom and drank some water. Not turning on the light so as not to disturb Luke. She wandered to the window. Pulled apart the curtains and looked out.

It was such a strange sight she wondered for a moment if she had fallen asleep after all. Maybe she was dreaming that a naked male was lying facedown and motionless in the middle of the parking lot.

She couldn't see his face but somehow knew it was Gray. She quickly pulled some clothes on. Eased the door shut behind her. As she approached him she was shocked to see signs of terrible violence that had been visited on his body. His back seamed with long gleaming scars and a ragged healed-over hole the size of a golf ball in his left buttock and his legs pocked with several smaller holes. His arms and legs were splayed out and formed a sort of X and his face was pressing at an angle into the pavement. His eyes were closed. He seemed unconscious. She knelt beside him and said: "Gray?"

He made a sound. He made it again. He kept making it and she leaned in close and realized he was saying in a faint whisper: "*Stop. Stop. Don't. Don't.*"

"Gray? It's Gina. Are you all right? Gray!"

She touched his shoulder and he fell silent and opened his eyes.

"What's wrong? Are you hurt?"

He didn't answer. His eyes began to move around a little but never looked at her.

"Come on. Get up. It's freezing out here."

She pulled at his arm and he got up slowly. Allowed her to lead him toward his room. She wondered if he was drunk or zonked out on drugs. Though he didn't seem like the drunk or druggie type. The door to his room was wide open. They walked in and she turned on the light and led him over to the rumpled bed.

"Okay. Lie down."

He did so like some obedient zombie. As she pulled the bedclothes over him she noticed more scars on the front of his body.

"Mom?"

Luke was standing in the doorway.

"What's going on? What's wrong with Gray?"

"Nothing. Go back to bed."

But he didn't move.

"Luke, did you hear me? Go! And shut the door."

Reluctantly Luke left. She looked back down at Gray and saw that he was looking up at her.

"Do you want anything? Some water?"

He shook his head.

"Are you all right?"

"Yes," he said then rolled over and closed his eyes. She watched him for a minute or two until she was satisfied he was no longer in some weird catatonic state but was simply asleep. Then she turned off the light.

Luke was sitting on the side of his bed waiting for her.

"Don't ask me any questions, okay?" she said. "'Cause I don't have any answers."

"Is he sick?"

"I don't know. I don't think so."

She sat down on the side of her own bed and looked at him.

"I know you like him. So do I. But we barely know him. And I don't have enough energy left to worry about him. I can only worry about you and me."

"Why does everything have to be like this? Why can't we just be normal?"

"I told you not to ask me any questions."

Saturday

" 'For thy sake we are killed all the day long. We are accounted as sheep for the slaughter.' "

The preacher paused. Looking out on the weeping people and people trying not to weep. They stood in their best clothes in the chill wind and under the cold blue blaze of the sky. Family members sat in folding chairs under a pavilion tent next to the two graves. Behind the family stood the Brady Bobcats football team.

"It was just another Wednesday morning for Ricky and Eric Vickers. The father a hardworking farmer. The son an athlete of great promise. Then death on his pale horse came riding onto the Vickers farm. You ask why and I say I don't know why. I don't know why Trish Vickers had her husband and her son taken from her. Don't know why Tiffany and Tara no longer have a loving dad and a big brother."

McGrath was near the back of the crowd. He hadn't gone to Deiter the Cheater's funeral yesterday and hadn't planned on coming today but at the last minute had jumped in his car and sped over from Oklahoma City. He looked at a clump of teenage girls all dressed up as if for the prom. Holding on to one another. Tears marring their makeup. Looking to McGrath less sorrowful than terrified like early Christians in the Colosseum being fed to the lions.

"It is like some dark kind of miracle. It is like we are people that have had their living hearts ripped right out of their chests and yet

continue to walk around and talk and to eat and drink and breathe—
that's what it's like to lose someone we love. And yet let us remind
ourselves that the Lord is our shepherd and none of his sheep will
ever be lost. Not even for a single second. 'For I am persuaded that
neither death nor life nor angels nor principalities nor powers nor
things present nor things to come nor height nor depth nor any
other creature shall be able to separate us from the love of God,
which is in Jesus Christ our Lord.'"

He read the sticker on the bumper of the car in front of him and
smiled a little. Maybe the Hokey Pokey *is* what it's all about.

His cell rang.

"McGrath."

"Well hey, Doug. What's shaking?"

"Frank! Where the hell are you?"

"Oh out west I guess you could say. Sorry I been outa touch."

"What's going on? Have you found Gina?"

"Well, yes and no. I think I know where she's at but it might take
me a day or two to get there."

"You okay? You don't sound so great."

"Oh I'm fine. I think the flu bug bit me but I'm just about over it.
So I hope you been keeping everything under your hat. As we dis-
cussed."

"I said I would for a few days. But it's already been a few days."

"Like I said. I need a couple days more. Then I'll get this thing
wrapped up. Help her and the boy start a bright new life in Butt-
crack, Nebraska. The waters will be smooth again in no time.
You'll see."

"I'm on my way back from Brady. I've been to a funeral. A double funeral in fact."

"Any progress in the investigation?"

"Well they thought they had an ID on the fat guy. The license
plates on the car that got burned up were missing but they were able
to get the VIN number."

"That's redundant."

"What is?"

"VIN number. What you're really saying is 'vehicle identification number number.'"

"They found out it was rented at the Tulsa airport by a Robert Cassato from New York City. Had an address on him and everything. But it turned out the name and address were phony."

"Too bad."

"But I think we can still assume he was sent by Cicala. And that he's gonna be sending more of his people after her. So you better find her before they do."

"You can count on me."

"So where is she, Frank? Why all the mystery?"

"In the Phoenix area."

"Is that where you are?"

"Yup."

"Maybe we should put some more men on this."

"How are you able to do it?"

"Do what?"

"Drive."

"Drive? What are you talking about?"

"How are you able to drive with your head up your ass? We *can't* put more men on it, Doug. We've fucked up and we don't want anybody to know about it. Remember?"

"Actually *you're* the one that's fucked up. She was your responsibility."

"You know something? You're my boss. So you're responsible too."

"You're not acting like I'm your boss."

"I'm trying to pull our nuts outa the fucking fire, all right? You oughta be grateful to me instead of giving me a hard time."

TerHorst felt genuinely indignant. As if all he were doing was trying to deal with some bureaucratic snafu. As if he were searching for Gina so he could help her instead of murder her and take her diamonds. His breathing was coming a little fast and his heart hurt and he rubbed his chest.

"Frank? You okay?"

"Yeah. Didn't mean to fly off the old handle, buddy."

"Forget it."

"Next time you hear from me it's gonna be good news."

"I hope so. I could use some good news."

TerHorst laid his cell down on the bedside table. Picked up the remote and unmuted the TV. There was a good game on. Number nine LSU and number three Alabama. He hadn't got a new roommate yet so he could watch the game in peace. Martinez had brought him some beef jerky and he tore the wrapper off and went to work on it. He was rooting for LSU. Not that he liked LSU. But he hated Alabama.

"Hi, Quetzalli," he said to the Guatemalan maid pushing along her cleaning cart. She showed her missing teeth in a smile and then he knocked on the door of room 21. The curtain twitched back and Luke peered out. So wary and watchful the two of them. Gray smiled but Luke didn't. He disappeared from the window then the door opened.

"Hey Luke. You guys ready?"

"Um . . . Mom's in the shower."

"Okay. I guess I should call Norman. Tell him we're running a little late."

"Mom said to tell you that we can't go."

"Why not?"

"She's not feeling very good."

"What's the matter?"

"She has diarrhea."

"Oh."

"She thinks it's something she ate. She's pretty sick. She has to go running to the bathroom every few minutes."

"She should take something for it. What's that pink stuff?"

"Pepto-Bismol. She did already."

The door was open only about a foot. Luke stood there looking up at him. He got the feeling Gina was on the other side of the door listening to every word.

"Well —tell your mom I hope she feels better."

"Okay."

"See ya."

"See ya."

Luke shut the door. Gina was sitting on the side of her bed.

"Jesus Christ. Why'd you tell him I had *diarrhea*? My god. Pepto-Bismol."

"I really wanna go. Why can't we?"

"Because. What do you want for lunch? Wanna call out for a pizza?"

"No. I wanna go to Santa Monica and have lunch with Gray and Norman."

"Pizza it is."

She went to her laptop to Google pizza in King Beach.

"I don't want pizza."

"Okay. Chinese."

"If you don't wanna go why don't you just let me go?"

"By yourself?"

He nodded.

"Forget it."

He walked over to his bed and just stood there. Then he toppled over and lay facedown upon it. Unmoving. Like a felled tree.

"Luke?"

No answer.

"Luke. Get up."

"I'm just gonna lie here. Never move again. Never talk to any-body. Then you'll be happy."

"Quit being difficult."

"*You're* difficult."

She went over to him.

"If I tickle you you'll move."

"You better not."

She thrust her fingers in his armpits and tickled him as he squirmed and shrieked.

"Stop it! No! Stop it!"

He jumped up off the bed. His face flushed and angry.

"That wasn't funny, Mom!"

"Then how come you were laughing?" She went back to her computer. "Come on, I'm starving. What do you want?"

"I'm not hungry."

"Fine. I'll just get what I want then."

"He looked sad. When I told him we weren't coming."

"Jesus, Luke. Enough already." Then she sighed and stood up. "I'll go talk to him. Okay?"

She knocked on the door of room 18. When Gray opened it he was on a cell phone. "Norman? Can I call you back?" And then to Gina: "Hey. How you feeling?"

"I'm okay. Can I come in?"

"Sure."

He closed the door behind them.

"Look," she said. "I'm not really sick."

"I kinda figured you weren't."

"I guess Luke's a lousy liar."

"It's good he's lousy."

"I don't know. Lying has its uses."

"Yeah. I guess it does. Wanna sit down?"

"Okay."

He pulled out a straight-back chair from a desk and she sat down. She looked at him and wondered what to say.

"So what's up? " he said.

"Do you remember last night?"

He looked puzzled. "What about it?"

"I found you outside. Just laying there. Without any clothes on."

He nodded. Seeming oddly unsurprised. He sat down on the bed.

"Then what happened?"

"I helped you up and brought you back in here. And put you to bed."

"I thought I'd dreamed it. You in here. But it was really you."

"What was the matter with you?"

"It was—kind of like sleepwalking I guess. It used to happen a lot when I was a kid. But I haven't done it in a long time."

"It's like you were having a nightmare. You kept saying *don't, don't.*"

"I probably was having a nightmare. I don't remember."

"Did you ever see a doctor or a shrink about it?"

"No. I didn't come from that kind of family. So you said I wasn't wearing any clothes?"

She nodded.

"I guess you're wondering what happened to me."

"If you wanna tell me."

"Sure. It's no secret. I was in an accident. A car wreck."

"Must've been a pretty bad one."

"Yeah. It was. I was laid up for quite a while. I know it looks bad. But I'm fine now. Anyway. Thanks for helping me out last night."

She nodded.

"Did Luke see me?" he said.

"Yeah."

"So you think I'm some kind of psycho? That's why you don't wanna have lunch?"

"Look. I just met you two days ago. I don't know what to think. I just know my first responsibility's to Luke. To protect him—"

"From me?"

"You know the only thing I know about you? You're a lousy liar. Just like Luke."

"What do you think I've lied about?"

"Well . . . I don't think you were in a car wreck. I don't think that caused what I saw last night."

"Are you some kind of expert in injuries?"

"I've seen gunshot wounds before."

"And you think I got shot?"

"Maybe. Among other things. Like I got no idea what happened to your back."

"Where have you seen gunshot wounds?"

She shrugged. "Listen. What happened to you. It's none of my business. I don't really care."

Gray was silent. They looked at each other.

"Actually I *do* care," she said. "But that's a problem too."

"Yeah. I know what you mean."

His cell rang.

"Hello? Uh-huh. Sure, I still wanna come. Hey Norman? Could you hold on a sec?"

He lowered the phone and looked at Gina.

"Wanna change your mind?"

Their waitress's name was Amanda. Pale and pretty with large green eyes. She approached their table with a pot of coffee.

"How is everything?" she said. With a big smile. Like they were the nicest customers she'd had all day.

"Very tasty," said Markus Groh.

She looked him over as she refilled his cup. "You look like somebody."

"Thank you. Much better than looking like nobody."

"I mean somebody famous. This English actor. I can't remember his name—"

"So is he very ugly?"

"Oh no. He's real cute. Got blond hair, blue eyes. A little dimple in his chin. Like *you*."

"Maybe I am this English actor. Did that cross your mind?"

"Are you?"

"No. Sorry to disappoint you."

She hung around the table. Liking Markus Groh.

"What *do* you do? If you're not an actor."

"I am in business. With *him*." Nodding across the table at Bulgakov.

"What kind of business?"

"Dima! How would you describe the business we're in?"

Barely perceptibly Bulgakov shrugged. He was holding a club sandwich in both hands and chewing through it with an insectile relentlessness. Staring at the TV behind the bar. A football game was on. Alabama and LSU. LSU ahead in the second quarter.

"You a football fan?" said Amanda.

"No. It's stupid game."

"We turn the living into the dead," said Groh.

"Pardon?"

"Our business. We turn the living into the dead."

She looked at him and then she laughed. "So where y'all from?"

"I'm from Austria."

"Kangaroos."

"No, that's Australia. Austria's a country in Europe. No kangaroos."

"I'll bet in zoos they got some."

"I'll bet you're right."

"Y'all want anything else?"

"Tea," said Bulgakov.

"Hot tea? Or ice tea?"

Bulgakov fixed his small hard eyes on Amanda's emerald eyes. "Hot."

Something about Bulgakov made Amanda's smile falter.

"Okay."

"And strawberry jelly."

"Tea and jelly. Coming up."

She smiled at Groh then walked away.

"It's stupid," said Bulgakov.

"What is?"

"To tell stupid waitress about us."

"Don't worry, Dima. She didn't believe me. No one believes the truth anymore."

They left the restaurant. Walked through downtown on Peachtree

Street. Markus Groh sunny, slim, and tall. Bulgakov dark and bandy-legged. His hair in a brutal-looking buzz cut. He lit a cigarette.

"I understand why you don't like American football," said Groh. "Incomprehensible rules. Muscle-bound oafs dressed up like riot police. But you don't really like any sport do you?"

"No."

"Why not?"

"It's waste of time."

"But what is time for? If not to enjoy? I've derived so much pleasure from sports in my life. We must find you a sport."

They reached the hotel. Bulgakov threw down his cigarette then spat over his shoulder three times. For luck. Groh watching him with a frown. Then a liveried doorman held the door open for them and they entered.

They crossed the lobby through dozens of convivial convention-eers wearing name tags. Stood waiting at an elevator then shuffled aboard with several others. Got out on the seventeenth floor.

They walked down a long hushed carpeted hallway. Gilt-framed mirrors reflecting their advance. A door ahead of them opened and a well-dressed elderly man came out. He had a white moustache that looked like a crescent moon. He nodded at them in a genteel way and Groh nodded in return. At the end of the hallway Groh and Bulgakov paused and looked back. Saw the elevator doors clos-ing and the old man disappearing.

They moved down another long hallway. Stopped in front of room 1737. They regarded the door as though it were a piece of art-work hanging on a gallery wall. Then Groh pointed at the peephole.

They took flesh-colored rubber gloves out of their pockets and pulled them on. There was a room service cart next to the door. Groh lifted a silver cover and looked at what was left of someone's lunch. A steak, a baked potato, asparagus. The vegetables had barely been touched. Maybe a quarter of the steak was gone.

"No appetite," he whispered. "You think he's nervous about some-thing?"

He replaced the cover then glanced up and down the hallway and took a silenced pistol from under his sports coat. He stood in front of the door and aimed his gun at the peephole. The end of the silencer about a foot away. He gave Bulgakov a quick nod and Bulgakov knocked.

The whole world for Groh was contained within the bright circumference of the peephole. It seemed at the same time tiny and the size of the sun. Seconds passed with the speed of centuries then the light from the peephole was blocked out. He gave the eye a half second to get settled in then fired.

A bullet hole obliterated the peephole and then they heard a thud.

"Let's make certain, Dima," murmured Groh but Bulgakov already had his electronic pick out. Groh picked up the ejected casing and checked up and down the hallway as Bulgakov worked at the lock. The hallway remained obligingly empty then Bulgakov turned the door handle. The door swung in a few inches and stopped. Bulgakov put his shoulder into it then the two assassins stepped inside.

A man was lying on his back. Gray trousers and a flowery yellow shirt. Socks but no shoes. A gory hole where his right eye had been. A small revolver was lying on the patterned gold carpet near his curled fingers.

He seemed dead but Groh shot him again to be sure. In the other eye. For symmetry's sake.

They shut the door behind them and walked back to the elevators. Stripping their gloves off as they went.

"Have you ever played tennis?" said Groh. "It's a wonderful game. And you Russians are becoming quite good at it. Especially the women. Sharapova, Kirilenko, Dementieva. And they're so beautiful!"

"What do you care? You are fucking faggot."

"Tennis, Dima. I will teach you tennis!"

————

Hidden away from the street in a courtyard filled with shrubs and trees was a restaurant named Secret. Reggae music was playing and sunlight poured down. Mostly young good-looking customers were sitting on long couches being served by waiters and waitresses who were all from Europe and who were also good-looking and young.

"This is a pretty hip place, Norman," said Gray.

"Well what the hell did you expect? I'm in with the in crowd. I go where the in crowd goes."

Gray and Norman and Gina and Luke were sitting at one of the tables along the side of the courtyard. Their waiter Vincenzo told them about the specials then opened a bottle of red wine. He had a gaunt goateed face that was ugly in a good-looking way.

"You got a great accent," said Gina.

"Oh thank you very much," Vincenzo said with a toothy smile.

"Where are you from?"

"Sardinia. It is beautiful, beautiful, beautiful!"

"Why'd you leave?" said Gray.

"Because of woman."

Norman turned his whole body and looked at Gray. "Cherchez la femme!"

"She was tourist. Most beautiful girl from New York. I fall in love. Follow her to New York. I come here to California on vacation. And it is beautiful, beautiful, beautiful! And I know that here is going to be my home!"

"I'm almost afraid to ask," said Gray. "But what happened to the woman?"

"She's here. With me. Five years. My wife!"

He laughed and poured some wine in Norman's glass. Norman sniffed and tasted it then grinned up at Vincenzo.

"Perfecto."

Norman had a New York steak. Gina the Kurobota pork chop. Gray the portobello mushroom. Luke the roasted chicken breast. And they got another bottle of wine.

Norman sliced off a big piece of steak and stuck it in his mouth. "Gray's a vegetarian," he mumbled through his meat. "Did he tell you that?"

Gina looked at Gray. "Oh yeah?"

Gray nodded.

"For how long?"

"About seven years."

"Any particular reason?"

"I was in Japan. I saw some fishermen string up a dolphin by its tail. It was still alive. The dolphin started crying out for help. And when other dolphins heard it they came swimming to the boat and the fishermen speared them."

Gina made a face. "Sounds horrible."

"Anyway. I decided I wasn't gonna eat meat anymore."

"I can understand you not wanting to eat dolphins," said Norman. "They're intelligent wonderful creatures. But cows and pigs are different. They were raised to be food."

"You ever been to a slaughterhouse?" said Gray. "I went to one in Texas. Just to see what it was like."

"And?" said Norman.

"I thought it was . . . evil. An evil place. I'm not gonna do anything to help keep a place like that in business."

"I'm not gonna eat meat anymore," Luke announced.

"Oh great," said Gina to Gray. "See what you've started?"

"Hey it wasn't me. It was Norman. He likes to cause trouble."

Norman smiled, nodded and chewed.

"What do you do for a living, Norman?" said Gina.

"I'm retired. Isn't that obvious?"

"What did you used to do?"

"I worked in the aircraft industry. I was an executive at Hughes Aircraft and later at Lockheed. I was involved in a big scandal there in the seventies. Nearly brought the whole company down."

"What happened?" said Gray.

"We were accused of paying twenty-two million dollars in bribes to members of foreign governments so they'd buy our military planes."

"Unjustly accused?" said Gray.

"You kidding? We were guilty as hell. Actually I've made a very minor mark on American history. You know how?"

Gray shook his head.

"Technically what we did—bribing foreign officials—wasn't against the law. So Congress took care of that by passing the Foreign Corrupt Practices Act. Never would've happened without me and my associates. That's pretty cool, huh Luke?"

Luke nodded uncertainly.

"Anyway. We all had to resign 'in disgrace' as they say. I invested all my ill-gotten gains in real estate and did pretty well. Became a wealthy man in fact. I had one hell of a life until a few years ago. When my wife died and then a week later I broke my fool neck. So, Luke! How's the homeschooling going? What did your mom teach you today?"

Luke looked at Gina.

"Nothing," she said. "Today's Saturday."

"Right," he agreed. "Today's Saturday."

Norman gave Gray a quick smirk. "Nothing better than Saturday when you're a kid."

"Yeah," said Luke. He looked at Gray. "What were you doing in the park yesterday?"

"It's called qigong. It's a combination of physical training and meditation."

"Is it like kung fu? Like those guys said?"

"Well it could be. 'Qi' just means energy and 'gong' means a skill cultivated through hard work. So it could be about fighting or healing or playing baseball or whatever."

"So what are you doing it for?" said Norman. "To be a better baseball player?"

"I think the whole higher purpose of qigong is to completely know yourself. Looking for your personal truth. Where you fit into the puzzle. So I guess that's what I'm after."

"See?" said Gina. "I knew you were a hippie."

"You've got him wrong," Norman said. "Can't you see that outlaw look in his eyes? He's probably doing qigong to make himself a better bank robber."

Gray laughed. Vincenzo came over. Picked up the bottle of wine and replenished all their glasses. Gray looked at Gina. Just as she moved her head into a slash of sunlight that lit up her tumble of black hair. And her red wine was lit up too.

"What a day in California, yes?" said Vincenzo. "It is beautiful, beautiful, beautiful!"

Fat raindrops began to splat against the windshield and Bobby Lamonica turned on the wipers. Moments later they were in the midst of a downpour.

"Jesus," Cicala said. "It's really raining cats and dogs."

"I never knew what that meant. Raining cats and dogs. Whatta cats and dogs gotta do with it?"

"They don't have anything to do with it. It's just a saying."

They were on 18th Street. Near the Hudson River. The rain on the roof was drowning out the radio and Cicala turned it up. A golden oldies station was playing "A Teenager in Love" by Dion and the Belmonts. *Each night I ask the stars up above . . .* What did teenagers know about love? About how beautiful girls turned into diapered old ladies that never stopped smiling?

They drove down to Chelsea Piers. Entered a parking lot. Bobby parked and switched off the engine and the golden oldies stopped and rain overwhelmed the windshield.

"I hope you remembered to bring an umbrella," said Cicala.

Bobby looked pleased with himself. "I didn't have to remember. I keep one in the trunk."

They got out of the black Lincoln and Bobby popped the trunk. It was empty except for a baseball bat.

"That doesn't look like an umbrella," Cicala said.

"It ain't. It's a baseball bat."

"I know it's a fucking baseball bat," said Cicala as he slammed down the trunk lid.

It was late afternoon but looked like early night. They walked stolidly through the rain. Hands thrust in the pockets of their dark overcoats. Looking like exactly what they were. Gangsters on a mission. Not hurrying because Cicala didn't believe in hurrying. People might get the wrong idea if they saw you hurrying. Like something was wrong. Like maybe you weren't on top of things.

He'd been bugged all day by a dream he'd had last night and now it began to bug him again. He'd been in some vile men's room with water all over the floor and had stepped up to a urinal and unzipped. And his penis had been like a soft rotten piece of wood and had broken off in his hand.

"Somebody musta stole it," Bobby said. "Some cocksucker."

"What are you talking about?"

"The fucking umbrella."

"Somebody went to all the trouble of stealing an umbrella out of the trunk?"

"Yeah. Some cocksucker."

He and Bobby went back a long way. To the old neighborhood. Everybody had called him Bobby the Hump then and some people still called him that. He'd had an illness when he was a little kid that had attacked his bones and left him with one shoulder raised and rounded. When Cicala was in his early twenties Bobby was a deformed little boy who was always hanging around pestering him for a job and whom he was always telling to beat it. But then one day he saw him take a tire iron to a grown man who had called him Bobby the Hump and he broke both his legs so Cicala let him start running numbers. Soon he was doing all kinds of things. Whatever you told him to do. He was still like that.

They walked to the marina where a big blue and white yacht was waiting. *Invictus* painted on its side. A young Chinese man in a dark suit was standing under an umbrella smoking a cigarette.

When he saw them he threw the cigarette in the water and hurried down the pier toward them.

"Mr. Cicala," he said, "you're getting drenched!"

He held the umbrella over Cicala and they walked toward the boat. Bobby trailing behind them in the rain but not seeming to mind.

"It's raining cats and dogs," he said.

They crossed a gangplank onto the boat and then the Chinese man led them into a small room. He helped Cicala take his overcoat off.

"May I get you something to drink? A cup of tea?"

"Coffee," said Cicala.

The man left. Cicala and Bobby sat down on a couch in front of a flat-screen TV. An infomercial was on. "Get Ripped in 90 Days." Cicala felt engine vibrations and looked out a window and saw the pier slowly sliding away. A very black man in a white jacket came in with a silver coffeepot and delicate cups decorated with rampant blue dragons. He also had towels which he handed to the men and then he poured them coffee and left without a word. Cicala toweled his face and what was left of his hair as Bobby loaded up his cup with sugar cubes.

The *Invictus* headed south down the rainy river toward Battery Park. Cicala could see through the deepening gloom the skyline of New Jersey.

Phil was fifty-seven. He was very sedentary, unfit and unhealthy till he started the program. Then he lost forty pounds of fat and gained twenty pounds of muscle in just ninety days and his wife told him he had the body and energy of a twenty-five-year-old. Then Phil's lean new body froze as the satellite signal was interrupted by the rain then Phil fractured into a myriad of glowing digital cubes and crumbled away into nothing.

The Chinese man returned. Told Cicala Mr. Li was ready to see him.

He had been here before and as he entered it struck him again as mysterious how the room seemed far too large to be contained within the boat. Mr. Li sat behind a big mahogany desk. Nothing on it except a Mac computer. Cicala walked across the polished parquet floor as Mr. Li stood up to greet him.

"It's good to see you, Mr. Cicala."

"Good to see you, Mr. Li."

They shook hands. Mr. Li's hand as soft and grip as weak as a girl's. Cicala sat down in a chair across the desk from Mr. Li.

"How is your wife?" said Mr. Li.

"Ah you know. The same. Thanks for asking."

Mr. Li nodded. The room was underlit and the glow from the computer screen washed over him. Making him pale and ghostly. He looked at Cicala. Waiting.

"Thanks for seeing me. I know it was short notice."

"My door is always open to you. I'm glad I was in town."

"You gonna be here long?"

"A few days. Perhaps a week. And then—" He made a motion with his hand. As though releasing an invisible bird.

"It's about my daughter-in-law," Cicala said. "My *ex*-daughter-in-law."

"Yes."

"We found her. But she got away."

"Yes."

"And the guy we sent after her. Toddo Palmentola. He got killed."

"Please, Mr. Cicala. Tell me something I don't know."

"That fucking marshal. He's disappeared. I think the cocksucker double-crossed us."

He saw Mr. Li's face, usually a mask of bland impassivity, betray a bit of distaste at his profanity.

"What is it that you want?"

"I want the marshal dead. I want my daughter-in-law dead. And I want my grandson back. But I need some help. We been RICO'd half to fucking death. I want you to put your best guys on it."

Mr. Li was silent. Cicala could faintly hear the rain still coming down hard. Could feel the soft motion of the boat as it made its way along a river now as dark as the Styx.

"It's unfortunate when one cannot control one's own family," Mr. Li finally said.

Cicala felt like Mr. Li had slapped him.

"I've done a hell of a lot for the System."

"And the System has done a lot for you."

"That's the way it's supposed to work. One hand washes the other."

"I can tell you this immediately. It's the policy of the System to maintain good relations with governments at all levels. We will not kill the marshal. We will not take the risk of getting in a war with the government of the United States over what is essentially a personal domestic matter."

"Okay. Forget the marshal. Luke and Gina. That's all I care about. What about the Russians?"

"The Russians?"

"Yeah. I hear everybody talking about the Russians. They say they're your best talent."

"Actually only one of them is Russian."

"Look, I don't care if they're from fucking Jupiter and Mars. They're the guys I want."

"I'll see if they're available. And then I have to check with the Directorate. The Directorate will say yes or no."

"How long's this gonna take? There's no time to waste."

"No time will be wasted. You'll hear from me soon, Mr. Cicala." Mr. Li stood up and extended his hand. "Give my regards to your wife."

His condo wasn't far from Secret. On the top floor of a twenty-eight-story building right on the beach. A wraparound balcony. Big elegantly furnished rooms. Lots of artwork from all over the world. Astounding views of the ocean, the mountains, and the city.

"I'd never leave," said Gina. "If I lived in a place like this."

"Oh you'd leave all right," said Norman. "Sure it's nice. But you can't help but get used to things. Take them for granted. Probably all kings think their castles are boring."

They were lounging around on a sectional sofa in the big-windowed living room. Drinking and listening to music on the surround-sound system.

"How long you lived here?" said Gray.

"Eight or nine years. My wife fixed it up like this. Nothing made her happier than remodeling. We had another place. Out in the desert east of San Diego. My wife turned it into a real Shangri-la. What it was was an old country club. Had a clubhouse, swimming pool, tennis court, and an eighteen-hole golf course. It was near this little town in the middle of nowhere. Tejada Springs. Back in the forties a bunch of rich guys from LA decided to make it this hot resort place. It was gonna be the new Palm Springs. They built this big fancy hotel and for a while they had Hollywood people like Clark Gable and Marilyn Monroe and Orson Welles staying there. But the hotel burned down in the fifties and everything just kind of fizzled out. All the new people left and they closed the country club down. It was taken over by coyotes and jackrabbits. We bought it for a song. We remodeled the clubhouse and made it our house. We both loved to play golf and so we had our own private golf course. I can't play golf now because of my neck. I hardly ever go out there anymore. I guess the coyotes and jackrabbits are taking over again. My guess is it won't be long before they take over everything."

"What do you mean?" said Luke.

"Well young man, what I mean is we're a doomed species. *Homo sapiens* as we amusingly call ourselves. Wise men. What a knee-slapper. We should call ourselves violent men. Stupid men. Greedy men. We've proved ourselves completely unfit for survival on this planet. Darwin's hammer will come down hard on us."

"I can't think like that," said Gina. "I gotta believe Luke's gonna grow up in a decent world."

"I'll bet Gray agrees with me."

"I understand what you're saying, Norman. But I guess I'm with Gina. Seems like you've gotta have a little hope."

"Well suit yourselves. I'm preparing for the worst. I've got plenty of bottled water and canned goods. Plus a gun in every room. Including both bathrooms and all the closets."

"You serious?" said Gray.

"You bet. When my wife and I lived in Bel Air we were the victims of a home invasion robbery. They didn't hurt us but they sure did scare us. They locked us in a closet. Anybody tries that again they're gonna be in for a big surprise."

"You wouldn't have a problem killing somebody?" said Gina.

"In a situation like that? Brutal cretinous thugs threatening me or people I care about? Hell no. I'd do it with pleasure." He turned his shoulders and looked at Gray. "What about you?"

"What about me what?"

"Think you could kill a man?"

Gray was silent. Fingering the cold metal of his can of Carta Blanca.

"He's all about peace and love," said Gina. "He'd try and reason with them."

"Where is it?" said Gray. "The gun in this room."

"Actually since this is such a big room I've got two guns. A .38 Police Special and a .357 Colt Trooper. They're well concealed but within easy reach. We could make a game of it. Like an Easter egg hunt. Whoever finds the most guns within, say, fifteen minutes wins."

Luke looked eager. "That sounds fun."

"I don't want Luke ever thinking guns are fun," said Gina. "Like they're some kind of toy."

"I think I've just been admonished. And correctly so."

It was late afternoon. Towering clouds were beginning to float in off the ocean. Gray went out on the balcony with his beer. Propped his elbows on the railing. Looked north past the Santa Monica Pier and Pacific Palisades. Mountainous purply clouds.

Purplish cloudlike mountains. It reminded him of something. Of other clouds and mountains. But where and when?

He heard the glass door behind him sliding open. He looked around as Gina stepped out. She brought her glass of wine to the railing and looked out with him.

"Fucking beautiful," she said.

"Mm-hm. That's Malibu."

"Where?"

"All the way up the coast there. It's twenty-seven miles long. Probably the longest skinniest town in America."

"You know LA well?"

"Not really. Just passed through a couple of times."

"Bet you've passed through a lot of places."

"I guess so."

"So how do you get around? Without a car. Hitchhike?"

"I've hitchhiked some. I walk a lot. Sometimes I rent a car. Sometimes I get on a plane."

"You ever planning on getting a regular job?"

"No plans at the moment."

"I don't mean to sound like your mother. But what are you gonna do with the rest of your life? Go to parks and walk around trees?"

"Keeps me out of trouble."

"What are you gonna do for money?"

"I've got a little saved up."

"I didn't know being a sailor paid that well."

"Oh yeah. It's very lucrative."

"I'm determined to get to the bottom of you."

He smiled a little. "I could say the same thing about you."

They were silent. Looking at each other. The way they had looked at the clouds and the mountains. And then they looked away.

She sipped some of her wine and sighed. "Shit. I been drinking too much. Ever since I met you and Norman."

"Gina? You can tell me."

"Tell you what?"

"Why you and Luke are running."

"What makes you think we're running?"

"It was obvious. From the first minute I laid eyes on you."

She didn't say anything.

"Maybe I can help."

"How could you help?"

He shrugged. "Sometimes it helps just to talk about it."

She looked up at him. The breeze off the ocean blowing her hair. She had an intense way of looking at you. Her eyes going back and forth from one of your eyes to the other.

"How do I know I can trust you?"

"Do you trust yourself?"

"Yes."

"What do your instincts tell you about me?"

They heard the door slide open. Luke was there.

"Norman wants to know if we wanna play Scrabble."

Gina looked dubious. "I don't know. I can't even spell cat."

"K-A-T," said Gray. "Come on. It'll be fun."

"Yeah, Mom. F-U-N."

"O-K."

It had stopped raining. They walked back to the car skirting water that had puddled on the pavement. Cicala deep within himself. Feeling a searing nostalgia for some simple time in his life that had probably never existed. All at once he noticed Bobby was carrying a furled umbrella.

"What's that?"

"An umbrella."

"I know it's a fucking umbrella. Where'd you get it?"

"Chuck let me have it. It was Chuck's."

"Who the hell's Chuck?"

"The Chinese guy. That was waiting for us. You know."

"A Chinaman named Chuck?"

"Yeah. He's a great guy. You know what? He loves the fucking

Jets. Knows all about 'em. Knows how many touchdowns Mark Sanchez threw in the third fucking grade."

"Now we got an umbrella. Now that it's not raining."

"But next time it rains we'll have it. If somebody don't steal it."

They reached the Lincoln. It made chirping noises and lights blinked as Bobby unlocked it. Cicala sighed.

"The fucking slants. They're taking over everything."

They stood on the balcony. Gray looking at her. With those calm gray-blue eyes.

"What do your instincts tell you about me?"

She didn't answer directly.

"Why didn't you kiss me yesterday? I wanted you to."

"I wanted to too."

"Are you shy? Shy with girls?"

He took her in his arms. Not shy at all. And he was kissing her exactly like she liked to be kissed. But wait a second. They wouldn't be doing this with Luke and Norman there. Maybe watching them through the glass door.

Luke and Norman had left of course. On an errand. To pick up some special dessert that Norman knew about. It would take them about half an hour.

She was naked. In the hot soapy water in the bathtub at their motel. She was thinking about Gray sliding open the glass door. Them stepping inside. She was about to see his body again. With its strange scars. His lean ravaged beautiful body.

By the time she came out of the bathroom Luke had gone to sleep. In front of an old Alan Ladd movie on TV. She sat down at the desk. She wanted to Google Gray. But she didn't even know his last name. Or maybe Gray was his last name. The only hard fact she had was the name of the ship he'd served on.

She typed "u.s. navy the thomaston" into her laptop. Fifteen thousand nine hundred entries popped up. In a minute or two she'd discovered the *Thomaston* had been built in Pascagoula, Mississippi, in 1953. Had participated in the Marine landings at Danang and Chu Lai in South Vietnam in 1965. And had been decommissioned on September 28, 1984. Gray looked to be in his early to mid thirties. Say thirty-four. Which in 1984 would have made him nine. Kind of young to be a sailor.

Meanwhile three doors down the sailor was asleep. He was toiling in his dream up a high craggy mountain. Amid tumbling purplish clouds. And he understood that the clouds and the mountains he had seen from Norman's balcony had not reminded him of something in his past but had been a foreshadowing of this. Of his ascent to the summit where he would meet the Monkey King face to face. Since long before he had been born the Monkey King had been awaiting him. The Monkey King's golden eyes could see through all illusions. At one touch from his dark wrinkled hand the sailor would shatter and the only thing left would be the truth. Or maybe Truth. And so the sailor climbed.

Sunday

He had a new roommate. Another old man. A Mexican. Manuel. But he wasn't obnoxious like the last one. He was fat and good-natured and he had a big fat family that clustered around his bed during visiting hours laughing and gabbing in Spanish like a hospital room was a fun place to be. He had a comely teenage granddaughter that hadn't gotten fat yet. She had smiled at terHorst once and he could have eaten her with a spoon. The only negative with Manuel was he was somewhat deaf and always had the audio on his TV turned way up. Right now he was watching an asinine Spanish-language talk show where the host, a fat balding guy in his fifties, was in the process of taking off his clothes so he could climb into a bubble bath where a big-titted blonde in a yellow bikini awaited. The studio audience was laughing uproariously and so was Manuel. He began to cough and his face turned red and terHorst grew a little alarmed.

"Hey Manuel, you okay?"

He nodded and waved him off. Still so choked with laughter he couldn't speak.

"Hey Manuel? Would you mind turning it down just a little bit?"

"Oh *si*. Sorry."

He was half watching Green Bay at Tampa Bay while he fooled around with his laptop. He was trying to figure out how Google Earth worked. He wanted to zoom in on King Beach but instead and maddeningly it kept returning to a neighborhood in Paris. Finally he gave up and checked in with the MobileTracker. Yup. They were still in King Beach. Obviously feeling safe there. Which puzzled him. He could have sworn that Luke had looked right at him as he was having his heart attack on the interstate. Seemed like knowing he was out here they would have vacated Southern California as quickly as they could. But maybe it was a matter of Luke seeing him in an unfamiliar context and just not recognizing him.

He set the laptop aside and interlaced his fingers on his stomach and settled in to watch the game. He was still weak but feeling better. He was hoping he'd feel well enough to travel in a day or two. All in all his stay at the hospital, except for the malevolent Muslim doctor who was scheming to kill him and make it look like a medical accident, hadn't been so bad. The food was terrible but Martinez snuck in lots of goodies for him—candy bars, trail mix, Fritos, and delicious chicken tamales his mother-in-law had made. He wasn't the introspective type but now he kind of enjoyed having the time just to think, remember, and daydream. His mind drifted away from the battle of the Bays and he began to daydream now. Imagining himself running his hands through a glittering pile of diamonds like a mad miser in a silent movie. When he was a kid his family had gone on vacation and stopped at the diamond mine in Murfreesboro, Arkansas. People paid a fee to look for diamonds and you got to keep whatever you found. He'd thought they'd all be handed picks and miners' hats with lights on them and they'd go deep down into a dark mine but it turned out to be a plowed-up field under a broiling summer sun. Within fifteen minutes of starting he'd actually found a diamond. A crummy little yellow one but a diamond nonetheless and it was like he'd been bitten by the diamond bug. He'd take Gina's diamonds from her and then have sex with her and kill her and then retire from the Marshals Service and move to some warm-weather Third World country. Where he could sell off a diamond every now and then and live like a king. Thailand maybe. Great food and plenty of cheap young poontang.

He'd been thinking about Luke. About what to do with him. The more he thought about it the more simply killing him along with his mother seemed like a waste.

But he had an idea. He had met a fascinating fellow. At a bar in the Miami airport. An Argentinian. Leopoldo Forza. Their planes were delayed and they had spent hours drinking single-malt scotch and talking. Forza had a PhD in economics. He was a professor at the National University of Mar del Plata and a published writer and a businessman who had his fingers in an amazing array of pies. He believed that since nature was amoral and man was a part of nature man too was amoral and anyone who believed in any kind of morality was delusional. Government in all its forms, said Forza, was in the process of fading away and its functions were being taken over by the market. No laws, rules, or regulations would be necessary or even possible since every atom of the earth and of all the creatures on it would be part of a system that would spin on its own forever like a top. All salvation and success lay in embracing that system. In merging oneself with it in a joyous mystic union. TerHorst was not sure how much he understood of all this but was intrigued by it but had reservations because he was a Christian. Professor Forza said just think of the market as the body of Christ.

They had stayed in touch and been discussing this and that and looking for something to work on together. And now he was re-membering what Forza had told him about a South American pedo-phile ring. There was a group of fabulously rich faggots who would pass a boy around till he lost his freshness and was disposed of. A cute Anglo boy like Luke would no doubt fetch a pretty penny.

They had croissants and coffee at the coffee shop then went for a walk. The Sunday morning shook as a plane flew up. All three watched till it diminished in the distance and the sunny serenity of the town was restored.

Gina winced a little and put her hand on her stomach.

"What's the matter?" said Gray.

"My stomach. It's kinda screwed up."

"Serves you right," said Luke.

"What do you mean?"

"You said you were sick yesterday and you weren't. So it serves you right you're sick today."

"Thanks for the sympathy. Anyway. It's all Gray's fault. And Norman's."

"Why's it our fault?"

"'Cause of all the wild partying you guys have made me do. My body's not used to it."

"Playing Scrabble for three hours is your idea of wild partying?"

"That's right. I'm a very conservative girl," she said and then to Luke: "Let's go back. To the motel."

"Why?"

"I just told you. I don't feel good."

"But why do I have to go? Why can't I just go with Gray?"

"Oh Luke. Do we have to fight about every little thing?"

"He can come with me," said Gray.

She was silent. Looking at Gray. Thinking it over.

"Gina, he'll be fine. You don't have to worry."

"I'll be fine, Mom."

"Okay. But don't go far."

"We won't," said Gray.

"And don't be gone long."

"We won't," said Luke.

Gina and her turbulent stomach hurried down Alejo Avenue toward the motel and Gray and Luke went up a side street. Past duplexes and quadriplexes and occasional small houses in a jumble of colors and styles. The lots small and virtually yardless and everything crowded together.

They went by without realizing the little yellow bungalow now painted white was where Norman and his wife had lived.

A Sunday morning lassitude prevailed. An old lady walking her old dog. A corpulent black cat dozing on a windowsill. A hungover-looking guy washing his beat-up car and water trickling along the curb. The street rose and circled around and led them to the lagoon. Luke saw the tall white bird hunting in the shallows.

Not a word had been said since they had left Gina.

"You don't talk very much do you?" said Luke.

Gray looked at Luke solemnly and shook his head and then they both laughed.

"Does it bother you?"

"No. Mom talks all the time. I get tired of it."

"Your mom's something special. I hope you know that."

"You really think so?"

"Yeah."

"But how do you know? You just met her."

"Sometimes you just know."

"What's your mom like?"

"She died. A long time ago."

"What about your dad?"

"Dead too."

Three ducks and their reflections glided over the lagoon. Clusters of grass eight or ten feet tall were scattered along the bank. A wind came up and blew the grass and in the shade that flickered like fire they saw a ragged man curled up on his side asleep. The windy grass made a *shhh* sound and they walked by him in silence.

"My dad's in prison," Luke said.

Gray thought about it. Looked at Luke.

"Will he be in for a long time?"

"Yeah."

"Do you miss him?"

"Sometimes. He was great sometimes. He'd joke around and we'd go bowling and sometimes he played video games with me. And I'd always beat him."

"But sometimes he wasn't great?"

"He was mean to Mom. He'd get mad and hit her. But she made it worse."

"How'd she do that?"

"She'd fight back. She'd curse at him and spit in his face. And that made him even madder and he'd hit her harder. And she'd keep cursing at him."

"I'm sorry, Luke. That must've been rough."

Luke seemed to want to say more but didn't and it didn't feel right to Gray to press him.

"Gray?"

"Yeah?"

"This stuff with Dad. It's a big secret. Don't tell Mom I told you. Okay?"

"Okay."

They reached the end of the lagoon and walked past the playground and the park seemed so pleasant they sat down at one of the tables in the picnic area just to take it all in. The kids on the swings and seesaws. Two skinny geeky guys throwing around an orange Frisbee. Half a dozen guys playing soccer. A teenage Latino couple cuddling on a blanket on the grass. All beneath the mellow early November sun and an endless azure sky.

And then Quex and Stitch entered the park.

They walked across the grass on their steel-toed boots. Said something to the cuddling couple and laughed. The teenage boy glared after them and the girl looked scared. The dog was with them. The battered half malamute. Trudging along at the end of his leash in his spiky punishment collar. They sat down in the shade of the single tree. They were carrying Cokes and white paper bags out of which they took burgers and fries and onion rings.

The teenage couple gathered up their blanket and left.

"That's your tree," said Luke.

"Well it's not *my* tree."

"It's where you do your qigong."

"I'll let 'em sit there. Just this once."

Quex and Stitch tore open plastic packets and squirted ketchup on the onion rings and fries. As they ate the dog stood a little ways off. Watching them intently. As if nothing else existed in the universe except their food.

Quex tossed him an onion ring and he snapped it up and gulped it down.

A minute or two passed. No more food was forthcoming. Quex and Stitch were talking and not paying any attention to the dog. Who began to inch closer. When his big head was within a foot of the onion rings Quex noticed and yelled: "Get away you fucker!" and hit the dog with his fist just below one of his tattered ears. The dog yelped and leapt back and the skinheads laughed.

Luke glanced at Gray to see if he had seen this. He had. But his face showed no emotion. Now he looked away from the tree and scanned the park in a general way.

"Hey Luke? I just remembered there's some stuff I have to do. Would you mind going back to the motel by yourself?"

"Right now?"

"Yeah."

He shrugged. "Okay."

"I'll see you in a little bit."

Luke nodded. Stood up and started walking off.

"Go straight back, Luke. Don't go anywhere else."

"I won't."

He walked off across the grass. Passing between the tree and the Frisbee guys. He reached the other side of the park where the public restrooms were. He looked back and saw Gray still sitting at the picnic table. Gray waved and he waved back and walked on and then when he was out of sight of Gray behind the restrooms he turned around.

He peered around the side of the building. Saw that Gray had left the picnic table and was walking toward the tree.

He entered the shade. Went straight to the dog and bent down and took his leash. Quex and Stitch stared at him.

"What the fuck you doing?" said Quex.

Gray kept his eyes on the dog. "Let's go, boy," he said softly.

The dog looked at him a moment. And then they walked away together.

Quex and Stitch just sat there. Lips covered in mustard and ketchup. Slack-jawed in astonishment.

"What the fuck?" said Stitch.

"Hey asshole!" yelled Quex. "Where you going with my dog?"

Neither man nor dog paused or looked back.

Quex looked at Stitch.

"You believe this shit?"

"Naw."

"Hey fuck!"

They threw down their burgers and jumped up and ran after Gray. Quex a little ahead of Stitch. Their boots pounding over the grass.

Luke watched them running. Watched Gray and the dog just keep walking. As though he didn't know they were coming and they were almost upon him and Stitch had taken a blackjack out of his pocket and Quex was reaching out for Gray's shoulder but as Luke stepped out from behind the building to shout a warning Gray pivoted. He grabbed Quex's arm and kicked back with his right leg and the flat of his foot drove through Quex's right knee. The joint collapsed and there were popping sounds as tendons snapped. Quex screamed and Gray twisted his arm dislocating his shoulder and forcing him down and then with his forearm he broke his elbow. His scream modulated into an unearthly shriek cut short when Gray slammed his knee into his mouth then he finally let him fall to the ground.

Now Gray looked at Stitch. He was standing a few feet away. His eyes were wide and he was breathing hard. Like he'd run a mile and not just fifty feet. He was holding the blackjack like it was a dog turd he'd picked up by accident. His voice quivered as he said: "Dude! Don't fuck with me! I'll go gorilla on your ass!"

Gray gazed down dispassionately on Quex. Twitching and groaning on the grass. Spitting out blood and teeth. Then he walked over to the dog. The dog seemed nervous and shied away.

"It's okay," he said as he knelt in front of him and unfastened his collar. Then he went back to Quex. He leaned over him and quickly slipped the collar on. Tightened it so the spikes pressed snugly against his neck.

"Oh man!" said Stitch. "What the fuck *is* this? Jesus!"

The soccer ball and orange Frisbee lay abandoned on the grass. The Frisbee throwers and soccer players observing Gray. Alarmed mothers were hustling their kids out of the playground. Luke watched Gray put his hand in the loop of the leash and begin to drag Quex toward the tree.

Quex began to cough and choke. He grabbed at the collar with his left hand. His broken arm and shattered leg slithering over the grass.

Stitch trailed along at a safe distance. As if he were a sympathetic but helpless onlooker and Quex some Christ being conveyed to his crucifixion.

When they reached the tree Gray wrapped one arm around Quex and hoisted him up. He whimpered and gibbered as Gray hung the leash over a low limb and pulled on it. When his boots were barely touching the ground Gray knotted the leash and left him there.

The dog was waiting for him and they walked away. As behind them Quex stood tippy-toe on his good leg and clawed at the collar. Stitch still at a distance. Making sure Gray wasn't coming back.

Gray was going in Luke's direction. He had stepped back behind the building and was standing with his back to the brick wall. But as soon as Gray and the dog came around the corner they turned and looked right at him.

"Why didn't you go back to the motel?"

Luke shrugged. He walked out. Saw that Quex was now stretched out under the tree. Stitch standing over him and talking on his cell phone.

"He's calling somebody," said Luke.

"Looks like it."

"What if he's calling the cops?"

"What if he is?"

"You took their dog."

"Whatever happens happens. I'll deal with it when it comes." He put his hand on Luke's shoulder. "Let's go."

They began to walk back toward the motel. The dog between them as though for years this had been his place. Luke saw that ugly sores ringed his neck.

"What are you going to do with him?"

"Keep him. Unless you want him."

"Yeah, Mom would love it if I brought *him* home."

"Don't tell her what you saw. Okay?"

"Why not?"

"I just don't think she'd be very happy about it."

"Okay. But she's gonna wanna know where he came from."

"We found him in the park. Wandering around. Lost."

Luke smiled. "He followed us home."

Gray smiled too. "Right."

It was a block to Alejo then a block to the motel. Luke unlocked the door to his room and looked in.

"She's in the bathroom."

Gray nodded. He stood there. Wanting to say something.

"What are you gonna name him?" said Luke.

"I don't know. Listen. I didn't want you to see all that. I'm sorry."

"I've seen lots of stuff."

He stepped inside and shut the door.

But Gray didn't go to his room. He and the dog headed toward town. There were things he needed to get him. Food. A new leash and collar. And something to put on his wounds.

They were met at the baggage carousel by a young man with a scarred acne-inflamed face and a snoutlike nose. The System's representative in Oklahoma City.

"I'll bet y'all are Mr. Smith and Mr. Jones," he said with a grin. Disconcertingly blue eyes blazing out of his red face.

"Actually," said Groh, "I'm Mr. Smith-Jones. My associate is Mr. Jones-Smith."

The man laughed and stuck out his hand.

"You wanna know something funny? My name really *is* Smith. DeWitt Smith."

"That *is* funny," said Groh, shaking his hand reluctantly. The man so startlingly ugly he didn't want to touch him.

"Y'all got luggage?"

"Yes."

DeWitt eyed the bags sliding by on the rumbling carousel.

"Well just let out a holler when you see your shit, I'll grab it for you."

"All right."

"How was your flight?"

"Quite dull. I'm pleased to say."

DeWitt laughed. "Yeah, I guess you don't want a flight to be real exciting do you?"

DeWitt decided he liked Mr. Smith-Jones but not Mr. Jones-Smith. You met a lot of cold-eyed customers in this line of work and Jones-Smith for shit sure was one of them. When he was a kid he'd been out on his granddaddy's farm and there was an old well covered with boards and he pulled a board off and looked down in it and cool dank air wafted into the summer sunlight and several daddy longlegs scuttled away and he couldn't see the water but only darkness and he imagined how terrible it would be to fall down in there and that's the feeling he got looking at Jones-Smith.

"That's mine," said Groh and DeWitt grabbed it and swung it off and Bulgakov's soon followed.

"Well let's act like cow shit and hit the trail!"

He energetically exited the terminal pulling along behind him the two wheeled bags. Groh and Bulgakov having to hurry to keep up. Exchanging a look behind his back. DeWitt was stoked. He didn't know what these guys were up to but they were obviously on some kind of high-profile mission and he was determined that his part of it was going to go off without a hitch. He knew the System was a meritocracy. Maybe he used to be some nobody from Ratliff City, Oklahoma, population 131, but now there was no telling how far he could rise.

They thought she knew nothing but she knew nearly everything. She knew that for all her outward jollity Latreece was knotted up inside because a lump had been discovered in one of her gigantic breasts and now she was having to suffer through the weekend waiting for the results of the biopsy. And she could smell it like the smoke from a faraway fire. Her son's anguish and anger at being locked up in Pennsylvania. And she knew that a crack team of assassins had just been dispatched to track down her runaway ex-daughter-in-law and that an hour ago her husband had gone into his socks and underwear drawer where he pathetically kept hidden his bottle of little blue pills and that this very moment he was downstairs in the maid's room with the maid who was patiently trying to coax an erection out of his crooked old cock. And the maid she knew was not what she seemed. Not a sweet simple laughing girl from South America but a schemer as ruthless and hard-hearted as she Millie Cicala had been before her stroke. The stroke that had not imprisoned her but had set her free.

It was like this. The parts of her brain that generated fear, worry, sadness, and wrath had been flooded with blood and destroyed. Spared had been more positive parts. People mistook her smile for the simpering of an idiot. Actually it was an expression of a bliss that started within her skull but seemed to extend to the farthest reaches of the universe. How could she be concerned about a husband diddling or trying to diddle the maid when she felt like a leaf being blown along in a prodigious hurricane of joy?

His mother had always said one sign of trashy people was they never made up their beds and when he was growing up he was at risk for a whipping if he didn't make up his. His mother inspecting the work like a Marine drill instructor. The habit had stuck with him. Even though he lived a solitary life and hardly anyone ever saw his impeccably made-up bed but him. His mother had given him a bedspread that her mother had given her. Once white but having taken on with the decades an ivory cast. Ornate nubby patterns woven in and a stringy fringe. He usually kept it folded in a drawer but had taken it out because he had visitors. It was tucked cozily around the pillows. Its fringe all around equidistant from the carpet. Weaponry spread out on it in hard shiny rows.

Mostly handguns. Both revolvers and semi-automatics. Half a dozen knives. And some silencers.

"Quite an arsenal, DeWitt," said Groh and DeWitt saw he had done well.

They both selected semi-autos. Groh a .32, Bulgakov a .45. And Bulgakov also took a Morseth boot knife with a four-and-a-half-inch blade. DeWitt could tell by the way he handled it that he liked knives. DeWitt didn't. He had seen his granddaddy slaughter a pig once. Slitting open its stomach when it was still alive and oinking. He hadn't eaten bacon for a month after that.

"What kind of car did you get us?" said Groh.

"Dodge Neon. I was told you didn't want anything too fancy."

Groh nodded. Looked at his watch. "Would it inconvenience you if we stayed here for a bit?"

"Inconvenience me, are you kidding? I'd love the company!"

They went in the living room. Groh and Bulgakov sat down on the couch. On the coffee table was a cow's skull with long curving horns.

"That looks like something out of a painting by Georgia O'Keeffe," said Groh.

DeWitt had never heard of Georgia O'Keeffe but just in case Groh was making some kind of joke he laughed.

"Could I get y'all anything? Something to drink? Or maybe some supper. I ain't a bad cook."

"Nothing for me thanks," said Groh.

DeWitt looked at Bulgakov. Who was ignoring him. Affixing a silencer to his pistol.

"Hey," said DeWitt, "it's Sunday night! You know what that means."

Groh looked at him blankly.

"Sunday night football!"

And he reached for the remote.

Gina dreamed about a poorly thrown bowling ball rolling noisily down an endless gutter then awoke to a plane taking off. She was lying on the bed with all her clothes on. The window was filled with dusk. She looked around and didn't see Luke. The door to the bathroom was open and he wasn't in there either and panic gushed through her and she said: *"Luke? Luke?"*

His head popped up on the other side of his bed.

"What?" he said irritably.

"What are you doing down there?"

"Reading."

"On the floor?"

"I like to read on the floor."

She sat up, sighed, rubbed her face and eyes.

"How do you feel?" he said.

"Better, I guess."

"Can we go and get dinner? I'm starving."

"Oh Luke, I don't feel like going out. Make yourself a PB and J."

"But that's what I had for lunch."

"It won't kill you to eat the same thing twice."

"I'm sick of sandwiches. This is like child abuse. Always making me eat sandwiches."

"Child abuse. Okay," she sighed. "Just let me take a shower first."

They walked down Alejo Avenue. Dusk turning into night and a single bright star shining behind them over the sea. They went in the Sea Horse and took a booth.

"Hey there's Norman," said Luke.

He was sitting at the bar with some raucous companions. Wearing a San Diego Chargers ball cap and watching the Eagles and Cowboys on TV.

"Maybe he won't see us," said Gina.

"Don't you like him?'

"Yeah. But I'm not in a Norman mood. He takes a lot of energy."

January came over with menus. They looked them over.

"I'm not very hungry," said Gina. "Think I'll just have a bowl of clam chowder. You gonna have a Pirateburger?"

"I don't eat meat."

"Oh yeah. I forgot. Mr. Vegetarian. So what are you gonna have?"

"I don't know."

He puzzled over the menu. The bar erupted in shouts as the Cowboys scored a touchdown.

"Come on, Mr. Vegetarian. Pick something."

"Leave me alone."

"Hey guys."

Norman had walked up. Drink in hand.

"Mind if an old coot keeps you company?"

"'Course not," said Gina.

He sat down next to Luke. A little red-faced. A whiff of alcohol coming off him.

Gina looked at his cap. "Are you a Chargers fan?"

"Yeah. I'm from San Diego originally. We had a fantastic win over the Giants today so I'm happy. You like sports, Luke?"

"I like to skateboard. And play soccer. But I don't like to watch sports very much."

"Good for you. I've probably wasted in toto several years of my life watching sports on TV. It's an interesting phenomenon. Sports fandom. You're in euphoria or despair because of the meaningless activities of a group of people who have nothing at all to do with you. Who don't even know you exist. The relationship's totally one-sided. It reminds me of the philosopher Spinoza's conception of God. He was a pantheist. Saw God as an impersonal force. And he said you can love God but you can't expect God to love you. Old Norm Hopkins can love the Chargers. But the Chargers will never love old Norm Hopkins."

January came back with glasses of water. "We know what we want?"

Gina looked at Luke. "I think we need a little more time."

"Okay. How we doing, Norman?"

"Just fine, January. And we'd be doing even better if you brought me another drink."

"You got it."

"Where's your partner in crime tonight?" he said to Gina.

"Gray? I don't know. We haven't seen him since this morning."

"I called his room but didn't get an answer. Maybe he's out walking his new dog."

"How'd you know about the dog?"

"Oh, everybody's talking about it."

She was puzzled. "Really? Why?"

Now he was puzzled. "Well it was quite an event from what I hear."

"What was? What are you talking about?"

"How Gray got the dog."

"He and Luke found it in the park. It was lost." She looked at Luke. "Right?"

Luke managed a feeble nod.

"Well that's extremely strange," said Norman. " 'Cause I heard an entirely different story."

Gray and the dog walked up over the dunes then down to the Sea Breeze Motel. He unlocked his door and they went in. The dog stepping on a picture postcard of the Sea Breeze.

He took the leash off and picked the postcard up. On its back was written:

I want to talk to you. Now!
Gina

The dog was lapping up water from a gleaming silver dish.

"I'll be back soon," said Gray.

He knocked on her door then waited and knocked again then heard her.

"Who's there?"

"Gray."

The door opened quickly and as she came out he caught a glimpse behind her of Luke who seemed to have been crying then she shut the door.

"What the fuck happened in the park?" she said. Her face rigid with anger.

"Sounds like you already know."

"Why'd you tell Luke to lie?"

"I didn't want you to be upset."

"You had no right. You endangered my son!"

"He was never in any danger."

"All 'cause of some stupid dog!"

"I saw an animal being abused and so I stopped it."

"You shoulda called the fucking Humane Society if it bothered you that much. Not got in a fight. Right in front of Luke."

"I'm sorry he saw it. I didn't want him to."

"Yeah. He told me. That you sent him back here."

"I did."

"He's just a little boy. He shouldn't be wandering around by himself. Anything coulda happened. There coulda been perverts in the park."

"There weren't."

"How do you know?"

"I looked."

She gave an incredulous laugh. "You think you're some kinda all-seeing person? You can see through walls? See around corners? You don't know who the fuck was in the park!"

"A ten-year-old boy oughta be able to walk a few hundred yards by himself in a peaceful town without his mother freaking out."

"It's none of your fucking business how I raise my son. *I* make the decisions for him. And this morning I made a bad decision. I trusted him with *you*."

"You can trust me. It wasn't a bad decision."

"You didn't just get in a fight. Over something that had nothing to do with you. You nearly *killed* that guy. You hung him from a fucking tree."

"I didn't come close to killing him. If I'd wanted to kill him I would have."

She stared at him.

"Who *are* you?" she said softly.

"I told you who I was."

"You told me a lot of lies."

"Like what?"

"You said you were a sailor. On a ship called the *Thomaston*. But you couldn't've been. It was decommissioned in 1984. When you were a kid."

Gray was silent.

"Well?"

Again. Silence.

"I don't know what's going on with you. Maybe you're not a liar. Maybe you're just . . . ill. But I can't take any chances. I don't want you around Luke anymore."

She opened the door and began to go through it.

"Gina—"

But the door shut in his face.

———

The town lay silent under the stars. They drove between Buster's Restaurant and the used-car lot. Past the big DEITER "THE CHEATER" CHEATS FOR LESS sign. The red and blue and yellow and green pennants hanging limp in the stirless air.

Groh loved coming to a new place. Not knowing what he would see or what would happen in the next moment. He wished he never needed sleep or rest but could ceaselessly, sharklike, be moving, moving, moving.

In this he wasn't at all like Bulgakov. Who was snoring now with his mouth open. He was the most incurious creature Groh had ever encountered. Nothing that happened between jobs mattered to him. Paris was the same as London and Mexico City as Hong Kong.

"Dima. Dima. Wake up. We're here!"

They glided through quiet streets past modest but well-kept houses filled with the sleeping citizenry of Brady. Oblivious to the fact assassins had come into their midst. Unless their passing somehow registered in their dreams. Caused them to moan and mutter and roll over and want to wake up. Groh parked in front of the Osage Creek Apartments. Turned off the engine and lights. They sat in the car staring at the building. Then they pulled on their flesh-colored rubber gloves and got out.

It was cold and their breath came out in gray puffs. Lights were on in one unit and they could hear faint music. Some wailing country song. Evoking a lonesome listener with a can of beer and a cigarette. But the rest of the units were dark and silent.

They found mailboxes. In locked metallic tiers. Bulgakov popped open the one labeled PETERSON with one of his lock-picking tools. Inside was a single postcard. Addressed to Occupant. Advertising HAPPY JACK'S BAR-B-Q. BRADY'S HAPPIEST PLACE TO EAT!!!

They went along a walk that ran in front of the building then up the flight of stairs to apartment 25. Bulgakov carefully removed the yellow X of police tape then went to work on the lock. On the other side of the landing was another apartment. Groh keeping his eye on the door in case it was opened by some nosy light-sleeping neighbor. Who would be in for a big surprise.

Bulgakov got the door open and they stepped in. Groh crossed the living room to a window that looked out on the street. The curtains were open and he closed them and they turned on small flashlights. Their beams wandered around the room. Bulgakov's stopped at the dark stains on the carpet where Deiter had died. Groh's played over the picture of the fox hunt.

"I went fox hunting once, Dima. Did I ever tell you?"

Bulgakov ignored him. Walked over to a desk and pulled out a drawer. They were looking for anything that might lead them to the woman who had fled. Telephone bill, credit card receipt, travel brochure. A computer of course could be a treasure trove. But after ten minutes they had come up with nothing. There were clothes in the closets and food in the refrigerator and fuzzy slippers beside the bed but it seemed that nothing useful had been left behind. Or if it had the police had already taken it.

Groh went into the boy's room. Luke's room. He knew what he looked like because he'd received e-mailed photos of him and his mother. A handsome boy. A beautiful boy. Something catlike about his eyes. Strange bewitching eyes. He would be kind to him after they killed his mother. Buffer him against Bulgakov's harshness.

His flashlight found another flashlight. The Harry Potter flashlight. He picked it up. Turned it on experimentally. So Luke liked Harry Potter. He'd buy all the Harry Potter books. So Luke would have something to read while he was in transit. And when he gave them to Luke he'd look up at him with those eyes and say: "How did you know I like Harry Potter?"

The light came on.

A young policeman was standing in the doorway holding his gun with a two-handed grip and pointing it at Groh.

"Put your hands up!"

Groh just stood there. Blinking in the sudden light.

"Drop the flashlights! Put up your damn hands!"

He tossed the flashlights on the bed and raised his hands.

"On your head! Put 'em on your head!"

Groh did so. The cop was wearing a name tag that said Butter-field. Looking at him you might have thought Brady was some special place where sixteen-year-old boys could be policemen.

"What are you doing here?"

Groh could feel fear coming off Butterfield like heat. This was probably the first time he'd ever pointed a gun at anybody.

"Gina and I are old friends. I'm quite distressed by her disappearance. She has some things of mine. Some books and photographs. I've come here to get them."

"How come you're sneaking around in the dark? How come you got them gloves on?"

Butterfield had advanced a few steps into the room. Groh looked at the tightly gripped nine-millimeter.

"How come your gun is shaking?"

"Get down on the floor! On your stomach! Let's go! Do it!"

But Groh just stood there. Seeing behind Butterfield the dark bulk of Bulgakov. Black sweatshirt, black jeans, black leather coat and sturdy brown boots. Which he was moving forward noiselessly on.

"My associate is behind you. He has a gun. He's about to kill you with it. Unless you follow my directions."

Butterfield gave an anxious laugh. Shifting his weight from foot to foot. Head and shoulders rocking a little.

"Yeah. Right. Get on the floor!"

Bulgakov pressed the nose of the silencer against the nape of the cop's neck. He flinched and cried out as if the metal were red-hot.

"Give me your gun," said Groh. "Grip first."

His hands now were trembling so much he nearly dropped the gun as he turned it around and presented it to Groh.

"Get on your knees."

His face contorting he dropped to his knees. Like an abject sinner finally giving in to God.

"Don't kill me. Please."

He swayed on his knees. Groh in front and Bulgakov behind.

"How did you know we were here?"

"I've got a wife. I've got a little baby. A boy!"

"Control yourself. Concentrate. Your life depends on it."

"Yes sir. Yes sir. I hear you."

"How did you know we were here? Did someone call you? If so, who?"

"Nobody called. I was just driving by. I check on this place ever' so often. 'Cause of what happened here last week. And I got suspicious."

"Why?"

"The curtains. The curtains in the living room winda. They were shut. They were open before. Mister don't hurt me. We're fixing to take our first vacation together. To Branson, Missouri. Next week!"

"Did you call for backup?"

"What?"

"Did you call for backup?"

"No. No sir. I didn't."

"The truth this time. Did you call for backup?"

And now Groh saw a clumsy attempt at cunning kindle in his eyes.

"Yes sir. I sure did! There's probably six or eight men out there right now. Waiting on you. They'll cut you down if you don't give up!"

Groh raised his eyes from Butterfield to Bulgakov. It was not even a nod he gave him but some subtle look and somehow Butterfield knew what it meant. He began breathing fast and his head lolled around as though it had become too big and heavy for his neck. Like a giant baby's head. Groh smelled urine and saw Butterfield was wetting himself.

Bulgakov reached into his boot. Butterfield glancing back.

"Oh God! Oh fucking God!"

Once Bulgakov, in an uncharacteristically loquacious mood, had told Groh about how he had killed prisoners in Chechnya. He'd pin their heads to the ground with his boot then stab into their throats till he cut the carotid. It was an effective but messy method. You often got blood all over you. But he had devised a better way. With hardly any blood. And now Groh watched as Bulgakov knocked off Butterfield's cap, grabbed the crown of his head and forced his chin down on his chest then shoved his knife into his neck just below the base of the skull. Angling the blade up into the brain.

He gasped and toppled over. Twitched a bit and was still.

Groh picked his flashlight up off the bed.

"All right, Dima. Move fast. But don't hurry."

They closed the front door behind them. Replaced the police tape. Went down the stairs. Both with their guns out. As they came out of the stairwell they found themselves face to face with another policeman. A very fat one coming down the walk. Wearing a thick plaid coat against the cold that didn't match his blue uniform. He too had his gun out but was too surprised to use it as Groh and Bulgakov instantly began to shoot him. But he didn't fall. Arms held out a little in front of him he stood there taking round after round like a man determined to set a record for how many times he could be shot and keep standing. Maybe some combination of heavy coat, armoring fat, and the decreased muzzle velocity of their weapons because of the silencers kept him upright. He was making peculiarly small noises considering what was happening to him. *Ah! Ah! Ah!* As if he were in front of his bathroom mirror plucking out nose hairs with a tweezer. But a bullet spang to the forehead ended it all.

"Markus!"

Bulgakov was pointing across the street. A man and his dog were standing under a streetlight. The man gaping at them. Then he and the dog took off.

Far too far for a shot. Bulgakov took off after them. Running by the two BPD cars parked out front.

The man heard Bulgakov's boots striking the street. Was horrified to realize one of the killers was chasing him. His dog, a brown medium-sized mutt, was bounding along beside him at the end of his leash, his loppy ears flopping.

"Come on, Lewis! Run!"

They reached the corner and turned down another street. He was a pharmacist. Who had trouble sleeping. He had run track for the Brady Bobcats two decades ago and had kept in good shape and was wearing Nikes and running very fast but looked back and saw Bulgakov round the corner swinging wide, arms furiously pumping, gun glinting as he ran through the luminous cone of another streetlight and he saw that he was even faster and closing the gap. He screamed at the silent houses: "HELP! HELP! CALL THE POLICE! CALL THE POLICE!"

The air next to his ear cracked as a bullet passed through it. He thought, *I'm being shot at* and the thought made him stumble and he let go of the leash as he flailed his arms wildly trying to keep his balance then a bullet smacked him in the back. He went down. Tumbling along the street. The rough pavement abrading his face but he felt nothing. He came up to his hands and knees. Saw his dog twenty feet in front of him. Looking back and barking. Uncertain what to do. "Run, boy!" he tried to shout but only whispered. And then Bulgakov was above him. His gun popped twice softly and the pharmacist dropped.

Bulgakov panted. Frosty breaths gushing out of him. He picked up the shell casings that had clinked onto the street. The dog was running back and forth and barking at him and unseen dogs as though in solidarity also began to bark. A light came on in one of the houses. Bulgakov put the casings in his pocket and looked at the dog.

Behind him headlights came sweeping around the corner. He turned and faced them. Prepared to kill again. But it was Groh in the Neon.

"Come, Dima! Hurry!"

Bulgakov jumped in and the car screeched off.

Lewis, leash dragging, walked back to the corpse.

Gray couldn't sleep. He lay in bed watching Turner Classic Movies. *Nancy Drew and the Hidden Staircase.*

The malamute had been sitting on the floor near the front door. Gnawing on the Nylabone Durable Pooch Pacifier Gray had got him. Now he stood up, stretched, and walked over to the bed. He looked up at Gray. One eye scarred and dim. One bright and brown.

"You can come up here, boy. Come on. Jump!"

He slapped the bed and the dog jumped up. He moved to the foot of the bed and circled around twice and then plopped down. He rested his head on one of Gray's knees. He blinked a few times. His eyes getting heavy. And then he sighed. There could be something weary about a sigh but this wasn't that. Clearly it was a sigh of complete contentment.

Gray wished he could live in the innocent black and white world of Nancy Drew. The events of the morning kept replaying themselves in his head. Maybe Gina was right and he had displayed bad judgment in rescuing the dog. He probably shouldn't have told Luke to walk back to the motel by himself. Not because realistically there was any danger but because Gina had put him in charge and she wouldn't have wanted it. And when you stepped through the door of violence anything could happen. It could have had an entirely different ending. The guy with the CRAZY WHITE BOY tat could just as easily have had a gun as a blackjack and Gray could be dead now.

But ultimately Gray felt it had all gone down the way it had to go down. He knew you didn't choose who or what you were willing to die for. It chose you.

Monday

What did it all mean?

Because it had to mean something. This was a universe of meaning. You couldn't escape it no matter how hard you tried. Booze, drugs, women were just distractions on the path that led you inevitably back to the Lord. And if He knew when a sparrow fell He sure as hell must have known about the heart attack.

Before two years ago he'd never been seriously sick. Hardly ever even caught a cold. And now . . . two heart attacks in two years.

The first one had changed his life. It had made him take stock of what was really important to him. And he had discovered what was really important to him was to make a lot of money so he could quit being a marshal and do whatever the hell he wanted. He hated working for WITSEC. Being at the beck and call of treacherous scumbags who had turned against their own people. But when given lemons you had to make lemonade. He had been put in possession of secrets. Big and valuable secrets. It had just been a matter of picking and choosing his spot. And then a year ago Gina and all her diamonds had fallen into his lap. But why a second heart attack?

It was a test, he guessed. Probably the only way to look at it. Like that big kid in Oklahoma had said: "Winners don't give up, they get up." Either you believed you had a destiny or you didn't.

He tried the MobileTracker again. It was still on the fritz. It had been so since last night. If it didn't come back and it turned out she had left King Beach then he was fucked. Utterly fucked.

His cell rang. McGrath. Great.

"Hey Doug."

"Something terrible has happened."

"What?"

"Three people were killed in Brady last night. Two cops. And a guy walking his dog."

"Shit."

"One cop was found in Gina's apartment. The other outside the building. The guy with the dog just down the street. It's pretty clear what happened. One or more of Cicala's guys broke in the apartment. Trying to pick up her trail. And the cops walked in on 'em. It's our fault, Frank."

"Like hell it is."

"I've gotta let them know."

"Know what?"

"The truth."

TerHorst began rubbing his chest in slow desperate circles.

"It's way too late for the truth. The truth will destroy our careers. Just give me one more day, Doug. And I'll bring her in."

"I don't think you've got any idea where she is. If you did you would've already got her."

"You want the truth? Here's the fucking truth. I've had another heart attack."

"What?"

"I nearly died. I'm in a hospital."

"You shitting me?"

"Would I make something like that up?"

"Damn, Frank. I'm sorry."

"I've been getting better. I'll get out soon. Maybe tomorrow. Then I'll get her. I know exactly where she is."

"Then tell me."

"I can't do that."

"Why not?"

"I gotta handle this myself."

"Something doesn't smell right. There's something big you're leaving out."

"Have I ever let you down?"

"No."

"When Alison got sick. I was there for you wasn't I?"

"You've always been there for me. Like I've always been there for you. That's irrelevant."

"Fifteen years of friendship? That's irrelevant?"

"I'm ending this. Today."

"Tomorrow, Frank. End it tomorrow. If I don't get her. Okay?"

"If you've really had a heart attack you should be taking it easy. Not running around Phoenix looking for Gina."

"Let me worry about that."

Silence on McGrath's end. And then he said: "I'll get back to you," and hung up.

TerHorst figured Dr. Goatfucker with all his dire warnings was wrong. That he indeed was well enough to travel. To track her down and kill her. Professor Forza still hadn't gotten back to him about Luke. His assistant said he was on a business trip in Asia. Maybe it would be best just to go ahead and off Luke too. He'd never much liked him anyway. The little cockknocker.

He tossed the covers off and swung his legs out of bed. He walked by Manuel who was dozing in front of one of his Mexican soap operas. Which were recommended by the presence of *muchas* spectacular *muchachas* whose breasts were always bursting out of bikinis or halter tops or low-cut blouses. He went to the closet and got some clothes and went in the bathroom and shut the door and took off his stupid nightgown and then Reverend Billy was yelling in his ear: *"The time has come, Brother Frank! The Omega Point! The End of Days! We're arming for Armageddon! And you're in my army, Brother Frank!"* And he was walking barefoot across a sulphurous smoking plain. Buzzards were circling overhead and a moon was out even though it was broad daylight. The moon was several times bigger than *the sun. There was a throbbing and commotion in the air and he realized it was invisible angels beating their wings. Circling him like the buzzards.*

He opened his eyes. He was sitting on the floor with his legs splayed out. The tile cold on his bare ass. His genitals drooping between his thighs. Purplish and inert-looking. He grabbed the toilet and hauled himself up and sat down on it. He felt a little dizzy and like he might throw up but sat there till it passed. Then he went to the sink and splashed his face with cold water.

He must have passed out. Because he'd jumped up out of bed too fast. After McGrath had gotten him all riled up.

He put his gown back on and tottered back to his bed. Feeling relieved. For a moment he had thought he'd been having another heart attack. Thought God was calling him home to glory.

Gray took Norman's rook with his knight.

"You've fallen into my trap, Gray. You're doomed now. No escape is possible."

"We'll see."

They were in the park at one of the picnic tables. The dog was snoozing in the shade of the table at Gray's feet. Norman contemplated the board. The black and white pieces gleaming in the sun.

"I lost a million bucks today," he said. "Give or take."

"How?"

"Stock market took a dive. Don't you pay attention to the Dow?"

"No. Gee. I'm sorry."

"Don't be. You reach a certain lucky level and it's like Monopoly money." He pushed a pawn forward. "Take your jump."

"That's in checkers."

"Oh. It's your move then. And the clock is running."

Gray immediately slid a bishop across the board. Norman peered down at it suspiciously. "What are you up to? You sly dog."

"You ever lost that much before? A million?"

"Oh sure. You win, you lose. Who cares? I'd give ten million bucks to have Mr. Jones alive and well. I had a dream about him last night."

"What did you dream?"

"I opened the front door of my condo and there he was. Just calmly sitting there. Licking his paw and washing his face with it. It turned out he hadn't gotten sick and died after all but had just got lost. And now he'd found his way home again. Oh I see. You're after my queen. Well we'll nip that in the bud."

A shadow swept across the board. Gray looked up and saw a seagull flying over. White and gray against the blue sky. Such graceful curves to its wings. He'd heard gulls called mean and filthy and the rats of the ocean but to him they'd always seemed ethereally beautiful.

"Your move. Quit stalling. You're headed for a checkmate and there's not a damn thing you can do about it. It's a helpless feeling isn't it?"

"I'm thinking about leaving," said Gray.

"Leaving? When?"

"I don't know. Today maybe."

"Today?! But you can't. We're playing chess."

"I'll finish the game. Don't worry."

"And where will you go?"

"Maybe Alaska."

"Why Alaska?"

"Never been there. Wanna see it before it melts."

"What about Gina? You gonna take her with you?"

"I don't think she'd walk across the street with me."

"She's pretty pissed huh?"

"Yeah."

"Sorry. Guess I let the cat out of the bag. Or in this case the dog."

"It wasn't your fault."

"I don't know why she's so mad. I think what you did was a good thing. Admirable even. Giving the village skinheads their comeuppance."

"I think what made her really mad was I put Luke up to lying to her. She saw that as a betrayal. And I can see her point."

Norman sighed.

"Gray, Gray, Gray. If I was your age and I had a chance at a girl like that I wouldn't let anything stop me. I'd climb a mountain or cross an ocean if I had to. Like Vincenzo."

"Who?"

"The waiter. From Sardinia. Who chased the girl to New York."

"Oh. Right."

"But instead you're running off to Alaska. With a one-eyed dog."

Gray was silent. He moved his knight again.

"You and Gina. You're quite a pair. I remember reading something in some goddamn book or other. About two locked boxes. Both boxes have keys. But the key to each box is in the other box."

Gray looked across the table at Norman.

"Okay."

"Those two boxes. That's what you and Gina remind me of."

"It's your move."

Norman returned his attention to the board.

"Well I'm going to do my best to talk you out of this Alaska nonsense. It's not easy to find somebody who's a worse chess player than me."

They looked kind of like seals. Dozens of them. Sitting on their surfboards in their glistening black wetsuits waiting for the next good wave.

"You should try surfing," she said. "I'll bet you'd love it."

"Mom," he said.

"It's probably a lot like skateboarding. And you're so good at that."

"I think this is a mistake."

"I'm tired of you second-guessing every little thing I do."

"This isn't a little thing, Mom! I don't think leaving Gray's a little thing! It's a big thing!"

"Hey calm down. Quit yelling."

"You didn't even let me say good-bye."

"You left him a note. That's plenty."

"He was our friend. We don't have anybody. We're all alone."

"How do you know he's our friend? We got no idea who this guy really is."

"He's a good guy, Mom."

"Is he? Do good guys beat people up and hang them from trees?"

"Sometimes."

"He's a liar. He hides things."

"We're liars. We hide things."

"For a real good reason. Luke, he put you in danger."

"No he didn't. I always felt safe when I was with him."

"So is that it? You want him to be our protector? You really wanna get him mixed up in our shit? You think that's fair to him? And anyway. It's not like one of your video games. That karate stuff doesn't work against guys with guns."

Luke gazed glumly out the car window. Not seeing the sparkling ocean. The steep brown mountains.

"You'll see. We'll have fun in San Francisco. We'll drive over the Golden Gate Bridge. Go to Chinatown."

"Mom, let's go back. I liked it back there. You did too."

"Luke. Enough already."

"We could get an apartment. I could start school."

"And what would I do?"

"Get a job as a waitress. At the Sea Horse!"

"You got it all figured out."

"Yeah. And Gray could be our friend. And Norman too. And we'd see them every day!"

"Give it up. It's not happening. We're not going back."

"Well maybe *I'll* go back then."

"What?"

"Maybe I'll run away."

She jerked the wheel to the right and the car left the road skidding to a stop in front of a pottery business with a sign that said: PRAY FOR OUR TROOPS. She reached over and grabbed his arm.

"Ow! Mom! You're hurting me!"

"*Listen.* Don't talk like that. If you ran away it'd kill me. I'd kill you if you ran away. Do you hear me?"

"Yes! Let go."

She let him go and guided the car back to the edge of the PCH. It was filled with fast traffic. She waited for an opening then hit the gas. The tires squealed and the car slithered back up on the pavement and accelerated up the road.

"You're losing it," he said rubbing his arm. And then they drove in silence through the rest of the twenty-seven-mile-long town.

"Looks like somebody likes Harry Potter."

The books on the counter made a stack over a foot high. DeWitt chuckled.

"They're not for me. They're for my nephew. It's his birthday."

"What's his name?"

"Bo."

"My first boyfriend was named Bo."

He watched her ring the books up. KIMBERLY said the tag that rode the swell of one of her breasts.

"How old were you? When you had your first boyfriend?"

"Six. He was six too. I broke his poor little heart."

DeWitt laughed. Paid for the books with cash and left. Walked through the parking garage of the mall lugging the heavy sack of books and feeling agitated and conflicted. Kimberly was cute and funny and about the right age and maybe she'd been flirting with him talking about boyfriends and all he'd done was laugh and walk out. He should've said what's your present boyfriend's name and she might've said well I happen not to have a present boyfriend and he could've said well that's funny I don't happen to have a present girlfriend either. Then who knew what would've happened next? A date? Many dates? Sex? Love? Of course there was nothing to stop him from turning around and walking back in the store and saying what's your present boyfriend's name. And then he'd see Kimberly recoil as she realized this pimple-faced asshole was about to ask her for a date. No, she had been nice to him probably because she was naturally nice and also it was part of her job to be nice. He'd never get a girl he didn't have to pay for unless and until he achieved success. If you had power and money you could look like the goddamn Elephant Man and get more girls than you could handle.

He drove back to his apartment complex. Knocked on the door of his bedroom. It was opened by Smith-Jones.

"Got you your books."

"Oh thank you so much, DeWitt."

Groh took the sack. Behind him DeWitt could see the other one—the dark scary one—hunched over a laptop.

"Y'all need anything else?"

"More coffee please."

Groh closed the door. They had been holed up in there ever since they got back in the early hours of the a.m. Working on their computer. Talking on their cells. DeWitt didn't know what was up but guessed it had something to do with the big news story of the day in Oklahoma: The two cops killed last night in Brady. Along with another guy. These on top of the three homicides last week in Brady.

He went in the kitchen. Put fresh french roast in the Mr. Coffee machine. It was usually best not to do much wondering but he couldn't help but wonder a little bit. He wondered if you could be charged with murder if you gave guns to somebody and they used them to commit murders but you didn't know that's what they were going to use them for. And he wondered what they wanted with the Harry Potter books. Maybe to hollow them out and make them into bombs.

He pondered two postcards. One said:

> *Dear Gray,*
> *Sorry we had to leave so suddenly. Without saying good-bye. Thanks for changing our tire and being so nice to Luke. I don't know where Luke and I are going, but I guess we'll get there someday.*
> *Say bye to Norman. I hope you find what you're looking for.*
> *Gina*

The other said:

> *Bye Gray. I'll miss you. I wanted you to teach me chee gong. I hope you think of a good name for the dog.*
> *Your friend,*
> *Luke*

He tossed the postcards down on the bed beside him. Put his hands behind his head. Settled in for some serious staring at the ceiling.

She raked leaves as the dusk came on. Into a big pile under the oak tree in the front yard. When she was a kid she and her siblings used to bury one another under piles of leaves. Hard to say what they had got out of that. Except that a ghostly sense of magic seemed to hover then over every object and action and so they had lain silently like they were waiting for something in the dusty crackling darkness under the leaves. There had been four of them and now one was dead and the other three had been knocked around to varying degrees by life and she felt the sadness in the dusk. How time passed and dreams dimmed. But there was still a little magic left. The brown brittle leaves reminded her of jigsaw puzzle pieces. And a chilly wind blew and the tree heaved and sighed as though under the sway of some mighty emotion and more puzzle pieces came spinning down. And then unexpectedly early her husband's car pulled into the driveway and since she loved him there was also a little magic in that.

McGrath got out. She leaned on her rake waiting for him. Bundled up although it wasn't all that cold and wearing work gloves and a scarf over her hair that was still short because of the chemo. A ruddy flush on her thin cheeks that was nice to see.

"You're home early."

"Am I?"

He gave her a quick kiss. Looked at the leaf pile.

"You're industrious."

"Yup. Feel like I could rake up all the leaves in the world."

He nodded. There was something in his face.

"Doug, what's wrong?"

"Nothing. You know. Work. I don't wanna bore you with the details."

"That's okay. Bore me."

"Maybe later. I need a drink first."

"I'll join you."

They went in the kitchen. It was a nice room and should have been since they'd just spent thirty-five grand remodeling it. McGrath hated wearing a coat and tie and the first thing he always did on coming home was take them off. The tie was a clip-on. He'd been wearing clip-ons ever since a muscular suspect he was trying to wrestle down had grabbed his tie and wrapped it around his neck and nearly strangled him with it. He hung tie and coat over the back of one of the chairs at the kitchen table. He had a .38 semi-auto in a shoulder holster and took it off and hung it on the chair too. Alison brought over a Smirnoff on the rocks. And a glass of white wine for herself. They said cheers, bumped glasses, and drank.

"Okay," she said. "So what's wrong?"

"You know what? It's official business. I can't really talk about it."

"I'll get you drunk and you'll tell me everything. Like you always do."

He laughed. Pulled a chair out and sat down.

"What's for dinner?"

"I thought I'd make that shrimp stirfry you like. And rice. And a salad."

That shrimp stirfry he liked. His doctor had put him on cholesterol medication and told him he had to lose thirty pounds and now Alison was fanatically feeding him "healthy" meals with everything good to eat strictly off-limits. If he didn't express open revulsion for one of her dishes that meant he "liked" it.

"Are you hungry now?" she said.

"Kinda. All I had for lunch was a banana."

"It's not good to skip meals," she lectured.

He sat at the table and drank his vodka and she started on dinner. He stared into the backyard at the ebbing light. This time of year always depressed him. Right after the end of daylight savings time when it suddenly seemed to get dark so fast. It was like the whole world was being swallowed up by night.

He still hadn't called terHorst back. He'd passed the day in a state of abject paralysis. While the killers were out there somewhere continuing their machinations. Their deadly hunt for Gina which seemed to be killing everyone *but* her. How could he possibly allow this to go on another minute? But how could he possibly explain so long a silence? And his old pal Frank. What was up with him? Was he really in Phoenix? Had he really had a heart attack? Maybe he didn't know him as well as he thought. He knew he liked money. He had always seemed to live pretty high for a U.S. marshal. It could be he had sold his soul to Cicala and now was looking for Gina not to save her but to kill her. It had always seemed strange that she had never called either Frank or him after she had run away. Because they after all were her putative protectors. But it would make perfect sense if she had concluded that he and/or Frank had disclosed her presence in Brady to Cicala. And if Frank was in league with the killers and he was in league with Frank that meant he was in league with the killers.

He finished off his drink. Got up to get another.

The doorbell rang.

"Honey," said Alison over the salad, "would you get that?"

"Sure."

He opened the front door. Three men were standing there. An older man flanked by two younger ones. The older man was wearing a long black and red plaid coat. McGrath looked straight into Mac Lingo's eyes. Saw something vulturine and malignant there. He stepped back and began to slam the door just as Lingo took a shotgun from under his coat. It looked something like a tommy gun with a short barrel and a revolving drum magazine. Loads of buckshot tore through the screen door and hit the wooden door blowing splintering holes in it and knocking it back open then McGrath took blast after blast in his chest and stomach stumbling backward and going down.

Alison appeared. On the other side of the room. Lingo fired again. The pellets spreading out and peppering a wall. But Alison was gone.

"Get her, boys!" yelled Lingo.

The Lingo brothers Steve and Ronnie pulled out handguns and went clomping over the hardwood floor. They went down a hallway and Ronnie stuck his head in a bathroom as Steve continued into the kitchen. A knife gleamed on the counter by bright salad ingredients. The back door was wide open. Steve hollered: "Ronnie, come on! She ran out the back!"

Steve went through the door as Ronnie came in the kitchen. The backyard was fenced in and private. With lots of trees and bushes and flower beds in it since Alison loved to garden. Ronnie stood in the doorway and watched Steve running around the dark yard waving his gun around and calling out: "Where are you, you fucking cunt?"

Ronnie turned. Looked around the kitchen. There was something odd about his body: a big head and torso and short arms and legs so he looked like a gigantic dwarf. He saw a door on the other side of the refrigerator. Walked toward it across the newly laid tile floor. Put his hand on the knob and jerked the door open.

It was a pantry. She was crouched on the floor. Pointing up at him her husband's gun. His face had time to register surprise and then she pulled the trigger.

But nothing happened. She sucked in her breath sharply. And then he snatched the gun away.

He looked it over. Grinning. A crooked tooth sticking up from his lower jaw.

"This kinda gun? First shot you gotta cock it. Like *this*."

And he pointed the pistol at her face and fired.

Things were looking up. Finally the MobileTracker had got back on track and just in time too because he had discovered they were on the move again. All afternoon he had observed the little blue car ticking its way up Highway 1 which ran along the California coast. Around seven it had settled apparently for the night in Monterey. And Professor Forza had called him back. From Ho Chi Minh City. Quite excited at the prospect of selling Luke to the South American queers. The plan was for terHorst to drug Luke to make him docile then drive him down into Mexico. Crossing the border at Tecate and then going into the Sierra Madre Mountains to the town of Santiago Papasquiaro. There was an airstrip there. He would hand Luke over to others who would accompany him on the next leg of his journey into degradation, torture, and death. And of course the best news of all was that the McGrath problem had been solved and the Lingos were on the road and headed for Barstow. He was feeling better but figured he still needed help. He'd promised the Lingos ten thousand for McGrath and another ten thousand for Gina. Which was peanuts compared to all the dough he'd already got from Cicala and would make off Luke. Not to mention the diamonds. But the Lingos were dumb as dirt and would never know the difference.

They'd drive straight through the night and should arrive tomorrow around noon.

the second week

Tuesday

They hadn't been able to sleep. And for much the same reason. He wondering where she had gone. And she wondering *why* she had gone.

He got up before dawn. Roused the dog and fed him. Then got dressed and put on his sneaks.

He and the dog walked across the silent parking lot of the still motel. Went up the dunes then walked across the sand. Till they reached the bike path where they began to run.

There were still stars over the ocean but in the east over the San Gabriel Mountains the sky was starting to brighten. In crowded LA it was nice to have the beach all to themselves. It was cold enough that their breath made clouds.

The dog loved to run. He would trot as Gray jogged along and then when Gray would sprint would break into a joyous gallop. He never seemed to get tired. His stamina surprising in such a decrepit-looking creature.

Gray knew the way to end suffering was to end desire. To snuff it out like a candle and accept completely every fact of existence at every moment of your life. But he found himself unable to accept the absence of Gina from King Beach. He could have kicked himself for not kissing her when she'd looked at him wanting to be kissed as they had sat on the dunes with the sun going down. If he had kissed her then maybe everything would be different now. She might be here and thus he wouldn't be feeling this yearning ache for her and worrying about whatever it was that was threatening her and her son and getting ready to go to Alaska and wondering where she had gone.

They were running north. Toward her. And her dark motel room in Monterey. They were supposed to go whale watching today. Before continuing on to San Francisco where they would . . . what? Wander around Chinatown like lost souls? Like ghosts or shadows? Observing life but not being allowed to be part of it? King Beach had been nice except for the planes and she was even starting to get used to them so what were they doing now hundreds of miles away in the Cannery Row Inn?

It was Gray. He had scared her. She didn't know what to make of his gentleness and violence and scarred body and sleepwalking and his lies or delusions about his past. And she hadn't been in love with anybody since she was eighteen and had met Joey and that couldn't have turned out any worse and since she was feeling stirrings of being in love with Gray she feared another disaster. Why couldn't she fall for stable hardworking guys instead of mafiosi and mysterious drifters?

And there was Luke. He adored Gray. And Luke hardly ever liked anybody. She and Luke had been battling so much she had become used to dismissing his opinions but at bottom he was a smart and decent boy and perhaps his instincts about Gray were right. Which would mean that in a life filled with blunders her running away from Gray would rank right up there with the biggest.

Luke was having a frustrating dream about a skateboard race and there were hundreds of cheering spectators but the course ran up a steep hill and his wheels kept coming off and then Gina's hand was on his shoulder.

"Luke. Get up. We're going."

He looked groggily up at her.

"Going where?"

"Back."

They shambled into the lobby and looked around. And people looked back at them. Like three coyotes had strayed in out of the desert. So hungry they had boldly walked right into a hospital.

TerHorst stood up and went to meet them.

"Hey, Mac."

"Howdy, Frank."

They shook hands.

"You look pretty good for a dying man," said Lingo.

"Thanks." He shook hands with the two brothers. "Good to see you boys."

Nods and grunts.

"I guess y'all must be tired," said terHorst. "After all that driving."

"Lingos don't get tired."

"But they get hungry," said Steve. "I'm starving."

"Me too," said Ronnie. "I seen a Denny's on the way in."

"We got time?" said Lingo.

"Sure," said terHorst. "I could use some decent food too. After this hospital garbage."

"Good," said Lingo as they headed toward the front entrance. "My boys do dearly love Denny's."

The Lingos were in a Chevy Suburban. With Missouri plates. Ronnie went with terHorst in his Land Cruiser. Ronnie driving. TerHorst happily lighting up a Hav-A-Tampa. These last few days he would have given his left nut for a Hav-A-Tampa.

He brought the MobileTracker up on the computer. Saw Gina was still traveling south on the 101. Seemingly headed back to LA. Which was fortuitous for terHorst. He wondered what was up with her. He almost felt a little sorry for her. The fly fleeing into the web.

"How's that thing work anyways?" said Ronnie.

"Well you know it's satellites and shit. I'm not a technological kinda guy."

"It's something ain't it? What they can do these days?"

"Yeah."

"Someday they'll be able to fly to the fucking moon."

"They've already done that."

Ronnie laughed.

"No. I'm serious."

"Yeah?"

"Yeah."

"When?"

"Late sixties. Into the seventies."

"Oh." He shrugged. "That's 'fore I was born."

Three crows at the edge of the street were ransacking a discarded bag of fast food. Ronnie swerved at them. TerHorst heard a soft bump and looked back. On the street a broken crow flopped and flapped.

They got off the 101 at the 405 which they took to the Jefferson exit. Both feeling buoyant like they wanted to laugh. Like their lives had taken an unexpected turn for the better.

"Gray'll be surprised to see us huh?" said Luke.

"Maybe he'll be mad. That we left without saying bye."

"He won't be mad. He'll be happy."

They drove down Alejo Avenue into King Beach. Went past the Pilates place and the coffee shop and the grocery store in front of which they'd first encountered Gray and then a plane flew up out of the hills and they turned into the parking lot of the Sea Breeze Motel.

Pete, the fat bearded clerk, looked up from a *People* magazine with "Nicole's New Baby!" on the cover. He seemed glad to see them.

"It's you folks again. Welcome back."

"Thanks," said Gina. "Could we have our old room?"

"I think that could be arranged."

They took their stuff into room 21 with a feeling a little akin to that of coming home.

"Let's go see Gray," said Luke.

"Okay."

They walked down to room 18 and Gina knocked on the door. Got no response. Luke tried. Nothing.

"He's probably out walking the dog," said Luke.

"Senora?"

Quetzalli was standing by her housekeeping cart a few doors down.

"Your friend? He is gone."

"You mean he checked out?" said Gina.

"*Si*. Checked out. This morning. He and dog. They go."

"Okay. Thanks."

Luke was staring accusingly at Gina.

"He's *gone*, Mom."

"It's not my fault."

"Yes it is. You should've called him. Before we left. Let him know we were coming back."

"Well maybe you should've made that bright suggestion this morning. When it could've done some good."

They walked disconsolately back to their room. Sat on the side of their respective beds and gave each other now-what? looks.

"We'll never see him again," said Luke.

Gina was quiet a moment and then said: "He's got a cell phone."

"Call him, Mom!"

"I don't have his number. But I know Norman has it."

"Call Norman!"

"I don't have his number either. But we know where he lives. Let's just drive over."

TerHorst and company were in LA. Heading west through heavy traffic on the Santa Monica Freeway. The navy blue Land Cruiser leading the silver Suburban.

After a brief stop in King Beach the little blue car was on the move again. Up Alejo and then north on Lincoln. Twitching toward Marina del Rey.

TerHorst took out his cell and tapped in a number.

"Yellow," answered Lingo.

"We oughta be making visual contact in fifteen or twenty minutes. Don't do anything without my say-so."

"Okay, boss."

TerHorst put away the cell. Delved in a paper sack for his medications. Goatfucker had given him a shitload. While basically washing his hands of him. Saying without a bypass he and his heart were history. But he didn't have time for a bypass. He unscrewed the top off his water bottle and washed down the pills.

"We'll be taking the Lincoln exit," he said.

Ronnie nodded.

It was a great fucking feeling. Working your butt off and never giving up and now it was all about to pay off. Diamonds. Thailand. Twelve-year-old pussy.

Little Feat! That was it. They were the ones that had the song with Tucumcari in it: *I've been from Tucson to Tucumcari Tehachapi to Tonopah . . .*

I've been from Thailand to Tucumcari . . .

"Frank?" said Ronnie.

"Yeah?"

"This girl? We're fixing to kill?"

"Yeah?"

"Think I could fuck her first?"

"If circumstances permit."

Ronnie grinned. Struck the steering wheel with the heel of his hand.

"Hot dang!"

"But we don't hurt the boy. Nobody touches the boy."

"I don't give a shit about no boys."

TerHorst's cell rang. He saw it was Dee. His daughter.

"Hey honey. How much you—?" Need he was going to say because God love her she hardly ever called him unless she needed money but he was interrupted by her screaming.

"Dee? Dee? Is that you? What's happening?"

The screaming stopped but then came sobs and whimpers.

"*Dee! Dee!*"

"Frank terHorst?"

It was a male voice.

"Who is this?"

TerHorst heard: "Make her scream again," and then the screaming resumed and terHorst clutched his chest and gasped.

Ronnie was looking over at him. His small piggish eyes puzzled.
"What the fuck's going on?"

"Is this Frank terHorst?"

"Yes!"

"We have your daughter. There's only one way you can save her.
And that's by doing exactly as I say."

"How do I know that's really her? It could be anybody."

"Hold on," said Markus Groh. He was outside Oklahoma City
driving fast in the Dodge Neon down Highway 77. Bulgakov was
in the backseat. Both booted feet resting on Dee terHorst. Her
hands were flex-cuffed behind her and her ankles were also flex-
cuffed and she was lying on her back on the floorboard. Her top
and bra had been pushed up to expose her breasts. Groh handed
the phone to Bulgakov.

"Talk to your father," Groh said to Dee and Bulgakov put the
phone to her ear.

"Daddy?"

"Dee!"

"They're hurting me, Daddy! Make them stop!"

"I will, baby!" terHorst cried. His damaged heart thumping.
"Don't worry!"

Bulgakov handed the phone back to Groh.

"Frank? Am I going to have your cooperation?"

"Yeah. You got it. What do you want?"

"I want to find Gina and Luke. Do you know where they are?"

"LA."

"Alive and well?"

"Yes."

"And where are you?"

"I'm in LA too. I was just about to pick 'em up. You work for Cicala?"

"It's my understanding you're tracking them by means of a GPS device hidden in their car."

"That's right."

"Continue to monitor their position. But do nothing else. Until we get there. Or we'll kill your daughter. Do you understand?"

"Yeah. Can I talk to her again?"

"Not now. But you needn't be concerned about her. We have no desire to hurt either her or you. All we want is Gina and Luke. Okay?"

"Okay."

"I'll call back soon with further instructions."

Groh hit the off button. He was exhausted. He'd barely slept in days. Bogota to Miami to Atlanta to Oklahoma City. And soon to LA. He popped a 4Ever Fit caffeine tablet into his mouth and chewed. Hearing soft weeping from the backseat.

Bulgakov gazed down upon Dee. Torture was simple really. You didn't need elaborate electrical devices or steel contraptions with screws and spikes. He hadn't met the man yet he couldn't break in under ten minutes with nothing but a pair of wire pliers. Often he didn't even have to actually apply the pliers. Just cupping the man's testicles in one hand and holding up in the other hand the pliers would do the trick. Women could sometimes prove more stubborn. But then all one had to do was to bring before them and start to torture someone they loved, husband, child, brother, mother, even their dog or cat and they would quickly sing like a bird. Assuming making them sing was the point. Sometimes the torture itself was the point. In which case there was no salvation in singing.

She looked up at him. Shiny snot pouring from her nose. From her eyes mascara-dark tears.

The torture of her had aroused him. He took out his knife and cut the flex-cuffs off her ankles then began to pull down her pants and panties.

"Don't," she said. "Please don't."

Groh looked in his rearview. "What are you doing?"

He was yanking hard at her clothes. Now he got them off her legs.

"Ya sechas viebu etu zirnuyu svinyu."

I am going to fuck this fat pig.

"Leave her alone," said Groh.

He unbuckled his belt.

"I mean it," said Groh.

He unbuttoned his jeans. Groh braked hard. Guided the car onto the shoulder. Whirled around and stuck his gun an inch from Bulgakov's forehead.

Bulgakov smiled. One of the few times Groh had ever seen that.

"You are going to shoot me? By the road? In fucking Oklahoma?"

"Put her clothes back on. Now."

He shrugged. Rebuttoned his jeans.

Groh put away his gun and drove back on the highway. In the process of taking off her pants Bulgakov had turned them inside out. Now as he turned them inside in he noticed she was watching him. From the floorboard.

"On ne sdelal tebe nikakikh odolzenii. Tebe bi ponravilos."

He didn't do you any favors, you pig. You would have liked it.

They crossed the lobby to a desk that had a security guard sitting behind it.

"Can I help you?"

"We're here to see Norman Hopkins," said Gina.

"Your names?"

"Gina and Luke."

He picked up a phone.

"Mr. Hopkins, it's Luther. Gina and Luke are here to see you?

Okay, I'll ask 'em." Luther lowered the phone. "He wants to know if you're the real Gina and Luke or just imposters."

"Imposters," said Gina.

"They say they're imposters. Okay," and he put the phone down. "He says in that case you can come right up."

They took the elevator to the twenty-eighth floor. Where Norman was waiting in his doorway with a huge smile. He hugged Gina and slapped Luke on the back.

"My god it's good to see you guys again. Come on in. Where you been?"

"We just took a little trip to Monterey," said Gina.

"Used to spend a lot of time in that area. Great golf in Pebble Beach. So you miss me, Luke? Is that why you came back?"

"Um . . . not exactly."

Norman laughed. "Well maybe you missed Gray."

Luke nodded. "Yeah."

"We missed you too, Norman," said Gina. "But they said at the motel Gray checked out. You have any idea where he is?"

"Sure. Right over there."

He pointed across the wide living room. Gray was out on the balcony. Standing with his back to them.

"I didn't tell him you were here," said Norman. "Thought I'd let you surprise him."

Gina and Luke walked across the living room toward Gray. As they went by the couch the malamute lifted up his big head.

"Hey boy," said Luke.

He was stretched out along the plump cushions. His tail wagging at the sight of Luke. Going bump bump bump against the couch. Luke leaned over and rubbed his head as Gina slid open the glass door.

Gray looked around. Gina liking what she saw in his eyes.

"Gina."

She joined him at the railing. "Looking at Malibu?"

"Uh-huh. Why'd you come back?"

She turned from the view to him.

"Why do you think?"

Gray was silent. He looked inside and saw Luke with the dog.

"They said you'd checked out of the motel," said Gina. "I was afraid you'd left LA. I thought I'd never see you again."

"I nearly did leave. I was thinking about it. But Norman talked me into staying. At least for a few more days. Then they kicked us out of the motel. Me and the dog. No dogs allowed. But Norman said we were welcome to stay here."

And then the balcony became crowded as they were joined by Norman, Luke, and the dog.

"Hey Luke," said Gray.

"Hey," said Luke. Grinning shyly.

"So you want me to teach you qigong huh?"

"Yeah."

The dog tried to sniff Gina's crotch. She pushed him away.

"Chill out, Rover!"

"I think," said Norman, "this calls for some form of celebration."

They put cotton on her eyes then tape over the cotton then big sunglasses over the tape. Then they unbound her hands and feet and allowed her to sit upright in the backseat of the Dodge. Riding along in darkness.

She could tell when they left the highway and started moving along city streets. She heard her torturer sniffling and Groh said: "Are you catching a cold?"

"Maybe."

"I have just the thing. Astra C. It's a mixture of vitamin C and herbs. Two tablets four times a day. If you intervene early enough it will knock the cold right out."

"What's this all about?" said Dee. "Who's Gina and Luke?"

Silence.

"Where are you taking me?"

"The less you know about where we're taking you the better for you," said Groh.

She had had a job interview. For an entry-level position at an advertising agency. She thought it had gone well and in a good mood was getting out of her car in front of her apartment and then they were there. In an uncanny way. As though suddenly solidifying out of the astonished air. The blond good-looking man and the thuggish dark one.

She could feel the car slowing and turning and then it stopped and the engine was shut off. Car doors opened and Bulgakov said: "Get out," and then from outside the car she heard Groh: "It's all right, Dee. Take my hand." She did so. Left the warmth of the car for the cold of the twilight she couldn't see.

"Hold on to my arm like we're lovers," said Groh.

She took his arm and they began to walk. She heard voices approaching. It sounded like two young men. Debating what they wanted to eat tonight.

"Look at me and laugh," said Groh. "Like I've just said something funny."

For a half second she thought of screaming for help. But instead she "looked" at him and laughed. The sound hitting her ears like the giggling of a lunatic.

The voices of the young men passed by. They went through a door into a building then up two flights of stairs. They walked and stopped then Dee heard knocking. A coded knocking. Two knocks then three. After a few moments a door opened and Dee felt Groh's hand on her back gently pushing her through it.

He took off the sunglasses and then the tape and cotton. The first thing she saw was a cow skull sitting on a coffee table. Beyond the table was a burnt-orange sofa. On the wall above the sofa was a framed velvet picture of a matador and a bull.

She turned around and gasped and took a step backwards and nearly tumbled over the coffee table. There was a third man in the room. Besides Groh and Bulgakov. A black ski mask over his head. A single wide hole for his eyes. He looked like a terrorist or an executioner.

"This is our associate," said Groh. "He's wearing the mask for his protection and for yours. He'll be taking care of you when we leave. He's under strict instructions to treat you respectfully. He's also under strict instructions to kill you if you try to escape."

The man in the ski mask stood motionless before her. Blue eyes staring out of the black.

"We're going to have to tie you up again," said Groh.

"You don't need to. I won't try and escape. I promise."

"Sorry."

"Well, can I go to the bathroom first? I need to go bad."

"All right." He looked at the man in the ski mask. "Watch her."

The man nodded. Bulgakov sniffled and wiped his nose on the sleeve of his coat.

"Let's get you your Astra C," said Groh. He and Bulgakov headed toward the bedroom. Bulgakov glancing back at Dee. Like a hungry wolf leaving a hunk of meat.

The ski-masked man led her down a short hallway. She went in the bathroom and started to close the door but he put out his hand and stopped it.

"I can't go with you watching me," she said.

He just looked at her. With those intense blue eyes.

"Just turn your back, okay? I won't escape."

He stood in the doorway with his back to her as she pulled down her pants and sat down on the toilet. She felt self-conscious about the noise as the pee tinkled down. She saw there was a combination bathroom and shower with a rectangular window of frosted glass high in the wall. She wiped herself and flushed and went to the sink and washed her hands and face and they went back in the living room. She sat down on the sofa and he began to tie her up. Because the flex-cuffs and the cow skull and the black mask and most of all his silence terrified her she began to cry.

There was a spiral notebook and a ballpoint pen on the coffee table. He picked the notebook up and quickly wrote something in it then held it up in front of her face. He had printed out the words in big awkward letters that looked like the product of a child.

i want hurt u. dont be scarred of me.

They had all climbed in Norman's '65 Chrysler and gone to the Gelson's Market on Maxella and shopped for dinner. Now they were all in Norman's big kitchen making dinner under Gina's supervision. Except Gray really wasn't doing much. Just sitting at the reclaimed-pine farm table drinking wine and watching. The menu in deference to Gray and Luke was vegetarian: battered and fried artichoke hearts as an appetizer, a green salad, cavatelli with rapini, and for dessert a raspberry cheesecake. The air was warm and smelled of sauce simmering and artichoke hearts sizzling and Norman had a Rolling Stones album blasting and Gina would glance over at Gray from time to time and she'd be smiling. The dog was walking around like he owned the place. Keeping a keen eye out for any food that might fall to the floor. Gray didn't really like to get drunk but did like to get a pleasant buzz and that's exactly what he had now.

Norman did like to get drunk and was drinking scotch. Now he pulled Gina into the middle of the room and she laughed and protested but he insisted and they began to dance.

Gray took a piece of cheese from a cheese plate. Chewed on it and watched Gina. And there was that look from her again. That smile.

"Mom!" said Luke. "The artichoke hearts are burning!"

She rushed back to the stove to save them.

"Gina," said Norman, "I'm very sorry to report this. But Gray's being a slacker. All he's doing is eating cheese and guzzling wine. While we do all the work."

"Get to work you lazy bum!" said Gina. Standing over the smoking pan. As Mick Jagger sang: *Such a pretty pretty pretty girl* . . .

"Be glad to. What do you want me to do?"

"You can help me," said Luke.

"Sure. What are you doing?"

"Chopping up stuff."

Gray joined Luke at the cutting board. Took a knife to an avocado. Not able to remember the last time he had been this happy.

The man who had kidnapped his daughter had called back and said it was too late for them to get a flight that night and terHorst should pick them up at LAX tomorrow at 10:35 a.m. And he reiterated his admonition not to get near Gina. So he and the Lingos had gotten rooms at the Paradise Motel on Washington Boulevard in Mar Vista and were now eating pizza at the Shakey's down the street.

"I don't like it one bit," said Lingo. "It ain't what we signed up for."

"Nothing's changed," said terHorst. "You'll get your money. What do you care?"

"Who are these fellers anyway?" said Steve.

"You've asked me that five times. And I keep telling you I don't know."

"I say we kill 'em," said Ronnie. "Pick 'em up at the airport and take 'em someplace and pop 'em."

"But then what would happen to my daughter?"

"I don't know."

"They'd kill her. That's what would happen."

"Is she purty?" said Steve.

"She's pretty. She tends to be a little overweight. She's always losing and gaining the same twenty-five pounds."

"I like fat women," said Ronnie. A gooey wad of pizza in his mouth.

"She's not fat," said terHorst. "And we're talking about my daughter here, Ronnie. So be careful."

"'Member Monica?" said Lingo.

TerHorst grinned. "Yeah. Sure. Monica."

"Who's Monica?" said Steve.

"Just this ol' gal me and Frank used to know. Back in the old days."

"Okay. But how come you brung her up?"

" 'Cause she was fat too. Like Frank's daughter."

"Now wait a minute, Mac," said terHorst.

Lingo laughed. A raspy cackle. He reached across the table and poked terHorst's arm with his finger. "I was just funning with ye."

Steve picked up their pitcher of beer and started to top off all their glasses. But terHorst put his hand over his. "No thanks. I've had enough."

Lingo squinted at him. "You look like ten miles of rough road."

"I just need a good night's sleep. You can't ever sleep through the night in a hospital," and then he looked at Steve. "So what's been up with you? I haven't seen you in a couple of years I guess."

"Well I took a job at the chicken plant. But I quit it last week."

"Didn't like it huh?"

"Oh naw, I loved it. I liked to kill chickens. But the goddamn foreman was always on my case. Always wanting me to show up on time. Shit like that."

"You still married to that girl? What's her name?"

"Niki. Naw. We split up."

"Was it like a mutual decision?"

"A what kinda decision?"

"Was it both of y'all's idea?"

His lower lip twisted to one side and he shook his head. "It was *her* idea. The bitch. Said I was a psychopath."

"My first wife said I was a psychopath." TerHorst took a bite out of his pizza wedge and thought about it. "Second one too."

He noticed that Ronnie's head was leaning over to one side and his eyes had assumed a glassy stare.

"Ronnie? Hey Ronnie?"

Ronnie was silent. A drop of drool had collected at the corner of his mouth. TerHorst looked over at Lingo. "Is he all right?"

Lingo nodded. "He's just asleep. He sleeps with his eyes open.

When he's real tired. Or when he's had a snootful. Hey Steve? How 'bout running up there and getting us another pitcher?"

Gray and the dog accompanied Gina and Luke to their car. Luke was holding the dog's leash. He began to pull Luke at an angle across the parking lot.

"Whoa, dog! Where you going?"

"He needs to pee," said Gray. "He's taking you to his spot."

The dog led Luke to a grassy square that had three Canary Island palm trees in it. Gina unlocked her car then turned to Gray.

"I'm glad you didn't leave," she said.

"I'm glad you came back."

She looked over at Luke. He was watching the dog lift his leg and water one of the palms. She looked back at Gray and, knowing it was what she wanted and not going to miss his chance a second time, he leaned down and kissed her.

They moved away from each other. Luke and the dog were walking back. They were unsure whether he had seen them.

He had. And he was glad.

That night the wind changed. No longer blowing in off the ocean but instead from the deserts to the east and northeast. The air warming up as it flowed down the mountains and gushed through the passes and canyons, picking up speed till it was gusting up to fifty miles an hour as it hit the coast. The slender trunks of the palm trees outside Norman's building bent in the wind and the tree in the middle of the park in King Beach thrashed in the wind and a foraging possum unnerved by the wind moved very fast for a possum across the parking lot of the Sea Breeze Motel.

TerHorst saw it. Disappearing into the shadows. Nothing on this green earth uglier than a possum. The motel was silent except for the moan of the wind and all its rooms were dark. He saw Gina's car. Walked across the parking lot to it. It was sitting in front of room 21. He gazed at the door and the curtained window. Presumably they were in there. Her and the boy. Twenty-five maybe thirty feet away. He had crossed half a continent and overcome a heart attack to finally find them and yet here he stood in this weird wind powerless to finish the job. It was the most frustrating moment of his life. But he had to remember the Lord didn't ever put a bigger burden on your shoulders than you could carry.

Tomorrow would be a good day. Everything would get wrapped up. He'd get his diamonds and Gina would be taken care of and his daughter would be released and he'd probably lose Luke to Cicala but you couldn't expect to get everything could you?

He knew he ought to go but he lingered in the wind. Staring at room 21 and then at the car.

He unzipped his pants. Pulled his penis out. Began to pee on the back bumper of the Honda.

He had a full bladder and peed for a long time. Smiling as he did so. A shining widening pool of piss forming behind the car. Then he zipped up and walked away on his ostrich boots. Still smiling.

Wednesday

He woke up at 3:03 a.m. He woke up every night or morning, however you wanted to look at it, at about this time. So he could lie
there for hours tormented by the past and the future and his bladder and his bowels and the ache in his hip and the ringing in his
ears. The only reason getting old was the least bit bearable was that
it happened gradually. They said if you dropped a frog in a pot of
boiling water it would jump right out but if you put the frog in the
water and then turned on the burner so the water would heat up
slowly the frog wouldn't notice a goddamn thing. It'd just sit there
in the pot till it got boiled alive. Same thing with getting old. If you
were young one day then the next day woke up and looked in the
mirror and found yourself old you'd go nuts, you'd jump off a fucking building or something.

He could hear Smitty snoring on the floor in his doggie bed.
The sound didn't bother him. In fact he liked it. Found it comforting another living creature was in the room with him. He wasn't
used to sleeping alone. Millie had slept beside him for over forty
years. He wondered if she was awake too. He had gone in to check
on her in the middle of the night a couple days ago and there she
was sitting up in bed. Eyes wide open gazing into the dark. Smiling eerily at nothing.

Latreece had told him she also often found herself waking up at
this hour. She said it was the haunted time. "The spirits they be
walking and the dead they be talking."

Gina would be dead soon. The Russians would kill her today in LA. And then they would do what Toddo Palmentola was supposed to have done. Bring Luke back to New York. But not to Cicala. They would keep him in some safe and secret place. And then— and this was the ingenious part—Cicala would call the feds! He'd say his grandson had been kidnapped and the kidnappers had contacted him and said Luke would be killed unless he paid a seven-figure ransom. He'd ask for their help in getting him back. How rich was that? Teaming up with the fucking feds. And then as the Fucking Bunch of Idiots launched a feverish manhunt the Russians would get careless. Would leave Luke alone and forget to lock a door or close a window. Luke would escape and call the cops. With his mom dead and his dad in the joint the logical place for him to go live would be with his grandpop on top of Todt Hill. Maybe the feds would be suspicious that Cicala had engineered the whole thing but fuck 'em. Let 'em prove it.

Luke would be happy with him. Luke loved him and he loved Luke. But there was something that had been worrying him and that was worrying him ten times as much at 3:06 a.m. Gina's parents were dead but she had a sister. Connie. A hairdresser. Living in Baldwin on Long Island. She was married to a carpenter named Tom. His fear was that Tom and Connie would go to court and try and take Luke away from him. On the grounds he was unfit to raise Luke because he was supposedly some sinister Mafia godfather. Like there was even such a thing as a godfather anymore. Godfathers went out with spats and fedoras. The facts were he was a successful businessman who could give Luke all the advantages and send him to the best schools while with Tom and Connie he'd be living a struggling two-bit kind of life in a town that used to be pretty nice but now had been taken over by the niggers. Maybe the solution was the Russians. Once they had finished the job with Luke they could go out to Baldwin and pay Tom and Connie a visit. Not killing them unless they had to. Just terrorizing them a little. But he'd have to get Mr. Li to sign off on it. And Mr. Li would have to go to the Directorate. Whoever the fuck they were. And assuming they even existed. Mr. Li portrayed himself as just another functionary in the System but sometimes Cicala suspected he ran the whole ball of wax and the Directorate was just a fiction he'd invented to hide behind.

At any rate it just wasn't fun anymore. There was blood in the water around Pat Cicala and the sharks were circling. It was no longer about making a living. It was all about just trying to stay out of prison. Maybe it was time to finally leave this life he had been leading. And he began to have a fantasy. He went in his wife's bedroom to find she had passed away peacefully in her sleep. And then he moved away from Todt Hill with Luke and Eliana. To Palm Beach. He'd always liked Palm Beach. And they lived in a house whose doors and windows were always open and there was always a warm sea breeze blowing through and the constant tinkling of wind chimes. And his health came back and he achieved mighty erections and made love to Eliana many times a day. And Luke grew up tall and strong—

There was a bad smell and for a moment he thought it was coming from himself but then he heard it: Smitty farting in his sleep. "Goddamn you, Smitty!" he said but he wasn't really mad and Smitty just went right on farting and snoring. He looked at the clock. It was 3:09.

The dog stood by the bed staring at Gray. Waiting for him to wake up. He had been standing there for five minutes. He had a full bladder and wanted to be taken out. Plus he was hungry. But Gray's breathing remained deep and even. Finally he gave up and walked away.

He went in the kitchen and sniffed at his food dish. As if food might magically have appeared there since he last sniffed it.

Taking his time and his claws clicking he walked the length of the living room. Feeling the building shaking a little in the wind. All night the wind had blown against the building and swirled around its corners and groaned and hissed and hummed and fallen briefly silent before blasting and shaking the building again. He walked to the glass door that opened onto the balcony. Stood there and looked out. With his one good eye.

All he could see was the sky. One last bright star sinking in the west. And from the east a slow steady suffusion of light.

Usually when they traveled it was the other way around. But now Bulgakov was awake and Markus Groh asleep.

They were in first class. Bulgakov in the aisle seat. Cleaning out the grit under his fingernails with a toothpick. Groh's seat was pushed all the way back and his head lolled to the side.

He made a faint sound and Bulgakov looked over at him. And then he made it again. *Uh.* A muscle in his cheek twitched. And then a little louder: *Uh! Uh!*

Bulgakov watched. Amused. He put the toothpick in his mouth and chewed on it. Groh's breaths began to come fast and shallow. *Uhhhhh!* he went and then with a loud climactic *UHK!* he jerked and woke up.

He seemed dazed. Looking out the window and then at Bulgakov.

"Oh Dima. I had the most terrible dream."

He had a faraway look in his eyes.

"I was walking through the woods and I came across an old man. Sitting at the base of a tree. A little girl was sitting in his lap. Her arms around his neck. At first I thought he was asleep but then I realized he was dead. There were maggots crawling across his flesh and the little girl began to pick them off. And she was singing a little song. Some nursery rhyme. As she picked off and cast away the maggots. And she looked up at me and smiled and I saw she was insane. And oh Dima, I was terrified! I ran through the woods as fast as I could. And then I heard a voice, a big booming voice it was like the voice of God and it said: *To the merciless no mercy will be shown!* And then I woke up."

Bulgakov looked at Groh. Chewed on his toothpick.

"What do you think it means, Dima?"

"It means nothing. It means shit."

"But I think some dreams are special. Some dreams do have meaning."

"You are like some old peasant woman. Scared by some fucking dream."

Bulgakov lost interest in the conversation and returned to his fingernails. Groh turned to the window. Looked down on the wrinkled brown expanse of the Great American Desert.

Joey was supposed to be at work in the furniture factory but instead was flat on his back on his bunk in his cell. Staring up at the bottom of Jamie's bunk. Jamie was supposed to be at the factory too. But Joey had arranged it so it was unnecessary for them to do things like actually report to work to be recorded as being there. He hardly ever went to work unless he was particularly bored and frustrated and in the mood to pretend he was sawing through the necks or hammering in the fucking heads of certain people.

He heard from above him: *Uh uh!* and then a long spasmodic *Uhhhh!*

"Jesus. What the fuck's going on up there?'

"Nothing, Joey."

"Are you jacking off your dick again?"

Now Jamie's reddish face and whitish hair appeared over the side of his bunk.

"I got to, Joey. I get so horny. I can't help it."

"But you have to do it when I'm around?"

"But you're always around. 'Cause I'm your guard."

"Whatcha got up there? A fuck magazine?"

"Nah. I don't need one. I just think about my wife."

"Your wife!"

"Yeah. What's wrong with that?"

"For chrissake, Jamie. You can think about any girl you wanna. Some fucking movie star with the biggest tits in the world. And you think about your *wife*?"

"Yeah. You've seen pictures of her. She's real good-looking. She's hot."

"But that ain't the point. Now *me* thinking about your wife. That'd make some kinda sense."

"I wouldn't like that. You thinking about her."

"I'm just using that as a for example. You wanna think about fresh cooz. Not something you already fucked a million times."

"But I like thinking about her. It makes me feel like—you know—"

"Like what?"

"Like she's here with me. For a couple minutes. I really miss her, Joey."

Joey sighed as though Jamie were a totally hopeless case.

"Okay, pal. Whatever flips your switch."

Jamie's head disappeared back over the side of his bunk. It was quiet for a few moments and then: "Joey?"

"Yeah?"

"You wouldn't ever do that would you?"

"Do what?"

"Think about my wife. While you was jacking off."

"Naw, Jamie. I wouldn't ever do that."

Jamie was thinking about his wife. Joey was thinking about his ex-wife. He'd got a call from Bobby the Hump this morning. Bobby had told him: "I'm buying a new car today." That was code for: *The shitstorm is gonna hit Gina today. That cunt will get hers and you'll be getting your son back.*

A guard came in the cell. "I got something for you, Joey."

Joey sat up. The guard handed him a brown padded envelope.

"Thanks, Carl."

"You bet."

The end of the envelope had been stapled shut but now was open after it had been searched for contraband. He looked at the return address. It was from his father.

He tilted the envelope and a book slid out. With a glossy red and yellow cover. He read the title: *The Power of Positive Thinking* by Norman Vincent Peale.

Snorting and blinking, hocking and spitting, scratching their armpits and yawning, the Lingo brothers straggled into the sunlight. They'd been up late drinking and doing drugs. They walked out to the sidewalk in front of the Paradise Motel. Lit up cigarettes and watched the traffic going by and the wind tearing down Washington Boulevard. They stood in identical poses. Weight on left leg. Right knee bent a little. Cigarette in right hand. Fingers of left hand stuck in pants pocket with thumb hanging out.

The tops of the palm trees tossed in the wind. Suddenly a palm frond plummeted down and crashed on the sidewalk about twenty feet away.

"Shit," said Ronnie. "That coulda kilt us."

"Kilt by a fucking palm tree," said Steve. "That'd be just our luck."

"It's hot."

"Damn hot."

"What the hell's it so hot for?"

Steve shrugged. Blowing out smoke that the wind ripped away. TerHorst and Lingo came strolling out.

"Morning, boys," said terHorst. "Sleep all right?"

They grunted without looking at him. Now all four stood in a row facing the street. Like the tumultuous doings of the wind needed an audience and they were it.

"You boys about ready to saddle up?" said Lingo.

"Born ready, Daddy," said Ronnie.

"Steve? You about ready?"

"Yes sir. I'm ready."

"Now we're gonna waste these dudes, right?" said Ronnie.

TerHorst slid his hand over his shaved head in exasperation.

"Ronnie, dadgummit, no! We're not gonna waste 'em. We went over all this last night. Weren't you paying attention?"

Ronnie gave terHorst a sly squint out of the corner of his eyes. Smiled so his crooked upward-sticking tooth was uncovered.

"Had you going, Frank."

Now all three Lingos began to chuckle. In their dry raspy fashion. TerHorst shook his head and managed to laugh some himself.

"Yep. Had me going."

"Ronnie, you crack me up," said Mac Lingo.

TerHorst watched a wind-blown crow careen by above them. All but tumbling end over end. Dust stung his eyes and the hot dry dusty air made it difficult to breathe. He'd had a hard night. Listening to the eccentric rhythms of his heart and imagining the brutish tortures his daughter might be undergoing. He probably hadn't been a very good father in the sense of spending a lot of time with her but he truly did love her and had always tried to give her everything she wanted. She'd never had much use for her mom. She'd always been a daddy's girl.

"I'm hungry," said Ronnie.

"Me too," said Steve.

"We got time to get some breakfast?" said Lingo. " 'Fore we go to the airport?"

TerHorst looked at his watch. "I think so. If we leave now. And eat fast."

"You know what I need?" said Norman.

"What?" said Gina.

"A Thomas Abercrombie."

"What's that?"

"A hangover remedy. Two Alka-Seltzers dropped in a double shot of tequila."

Luke made a face. "Sounds gross."

"So you're not feeling so hot?" said Gray.

"No," said Norman, "but I'm okay with it. Last night was terrific fun. What was it Hemingway said? Take what you want and pay for it."

They were on Alejo Avenue. Sitting at a table in front of the coffee shop. They were having coffee and orange juice and muffins and croissants. The dog was lying by Gray's feet. Chomping on a chunk of muffin snuck to him by Luke. The wind snatched away Gina's paper napkin and sent it flying down the street.

"What's with the fucking wind?" she said.

"It's the Santa Anas," said Gray and looked at Norman. "They blow about this time every year right?"

"Yeah. Fires'll be breaking out everywhere before the day is out. You'll see," and then he grinned. Adjusting his Maui Jim sunglasses. "Well. Look who's coming."

It was Stitch. Striding down the sidewalk at a great rate. His boots clomped and his skinny arms swung and then he saw them. Norman and Gina and Luke. And the dog. And Gray. All looking at him.

He clearly was startled. His eyes darted about as though he were seeking an escape route. But then he recomposed himself. Fixing on Gray a resolute glare as he walked by. Gray looking mildly back at him. The dog growling softly.

"Top of the morning to ya," Norman said as he doffed his OLD DUDE baseball cap. But Stitch ignored him and then they were all looking at his back as he continued down Alejo. A crazy white boy in a hurry.

"I think that young man has a bright future. He will go far," said Norman.

"I wonder how his friend's doing," said Luke.

"Let's just change the subject hm?" said Gina.

"I think we should go someplace," said Gray. "Do something."

"Like what?" said Gina.

"I don't know. Something fun."

"Can we go to the amusement park?" said Luke. "I saw it from Norman's window. It was on the water."

"The Santa Monica Pier," said Norman. "An LA institution. I recommend it highly."

"So you wanna go?" said Gray.

"Love to. But I can't. I've got an appointment. With one of my many doctors."

"Everything's okay, I hope," said Gina.

"Oh yeah. It's just routine." He looked musingly down at the dog. "You gonna take that hideous beast you call a dog with you?"

"Sure," said Gray. "Why not?"

"Aren't you afraid he'll cause a panic? Small children might get trampled in the stampede to get off the pier. Besides. They're not gonna let you take him on the rides."

"Can he stay at your place?"

"Of course."

Gina looked at Gray across the table. "We can take my car. Then we can drop you off at Norman's later."

"Sounds good," said Gray.

They walked west toward the motel. Gray, Gina, and Luke. They saw a jetliner coming toward them. Gliding in over the ocean.

"It's coming from the wrong direction," said Luke.

"It's because of the wind," said Gray. "Planes always take off and land into the wind."

Looking out of the plane's third window from the front was Markus Groh. With Bulgakov asleep they had returned to their customary states of consciousness when traveling. Groh observed the approaching coast. The wide beach. The crowded clutter of houses and apartment buildings. A playground. A lagoon. A street on which he could see traffic moving and people walking. And then water gave way to land and the plane was floating over tan sand and a gray road and grassy dunes and then its wheels touched down.

They parked their SUVs in a parking structure then headed for the terminal. TerHorst puffing on a Hav-A-Tampa and very nervous. Because Gina was on the move again. She was heading north through Venice on Pacific Avenue. For all he knew she had just checked out of the Sea Breeze Motel. Literally at the very last minute for all he knew it was all going to slip away because Application MobileTracker could conk out again at any moment, perhaps permanently this time, and Gina and Luke would be lost. All because he had to go to the airport and pick up these two monsters who had kidnapped and tortured his daughter. And raped her for all he knew.

He discarded his cigar and they went in baggage claims. They were a little late because it had taken them a while to find a Denny's. Passengers from the Oklahoma City flight were standing around a carousel but the luggage hadn't started rolling out yet.

"We know what these jokers look like?" said Lingo.

"No. But they're supposed to know what I look like."

"Hey lookie there, Ronnie," said Steve. Elbowing his brother.

The mouths of both brothers fell open a little as they regarded a long-haired lissome creature in short shorts. She was standing next to her parents. She looked to be about thirteen.

"Shit far," said Ronnie.

"Look at the fucking legs on her."

"I see 'em, bro. I see 'em!"

"Now settle down, boys," said their patient dad. "We're here on bi'ness."

"Hello, Frank."

TerHorst turned around. Groh and Bulgakov were standing there. Having crept up on him like Indians.

"Thanks for meeting us," said Groh.

"It's not like I had a choice."

Now Groh and Bulgakov looked over the Lingos who in return looked over them.

"That's Mac," said terHorst. "Ronnie. And Steve."

"I'm Jack," said Groh. "And this is Bill."

"Jack and Jill you say?" said Lingo.

"*Bill,*" said Groh. Smiling. As Bulgakov glowered.

"Can I have a word with you, Frank?" said Groh.

They moved off some from the others.

"I don't think we really need your friends," said Groh.

"Well I think we do."

"They strike me as . . . undisciplined."

"I've worked with 'em before. They're disciplined enough."

"Bill and I are used to working alone."

"Let's lay all our cards on the table."

"Go ahead."

"The truth is I don't need you and you don't need me. But we each got something the other wants. You got my daughter. And I got this GPS tracker. You with me so far?"

Groh nodded.

"Now once I take you to the tracker and you get what you want, how do I know you're not gonna put a bullet in the back of my head at the first opportunity?"

"Our directions were explicit. We're to work with you and not hurt you in any way."

"Well I think you're a damn liar. I think Cicala hates my guts and wants me dead."

"What makes you think I work for Cicala?"

"If not him then who?"

"I can't tell you that. But I promise you have nothing to worry about."

"So I'm supposed to just trust you then. You and your degenerate buddy over there. I guess he's the one that was making my daughter holler, right?"

"You brought this on her, Frank. By not living up to your agreement with Mr. Cicala. That was why we were brought in. To sort things out. To make things work. And our success rate at that is one hundred percent."

The two men looked at each other. As the Lingos stretched and scratched. And as Bulgakov stared at the leggy young beauty. Who had become aware of his attention and was now squirming and flushing and tugging self-consciously at her hair.

"I'm not going off alone with you and your buddy," said terHorst and then he jerked his head at the Lingos. "They go with us."

"Okay." Groh cocked his head a little and took a look at ter-Horst. "Are you feeling all right? You look a bit pale."

"I'm feeling just fucking fine, thanks for asking."

They returned to the others. The carousel had come to rumbling grumbling life and luggage was sliding down the chute. Groh saw the bag containing his Harry Potter books was one of the first off. Which he considered to be a good sign.

They went in the Heal the Bay Aquarium at the foot of the pier. Saw eels and anemones, horn sharks and swell sharks, flag rockfish hiding in the kelp and blue-banded gobies. And their unanimous favorite, moon jellies. Tiny exquisite shimmering barely there jellyfish. Even their scientific name was beautiful. *Aurelia aurita.* Then they left and walked up the pier. The bone-dry wind blowing at their backs.

They passed vendors of T-shirts, pirate hats, and mermaid jewelry. You could buy if you were so inclined "your name on a grain of rice." A woman with long silvery hair who would draw your picture for twenty dollars had on display sample portraits of famous people like Marilyn Monroe and Barack Obama. A legless guy in a wheelchair played a saxophone that shined in the sun.

The pier was crowded with people who had come here to escape the heat but the heat had followed them.

Luke bought a white baseball cap with SANTA MONICA LIFEGUARD on it in red letters. He put it on and then: "Look!" he said.

Gray and Gina looked toward where he was pointing.

From a fire in the hills above Malibu smoke streamed out over the sea.

The blue car with the red circle around it was stationary. In Santa Monica. Next to the beach by Appian Way.

TerHorst was driving away from the airport on Sepulveda. Groh sat beside him. In the backseat were Bulgakov and Ronnie. Ronnie's assignment to make sure Bulgakov didn't shoot him.

Groh and Bulgakov were checking out the weapons the Lingos had provided them. Semi-auto pistols. Plus a boot knife for Bulgakov. The Lingos always carried an arsenal around with them wherever they went.

Ronnie was drinking a can of an energy drink called Shark. He was watching Bulgakov testing the edge of the knife.

"Daddy kilt a gook with a knife," he said. "When he was in Nam."

Bulgakov ignored him.

"You want a Shark?" said Ronnie.

Bulgakov shook his head.

"Hey Jack? You want a Shark?"

"No thank you, Ronnie," said Groh.

TerHorst glanced at his rearview. Making sure Mac and Steve were still behind them in the Suburban.

Groh looked at the MobileTracker display. At the motionless car and circle.

"You know, Frank, I don't know why you want to come with us. Wouldn't it be better for you if the boy didn't see you?"

"I'm coming," terHorst said. Thinking about the diamonds. And then he winced. His gut was cramping up. The medication was playing hell with his digestive system. He'd just have to tough it out till he made it to a restroom.

They were thrust forward into the blue. Into the sky scoured clean by the wind and the glittering water that stretched out till it met the sky. And then they were swept down and backwards and then up and forward again into the blue.

Gina was afraid of heights. She tensely clutched the rim of the octagonal yellow basket.

"It was a bad mistake getting on this fucking thing," she said.

Gray and Luke looked at each other and laughed.

"Don't laugh! We're not even strapped in. We could fall out!"

"Mom," said Luke, "there's no way we could fall out."

"The wind could blow the whole Ferris wheel down. And then we'd all fall out!"

Gray hadn't been on a Ferris wheel since he was eight years old. He'd been a little scared then like Gina. But not because he was afraid of heights. It was night and a storm was coming on. When the Ferris wheel lifted him above the trees he could see miles off dark clouds being lit up with lightning and he imagined the lightning striking the Ferris wheel. But he loved it now. What a view. He could see all of Santa Monica Bay from the Palos Verdes Peninsula to Point Dume. And the entire LA basin with its millions of souls living out their lives seeking their disparate destinies and downtown with its skyscrapers and beyond it huge mountains standing out with startling clarity in the unsmogged air. And planes lined up out over the ocean descending into LAX and storks, so ugly and un-gainly when you saw them perched on the railings of the pier, glid-ing just above the waves with an ineffable grace and beauty. But the best part of the view, sitting across the basket from him, was Gina.

The Ferris wheel slowed then stopped. With them at the top. Basket rocking. Gina seemed alarmed.

"What's going on?"

"They're letting people off, Mom," said Luke. "The ride's almost over."

They found the Honda Accord in a parking lot just south of the pier. In the southwest corner of the lot. Space 122. The lot was about half full. No attendant. You paid a machine six bucks.

They parked their SUVs in the lot. Climbed out and walked over to the Honda and stared at it. All three Lingos lighting up cigarettes. Having to shield their lighters from the wind.

TerHorst turned toward the pier. The yellow and red baskets of the Ferris wheel were going round and round.

"They're probably up there."

"Well let's go get 'em," said Mac Lingo.

Groh squeezed his lower lip between his thumb and forefinger. Contemplating the pier.

"Perhaps we should stay here. And wait for them."

"What's the point of that?" said terHorst.

"Fewer people around. Fewer witnesses."

"They might not be back for hours. And we're supposed to stand around with our thumb up our ass?"

"Yeah," said Ronnie, "fuck that."

Groh looked over his crew. Bulgakov. Dressed all in black. Sweating in the heat. TerHorst. Pasty-faced and burning-eyed. Looking like he might keel over with the next step. And the Lingos. Intriguing people. Of a particular American inbred-idiot type that he'd never encountered firsthand before. TerHorst had a point. Best to get this over with quickly. Before something went badly wrong.

"Let's go," Groh said.

Bulgakov spat over his shoulder three times.

They walked toward an exit that led to the beach. As the wind gusted past them even harder than before. As a white plastic bag flew by and palm trees leaned. It was like a dry hurricane was hitting the beach from the wrong side.

"We don't want to cause a scene," said Groh. "We'll take them with us and then deal with the woman elsewhere. And whatever happens, no one hurts Luke."

They stopped at the machine and fed it money. Steve was looking up at the sky with a strange smile. Mac looked up too but didn't see anything.

"What's going on with you, boy?"

"Huh?"

"You're grinning like a possum eating shit."

Steve shrugged. "Guess I'm just in a good mood, Daddy."

"Someone needs to stay here," said Groh. "In case they come back before we find them."

"Well I ain't staying," said Ronnie.

"Steve'll stay," said Lingo.

"If you see them," said Groh to Steve, "just call us on your cell. We'll come back immediately. *Don't* try to do anything yourself. Do you understand?"

"Yes sir. Roger that."

A tablet of Artane was dissolving under his tongue. His fifth of the day. He watched them walk away then looked back up at the sky.

He could hardly see it. It was almost completely transparent. It was like a perturbation in the blue. But it was definitely there. A laughing dragonlike creature. With mile-wide wings.

They sat out on the deck of a Mexican restaurant at the end of the pier. Eating corn chips dipped in a bowl of chunky guacamole. Luke drinking a Coke and Gray sipping a *cerveza* and Gina getting a little buzzed on a bloody mary.

Dozens of pigeons were hanging around the tables waiting for food to fall off. The more aggressive would go right up on the table tops and try to steal some morsel literally from under the customers' noses. Gray reflected that probably countless generations of them had lived and died around the pier. Maybe Santa Monica Pier pigeons had evolved into a whole different subspecies.

Luke threw them a chip and they swarmed around it in a fluttering frenzy. They had avid orange gleaming eyes.

"Hey don't do that," said Gina. "Don't feed them."

"But they're hungry, Mom."

"They're all so fat they can hardly move. And they're filthy. They carry diseases."

"Look! There's one with just one leg!"

"Uh-oh. Gray'll probably wanna adopt it. Make it his new pet."

"That's a good idea," said Gray. "I could teach it to ride on the back of the dog."

"Yeah," said Luke. "Cool."

"Ready for that roller coaster?" said Gray.

"Yeah, right," said Gina. "I barely escaped with my life from the Ferris wheel and now I'm gonna hop right back on a roller coaster."

"I'm ready," said Luke.

Gray paid the check and Gina slung her purse over her shoulder and they left. As the pigeons attacked the table and fought over what had been left there till a waiter shooed them away. As terHorst and company entered the aquarium and hunted for Gina and Luke among the luminous tanks.

A black guy with Rasti hair was playing the steel drum accompanied by recorded music. It was a bouncy Caribbean tune and Gray, Gina, and Luke stopped to listen.

"You're great!" Gina said to the guy and he smiled at her then she started dancing along.

"Let's dance," she said to Gray.

"Sorry. Don't know how."

She turned to Luke. "I know *you* know how."

He shook his head. "No way."

"Come on. You're a great dancer."

"Mom . . . are you drunk?"

"I've only had one drink."

"That's all it takes with you."

"Come on, Luke!"

She handed her purse to Gray and took Luke's hands and danced. Luke reluctantly going along. And Gray noticing again how heavy her purse was.

They stood around at the foot of the pier. Watching people coming and going.

"You stay here," Groh said to Ronnie. "If you see them do nothing. Except call us. Okay?"

Ronnie looked at his father.

"Do what he says," said Lingo.

"I'm outa cigarettes," said Ronnie.

"Take mine," said Lingo and handed him his pack.

Groh, terHorst, Lingo, and Bulgakov headed up the pier.

"Spread out," said Groh. "Act naturally."

They tried to amble along like tourists instead of psychos and assassins. They passed the T-shirt and junk jewelry vendors. Lingo looked with amusement at a couple of black guys standing at the railing with fishing rods and lines in the water. "Niggers love to fish," he said.

Groh and Bulgakov went in a video arcade and prowled around. Bulgakov stopped and stared at a boy playing one of the machines. Longish brown hair. Ten or eleven. Bulgakov looked at Groh. Groh shook his head.

TRAPEZE SCHOOL LEARN TO FLY! said a sign. A well-built young man bare to the waist was trying to teach a fat girl in a safety harness how to fly. TerHorst paused to watch. Unscrewing the cap from a bottle of water and taking a long drink. Then he began to walk over the worn planks of the pier again.

He could feel the unnatural wind sucking the moisture out of him. He felt like a desiccated dusty shuffling thing. A mummy in a horror movie. The amusement park was up ahead and to his left. The Ferris wheel was turning. The roller coaster cars were zooming. Breathing heavily he squinted at the passengers. Looking for Luke's brown head. Gina's black hair.

They walked back into the amusement park. A Buddhist monk was walking toward them. Shaved head, saffron robes, sandals with black socks and wraparound shades. Gray couldn't see his eyes but he could tell he was looking at him. With a hint of a smile. He seemed on the verge of speaking to him. He walked past and Gray looked back and saw the monk had stopped walking and was watching him.

"Hey," said Gina, "let's do our pictures!"

She was pointing toward a booth where you could get three photos taken for six dollars. They walked over to it and Gina pulled the curtain back.

"We can't all fit in there," said Luke.

"Sure we can," said Gina. "You can sit on my lap."

Gray glanced around. Saw that now the monk was gone.

"I don't wanna sit on your lap," said Luke.

"Don't be difficult."

"Mom, I'm not being difficult. I don't even wanna do my picture. You guys go ahead."

"You sure?"

"Yeah."

"Wait right here. Don't wander off."

"I won't."

Gina looked at Gray. Who had been paying no attention to the conversation. Who had been unsettled by the monk and whose gaze was now moving around the amusement park. Fixing on no one or nothing in particular.

"Everything okay?" she said.

He looked at her and smiled a little. "Yeah. Fine."

"Come on!" she said grabbing his hand and pulling him in the booth. They sat down and she reached across him. Snapped the curtain shut then immediately put her mouth on his. As he kissed her he could feel her body pressed up against him. Its heat and softness. Then they pulled apart and turned to the business at hand. He put in money and a recorded voice began to explain their options. They could choose romance or outlaw themes. In color or black-and-white or sepia.

"I think Norman would be very disappointed if we didn't choose the outlaw theme," said Gray.

"I agree."

Luke waited. Beyond the curtain in the wind. With boredom setting in fast.

He noticed a sign for a men's room about twenty feet away.

———

Gray and Gina in the photo booth mugged for the camera. Hearing but not paying any attention to the sound of boots clomping past on the wooden planks.

TerHorst entered the men's room. Passing within a few feet of Luke who was at a sink in front of a mirror washing his hands. Luke saw terHorst in the mirror walking quickly toward a stall. He went in and shut the metal door behind him.

It had hardly seemed real to Luke it had all happened so fast. He dried his hands on a paper towel and moved away from the sink. Bent down and looked under the door of the stall. Saw terHorst's golden ostrich-skin cowboy boots.

Luke ran out. Just as the curtain in the booth was pulled back and Gray and Gina emerged.

"Mom! Mom!"

"What is it?" said Gina.

He pointed back at the men's room.

"He's in there!"

"Who?"

"Frank!"

She rolled her eyes. "Luke—come on."

"He is, Mom! He's using the toilet! Right now!"

"Who's Frank?" said Gray.

"Nobody," said Gina. "The boogeyman. Luke's imagining it."

Luke pulled on his mother's arm. "We gotta run!"

"Luke, stop it! We have to wait for our pictures—"

"Let's go," said Gray.

He put his hands on their backs and firmly pushed them. Into the wind and toward the beach. Gina looked at him with surprise.

"The truth," he said. "Who's Frank?"

"Mom, tell him!"

"A U.S. marshal. From Oklahoma. He's looking for us. He wants to kill me."

They moved through a throng of tourists chattering in Chinese.

"Is he alone?" said Gray.

"I don't know."

"You got a gun in your purse. Right?"

She looked surprised again. "Yes."

"Give it to me."

She hesitated.

"Mom," said Luke, "give it to him!"

She went in her purse and took out the Glock and handed it to him. He slipped it under his T-shirt into the waistband of his jeans.

Luke cast a panicky look back over his shoulder. "Come on, let's hurry!"

"Settle down," said Gray. "Be calm. Blend in."

TerHorst came out of the men's room. Looking pale and shaky. He saw Groh and Bulgakov approaching. "No luck?" he said.

Groh shook his head. Bulgakov lit up a cigarette.

"Maybe they not come out on fucking pier."

"That's possible," said Groh.

The three men were standing in front of the photo booth. Mac Lingo came around the corner. Eating a foot-long hot dog.

"You got chili on your chin," said terHorst.

Lingo laughed and wiped it off with a finger which he then stuck in his mouth. "I do love chili."

The Chinese tourists walked by. One of them began filming Lingo and his hot dog with his cell phone.

"Hey gook!" snarled Lingo. "Knock it off!"

The tourist looked frightened. The booth suddenly ejected a glossy strip of paper. Groh looked at it curiously. Picked it up.

"My god," he said then handed it to terHorst. "Isn't that her?"

It was like an Old West poster: WANTED DEAD OR ALIVE REWARD $50,000. With three sepia-tinted photos of Gina and Gray.

"Well I'll be fucked."

"Who's the guy?"

TerHorst looked at Gray. "I've got no idea."

———

Ronnie leaned on the railing and watched the fire. Smoke streamed from his cigarette. Smoke plumed out over Malibu and the sea. He had always loved fires. One of his favorite things when he was a kid was to construct elaborate miniature forts in the backyard out of cardboard and sticks and scraps of wood. Defend the forts with plastic green army men then burn them down. It had been awesome to watch the army men melt and the forts collapse. His sister's blue-eyed white kitten Magic had perished in one of the blazes.

His cell rang.

"Yo!"

"She's on the pier," said Groh. "Probably headed your way. We don't know if the boy's with her. But she's with a guy. Thirtyish, short hair, T-shirt. Call me if you see them. Okay?"

"Sure thing, pardner."

Part of the pier was a parking lot and Gray, Gina, and Luke were walking through it. Their shoes making hollow sounds against the planking. Gina and Luke feeling desperate and Gray filled with something like a bright humming emptiness. A receptivity to all that was in this speck of space at this point of time.

He saw a break in the railing and realized they could get off the pier without going to the end. They went down a flight of wooden steps to the beach. Just as Groh and terHorst appeared behind them in the parking lot.

An asphalt path ran next to the pier. Bisecting the bike path and ending at the boardwalk. As they walked down it Gray took out the pistol and racked a cartridge into the chamber. He tucked the gun back under his shirt and Gina and Luke gave each other a quick look.

They paused at the bike path to allow three speeding bikers to pass. "Are you sure you saw him?" said Gina and Luke said: "I'm positive!" and then they crossed the path.

They walked by a volleyball game. A guy and a girl were playing a guy and a girl. The guys in baggy shorts, the girls in bikinis. The girls were lean and lovely and had attracted Ronnie's attention. And then he saw them: woman and boy and guy in T-shirt. Trying to sneak away like cornered rats and he laughed because he had caught them.

They neared the boardwalk. Gray looked up and saw at the foot of the pier the hulking form of Ronnie. Excitedly talking on his cell phone and looking straight at them.

"You recognize him?" said Gray to Gina and she looked and shook her head.

"He's with Frank," said Gray.

"What do we do?"

"Just keep walking toward the car."

As if in some anguished dream dreamt in the throes of a high fever terHorst found himself running across the parking lot on the pier through the hot wind. Cowboy boots weren't made for running and he felt clumsy and ungainly in them like an animal that some-one had put boots on as a joke. His tie was flapping and in his chest his heart was like a balloon being blown up bigger and bigger till it was only a breath or two away from popping.

He was running after Groh. Groh reached the railing and looked toward the boardwalk. Almost immediately he saw Gina and the guy and the boy, yes, Luke himself finally in the flesh. In a white cap. They were walking by several pairs of people playing chess on boards built into the tops of tables. They weren't acting like they knew anyone was after them but they must have seen terHorst. Otherwise why would they not have waited for their photos? Why had they departed the pier so suddenly?

The guy in the green tee. An unknown factor. Probably he wouldn't present much of a problem but one couldn't assume that.

Groh saw that Ronnie had left the pier and was heading down to the boardwalk. He didn't see Bulgakov and Lingo. They must still be on the pier. He looked down the beach to the parking lot where the Honda and their SUVs were. Steve was wearing a florid Hawaiian shirt so was easy to spot. Standing at the edge of the beach and looking up at the sky. Groh glanced up but didn't see anything. He had put all their cell numbers on speed dial and now called Steve.

He didn't react as the phone rang. Just kept standing there with his head cocked upward.

"What the hell is wrong with him?" said Groh.

TerHorst tried to say something but nothing came out. He was standing by Groh grasping the railing as though it was all that was keeping him upright. His face was the color of raw oysters.

The wind rushed and gusted and a Hasidic Jew's black hat blew off and he chased it over the sand and they were being hunted by men who meant them harm. It was like the nuts and bolts of the world were coming loose but Gray was seeking that still place. That central silence. Where nothing existed least of all himself.

They approached the parking lot. Saw a man in a Hawaiian shirt staring at the sky.

He had first pilfered the Artane from his grandmother who was taking it for her Parkinson's. He had liked the high and had quickly found a quack doctor who would supply him with all he needed. And now he stood beneath the mighty beating of the blue wings of the laughing dragon. Such a wind did the wings create that he struggled to stay put. At any moment he might be lifted right off his feet. Might be transported right off the beach and be born along forever at ever-increasing speeds by the scorching wind of heaven.

His cell rang again. He was going to keep ignoring it but then recalled he was on some kind of mission. That was why he was standing here in the first place. As he started to take the cell from his pocket he saw Gray, Gina, and Luke.

"That guy," said Gina. "He's looking at us."

"I know," said Gray. "Keep walking."

Steve watched them go up some wooden steps then pass into the parking lot. He pulled the folded-up photos of Gina and Luke out of his back pocket. It was them all right. Trying to escape. He had to stop them and he would stop them. Everything depended on them being stopped.

He began to run.

"Gray, he's coming!" said Luke.

Walking up the boardwalk Ronnie saw him too. "Steve!" he yelled and began to run.

Bulgakov and Mac Lingo were behind Ronnie. Seeing Ronnie run, they ran.

Groh and terHorst were on the asphalt path that paralleled the pier.

"What's that idiot doing?" said Groh as he watched Steve. And he left the path and ran across the beach. Angling through the volleyball game. TerHorst and his ostrich boots stumbling after him.

Steve ran up the wooden steps. His hand went under the palm trees and hula girls of his shirt to get his gun.

"Get down!" said Gray. Roughly shoving Gina and Luke behind a Chevy sedan. And then he pulled the Glock out.

Steve was charging across the parking lot. His eyes wide and his .38 revolver stuck out in front of him. He felt that he was flying more than running. His feet barely touching the ground. Joy was surging through him and cutting loose with a guttural yell he fired a wild shot.

Gray put two rounds into his center of mass. He crumpled and skidded and his gun skittered away. He came to rest on his back. Still alive. Looking up at the sky.

"Steve!" bellowed Ronnie as Gray hustled Gina and Luke to the Honda.

"Come on, get in!" he said and they all piled in, Gina in the front seat and Luke in the back and Gray turned on the engine. He put it in reverse and hit the gas. The car screeched back. Nearly colliding with another car that had just entered the parking lot. Not under-standing what he had blundered into, the driver angrily leaned on his horn. Gray put the car into forward. The way out was straight ahead. Past Steve. Gray gunned it and the car leapt forward and then Ronnie was there. On the other side of Steve. Pointing his silver-plated pistol at the Honda.

"Down!" yelled Gray. Gina and Luke both ducked as Ronnie's gun went *pop pop pop!* Holes surrounded by frosty circles appeared in the windshield. Gray veered and tried to run down Ronnie. The left front and rear tires bouncing over Steve's body and Steve screamed and then the car clipped Ronnie's leg as he dived aside. Then Gray ripped the wheel to the right and took off through an open lane that led to the exit. Ronnie regained his feet and pointed his gun and fired. The bullet took out the back window. Shattered glass rattling down on Luke as he crouched in the backseat. Before Ronnie could fire again he was flattened from behind by Groh. Groh stood over him and shouted: "Stop shooting, you fool!"

The car reached the street and went left and disappeared.

Steve gazed at the sky. It was blue and endless. Empty and blue. He could feel it absorbing him. Turning him blue. He was becom-ing the sky.

Ronnie crawled over on his hands and knees and looked down at Steve. He forced a grin that bared his snaggly tooth.

"You're gonna be okay, bro. Don't you worry none."

Steve made a noise like a bubbling croak then disgorged about a quart of blood on himself and died.

Bulgakov came up with Mac Lingo.

"He's dead, Daddy," said Ronnie. "Steve's dead!"

"Oh lordie! Oh lordie!" wailed Lingo.

Beachgoers were aghast at the scene in the parking lot. They gaped and cringed and cried out and hid. TerHorst staggered up. Took out his badge and held it up high. "Police! This is a crime scene!" And then he bent over and vomited.

"Let's get fucking out of here," Bulgakov said to Groh.

Groh grabbed terHorst's arm and pulled him to the Land Cruiser.

Mac Lingo and Ronnie picked up Steve's body and carried it to the Suburban.

Moments later both SUVs were gone and the parking lot was as it had been. Save for the broken glass and puddles of blood.

He drove south on Ocean. Traveling fast but not doing anything crazy. Constantly checking the rearview.

"Any idea what kind of car Frank's in?"

"In Oklahoma he had a dark-blue SUV," said Gina. "I don't know what kind."

"A Land Cruiser," said Luke. Looking back through the jagged hole where the rear window used to be. "I saw it in the parking lot."

"Keep an eye out for it," said Gray.

"I will."

They crossed Pico then Gray took a sudden left on a street called Bay.

"Where are we going?" said Gina. Her voice tight and high.

"Away," said Gray. "From them."

"And then what? What's the plan?"

The plan was to try and stay alive for the next ten minutes. If they were successful at that then they'd try and stay alive for ten more minutes. "We'll figure it out," he said. "So is there any reason not to call the cops?"

"We can't call them. They think I killed somebody. In Oklahoma."

"We're not in Oklahoma, we're in LA—"

"*You think I don't where the fuck we are?! I can't trust them! I trusted them once and they tried to kill me! I can't trust anybody!*"

"Okay, okay, simmer down."

He turned again. Right this time.

"How about it, Luke?" he said. "Think we're being followed?"

"I don't think so."

The 10 freeway was just blocks away. Gray had debated whether to jump on it and get out of the city as quick as he could. That had seemed to make the most sense. Which is why he had decided not to. Because unless their pursuers were stupid they would be thinking along the same lines. The best thing was to drive randomly. Till they lost themselves in LA's vastness. Its endless reticulation of streets, lanes, drives, roads, avenues, circles, boulevards, and ways.

The little blue car ticked along on the MobileTracker. East on Hollister. South on Sixth.

TerHorst in the backseat shook out a couple of pills into his palm. Clapped them in his mouth and washed them down with water.

Groh was behind the wheel. Watching him in the rearview.

"That was a fiasco," said Groh. "Because of your friends, Frank."

"Too bad they all don't get fucking killed," said Bulgakov.

"Maybe they will," said terHorst. "Maybe we all will."

"We'll all be fine," said Groh. "We'll catch up with them in a few minutes. They won't be expecting us. They'll think they've lost us. We'll move fast. Bang. He's dead. Bang. She's dead. Then we'll take the boy with us. Do we all understand?"

"Sure, Jack," said terHorst. "But what if that skinny son of a bitch decides to go bang bang right back at us? He seemed to be a pretty good shot."

Bulgakov gave his version of a smile. A contemptuous curl of his thin lips.

"He will be no problem."

They turned east onto Ocean Park. Immediately running into a lot of traffic.

Gray noticed their shot-up car was drawing looks from other drivers. It probably wouldn't be long till a cop pulled them over to see what the deal was. If Gina was expecting him to shoot it out with the police like John Dillinger she was going to be disappointed.

They topped a hill. Below them was the intersection of Ocean Park and Lincoln. Now he could see why the traffic was screwed up. The wind storm had knocked out the power and the traffic light was out. Turning the intersection into an anarchic snarl of honking cars and red-faced drivers.

"See, Mom?" said Luke. "I was right. I *did* see Frank."

"Yes," said Gina. "You were right."

"I was right *both* times.

"What do you mean both times?" said Gray.

"I saw him last week," said Luke.

"Where?"

"When we were coming out here. What was the name of that town, Mom?"

"Barstow. We spent the night there."

"Mom got scared and we left. And then I saw Frank by the side of the freeway. He was standing outside his Land Cruiser. He'd been stopped by the cops. I was sure it was him. But Mom didn't believe me."

"How do you think he traced you to Barstow?" said Gray.

"I've got no idea," said Gina. "It didn't seem possible. I guess that's why I didn't believe Luke."

Traffic was lurching forward a few feet at a time. Gray kept glancing at the rearview.

"How long have you had this car?" he said.

"About a year," said Gina. "I got it when we moved to Oklahoma. We were in witness protection. Frank got it for us—"

Gray slammed the car to park and opened his door. "Get out."

"What?"

"Get out! Now!"

They all three bailed out of the car. As people in other cars stared.

"Gray," said Gina, "what's wrong?"

"Frank put a tracking device in the car. They'll be here any minute." And then he said: "Run!"

"There they are!" said Groh.

The Land Cruiser was coming down the hill on Ocean Park. They saw below them the guy and girl and kid running away from the Honda. Dodging through the stop-and-go traffic.

"Dima! Get them!"

Bulgakov opened the door and jumped out. Dodged through the traffic too.

Groh and terHorst saw Gray and Gina and Luke reach the intersection. Go south on Lincoln. Disappear behind a bright-blue building.

Bulgakov was on the sidewalk now and running down the hill. So fast he seemed at each instant about to lose his balance and fall and yet somehow he maintained a frantic breakneck equilibrium.

TerHorst leaned forward from the backseat. His shaved head shined with sweat. Through clenched teeth he screamed: "Run you ugly bastard! Run!"

It was a grungy stretch of Lincoln. They ran past a Vee Dub repair shop, a laundromat, a muffler shop, a used-car lot. Gina having trouble keeping up. She wasn't as fast or fit as the other two plus her big purse on its long strap kept banging around against her side.

"Hurry, Mom!" said Luke.

"I am!" she said.

"Let's cross," said Gray.

They cut across Lincoln. Whose traffic was as messed up as Ocean Park's. Bulgakov came to the intersection and looked down the street and saw them. He headed across the street too. They reached the other side and went up a side street and out of sight.

They hadn't looked back at him. They didn't seem to know he was there.

He ran past a cronish-looking homeless woman. Squatting amidst a nest of bags, rags, and empty plastic water bottles.

"Slow down, sonny!" she yelled at him. "You'll hurt yourself!"

He did slow down as he neared the side street. Pulling his gun out and peering cautiously around the corner.

It was aptly named Hill Street. Going straight up a steep hill. A few cars were parked along its sides but otherwise it was empty.

He started running up the hill. Arms and legs attacking the incline. His breath coming in short sharp huffs. Drops of sweat flying off him and blotching the pavement.

The street led up into a residential neighborhood. As he approached the top he passed a parked car pointing down the hill. A couple of feet behind the car nestled against the curb was Luke's white Santa Monica lifeguard cap.

Bulgakov quickly crouched and holding his gun out with both hands scuttled around the car.

He saw nothing except a strip of grass and the sidewalk.

Gray popped up from behind a privet hedge on the other side of the street and fired. Bulgakov at the same moment seeing him out of the corner of his eye and lunging for cover behind the car. Gray's shot missed. Bulgakov's body in midair twisted and he got off a shot as Gray fired again. Gray heard a bullet rip by above him and saw Bulgakov's head snap around and a red flash of blood and then he fell behind the car and out of sight.

"Did you get him?" said Luke. He and Gina were peeping over the top of the hedge fifteen feet away.

"I don't know. Stay down."

Gray pushed through the hedge. He was about to cross the street. To finish Bulgakov off if need be. But then he looked down the hill and saw the Land Cruiser on Lincoln. Starting to make the turn onto Hill.

"Let's go!" said Gray. "Come on!"

He and Gina and Luke ran up the street past well-kept houses and wind-whipped evergreen and palm trees. Went down another street and disappeared.

The Land Cruiser came slowly up the hill. Groh and terHorst looking around at the empty street.

"Where the hell'd everybody go?" said terHorst.

Suddenly a blood-covered figure staggered out in front of them. "Dima!" said Groh.

They drove up to Bulgakov and jumped out. He looked at them woozily. His face ashen. His hand pressed to a copiously bleeding wound on the left side of his head.

"What happened?" said Groh.

"Gavnyook v menia vistrelil." The fucker shot me. Groh and terHorst grabbed his arms and pulled him to the SUV. TerHorst was smiling.

"No problem," he said. "Right, amigo?"

They walked east on this street and that through the catastrophic day. Smelling smoke and hardly talking and looking back over their shoulders. Prepared to run like hell again at every instant. Till they came to a park.

Dust blew over a deserted baseball field. On a basketball court several middle-aged white guys were playing badly but with great enthusiasm. A young Asian woman sat on a bench holding her baby. Raptly watching it as it sucked on a bottle as if nothing else in the history of the earth had ever been as interesting as it.

They walked across the grass till they reached some trees. They plopped down in the shade and looked at each other. Trying to think of something to say.

"I'm thirsty," said Luke finally.

"Me too," said Gina.

Gray nodded. He pulled out his cell and began to put in a number.

"Who you calling?" said Gina.

"Norman."

The phone rang twice then Norman said hello.

"Hey it's Gray. You know where Clover Park is?"

"I do."

"Could you come pick us up here?"

"Sure. You have car trouble?"

"You might say that. And bring water. And my rucksack. And the dog."

"Okay. What's the deal?"

"I'll tell you when you get here. But I gotta warn you. There's some danger involved in this."

"For me?"

"Yeah."

"Hm. Sounds interesting. Be there in fifteen minutes."

Gray put away the cell. The wind roared above them in the leaves. Breaking the shade up into bits of shadow and glittering light. Gray looked at Gina.

"Okay," he said. "Frank's a marshal. And you were in witness protection. What's the rest of the story?"

"I married a guy named Joey Cicala. He's from this big mob family in New York. He turned out to be an asshole. He beat me up. Beat up Luke. He told me if I ever tried to leave him he'd kill me. And he would've. No doubt about it. I figured the only way Luke and me could get away was if he was in prison. So that's where I put him."

"How'd you do that?"

"I called up the U.S. attorney's office. They'd been after the Cicalas for a long time. And I told 'em everything I knew."

"You became a rat," said Luke. With a touch of reproach.

"That's right. I became a rat. To save both our fucking lives. I even let 'em put a bug in our house. This went on for a couple of years. Till they had what they needed to arrest Joey and some of the other guys. Then Luke and me went into protection."

"They wouldn't even let me say good-bye to my friends," said Luke.

"Yeah, it was rough," said Gina. "While they were getting ready for the trials they kept moving us around. Motels, apartments, houses in the country. And we were always scared."

" 'Cause they had a contract out on Mom for a million bucks!" said Luke. With a touch of pride.

"That's what we heard anyway. When the trials were over they didn't need me anymore. So that's when we got shipped out to this little town in Oklahoma."

"And Frank was assigned to your case," said Gray.

"Yeah. We lived there about a year and everything went okay. Then last week this guy showed up at our apartment. I had a friend over for dinner and—and he killed him. And then he came after me. But we got away."

"How'd you manage that?"

"Mom threw boiling water in his face!" said Luke. "And then she hit him in the head with a pot!"

Gray looked at her. Smiling a little. "You did?"

"Yeah. I can't believe it."

"Did you kill him?"

"No. But somebody did. His body was found outside of town the next morning. On a farm. He'd been shot. And the guy that owned the farm and his son had been killed too. So that's three innocent people that are dead. Because of me."

"It's not your fault."

She shrugged. "Anyway. I found Frank's cell phone number in the guy's pocket. I guess my father-in-law must've got to him. Pat Cicala. Pat the Cat. Maybe you've heard of him."

Gray shook his head.

"You should know what you're getting into," she said. "He's a powerful guy. And he wants me dead. And he wants Luke back."

Luke gave Gray a level look through the flickering shade.

"Don't worry, Mom. Gray won't let that happen."

The red '65 Chrysler convertible eased down the street. Its top up against the brutal sun. Norman peering out from under his baseball cap. The dog sitting up like a person on the seat beside him and looking out too.

And then they saw them. Emerging from the clump of trees. Norman pulled over to await them. The dog whimpering faintly as he watched them come.

Gray opened the passenger door. Gina and Luke got in the backseat and Gray in the front.

"Here we go," said Norman. Handing them bottles of water.

All three took long guzzling drinks. Gray wiped off his mouth with the back of his hand.

"We need to get out of town," he said. "Now. We need a car."

"Okay. Take mine."

"Don't you need it?"

"I got another one. A boring Beamer. I just drive this one for fun."

"We can't take you home."

"No problem. I'll just call a taxi. But you gotta tell me what's going on."

Gray looked at Gina.

"We're in witness protection," she said. "'Cause I testified against my husband and put him in prison. And he's from this big mob family and now they're after us."

"What's your husband's name?"

"Joey Cicala. He's my *ex*-husband."

Norman stared at her. "You're Pat the Cat's daughter-in-law."

"You've heard of her?" said Gray.

"Sure. I'm a normal person and keep up with the news. Unlike you," and then he said to her: "Didn't you wear some kind of disguise when you testified?"

She nodded. "A head scarf and dark glasses."

"I remember. You seemed very glamorous and mysterious."

"Yeah, that's me. Glamorous and mysterious."

"Look," said Gray. Eying every car that passed. "We gotta get going."

Luke was leaning over the seat and scratching the dog's head. "But *where?*" he said. "We gotta get going *where?*"

"Someplace we can lay low. Till we can figure out the next step."

"What about my house?" said Norman.

"The one in the desert?"

"Yeah, the old country club. In Tejada Springs."

Dr. Pol-Lim drove up from Long Beach in his Lexus 350 to the Paradise Motel. He was paid a nice monthly fee to be instantly available 24/7. His patients loved him and didn't mind him occasionally dashing out in the middle of an office visit and speeding away dynamically in his matador-red car.

He had decided to become a doctor in the late eighties. When he was a sullen teenager working in his brother's doughnut shop. His mother had begun to experience periods of inexplicable blindness. And then, bizarrely, as if some terrifying virus were on the loose, several of her friends began to lose their sight too. Finally there were over 150 Cambodian women going blind in Long Beach. No physical cause for their condition could be found. But it turned out they had something in common. All had survived the genocide in Cambodia in the seventies and all had witnessed *with their own eyes* horrible things. In Pol-Lim's mother's case she had seen her husband be chopped to death with hoes wielded by half a dozen demonic children. The problem wasn't with their eyes but with their shattered souls and his mother and most of the other women began to get better when they realized that.

Pol-Lim had spent a lot of time driving his mother around to various doctors and had found himself fascinated with the medical world. His brother's doughnut business had taken off and he had opened several more shops and was on his way to becoming a wealthy man. He put Pol-Lim through college and med school. Then a few years ago he had approached Pol-Lim with an opportunity. He had a silent partner in his international doughnut empire that was in need of a doctor in the LA area who would operate outside the system. That silent partner was the System.

Bulgakov was impassive as the doctor cleaned and dressed his wound. Groh stood by watching. His arms crossed on his chest. Suddenly Bulgakov sneezed.

"Gesundheit," said Groh. "Have you been taking your Astra C?"

"I have been taking it up my ass," said Bulgakov. "Then shitting it out."

Dr. Pol-Lim chuckled. He always enjoyed his jobs for the System. Briefly leaving his quotidian practice in Long Beach to step into a twilight realm of mystery and danger. Never understanding who was who or what was what. Feeling like some minor character in an enthralling novel he would never get to read.

"You're very lucky," said Dr. Pol-Lim. "If the angle had been slightly different the bullet would have penetrated your skull."

"No chance of that," said Groh. "His skull is several centimeters thick."

The doctor laughed again. The blond man was delightful.

"Not fucking lucky," said Bulgakov.

"No?" said Pol-Lim. "Then what were you?"

"Quick. I was fucking quick."

The man was a killer. No doubt of that. Pol-Lim had seen much killing in Cambodia when he was a small boy but had never been able to understand it. He could as easily gouge out his own eyes as take the life of another. But in the end life and death were but different aspects of the same illusion. So the Buddha taught.

"You've suffered a concussion," said Pol-Lim. "A mild one, I believe. Your neurological signs are good. But just to be on the safe side I'd like to bring you in for a CT scan. To make sure there's no bleeding under the skull."

"No," said Bulgakov. "No fucking CT."

"I'm afraid there's no time for that, doctor," said Groh.

"I see. Well, keep a close eye on him. If he becomes lethargic or dizzy or begins to vomit or lose consciousness, call me immediately."

"I will," said Groh.

As the doctor finished up with Bulgakov Groh left. Went down a couple of rooms and knocked on the door.

It was opened by terHorst. Who was standing in a swirl of Hav-A-Tampa smoke and holding his gun.

"Can I come in?" said Groh.

"Sure. My shitty little room is your shitty little room."

TerHorst shut the door behind them. "How's your buddy?" he said.

"The doctor says he's going to be fine."

"That's great news. I was worried sick about him."

TerHorst plopped down on the bed. Propped himself up against the pillows.

The TV was on. Showing local live coverage of the fires. People fled through smoke and sparks. A helicopter dropped water.

"Looks like the whole fucking state's burning up," said terHorst.

Groh sat down in the room's one chair. "Have you heard from your friends?"

"Just got off the phone with Mac. They're on their way out to the desert. To bury Steve."

"I assume they're not coming back."

"Oh they're coming back all right. To finish the job."

"We can finish the job better without them."

"Look, Jack. The Lingos are country people. That fella whoever he was killed their blood kin. It's an eye for an eye. Blood for blood. That's the code of the country. They're not gonna stop just 'cause you or I tell 'em to. They'll stop when flies are crawling around on that fella's eyeballs."

Groh looked at the nine-millimeter. Which terHorst was holding lazily across his lap.

"You don't need that with me."

TerHorst blew out a slow cloud of smoke.

"See, I'm thinking like this. I'm thinking you're thinking you don't need me anymore. 'Cause they ditched their car and now my cool little GPS gizmo isn't worth diddly-poo." He lifted the pistol up. "This is just to remind you that I'm still relevant you might say."

"It's all about the diamonds isn't it?"

"What diamonds?"

"Gina's diamonds. Don't worry. We have no interest in them. You'll get what's been promised to you. Just let me and my associate do our work. We work best alone."

"I'm part of this. The Lingos are part of this. And that's it. And don't forget I'm a U.S. marshal. If I want to I can have a team of twenty marshals here in twenty minutes. I'd probably get some kind of dadgum medal for bringing you boys in."

"Hm. If you did something like that I wonder what would happen to your daughter."

TerHorst smiled. "Well, Jack. Looks like what we got here is an old-fashioned Mexican standoff."

He looked back at the TV. Frightened horses galloped through a pasture. As orange flames jumped in the distance.

"Poor horses," said terHorst.

Groh stood up. Walked to the door then stopped.

"The doctor's still here."

"So?"

"Maybe you'd like to see him."

"Why?"

"You're obviously ill."

"Thanks for your concern. But I'll be just fine. Do you know why?"

Groh shook his head.

"I don't walk in fear, Jack. I have the Lord holding my hand. Every step of the way."

The red Chrysler went east on I-10 into the teeth of the wind. Past Pomona they saw smoke beyond the hills. They took the 15 south.

Near Lake Elsinore a hillside was on fire. A DC-10 swooped low and dumped orange dust. Smoke blew over the interstate and the sunlight dimmed and the traffic slowed. "Look at the sun!" said Luke, pointing. In the backseat with the dog.

It was eerie like a pink moon and you could look right at it.

They had all been silent for a long time until Luke spoke. What had happened seemed too big for words. And the magnitude of the unknown they were headed into made words seem insignificant. Gina looked over at Gray. He seemed cold, focused, and inside himself. In thinking him some gentle hippie she had never been so ridiculously wrong about anything in her life. He was clearly some kind of expert killer and she was glad. She hoped he was the best killer in the world.

It had been too dangerous to go back to the motel to get their things so she and Luke now had nothing. The process had been one of stripping down. Of leaving behind. In the beginning the big house in Massapequa Park. Stuffed with all the paraphernalia of the good life. And then the two-bedroom apartment in Brady. And then two suitcases and the single room at the edge of the sea. How might the process continue? She and Luke were still wearing clothes. Next might be wandering naked in the wilderness. And what came after that?

But thank god she still had her purse. With all of her diamonds and much of her money.

They left the interstate at Temecula and stopped at a shopping center. Luke led the malamute over to some shrubbery and he lifted his leg and unloosed a powerful pissing. They went into a gun store where Gray bought ammunition for the Glock 19 then they went into a DeeLishus Donuts! shop. One of the chain, it so happened, owned by Dr. Pol-Lim's brother. They got doughnuts of varying kinds and Gina and Luke got Cokes and Gray a tall cup of iced coffee. When they returned to the car a skinny guy with a red beard was sitting astride his Harley and looking the car over.

"That's a great car, dude," he said.

"Thanks," said Gray.

The guy took a look at the dog.

"But that's a real ugly dog," he said and roared away.

They went south on the 79. The road slowly rising. Taking them into pretty country. Fields and trees. It was windy here too and the trees thrashed about but they saw no fires. Then they took the S-22. Up into the San Ysidro Mountains. Passing through pine and oak and juniper forests. One of only a few cars on the road. And then as the sun was setting they reached the top of the mountains and everything changed.

The Sonora Desert stretched out before them. Hundreds and hundreds of miles of it. Like a frozen brown ocean. Gray took the Chrysler down into the giant shadow of the mountains. The road switchbacked and switchbacked and switchbacked and switchbacked. It took them twenty-five minutes to get to the bottom and Tejada Springs.

S-22 turned into Palm Canyon Drive. Following Norman's instructions they turned left at Tejada Springs Road. There was a gas station/grocery store and a souvenir shop and a bleak motel and a café and a forbidding-looking bunkerlike bar with three motorcycles and a pickup truck parked out front and a hardware store. But several abandoned buildings gave the place a ghost-townish feel.

They drove through the deepening twilight. Peering at a straggle of shabby houses that had lights on inside but no apparent people. They went by something called the Lucky Horseshoe Trailer Park. Which looked as thought it might better have been named the Last Gasp Trailer Park or the Trailer Park of Broken Dreams. They turned right on Rango Road and there weren't any more houses but just the desert and after about a mile they turned right on Desert Club Drive. Another quarter mile brought them to Norman's house.

It was a low wide adobe building surrounded by palm trees. California fan palms with thick trunks and tall thin Mexican fan palms and date palms. A weathered wooden sign said: DESERT CLUB OF TEJADA SPRINGS. They got out of the car. It was very quiet. The palm trees were as motionless as palm trees in a painting. No wind on this side of the mountains. No car or plane noise. The chittering of a bird drifted in off the desert. As it sang its last song of the day.

The dog walked over to one of the palms, sniffed its trunk and peed on it.

Gray opened the front door with Norman's key then quickly punching the code Norman had given him into a keypad disarmed the burglar alarm.

They passed through an entrance hall. Found themselves in a room that spread across the whole back of the house. There was a sunken round cocktail bar and a stone fireplace. Lots of Native American artwork. Navajo rugs on the terra-cotta floor. The back wall was all glass. Through it they could see cactuses and palm trees and an oval swimming pool.

They slid open a glass door and stepped outside.

The pool looked as though it hadn't had water in it for years. The bottom was covered with dirt. A pair of palm fronds had grown crisp and brown.

"Is that a *snake?*" said Gina. Looking at a sinuous dark shape near one of the fronds.

"Don't worry, Mom," said Luke. "It's dead."

They stood there and let the silence and stillness seep into them.

"Where's the golf course?" said Luke.

"Guess it's out there somewhere," said Gray.

They were there for a couple of heartbeats then were gone: three shadows trotting through the dusk on the other side of a netless tennis court then disappearing behind some rabbitbrush bushes.

"Did you see that?" said Gina.

"Was that coyotes?" said Luke. Excited.

"Yeah," said Gray.

"Great," Gina sighed. "Snakes and coyotes. Just what I need."

Gray gazed through the failing light. Hoping to see them again. Their heads had been turned toward them as they moved by. The coyotes unmistakably had been checking the newcomers out.

Groh and Bulgakov put on their flesh-colored gloves. It took Bulgakov only seconds to break into room 21. They didn't waste any time looking through stuff but just carried it all out to the Land Cruiser. There wasn't much and it didn't take long.

Groh took a last look around the room. Saw a sock peeking out from under one of the beds. He picked it up. White with black and red stripes around the top. Luke's sock. No sign of its mate. Something poignant about it. Just that single sock.

Poor boy. He must be so afraid.

They sat on the couch watching *The Farmer Takes a Wife*. The city girls were having a milking contest. Their shapely behinds planted on stools as they tugged at the teats of the cows. The squeamish girls squealed and giggled and the cows looked nervously back over their shoulders. While the handsome young farmer, hands on hips, observed. Shaking his head with an amused sigh.

The man in the ski mask laughed. It was the first sounds she'd heard him make other than a throat-clearing or two. She looked at him and he looked back at her. The skin around his eyes was crinkled and she could tell he was smiling.

"I think he likes Alicia," said Dee. Referring to the hot-blooded little Cuban masseuse from Miami. "I think she's his favorite."

He shook his head. Picked up the spiral notebook and wrote something then showed it to her.

kristen. shes mor his tipe.

Kristen was the tall tan nanny from Dallas. Who read the Bible every night and claimed to be a virgin.

"Kristen? Really?"

He nodded.

"I think she's too goody-goody."

He shook his head.

"Huh. Well, maybe. What about Alexandra?" The sophisticated art student from Manhattan.

He wrote again in the notebook.

shes a bitch. shes evul.

She laughed. "Yeah, I can see that. She is kind of a schemer isn't she?"

He nodded.

"How come you won't talk? Cat got your tongue?"

He wrote in the notebook.

4 yur on pertekshun. so u want recugniz my voyce. so we can let u go.

"Would you do me a favor? Would you untie my hands?"

He shook his head.

"Why not? I won't try and get away. I promise."

He shook his head again and turned back to the TV. Monica, the waitress from Chicago, had just had her pail kicked over by her cow and milk splashed her legs and the other girls all laughed at her and she got hysterical and began to cry and the young farmer rushed over. But ignored Monica and tried to calm down the cow. It was pretty funny but he didn't laugh.

"Are you mad?" said Dee.

He looked at her again. His eyes were so blue. She wondered what he looked like without the mask.

"Well are you?" she said.

He wrote in the notebook.

corse not. i culdnt never be mad at u.

Norman had a freezer full of meat and chicken and frozen dinners and a pantry full of food in cans and tins and packages and jars. Gray defrosted some hamburger meat in the microwave and browned it in a skillet and gave it to the dog and Gina put a couple of frozen pizzas in the oven. Pepperoni for her and mushroom and black olive for Luke and Gray.

They ate at the sunken bar in the club room. Looking out on the empty swimming pool and the dark desert.

"Norman's got enough food out here for an army," said Gina.

"Guess he's preparing for the end of the world," said Gray.

"Mm. This is good," said Luke. Chewing on the pizza.

"*This* is good," said Gina. Lifting her glass of South African red wine.

"You see that wine cellar?" said Gray. "He's got enough wine for an army too."

"Gray? Those guys?" said Luke. "You shot?"

"Yeah?"

"You think they're dead?"

"The first one, yeah. The second one—I don't know. I don't think so."

"That reminds me," said Gina. "Thanks."

"For what?"

"For what? You saved us."

"I saved myself too. It was self-preservation."

"Cut the shit. I said thanks. Just say you're welcome."

"You better say it," said Luke. "She won't stop until you do."

Gray laughed. "Okay. You're welcome."

"Tomorrow?" said Gina. "You're gonna tell me exactly who the hell you really are. But not tonight. I'm too tired tonight. I just wanna drink myself to sleep."

The dog was sitting by Luke's chair. Gazing up intensely at him as he ate.

"Can I give him some?" said Luke.

Gray shook his head. "He's had his supper. I don't wanna turn him into a begger."

TerHorst lay on his bed watching the fires on TV. Much more beautiful at night. Tornadic swirls of flame. Golden sparks flying upward into the black. Hundreds of homes destroyed already. Tens of thousands of people fleeing. A tiny foretaste of what was to come. Because next time around you could take it to the bank the world would be destroyed by fire. That was the message of the rainbow.

There was a knock on the door. TerHorst took his gun with him over to the peephole. Saw Mac Lingo and let him in.

He was sweaty and grimy and had some of his son's blood on him. He walked past terHorst and sat down heavily in the chair.

"You get it done?" said terHorst.

Lingo nodded. His eyes dark hollows in his buzzard face. "It's been a hard day."

"I know." He put his hand on Lingo's shoulder and gave it a squeeze. "We all have to eat a peck of dirt."

"Ain't that the truth."

"Can I get you anything?"

Lingo shook his head. TerHorst was feeling dizzy. He went to his bed and lay back down.

"Well Mac. He's in a better place."

"That's right. That's right."

"How's Ronnie taking it?"

"His heart is broke. Steve was a people person. But Ronnie's always been kindly a lone wolf. His onliest real friend was Steve."

"Where'd you bury him?"

"Out in the Mojave Desert. Right next to this ugly-ass little tree." He pulled out a cigarette and lit it. "We stopped off and bought a shovel but we ort to of bought a goddamn jackhammer. Ground was like fucking concrete. Then I wanted to say a few words over him. When I was a boy my grandmama'd give me a nickel for ever Bible verse I learnt and I learnt a bunch 'cause I liked to get nickels but I couldn't think of a damn thing. So I just said the Lord's Prayer. What I 'membered of it."

"Lord's Prayer's always good."

"When this is all over with we'll go back and dig him up. Take him back home. Put him in the cemetery with all the other Lingos."

"You sure you'll be able to find him?"

"I made a map. I learnt how to do that when I was a army scout in Nam. But first we gotta get the son of a bitch that kilt him."

"We'll get him."

"Not only did he shoot my boy. He run him over."

"I know. I saw it."

"Run him over like a dog."

"We won't just kill him, Mac. We'll make him hurt."

"That's right. Make him holler first."

Lingo's eyes drifted over to the Hadean scene on the TV. Conflagration and collapse. Panic and running.

"Set far to him. That's what we'll do."

"Mr. Cicala will not be pleased," said Mr. Li. Not pleased himself.

"I don't like to make excuses, Mr. Li," said Markus Groh.

"I know."

"But the problem is terHorst. And his friends. They almost got Dima killed today. And they prevented us from successfully completing our assignment."

"You have no idea where they've gone?"

"None. Dima is searching their computers now. But so far he's come up with nothing useful."

"And this man. You have no idea who he is?"

"No. But he's clearly a professional. He makes the job more challenging but as I said. The problem is terHorst. He is physically ill. He is mentally unstable. And his associates are imbeciles. He insists on being a part of this. And yet we no longer need him."

Mr. Li's round bland face was pale in the glow of the Mac computer. He closed his eyes. Softly traced the arc of one eyebrow with the tip of his finger.

"Mr. Li?"

"Yes. I'm here. What do you propose to do?"

"Deal with the problem directly. It can all be taken care of in the next five minutes."

"I'm sorry. But that is a hornet's nest we are unwilling to stir up."

"It would be handled with the utmost circumspection."

"I'm sure that it would. But the answer is no."

"I understand. I'll be in touch."

"Thank you."

He put the phone down.

A cup of herbal tea steamed on his desk. He picked it up and sipped it.

He could feel a headache coming on. His headaches were savage and resistant to medication and he knew he would probably be awake all night. As the *Invictus* beat up and down the dark river.

The boat's name came from the poem by W. E. Henley. Which began—

> *Out of the night that covers me,*
> *Black as the pit from pole to pole,*
> *I thank whatever gods may be*
> *For my unconquerable soul.*

Mr. Li loved English literature. He had even gone to England as a young man to study it at Cambridge. Perhaps that love had something to with his having a splash of English blood in his veins. His great-grandfather had been an Englishman. Ronald Aldersey. A teacher in a British school in the International Settlement in Shanghai. Tall, thin, cerebral, lustful, romantic, and tubercular. One night in his white pongee suit he had gone for a stroll down Foochow Road. He entered a second-rate teahouse called the Garden of Supreme Happiness and saw for the first time a sing-song girl named Mei-ling.

She was fourteen. Less than half the age of Aldersey. She was from a small village. Her parents had sold her to a man who had sold her to the teahouse. Girls were not valued much in China.

There was a saying: "Eight saintly daughters are not equal to a boy with a limp."

Aldersey wanted to take her to a room upstairs and began to negotiate with the vile old madam. She said Mei-ling wouldn't come cheap because she was the freshest flower in the Garden of Supreme Happiness. He didn't for one second believe she was a virgin but because he had never seen such beauty in physical form he didn't haggle with the woman for long.

When Aldersey was finished he saw blood on the sheets. He clutched her to him and stroked and kissed her hair and begged her forgiveness for taking her innocence. But Mei-ling actually had lost her virginity more times than she could count. With the help of a vial of chicken blood she kept under her pillow.

He saw her as often as he could. When she became pregnant he just assumed the baby was his. She wanted to get rid of it but he wouldn't let her because he loved Mei-ling and wanted her to have his child. And she loved Aldersey because he was kind to her. She had never known such kindness or indeed any kindness at all.

His life began to seem impossible to him. He lost weight and slept little. Occasionally he would cough up blood. He had a beautiful sonorous voice and Mei-ling liked it when as part of his efforts to teach her English he would read some favorite piece of literature aloud to her. When he reached the end of *Romeo and Juliet* he became choked up and couldn't continue because he saw Aldersey and Mei-ling as a doomed couple too.

He had always intended to go back to England because he loved it there and missed his family. But he could imagine his parents' reaction if he brought back a barely pubescent Chinese girl. They would disown him if he married her. The thought of losing his family was unbearable to him. But it would be likewise unbearable to lose Mei-ling.

Fate solved the problem for him. His mouth one morning suddenly gushed blood and he fell to the floor in front of his horrified students. He died in Shanghai General Hospital two days later. The weeping Chinese child with the huge belly had been turned away from the hospital by stern nurses. When word came that Aldersey was dead she walked to the Whangpu River with the intention of throwing herself in. But then with her too there was a gushing as her water broke and she lay down on her back on the muddy riverbank and gave birth to Mr. Li's grandfather. Who had Aldersey's blue eyes.

Mei-ling survived famines, floods, earthquakes, plagues, wars, and revolutions. Gradually turning into a shrunken bony humpback with a few hanks of white hair clinging to her head. Finally dying shortly after Mr. Li was born.

With a sigh Mr. Li peered at the screen and maneuvered the mouse. There was always work to be done somewhere in the world. This business with Cicala's family was really quite vexing. Sometimes it was the most trivial things that took up the most time. But ultimately like all things human it was temporary. As evanescent as the scent of a flower in a garden at dusk. As the steam off his cup of tea.

The barking of the dog awoke him. He got out of bed and pulled his jeans on and picked up the Glock off the bedside table.

He went out of the bedroom. Walked down a hallway to the club room.

The malamute was standing at the glass wall barking barking barking.

Gray walked across the dark room and joined him.

"What's out there, boy?"

He looked out at the empty pool. The cactuses and palm trees. Everything was still and quiet. Except for the dog.

"What's going on?"

It was Gina. Coming in with Luke. Both of them disheveled and blurred from sleep.

"Don't know," said Gray. "Something spooked the dog."

"Oh god," said Gina. "You think they've found us?"

"Maybe it's the coyotes!" said Luke.

"It's probably nothing," said Gray. "But I'll take a look around."

"Can I come?" said Luke.

"No. Stay with your mom."

"Be careful!" said Gina.

He slid open the glass door and the dog charged out. Still thunderously woofing. He ran past the swimming pool but then Gray called out: "Hey boy! Stop!" If it was coyotes Gray didn't want the dog tangling with them. Your average skinny scruffy coyote could kill a dog three times its size in seconds.

The dog waited for him and they walked out together past the palm trees. Gray holding the gun by his side. The gravelly ground crunching softly under his bare feet. The dog barked again and then Gray saw it: a plump skunk its tail held high waddling away down a shallow arroyo.

Gray smiled. Dropped to one knee and rubbed what was left of the dog's ears and gave his scarred muzzle a kiss.

"Good boy! What a guard dog!"

The dog seemed to grin as he accepted the congratulations. His tongue hung out and he panted happily. But when he made a move to go after the skunk Gray gave his collar a firm jerk. "Better quit while you're ahead, buddy."

Gray knew he should go back. Ease Gina and Luke's minds. But he found himself lingering there at the desert's edge. The ruins of the golf course stretched out before him like a golf course on the moon. It was lit by the light of more stars than he had seen in quite some time. The mountains blocked off the light and pollution from the big cities to the west. He could see the faint cloudlike luminescence of the Milky Way. Suddenly he felt staggered by the fact that such a minutely tiny thing as himself could be standing here with his feet in the dirt beholding the Eternal and the Infinite.

The dog looked up at Gray and whimpered a little. Ready to get a move-on. To chase the skunk or do *some*thing. But Gray continued to look at the sky. He felt a swirl of vertigo. As if gravity might stop and he might drop into that blazing abyss of stars.

Billions of billions of stars, the scientists said. And probably millions of millions of worlds where life existed.

He wondered if all worlds were as beautiful as this one. As cruel as this one.

Thursday

"What is wrong, Mr. Pat?"

He was at the counter in the kitchen. Pouring himself a cup of coffee.

"Every fucking thing is wrong."

She walked over to him and put her hand on his chest. Gazed up at him with those preternaturally big and dark eyes. Looking as she well knew incredibly adorable.

"Tell me. Tell Eliana."

"Ah don't worry about it. Nothing I can't handle."

He took his coffee over to an oak table. Which looked out on a terrace and the garden. He blew on the coffee and sipped it and pondered the call he had just gotten from Mr. Li. Informing him of the debacle of yesterday.

He couldn't believe Gina had managed to slip away from them for a second time and was now probably speeding away down some highway laughing at them the cunt. With Luke. And now this mysterious protector. Who had managed to make the Russians, Mr. Li's best guys, look like the Keystone Cops.

It was a cold blustery day atop Todt Hill. Rain had been spattering down periodically. In the garden sodden leaves were lying around the bases of the bronze statuary. Their patinas going dull and dark in the elements. Angels and saints and the Virgin Mary weeping over her dead son. Of course it was all a big charade. He wasn't really dead because He was the son of God and would pop up again in three days. So what was this big fucking sacrifice supposed to be about? When Pat the Cat died he wouldn't pop up again in three days, he'd be just more rotting garbage buried in the dirt. And who would weep over him? His wretched wife with half a brain? His little spick mistress who pretended to love him as she plotted to get her hands on every nickel he had? His jerk-off son in Lewisburg? Bobby the Hump?

Luke. Luke would. He was tenderhearted, probably too tenderhearted for a boy, he had seen him cry over a bird he'd found floating dead in the birdbath. He loved his grandpop and would certainly when the time came weep for him.

"I make you breakfast," said Eliana. "*Arepas*. Like you like. With *perico*."

"I'm not hungry. My stomach hurts. I think I got stomach cancer. Like my father."

"Oh you no have cancer, Mr. Pat. You are silly. A *silly* boy." And she reached out and ruffled what was left of his hair and elicited a smile.

"Eliana?" he said

"Si?"

"Do you love me?"

"Oh yes, Mr. Pat. So much."

She was about to lean down and kiss him but then they heard Latreece coming. Eliana began to move about in an efficient maidlike fashion.

Latreece was softly singing a Bob Marley song. "Three Little Birds." She was in a buoyant mood. The biopsy had come back negative. Death had been sitting on her shoulders like an evil gnome straddling her neck, pulling on her hair and then *poof!* it was gone. She smiled absently at Cicala and the maid. Part of her knowing something was going on between them and the rest of her not wanting to know. She began to knock about the kitchen making breakfast for herself and Millie Cicala.

There was an electronic device hidden in the light fixture that hung over the table Cicala was sitting at. Though famously careful and paranoid he had been bugged successfully for over a year. Somewhere in the city in a little room a man with earphones on and expressionless eyes was listening to Latreece singing: *"Every little thing gonna be all right!"*

As the sun rose up out of one end of the desert Gray at the other end buried the snake. It was about four feet long. Broad brown bands alternating with narrow creamy ones. He guessed that possibly in pursuit of prey it had fallen into the pool and, trapped there, had perished.

The malamute watched him shoving the shovel into the hard ground. It made clunking scraping noises then he heard the scrannel cries of crows. They were flying around in the distance dark against the sun. He had always liked crows. They were brash and smart and brave. They seemed to love life. They would still be flapping and strutting around like they owned the planet when the last human had turned back to dust.

Luke came walking up. Wagging his tail, the dog went to meet him.

"Morning," said Gray.

"Morning." Luke yawned and petted the dog. Looked at the hole and the snake lying by it. "What are you doing?"

"Burying the snake."

"Why?"

"I didn't want to just leave it in the pool. I don't think your mom liked looking at it."

"But why are you burying it?"

"I don't know. What would you have done?"

"Thrown it in the garbage?"

"But I don't think of it as garbage."

"It's just a dead snake."

"I think all life should be treated with respect."

"What about that guy yesterday? In the parking lot."

"What about him?"

"You didn't treat his life with respect."

Gray stopped digging, leaned on his shovel and thought about it.

"I had to do what I did. I was defending you, me, and your mother."

He decided the hole was deep enough. Picked up the snake and put it in. Luke wrinkled his nose.

"How can you stand to touch it?"

Gray shrugged. He began covering up the snake with dirt.

"What is it?" said Luke. "A rattlesnake?"

"No. It's a kingsnake. They eat rattlesnakes."

"Wow. And they don't get poisoned?"

"They're immune to the poison."

Gray stepped on the dirt on the grave of the snake, tamping it down. For just a moment the bottom part of the circle of the sun seemed to be resting on the horizon line. Making it look like the sun wasn't millions of miles away but was a great glowing object sitting in the desert. Something you could walk right up to and look up and marvel at.

They started to walk back toward Norman's house. The attenuated shadows of the man and boy and dog extending far ahead of them.

"Your mom up?"

"No. I think she's still asleep."

"She must be really tired. Yesterday was a long day."

"Yeah."

"You hungry?"

"Yeah."

"Me too. You like oatmeal?"

"Um . . . it's okay."

"I got a special way of making it. I guarantee you'll like it. Want me to teach you how?"

"Okay. But . . ."

"But what?"

"Will you wash your hands first?"

Gray laughed. "Sure."

———

A brownish pall hung over the land. Bits of ash drifted down. Like a gray infernal snow. It was ninety degrees at nine a.m.

The sun at their backs Groh and Bulgakov walked down Alejo Avenue. Groh was drinking Gatorade. Bulgakov was wearing a baseball cap that hid most of his bandage.

"You okay?" said Groh.

"Quit asking every fucking five minutes."

"Okay. But how are you feeling?"

"Like I was shot in fucking head."

A woman was coming toward them. Walking a little dog. With a nice smile Groh accosted her.

"I'm sorry to bother you but we're looking for some friends."

"Oh?" she said. Smiling back. A lush redhead in her fifties. Her dog began to bark at the men. "Pogo! Quiet!"

Groh handed her the photos of Gina and Luke and one of the three pictures showing Gina and Gray as outlaws. TerHorst and the Lingos had the other two.

"We were supposed to meet them," Groh said, "but there was a mix-up. And we've lost their phone numbers. Perhaps you know them or have seen them."

"Mmm," she said. Frowning at the pictures. "I'm afraid they don't look familiar." She handed them back. "Sorry."

"Oh that's all right. We'll probably bump into them when we go around the next corner."

A gust of wind blew off Bulgakov's cap. He hurried to get it. The woman looked at the bandage.

"Oh what happened to your poor head?"

"A minor traffic accident," said Groh.

The flurry of activity had set Pogo off again.

"Pogo!" said the woman. "Bad dog! Quiet!"

Groh looked down at him. "What kind of dog is he?"

"A poodle-Pomeranian mix. Aren't you, Pogo?"

"Well thank you. Have a nice walk."

"I hope you find your friends."

"We'll find them. I'm sure of it."

Groh and Bulgakov watched the woman and her dog walk away. She had a big stride and the dog trotted briskly to keep up.

"What a cute dog," said Groh.

Bulgakov grunted.

"Don't you like dogs, Dima?"

"They're okay. If you cut off all the fat. The fat has bitter taste."

They drove down the half-abandoned main drag of Tejada Springs. Went into the gas station/grocery store and got milk, cheese, bread, eggs, some fresh fruit and vegetables, and Honey Nut Cheerios. Luke's favorite cereal.

The guy behind the counter was wearing an orange T-shirt that said HAPPY CAMPER 1980. His skin and the whites of his eyes were yellow from a bad liver. He gazed past Gray through the grimy front window.

"Isn't that Norm Hopkins's car?"

"Yeah," said Gray. Counting out some money.

"Where's Norm?"

"In LA."

The man's yellow eyes took in Gina, Luke, and the dog.

"You friends of Norm?"

"Yeah."

"Great guy. Norm."

"He sure is."

The man went in the cash register and gave Gray his change.

"Visiting? Or just passing through?"

"Visiting."

"Staying out at Norman's place?"

"Yeah."

"You know it used to be the old country club. Movie stars would go out there to play golf. They say Bing Crosby played out there. And they say Marilyn Monroe went skinny-dipping in the swimming pool one night."

They left the store and walked back to the car.

"Why'd you tell that nosy asshole where we were staying?" said Gina.

"This is a small town," said Gray. "Everybody's gonna figure it out that we're out there. And if I lied it would look suspicious."

"Yeah, Mom," said Luke. "Gray's got it all under control."

"Oh I'm sorry," said Gina. "I forgot Gray's such a genius. In the future I'll keep my mouth shut."

"Good idea, Mom. Ow! Stop it!"

She had grabbed his ear and was pulling on it. Gray laughed. And then he saw the birds. Out over the desert. Dozens of them drifting around in a slow circle. An indolent swirl. Gray realized with surprise they were seagulls. Their presence here making no sense so far from the sea.

DeWitt sat on the commode with his eyes closed. Imagining making love to Dee on top of the antique bedspread. And then he groaned and came. The blissful images faded away. He opened his eyes.

He got up and went to the sink and washed his hands. Regarding his face in the mirror. It had been doing a little better lately but had erupted overnight. Not surprisingly. His acne was tied up with his emotions. When he was agitated it was worse. And he found Dee agitating.

His teenage years had been blighted by his acne but he had assumed when he hit his twenties it would go away like it did with everyone else but here he was nearly thirty and it was as bad as ever. Oklahoma's best dermatologists had pronounced themselves baffled and beaten by his acne. He had tried herbs and acupuncture and homeopaths and hypnotism and had even gone to a faith healer who would make crippled old men jump up out of their wheelchairs and dance a jig but nothing had worked. And therefore he would never possess a girl like Dee except in his panting pathetic dreams.

His cell rang. It was Groh.

"How is she? Any problems?"

"She's doing just fine," said DeWitt. "No problems a-tall."

"Good. Her father wants proof of life. Please call him. On her cell phone. Make it short."

DeWitt put his ski mask back on and went into the living room. She was tied up on the couch. She loved his big new high-def TV that got a gazillion channels. Right now she was watching a shopping channel. An aging supermodel was hawking a line of skin care products. With a secret tri-peptide complex.

"I gotta get me some of that," said Dee.

He picked up the notebook and wrote: *dont b sily. u got skin like a litle baby.*

"Aw you're sweet. You're a liar but you're sweet."

She had begun to flirt with him but he wasn't fooled. She was his captive and he had life and death power over her so naturally she was going to be nice to him. Maybe she was hoping he would let down his guard and she could escape but that wasn't going to happen. He prided himself on always getting the job done whatever it was. *Just do the job.* That was the beauty of the System. It needed all kinds. Cold-blooded killers like Smith-Jones and Jones-Smith and easy-to-get-along-with eager-beaver can-do fellas like himself.

He unbound her wrists and ankles. He had begun experimenting with giving her a little more freedom in his presence. As long as he never turned his back on her it should be okay.

"Whew," she sighed rubbing her wrists. "Thanks."

He wrote in the notebook: *im caling yur daddy. b carful what u say.*

"Oh I'll be careful. Don't worry."

224 / *Tom Epperson*

He tapped in the number and then heard terHorst: "Baby? Is that you? Dee? You there?"

He handed the phone to Dee.

"Daddy?"

"Dee! Honey! Are you all right?"

"I'm fine, Daddy," she said and began to cry.

"Why are you crying?"

"I don't know, Daddy. I miss you."

"Oh I miss you too, baby. I'm gonna get you home soon. You'll see."

"Okay."

"How are they treating you? They're not hurting you anymore are they?"

"Nobody's hurting me. They're treating me fine."

"What kind of place are you in? How many people are there?"

Dee looked at the man in the mask. His blue eyes burned into her. Sometimes it seemed like they never blinked.

"Dee?"

"I can't talk about it."

DeWitt held out his hand for the phone.

"I gotta go now."

"Dee! Wait—"

"Bye, Daddy."

"Dee!"

But the line was dead.

"Fuck," said terHorst.

He was lying in the unmade bed. In the air-conditioned box of the motel room in Mar Vista. Feeling too ill to join the others in King Beach. His heart beating like a kettledrum.

The TV was on. It hadn't been off for a long time. It was like a fireplace with a fire always going in it. The fires were even more widespread and fierce today than yesterday. He would flip from channel to channel. It was hypnotic watching the fires. He felt like he too was burning up.

He got up and went to the window and pushed aside the curtains. Watched the wind whooshing down Washington Boulevard.

Today was the McGraths' funeral. Probably happening right now. He had called into the office and talked to Linda, the departmental secretary, and told her he couldn't come because he was holed up at home with the swine flu. Didn't want to spread it around. Great thing about cell phones was no one ever knew where you were calling from.

He remembered how broken Frank had been when Alison had gotten sick. He had got drunk and cried and he had never seen Frank cry. Cancer. What a god-awful thing. Alison had always been so pretty, like a fragile flower, and then she had begun to just wither away.

Life.

Death.

It might seem to be complicated but it was all extremely simple. God created Adam and Eve with perfect bodies and flawless immune systems. No cancer, heart disease, diabetes, lockjaw. They could just lie around in the shade of the garden and fuck each other's perfect bodies forever. But Eve listened to the snake instead of God. And now we all got sick and died like wretched animals or got run over or murdered or struck by lightning. It was all Eve's fucking fault.

He fired at the targets: three cardboard boxes on which he'd drawn concentric circles. He was rusty. The fact he hadn't killed the guy on Hill Street had proved that.

Five he knew about had been after them. The guy in the Hawaiian shirt. No longer a factor. Frank terHorst. A law officer with presumably at least some limited skills. The oafish guy with the big trunk and stubby limbs who had shot at him through the windshield. The fact he had missed suggesting he was a garden variety thug and not a real talent. The blond guy he had glimpsed in the rearview mirror knocking down the thug when he was firing at the car. Indicating this was not purely a kill job but they wanted at least one of them, almost certainly Luke, alive. His capabilities were unknown but Gray wouldn't have been surprised if they were equal to those of the guy with the buzz cut. Who was alive not only because Gray was rusty but because he had reacted with such startling speed.

So four were left he knew about and maybe others. Maybe many others. Maybe it would come down like it had at the presidential palace in Kangari. As they had come swarming over the lush and perfect lawns. Crazed on palm wine and cocaine and convinced his bullets wouldn't hurt them. The blue and yellow lizards skittering out of their way.

The targets were set up in a deep ravine. North of Norman's golf course and south of a jumble of rough eroded hills. He wasn't just standing straight up and banging away. He fired from prone and crouching positions. He ran toward the targets and fired. Stood with his back to the targets and whirled around and fired. Dived this way and fired and that way and fired and did twenty-five rapid push-ups and jumped up and fired then somersaulted and fired again and fired with his eyes closed and splashed water in his eyes and fired and practiced a quick draw like Wyatt Earp and fired and reloaded and spun around and around like a little kid and made himself dizzy and fired.

This was something the major had drilled into him. In a combat situation if you hadn't practiced something you would never do it. At least not successfully.

Luke listened. Just barely able to hear the distant popping of the Glock.

"Why can't I go watch?" he said.

"Because," said Gina.

She was sitting at the circular bar. Sipping wine and slowly turning the shiny pages of a two-year-old *Vanity Fair*. Looking at the ads. At the inhumanly attractive male and female models.

Luke turned away from the tall wall of glass. The dog walked along with him to the bar.

"How much longer are we going to be here?" he said.

"I don't know."

"I don't have anything to do."

"Read. Watch TV. Or I could homeschool you. What's eight times eight?"

Luke didn't answer. Watched his mother drink the wine.

"Are you becoming an alcoholic?"

"No."

"Can I have some wine?"

"Of course not. Are you crazy?"

"Jeff's parents always let him drink wine at Passover."

"This isn't Passover. We're not Jewish. You're not Jeff."

Luke and the dog went into his bedroom. He flopped onto the bed. Webbing his fingers behind his head he stared up at the beamed ceiling.

He was on his skateboard. The dog was trotting along beside him. They came to the top of a hill. They saw Gray below them.

He was in trouble. Surrounded by bad guys. He was fighting bravely but he was running low on ammo.

"Let's go, boy!" said Luke.

He bombed down the hill. Going faster than he had ever gone. The dog was running beside him. The wheels of the skateboard made a roaring noise on the street. The dog was barking. Luke pulled out his gun and began to fire away.

Gray looked up the hill and grinned.

"Luke!" he said.

The bad guys were firing at Luke. He could hear the bullets whistling past him. He crouched low and kept shooting. A bad guy screamed and fell down and another bad guy did the same.

Gray was out of bullets but started doing his qigong on them.

The dog leapt on one of the bad guys and his teeth tore at his throat.

Luke zipped in on his skateboard among the bad guys. Two of them fired at him but he ducked and they hit each other!

The surviving bad guys began to run away.

"You got here in the nick of time, Luke!" said Gray. "Thanks for saving me!"

"No problem," said Luke.

The dog barked and Luke and Gray laughed—

They wandered through the heat, wind, smoke, and ash. Striking out every time when they showed their pictures to people. Who couldn't wait to get away from them. As though they'd just been accosted by father and son Grim Reapers.

Ronnie was limping a little. His left leg bruised and swollen where the Honda had hit it.

"I'm thirsty, Daddy."

"Here," said Mac Lingo. Thrusting a big plastic bottle of Dr. Pepper at him.

"Naw. I'm thirsty for a beer."

They went in the Harbor Room. A sign said: THE SMALLEST BAR IN LOS ANGELES. They sat down at the bar and got draft beers.

It was a small bar all right. Ronnie by himself seemed to take up about a quarter of it.

"You got a moustache," Ronnie said.

Lingo grinned and slowly right to left licked the foam off his upper lip.

"Take a gander at these, chief," he said to the bartender. "Any of 'em look familiar to ya?"

The bartender frowned at the photos. Cocked his head a little as he looked at Gina.

"I don't know. Her maybe."

"Yeah?" said Lingo. "You seen her? Maybe she's been in here."

"No, I don't think she's been in here. Maybe I've just seen her on the street. Or maybe not. Maybe I just *wished* I'd seen her. She's really hot."

Lingo looked fondly at the photo. Like he was Gina's doting dad.

"Ain't she though? She's a right purty little gal. Yes sir."

"Well you seen her or not?" said Ronnie. "How about a straight answer?"

"I don't think I've seen her," said the bartender. Looking the Lingos over. "How come you wanna know?"

"We're PIs," said Lingo. "On a case."

"I see," said the bartender then deciding his only other customer was in urgent need of attention moved away.

"Daddy?"

"Yeah?"

"You think Steve's in heaven?"

"I don't think there's no doubt about it."

"What do you think he's doing up there?"

"Got no idea."

"You think they got hunting and fishing up there?"

"I don't know."

"I hope so. Steve loved hunting and fishing."

They finished their beers and Lingo paid up. Leaving the bartender a quarter tip. As they got up to go Norman came in. He stepped aside for them but in the confined space their bodies swayed and bumped up against him and Ronnie glared at him and he could smell their sour odor. Then they were gone.

"Them was some weird dudes," said the bartender. Watching them amble past the window.

"Yeah?" Norman said. Sitting down at the bar. "Well King Beach is full of 'em."

"What'll it be, Norman?"

"Dewar's. Rocks."

Groh perused one of the Harry Potter books. Didn't find much to engage him but then he wasn't a ten-year-old boy.

Bulgakov had turned pale and tottered as they walked by the lagoon and had had to sit down on the grass. Groh had wanted to call Dr. Pol-Lim but Bulgakov resisted so they had compromised by returning to the motel to rest for a bit. Leaving the vengeful

Lingos to carry on the search. Probably doing more harm than good but Groh was stuck with them for now.

He couldn't get it out of his head: the image of Luke in his white baseball cap dodging through traffic. Fleeing down Lincoln Boulevard. Running away from *him*. If only he knew that all Groh wanted to do was to protect him. To deliver him safely to his grandfather.

The corrupt old gangster that was his grandfather.

He wasn't in the habit of speculating about the fates of nontarget individuals he encountered on his assignments but there was something special about Luke. Such a beautiful child. He deserved to grow up in a beautiful place. Where all the sadness, evil, and filth of life wouldn't be allowed to touch him.

He was toying with an idea.

In this line of work you didn't grow old. Someday the odds would catch up with you and you would die. Killed by someone as good as you were or maybe just by some lucky idiot.

And maybe that time was soon. Maybe that time was *now*. That terrible dream he had had on the plane. The mad little girl sitting in the lap of the maggoty old man. And the voice: *To the merciless no mercy will be shown!* How could he have been given a clearer warning?

He wasn't like Dima. Dima enjoyed it. The actual act. But for Groh it was about the hunt not the kill. And he could get that thrill in some other way.

By saving Luke for instance. Spiriting him away from Cicala and the System.

There was a place. An island. In the South Pacific. Off the beaten track. Owned by an Australian billionaire of his acquaintance. Who kept it for the most part unspoiled. Edenic. There was just one tiny town to service the handful of tourists he allowed in. His own friends mostly. It was his plaything was the island. Groh had often daydreamed of retiring there. He could open a bar. Call it Happy Jack's. Wear a Hawaiian shirt and flirt with the tourists. He and Luke would be so happy there. Money would be no problem. He had stashed away a good deal of it in impregnable accounts in the Cayman Islands.

Of course the System wouldn't be pleased with his disappearance. His farewell to arms. Someday someone would come for him. The way he had come for so many others. Or maybe not. Maybe the System was so enormous and he and Luke were so insignificant they would slip through the cracks. Be left alone to live out their lives in their island paradise.

He sat in the chair with the book. Fingering its pages. Smiling a little. Was this only an idle fantasy? Or the beginning of momentous change? Too early to tell.

There was a knock on the door. He put down the book. Took his gun to the door with him. But it was just Bulgakov. Looking better.

"Nu davai," he said. "Davai naydiom etich yobarei."

Come on. Let's find those motherfuckers.

Norman had lots of books. Gray browsed amongst them. Finally plucked out one with an attractive title. *Wanderer.*

It was by the actor Sterling Hayden. Gray knew him from only two roles: General Jack D. Ripper in *Dr. Strangelove* and the corrupt police captain shot in the throat while eating spaghetti in *The Godfather.*

He took the book and a glass of lemonade out on the patio. Sat down in the shade in a lounge chair.

The book was half autobiography and half an account of a voyage Hayden took across the Pacific in 1959 in his schooner *Wanderer.*

Don't talk to me about finding yourself. Only as you are lost is there any hope for you.

He read for about twenty minutes. Liking the book. But growing drowsy.

He took a sip of lemonade.

He saw some movement out of the corner of his eye. Two mice with white feet scampering past a cactus.

It was so quiet that soft sounds sounded loud. The thrumming wings of a hummingbird floating among some flowers. The stirring of palm fronds in a light breeze. The buzz of an insect.

The sky was blue with just a few vagrant shreds of clouds. The day was heating up. A Cooper's hawk was riding the thermals.

Mice beware.

He watched the hawk slowly circling. It put him in mind of the seagulls he had seen this morning. So strange. Maybe they hadn't even been there. Maybe it was a vision of some sort.

His eyes closed. He was wandering. Drifting. Circling. With the hawk. With the gulls.

He heard something and opened his eyes.

Gina was walking past. She grabbed a lounge chair and dragged it clattering over the flagstones till it was next to Gray's chair. Then she sat down and faced him.

"Now," she said. "Tell me."

He enlisted in the army a month out of high school. Took to it immediately. He was a shit-hot soldier. He was sent to Haiti in 1994 as part of Operation Uphold Democracy. Its mission: to throw out the bad guys and replace them with the good guys. Not much happened. It was boring upholding democracy. He and his unit seldom ventured beyond the perimeter of their base. They sought shade from the hot sun and smoked and spat and played cards and stared out at the ragged Haitians clustered beyond the fence.

At night after the others had gone to sleep he began to slip away. Into the dismal slums of Port-au-Prince. Carrying only a sidearm. Not that he seemed to need it for everyone seemed to love him. They smiled and laughed and crowded around and grasped his arm and pressed food and drink upon him. As if his appearance in their midst was a harbinger of good times. Of plenitude and balmy days. Of no more mud slides obliterating their mud huts or babies dying of diarrhea or men with machetes coming for them in the night.

There was no power and he walked through a hot steaming

darkness. Lit here and there by lamps and fires. It could have been a thousand years ago. One night near the waterfront he heard someone crying out and then he heard talk and laughter. He moved toward the sounds and came round a corner. Behind a warehouse in the orange light of a kerosene lantern three Haitian soldiers were raping a young girl. She was maybe twelve or thirteen. She was naked. Her grimy green dress lying near her. The soldiers were drinking one-liter bottles of Presidente beer. Their weapons were leaning up against the warehouse wall.

He unholstered his M9 Beretta and as he stepped forward into the light cocking the pistol they looked at him.

"Let her go," he said.

Maybe there was something in his eyes. Maybe they saw something there that made them think that just letting her go wouldn't be enough and that was why they made a lunge for their rifles.

He put two rounds into the center mass of each.

The girl got up. Blood running down her legs. She picked up her dress and looked at the soldiers and then at him. He tried to smile reassuringly. Putting his hand out toward her.

"It's okay."

But she darted past him. Clutching the dress against her chest.

"Wait!" he said but she disappeared into the dark. Her dark slender form seeming to merge with the night.

He turned back to the soldiers.

Two were lying facedown and looked dead. The third was looking right at him. Sitting with his back propped up against the warehouse. He mumbled a few words in Creole. Then coughed and put his chin on his chest and died.

It had all happened so fast the contents of a bottle of Presidente beer that had been knocked over were still gurgling out onto the ground.

He wasn't sorry he had killed them. He wished they would come back to life so he could kill them again.

He went back to the base. Never told anybody what had happened.

His unit left Haiti after five months and went back to the States. He had been in the army nearly three years and planned to re-up but then one night got in a fight with another soldier. Busted him up so bad he was told he would be brought up on charges. Unless he left the army voluntarily.

He drifted. Drank. Smoked weed. Got in more fights. Wound up in Seattle where he worked construction. And then in the back of a magazine he saw a classified ad. *Experience working in hostile environments.* Which is how he wound up in Miami at the head-quarters of the Argus Defense Group.

It was a private security company that worked in "developing" countries for western corporations. Which were basically in the business of extracting stuff from the earth. Like oil, copper, gold, and diamonds. Argus provided protection for their operations against bandits, guerillas, terrorists, radicals, and other assorted riffraff. It also trained local forces to do the job. Another service Argus offered was PSDs. Private security details. Which were bodyguard units for the rich and powerful.

Argus was run by a retired British SAS major named Sandy Hobbes. One of those tough terse born-to-lead fellows. Craggily handsome though half his right ear was missing. Nobody knew what had happened to it and nobody ever dared ask.

"We're not a bunch of wild-eyed mercenaries running about shooting people," the major told Gray at his job interview. "We're professional and disciplined. We're the ADG. We're the best in the world at what we do. Any questions?"

"Yes sir. What happened to your ear?"

He was on the receiving end of an interminable look from Major Hobbes's ice-blue eyes.

"None of your bloody business," he said finally. "All right. We'll give it a go."

"I'm hired?"

"Yes. Now get out. I'm busy."

And so he worked for Argus for a dozen years. In Africa, Asia, Latin America, and the Pacific. Plunging into this rain forest and helicoptering to the top of that mountain. The major took a special interest in him. Which manifested itself in his being even harder on Gray than on the other men. Once he asked the major about it.

"To whom much has been given," the major said, "much will be expected."

Which flummoxed him. He didn't think of himself as someone who had received much. Who had any particular gifts. Actually he thought of himself in exactly the opposite way. But he didn't want to let the major down. He worked on himself as if he were a sculptor trying to find the perfect shape in the block of stone. Chipping away at his own laziness, apathy, fear, and ignorance. Not only did he need to be in the best physical condition he had to be the best shot. The best at hand-to-hand combat. The steadiest under pressure. The one most willing to throw his own life away in a moment if the exigencies of the job called for that.

He slew more men. Two in Peru. Shining Path guerillas attacking a silver mine in the Andes. One in Malaysia. A worker at an oil palm plantation who had gone mad and run amok slashing several coworkers with a parang. Five on an oil platform off the coast of Nigeria. Gunmen had taken the rig over and were holding several western workers hostage for a huge ransom. One of the workers became ill. After a lengthy negotiation the gunmen allowed a doctor aboard. Except it wasn't really a doctor. Gray pulled a Czech Skorpion machine pistol out of his medical bag and that was that for the gunmen. Two in Medellín. *Sicarios* on motorbikes attempting to assassinate the newspaper publisher he was guarding. The publisher was unhurt. But Gray was shot up badly and spent weeks in a hospital. And one in the Congo in Kinshasa. In a bar called Chez Ntemba. A drunken South African mercenary accused him of making eyes at his unappealing prostitute-girlfriend then came at him with a knife. Saying he intended to cut out those offending eyes. He struck the South African in the neck. Bursting an artery and killing him. Through it was clearly self-defense he was arrested by the police and charged with murder and thrown into a hellish jail. It cost Argus $30,000 in *matabiches*—bribes—to get him out.

Which Major Hobbes, furious at him for getting in a bar fight, informed him would be taken out of his future paychecks.

Eleven. He had killed eleven. All with the same cold satisfaction he'd felt when he'd dispatched the soldiers in Port-au-Prince.

His employment with the Argus Defense Group came to an end in Kangari.

It was a tiny country in West Africa. Not an object of corporate interest till the early nineties when oil and gas fields were discovered offshore. ADG had a twofold presence there. Protecting the offshore fields and protecting Albert Bangura. Kangari's most recent president.

He was the third in the last five years. One had been killed when his helicopter mysteriously exploded in midair. And one had been shot by a firing squad following a coup. On the orders of his former minister of health, Albert Bangura.

Dr. Bangura had been a pediatrician before he entered government. He was forty-three years old. He had three wives and ten children. He presided over a country rent by civil war. The Revolutionary Army of the Lord rampaged over the bleeding burning land. Committing ghastly atrocities. Though the government forces weren't much better. No apparent ideological or ethnic differences divided the two sides. It was all about controlling Kangari's newfound wealth. Cruelty and greed versus greed and cruelty.

The major had put Gray in charge of Bangura's PSD. The president was already being guarded by a detachment of Kangaran soldiers but he didn't trust them. He wouldn't even allow any ammunition to be issued to them. They hung around the presidential palace with their empty weapons smoking *gbana* and leering whenever she appeared at his youngest wife. Who was quite beautiful. With her long graceful limbs and shy smile.

Gray had liked Bangura from the moment he had met him. He was short, energetic, and charming. He smiled almost all the time and laughed frequently. A booming unlikely laugh coming from so small a man. He didn't seem like the type to have engineered a bloody coup. But every now and then when he didn't think anyone was watching you might get a glimpse of a different Bangura. His features becoming hard and cold and his eyes cautious and calculating.

And you heard stories about him. After the previous president had been executed he had had his heart cut out and had cooked and eaten it. He never made a move without consulting a battery of fortune-tellers and astrologers. He practiced witchcraft. That explained his improbable rise from pediatrician to president. There was a secret chamber in the palace where to the wild pounding of drums ancient juju rituals were performed. Animals were sacrificed. And his political enemies. And small children. And demons would appear and have sex with humans. Including Natalie, Bangura's youngest wife. Or in another version of the story Natalie was herself a demon.

But if Bangura was consorting with dark forces their power seemed to have waned because news from the war got steadily worse. Sulima fell. Then Dalao and Zorzor. One of his best generals went over to the RAL and took twenty Chinese-made Type 59 tanks with him. A thousand soldiers were captured and massacred and their bodies thrown to the crocodiles in the Lubutu River. And Malamba the rebel leader went on the radio and promised Bangura a terrible death if he didn't depart Kangari immediately.

In the presidential palace the Argus operatives cleaned their weapons and waited. The sat phone rang. It was Major Hobbes.

"You're clearing out," he said. "Tonight."

"Why?" said Gray.

"The situation's very dangerous."

"I didn't think this job was about being safe."

"You're a security detail. You're not the fucking three hundred Spartans. Anyway the job's over. The contract's been canceled."

"But that doesn't make any sense, major. Why would Bangura cancel the contract now?"

"Our contract wasn't with him."

"Who was it with then?"

"Can't tell you that. But the point is the powers that be have decided Malamba's not such a bad chap after all. He's someone they can work with."

The powers that be. Presumably the CIA or MI6.

"But what about Bangura?" said Gray.

"It's up to him. He can have a nice cushy life on the French Riviera. With all the other retired dictators. They're trying to talk him into it. But he thinks he's a man of destiny. And all that rot."

Gray went to see Bangura. Who greeted him with a sad smile.

"So you're leaving?" he said. "So soon? We were just getting to know each other."

"You should leave too, sir. The situation's getting critical."

"All the more reason I should stay. I can hardly desert my country in its time of need."

"I understand. But sometimes you reach a point when all is lost."

"But all is *not* lost. One mustn't listen to the exaggerations of my enemies. I've seen the intelligence. The tide is turning in our favor. Soon the terrorists will be on the run!"

"I hope so. But just in case. Shouldn't you at least get your family out? Wouldn't that be one less thing for you to worry about?"

Reluctantly Bangura went along with that. The plane that took out the Argus PSD that night also carried Bangura's older two wives and his ten children. Natalie, who had no children, begged her husband to let her stay and he agreed. Also staying behind was Gray.

As he watched the plane lifting up into the black sky he called the major. Who was apoplectic.

"For fuck's sake!" he said. "Have you lost your mind?"

"It just doesn't seem right to leave him, major."

"If he's too stupid to get out while he has the chance that's his fucking problem. Now this is an order. Get on the next plane out!"

"Sorry, major."

"How much is he offering you? Must be a bloody fortune."

"He's not offering me anything."

"He's not worth it, you know. He's not Nelson Mandela. He's just another cheap crook. Robbing his own people blind."

"You always said your job on a PSD is to protect the principal. No matter what. That's what I'm doing."

"Listen to me, you stubborn bastard. Bangura's a dead man if he doesn't leave and so are you. And you know Africa. You'll be lucky if you only get killed. They'll skin you alive if they can and wear you like a fucking coat."

"I'm sorry about this, major. I want to thank you. I owe you just about everything. I have to go."

He put away the sat phone. Got in the back of the limo with Bangura and headed back to the palace.

"Did you stay for her?"

He looked at Gina.

"For Natalie?" she said.

He drank some lemonade. The ice in it all melted now.

"That's funny. Bangura asked me the same question."

Bangura laughed. Gray could feel the seat shaking Bangura was laughing so hard.

"Forgive me," he said. "But I've never seen you taken aback before. You looked really quite surprised!"

"It doesn't have anything to do with her."

Bangura leaned toward him and patted his knee.

"Don't worry. I don't suspect you of anything. You are that truly comical figure in this modern world. An honorable man! *But* you are a *man*. And Natalie is so beautiful. So kind and so sweet. She would make any young man's heart skip a beat. Some Courvoisier?"

"Sure."

Bangura poured them each a cognac. Out of a crystal decanter. Gray sipped it as he looked out the tinted windows of the silver Mercedes limousine. They were part of a caravan of vehicles. Lights flashing, horns honking, sirens blaring. Make way for the president! But still progress was slow. The streets of the capital city were rough and potholed and always crowded. And refugees were coming in from the countryside. Thousands and thousands of them. Running away from the fighting. If it could properly be called that. Because rebels and soldiers alike preferred slaughtering the helpless to fighting each other.

He saw a thinker walking slowly along. A ragged man wearing rubber sandals cut out of tires. His head inclined as though he were deep in rumination. That's why they were called thinkers. They all walked like that with their heads down. You saw them all over the place. There was a muscle at the back of your neck and if it got cut your head flopped forward on your chest. You couldn't lift it. This was something the rebels did rather than simply kill people. It was like sending them forth wearing a sandwich board sign that said: THE REVOLUTIONARY ARMY OF THE LORD IS COMING!

The next morning Bangura sat beneath a big oil painting of himself. He was having a meeting with his top generals.

"Why is *he* here?" said General Garba. Glaring at Gray. Who was sitting off to the side wearing Oakley sunglasses with an M4A1 carbine across his lap.

"To protect me," said Bangura.

"From whom? From *us*?"

"Of course not. From the terrorists."

Garba's uniform was gaudy with medals and ribbons. He had bulging bloodshot eyes. He was sweating and clearly drunk.

"Our own men can do that. You think because he's *white* he can do a better job?"

"Of course not."

"How do you know he's not a *spy*?" Thumping his fat fist on the table. "For the RAL?"

"That's ridiculous. Now let's proceed."

After the meeting Bangura seemed exhilarated. "What did I tell you?" he said to Gray. "Things are looking up."

"Can I say it straight?"

"Please."

"They're blowing smoke up your ass."

Bangura's face became solemn. "Go ahead."

"The last thing these guys want to do is fight. They've got one foot out the door already. Garba for instance. He's not really a soldier. He's in the timber business. He's sending millions of dollars of hardwood to Europe. He'd cut down every tree in Kangari if he had the chance."

"How do you know this?"

"Everybody knows."

Bangura walked over to the tall windows. Stood there looking out.

"It's nice to be the president," he said. "Even of an inconsequential little country like Kangari. I'm not prepared to give that up."

Gray was everywhere with Bangura now. Striding beside him down long echoing hallways. Sitting near him as he took his afternoon nap. And grim as a guard at Buckingham Palace standing in front of the door to the bathroom as Bangura used its gold-plated fixtures.

He dined with Bangura and his wife that night. The three of them alone at a long candlelit table. Reflections of the candles' flames flickering above them in the chandeliers.

They were eating broiled fish. Bangura chuckled.

"What is it?" said Natalie.

"They say I'm a cannibal. But I don't even eat meat." He winked at Gray. "Bad for my cholesterol," and then he said: "In the midst of all this bleakness my wife and I have wonderful news."

"What?" said Gray.

"Natalie is with child."

"Congratulations," said Gray and they toasted the child and her.

After dinner they went out on the balcony with their glasses of wine. A sweet rotten smell blew in on a breeze. It was the rainy season. Lightning flashed in the distance and thunder grumbled.

"More rain," Bangura sighed. "Why couldn't I have been the president of a dry desert country?"

Then they heard faint booms. Which weren't thunder. Which were the war. Getting close.

Bangura sighed again. Went inside to get more wine.

Gray and Natalie looked at each other. Both shy. Trying to think of something to say.

"That's great," said Gray. "About the baby."

She touched her stomach. Thought about it.

"Is it?"

"Why wouldn't it be?"

"The world is filled with . . . such suffering. Is it right to bring a child into it?"

"Maybe your child will grow up to be a great man. And he'll help people who are suffering."

"Yes," she said, "maybe *she* will do that."

They both laughed. As Bangura came back out. Looking delighted.

"Ah laughter," he said. "A much better sound than explosions, yes?"

A few nights later he dreamed of her. He was walking across a field of wheat with her. In America. The wheat field was vast. You couldn't see the end of it. It rippled in the wind like waves in an ocean.

"I'm tired," said Natalie. "Will we ever get to the other side?"

He woke up. It was morning. One of the blue and yellow lizards that were ubiquitous in Kangari was doing quick push-ups in a splash of sunlight on his windowsill.

He got up and got dressed hastily. With the feeling that he had overslept. That something momentous might have happened and he had missed it.

He found Bangura in his office. With a couple of his worthless and worried-looking advisors. Whom he quickly dismissed.

"What's going on?" said Gray.

"Look out the window."

Gray saw columns of black smoke rising out of the eastern part of the city.

"The terrorists," Bangura said. "They've arrived."

The news for days had been dreadful. RAL rebels burning alive a hundred children in a school in a nearby town. General Garba flying to Morocco. In a Kangari Air Force transport plane packed to the gills with girlfriends and loot. And this morning Type 59 tanks had been spotted on the edge of the city and worst of all the airport had fallen into RAL hands.

There was a military airbase about eight miles away. A helicopter from there was expected within the hour. It would pick up Bangura and his people and fly them back to the base. And then they would board a plane and by the skin of their teeth escape the catastrophe of Kangari.

Gray suggested it might be time to give the Kangaran soldiers guarding him ammunition for their guns. Bangura agreed it indeed was time but said unfortunately they had deserted last night en masse.

Gray was silent. As it sunk in that now the only thing standing between Bangura and the Revolutionary Army of the Lord was Gray.

"If fate is unkind today?" Bangura said. "I mustn't be allowed to fall alive into the hands of the terrorists. And my wife as well. She must be taken care of. Do you understand?"

Gray nodded. Knowing he would be keeping a bullet in reserve for himself too.

Gray and Natalie and Bangura and three of his advisors and their family members gathered by the helipad on the spacious green grounds of the presidential palace. About fifteen people in all plus a pet parrot in a cage. And they stood by their luggage listening anxiously for the approaching throb of the helicopter but heard only the thuds and thumps of explosions and the rattle of gunfire. Then it began to grow very dark. Black clouds rolled in and the wind sprang up and a few big raindrops began to fall. And then the sounds of battle became muted under a roar of rain. The blue and yellow lizards ran for cover. Palm trees bent in the wind and the parrot squawked its displeasure. The people became afraid it would be too stormy for the helicopter to land and they would be trapped here by the helipad and butchered in the rain then there it was! Drifting in over the palace walls! The people laughed and cheered. It would be life today and not death, a future and not nothingness. Gray looked at Bangura's wife and she looked up at him and smiled. Her teeth so white in her dark face and the dark rain and then there was a boom and a flash of light.

A rocket-propelled grenade had hit the tail rotor of the helicopter. It veered and gyred out of control. It seemed to be coming straight for them. Everybody ran and then the helicopter crashed on top of the luggage and the screaming parrot and was transformed into a boiling orange ball of light.

Gray saw the rebel that had fired the RPG. Standing with two others near the base of a big fountain superfluously adding its water to the rain. They seemed transfixed by the sight of the burning chopper. Gray shot them. His M4A1 on full automatic. They were hit many times, two flopping onto the ground and one falling into the fountain. And then came gunfire from another direction. The top of the head of the minister of the environment was blown right off. His wife, a very fat woman, held her own head and began to shriek then bullets ripped into her too and she fell down beside him. Gray heard a shrill whistle as he shoved Bangura and his wife to the ground and then he saw them. The SBU. The small boys unit.

Both sides in the conflict used child soldiers. They were easy to train. A kid could be taught to kill with a Kalashnikov in thirty minutes. They were given alcohol and drugs and told to attack and were as brave as adults and perhaps even more cruel. Known for perpetrating fiendish tortures on prisoners and giggling as they did so. As if they were playing a particularly fun game. They died in droves but it didn't matter because there seemed to be an inexhaustible supply of children in Kangari.

There were seven in the SBU. Ranging in age from maybe nine to fourteen. Firing assault rifles as they charged across the grass. They were led by an adult. Wearing a red beret and a red bandana tied around his neck and blowing a silver whistle. Gray shot him first but the children kept coming and he shot two of them then ran out of ammo. The children kept running and stumbling through the rain and firing as he popped in a new mag and more of Bangura's people were hit and then he shot the other five children. They went down but two kept moving and he shot them until they were still—

"My god," said Gina.

He looked at her. Her face was pale and tight.

"Why'd you shoot them? The ones that were wounded?"

"They still had weapons. They were a potential threat."

"I don't know if I wanna hear any more."

"Okay."

Then "No," she said. "Go ahead."

Black smoke swirled up from the burning helicopter as the survivors scattered.

Gray knew their only hope was to drive to the airbase. They ran to a white Land Rover and Bangura and his wife got in the back and down on the floorboard and Gray took off. They didn't encounter any more rebels as they drove out through the wide-open wrought-iron gates of the presidential palace and onto the streets of the city.

Ordinarily he would have reckoned the odds of their making it out of the city alive at no better than a hundred to one but the storm was working in their favor. It was more pleasant to rape, plunder, and commit atrocities in bright sunny weather than in a violent thunderstorm. He expected that most of the rebels would be seeking shelter. Also the rain on the windows would make it harder for the casual looker to see inside. And their vehicle was not one that would attract undue attention. White Land Rovers were everywhere. They were the hot car in Kangari for those who could afford them. So with a little bit of luck by the time the storm had passed they would have slipped out of the city and be barreling down the highway that led to the airbase.

Despite the rain the streets were crowded with people fleeing the rebels. In cars, buses, donkey carts, on motorbikes and bicycles, and on foot. The going was slow. Gray drove with his pistol in his lap. Peering ahead through the thrashing wipers.

"What's going on?" said Bangura from the backseat. Starting to rise up. "What do you see?"

"Stay down!" Gray hissed. For suddenly he was seeing red-bereted rebels everywhere. Not at all daunted by the rain. Seeming to revel in the godforsaken motherfucking rain. Swaggering along, swigging out of bottles of Red Heart Rum. Pulling people out of their cars and robbing them. Lugging stuff out of stores and loading it into SUVs and trucks. He had driven into their midst like some slow cumbersome beetle blundering into an ant nest.

Two rebels came walking toward the Land Rover. Wearing incongruously friendly smiles. Like benign cops on the beat.

"Don't move," Gray whispered.

One of the men leaned down and still smiling peered in the rain-dripping window at Gray. Motioned to him to lower it. He hit the switch and as the window buzzed down lifted the pistol. The man having just enough time to look startled before he was shot in the face. As he dropped out of the way Gray shot the man standing behind him twice in the chest.

He saw ahead what looked like an alley running between two buildings. He twisted the wheel and surged forward and slammed into the car ahead of him. Backed up and swung around it and just as the Land Rover was riddled with automatic weapon fire, windows shattering and Bangura cursing and Natalie screaming, turned into the alley.

Which actually wasn't an alley at all. Only a space between the two buildings ending in a hog wallow and a mud wall. He drove down it as far as he could thinking *So this is it.* He had always wondered what it would look like. The place where he would die.

More bullets hit the SUV blowing out the back tires. He looked at the pigs. There were eight of them. Lean, black, and muddy.

"What should we do?" Bangura yelled.

"Get out!" said Gray. "Keep your head down!"

They all three jumped out and took cover behind the vehicle. Gray fired his carbine toward the street. The rebels did their usual spray-and-pray technique. Sticking their weapons around the corners of the buildings and firing off wild blind bursts. But one who looked about eighteen and must have seen too many American action movies ran out and stood there in the rain with his feet wide apart screaming at the top of his lungs as he fired. His face contorted. The spent shell casings tumbling out. Gray sent a tight pattern of bullets into his rib cage and ended the nonsense. He thought how it sucked he was going to be killed by such lousy rotten soldiers. Not soldiers. Cowards. Butchers.

Behind them the black pigs ran around in the mud and squealed.

He heard his name being called and looked down at Bangura.

"Now!" Bangura said. "Do it now!"

Gray looked at Natalie. Her face was lifted up toward him. Her eyes were blinking as the rain ran into them. She seemed to be crying but it was hard to tell.

He nodded. Unholstered his pistol.

She covered her face with her hands. Bangura scrunched his eyes shut.

He pointed the pistol at Natalie's head. His heart was beating so hard his whole body seemed to shake with it. He watched drops of rain falling off the barrel of his pistol. And then he heard a dull *splat* behind him.

He looked around. A grenade was there. Half buried in the mud. Thrown by someone on the other side of the mud wall or perhaps by an enterprising rebel who had climbed up on one of the buildings. He was going to pick it up and throw it over the wall but he hadn't moved toward it more than a fraction of an inch when it went off.

A speck of dust was floating down into a gigantic black canyon. And he was both the canyon and the dust. He had never felt such peace. And then a ringing noise filled the canyon. It got louder and louder. Till the speck of dust was gone and the canyon too and there was only the ringing—

He was lying on his back in the mud in the rain.

A rebel was standing over him but wasn't paying any attention to him. He pushed himself up on one elbow.

The rebels were celebrating. Laughing and climbing all over the Land Rover and firing their weapons in the air. They obviously recognized Bangura and his wife. Who had both been wounded by the grenade but were still alive. The rebels were carrying them away. Bangura's jaws were clenched but his eyes were big and wild. Natalie was screaming and weeping but she made no sound. Nobody or nothing made any sound. The grenade blast had deafened Gray and set his ears to ringing.

The rebel, noticing Gray was awake, clipped him in the temple with his rifle butt. Knocking him senseless again. The next thing he knew he was being dragged down the street. He didn't see Bangura and his wife. The rain had stopped. He had sustained shrapnel wounds from the grenade but nothing that seemed too serious. The mud having dispersed the force of the explosion and almost certainly saved him. Though the fact his injuries weren't mortal seemed a moot point now.

They took him into a church. Others were already there. Men, women, and children. Some already murdered and others being murdered and the rest to be murdered soon. He still couldn't hear anything. He shut down another of his senses and closed his eyes. Resolving to open them no more.

They stripped off his clothes and tied his wrists up and hauled him into the air so he was dangling. He was flogged with belts and whips awhile then his back was sliced open. Gunpowder packed into the slits and lit. It was a strange sensation to scream and not be able to hear yourself. He kept his eyes shut. He hoped he would lose consciousness again but that didn't happen.

Then the torture stopped. He hung there in the silence and darkness an indeterminable time. And then he smelled smoke.

He opened his eyes.

The church was on fire. The rebels had cleared out. Leaving

behind their victims. Most dead but a few still living. Tied up and helpless like Gray.

The flames licked up the walls and into the rafters. He saw a pigeon up there fluttering around in a panic. Trapped too. Behind the altar was a bronze statue of Jesus on the cross. Behind the statue an actual man had been crucified. A priest. Hands and feet nailed to the wall. His eyes closed, his head lolling around, and his lips moving in prayer.

Gray began to cough as smoke filled the church. He hoped the smoke killed him before the fire did.

And then three of the rebels came running back into the church. Bandanas pressed to the lower half of their faces against the smoke. They went straight to Gray and cut him down and carried him out. It turned out a debate had been taking place. Between the rebels who thought Gray should be killed and those who thought a white American mercenary might fetch a large ransom. The latter camp was vindicated when Major Hobbes flew in a couple of days later on a chartered jet with a satchelful of cash then immediately took off with Gray on board.

They flew to London where Gray spent a week in the hospital then they went to Miami where he was put in another hospital. His injuries healed well but at first brain damage was suspected. Because he didn't speak and didn't seem to understand or respond to others when they spoke. The major came to visit him every day but Gray never seemed to take any note of him. He would eat and drink and could walk when he was led around by the hand but there seemed to be no mental functioning going on. But the tests on his brain came back negative and in truth a part of him was aware of everything. Knew when a nurse was wearing a new perfume. Saw Major Hobbes when he broke down one day as he stood by his bed looking down at him. Tears coming out of the icy blue eyes. But the rest of him was elsewhere. It was as though he had fallen into a bubbling volcano of shame and guilt and horror. Where he had to confront, again, again and again, the fact he had killed children. And hadn't protected the principal. Or his wife. And where ceaselessly he would see the inside of the church. The priest on the wall. The silent slaughter of the innocents.

And then one day he threw the sheet off and got out of bed and left the hospital room. He walked through the corridors in his flimsy gown and he might as well have been invisible for all the attention that was paid to him then he found what he was looking for. The outside.

He walked out onto a patio. There were several hospital workers there smoking cigarettes but none of them looked at the scarred man in the hospital gown as he walked barefoot to a railing and looked out on the day.

It was paradisal. Palm trees and flowers and the scent of flowers and a warm breeze. And it was as though he came back into himself. And it was overwhelming that he had made the journey from the burning church where he had hung by his wrists to here. It was a million-to-one chance he was still alive. And that must mean something, mustn't it? That he was still alive?

He loved the major but knew he could never work for him again or for anyone in the major's business.

After he got out of the hospital and when he felt strong enough he went back to Africa. Not to Kangari. To a more peaceful country. Where he had been before.

He had been told about a mountain. It was a holy place to the people who lived near it. They thought God was on the mountain. And if you wrote down a prayer on a piece of paper and then went up on the mountain and put the piece of paper under a rock God would answer your prayer. And that is what Gray did. And on the piece of paper he put under the rock was written: *Tell me what I ought to do.*

His mouth was dry. He finished off the lemonade. He watched one white-footed mouse chase the other past the pool.

"So anyway. That was two years ago."

"Well?" said Gina.

"Well what?"

"Did He tell you? What you should do?"

"No. Still waiting."

Gina thought about it all.

"What happened to Bangura?" she said. "And Natalie?"

"They were taken to Malamba. The rebel leader. Who's now President Malamba. He had them killed. I don't think you want to know the details."

She sighed. "That poor girl."

Then she looked at him.

"So you were in the army. Not the navy."

He nodded.

"Then how come you told me you were a sailor?"

"You know what? I think I'm about talked out for today."

He got up from the lounge chair and stretched.

"Why don't we get outa here? Go for a drive or something."

The doorbell rang. It was the Chinese food delivery guy. He barely spoke English. DeWitt gave him a good tip because he liked him because he was always smiling and friendly. And now he smiled and bobbed his head and said thank you five times.

He moved the skull over and put the food out on the coffee table. Because she liked to eat in front of the TV. He went in the kitchen and got a plate and silverware and paper napkins that had cute pictures of cats and dogs playing baseball on them. Just the one plate because his ski mask didn't have a mouth hole so he would be eating later. He went back in the living room and put down the place setting and looked things over and remembered she needed something to drink and went back in the kitchen and got her a bottle of Corona. She liked Corona. Then he put his ski mask back on and went in the bedroom.

She was lying on the bed bound and gagged. Staring up at him reproachfully. She had promised to remain quiet and out of sight and not do anything stupid when the deliveryman came but *sory. i cant take no chancis* he had written her and she had cussed him out mercilessly as he put the flex-cuffs on her. And now the first word out of her mouth when he took the gag out was: "Butthole!"

But she quickly regained her good spirits as she sat in front of the TV eating her Chinese food. Sweet and sour shrimp. Beef with broccoli. Pineapple chicken. Fried wonton. Steamed rice.

"This is the best Chinese food I've ever had," she said.

He nodded.

"What's the name of the restaurant?"

He didn't answer.

"You won't tell me the name?"

He shook his head.

"Oh I get it. You think it might be a clue. About where we're located."

She watched his eyes crinkle up. Which meant he was smiling.

"You don't miss a trick do you?" Then she took a drink of her beer and said: "Did you like my wings?"

He had let her take a shower today. He had stayed in the bathroom with his back to her. Not trusting her alone with that little frosted-glass window. Not that she could get out of it but she might raise it up and start yelling or something. When she'd finished her shower she had asked for a towel and as he had handed it to her he had caught a glimpse of them. Her wings. Tattooed on her shoulder blades.

He nodded.

"Daddy hates 'em. He thinks tattoos are skanky."

Generally speaking he thought the same but he really had liked her wings. Why wings, he wondered. He thought about her turning the water off and sliding open the shower door. He had seen some of her nakedness because she had wanted him to see. She knew she was driving him crazy. Women always knew.

"What's this all about? Why are they doing this to Daddy?"

He wrote in the notebook then held it up in front of her.

i dont no. onist.

"You are honest aren't you? I can see it in your eyes."

She put down her fork and looked at him. Chewing on her Chinese food.

"You got the most amazing eyes. Did anyone ever tell you that?"

Sure. His mother. She was always saying that. *DeWitt's got the purtiest eyes.*

He knew he could have her any time he wanted but under the circumstances even if she seemed willing it would still be rape and he wasn't raised to be a raper.

"Wonder what my fortune cookie has to say."

The cellophane wrapper made a crepitant noise as she tore it off the cookie and a chilling thought suddenly came to him: What if his cell phone was to ring and it was Smith-Jones telling him everything had gone to hell and he had to get rid of Dee? Take her out in the woods and—?

"*Do it now!*" Dee read. "*Today will be yesterday tomorrow.* Huh. Now that's real true isn't it? Time sure passes fast. I mean in five years I'll be thirty. Thirty!"

She handed him the other fortune cookie.

"What does yours say?"

He removed the wrapper and cracked the cookie open and took out the fortune and read it.

"What's it say?" said Dee.

He handed it to her.

"*The time is right to make new friends.* That's a nice one! So now we gotta eat our cookies so our fortunes'll come true."

She popped hers into her mouth. He turned away from her. Slipped his mask up past his mouth and put in the cookie and pulled the mask down and turned back to her.

They looked at each other. Chewing. Crunching.

"What do you look like under that mask?"

He picked up the notebook and wrote in it.

ugly.

She gave a laugh. "Yeah, right."

They drove down Tejada Springs Road in Norman's big red Chrysler. The top down. The dog in the back with Luke, grinning into the wind.

They stopped at the Tejada Springs Café. The woman working there didn't mind them bringing the dog in. They sat at the counter and drank chocolate milkshakes. On the wall behind the counter was a marvelous mural showing sly sharp-faced foxes wearing fancy suits and playing tricks on people. Stealing an apple pie off a windowsill. Cheating at cards. Giving a fat sleeping man in a rocking chair a hotfoot. In one corner the muralist's name was signed: Ananda.

"Who's Ananda?" said Gina.

"She was this little hippie girl," said the woman. Whose graying hair was held in place by a glittering rhinestone band. "Came through here back in the sixties. Driving this beat-up yellow Volkswagen she called Gertrude. She told the owner she'd paint his wall up for him if he let her eat here for free."

"How long did it take her?" said Gray.

"Maybe five or six weeks. She camped out in the desert. Everybody said she was high on LSD all the time. And that at night she'd paint herself up like an Indian and dance around the fire naked."

"Cool," said Luke.

"So what happened to her?" said Gina.

"Well when she finished," said the woman, "she got in Gertrude and just drove away. Maybe that's what she *did*. Went around the country painting foxes."

"Maybe she's still doing that," said Gina. Wishing she could be doing that.

They got directions from the woman and drove out to the site of the old hotel that had burned down in the fifties. Where the movie stars used to play. It was at the end of a crumbling asphalt road not too far from the Lucky Horseshoe Trailer Park. All that was left of the main building were the concrete foundation and the remnants of a stone fireplace. Rising up like some rough Paleolithic altar. The swimming pool where the golden bodies of the demigods of filmdom once had swum had been filled in. Had become the habitat of snakes and lizards.

They saw the long ears of a jackrabbit. It was standing up and taking a good hard look at them. Then the dog went woofing after it and it took off. Swerving this way and that. Moving twice as fast as the dog on its long hind legs.

Gray cupped his hands around his mouth and yelled: "Give it up, boy! You'll never catch it!"

The dog broke off the chase. Trotted back toward them with his tongue hanging out.

Back of where the hotel used to be were the ruins of ten or twelve adobe bungalows. Doorless and windowless. Holes in the roofs or no roofs at all. Gray, Luke, and the dog headed into one to explore it. But Gina paused at the gaping doorway. It looked very snaky and ratty in there. The floor covered with bottles and cans and fast-food wrappers. So she took a pass.

She was left alone. At the base of the mountains. At the edge of the desert. Feeling specklike in the immensity. She couldn't get over how quiet it was. What sounds there were—wind stir, bird chirps—seemed to be just another aspect of the quietness. She gazed east. It was late in the day and the desert was being eaten up by the giant shadows of the mountains. Either this was a dream or the world they'd left of cities and people and clamor and cars was a dream. Because the worlds were too different for them both to be real.

Behind her she heard someone cough.

She whirled around.

A man was standing there. Blubbery, bearded, about fifty-five or sixty. His skin burnt orange-brown by the sun. He was wearing nothing but lime-green shorts, flip-flops, and a straw hat. And a holster with a revolver in it.

"You know who used to stay here?" he said.

She shook her head.

"The Wizard of Oz!"

"Really?" she said, deciding the man was insane and then she called out: "Gray? Luke?"

The dog came out first and began to bark at the man. And then came Gray and Luke.

"Hush, boy!" said Gray. As he looked at the gun.

"I was just telling your wife that Frank Morgan used to stay here. You know the actor that played the Wizard of Oz? In this very bungalow!"

"Is that so," said Gray.

"My name's Swanson," said the man. "Swannie people call me. I live over at the trailer park." Swannie pulled at his beard. "So you folks must be the ones staying out at the old country club."

"That's right," said Gray.

"Just visiting? Or moving here?"

"Visiting," said Gray.

"Oh. Too bad. This town could use some new blood. I've lived here my whole life. When I was a kid some of the Old People were still around."

"Who were the Old People?" said Luke.

"The Indians. That's what they called themselves. And they called us the New People. I guess we're the Old People now. But we're gonna end up like the Indians if we don't get us some new blood."

"What's the gun for?" said Gray.

"Protection."

"From what?"

"Whatever. Don't let it make you nervous. I'm the most harmless guy in the world," and then he said to Luke: "Have you seen it, son? The white horse?"

Luke shook his head.

"Me neither. But I hope to one of these days. Or nights. You only see it at night."

"What's so special about it?" said Luke.

"Well you know it's not a regular horse 'cause you can see clean through it. It's a spirit horse. The Old People told me about it. They said if it likes you it'll let you climb on its back. And it'll take you wherever you wanna go. It'll take you to the other side of the universe. If that's where you wanna go." And then he laughed. "Well I better be getting back. It's getting near suppertime. And if I'm late the old lady'll bounce a rolling pin off my head. Enjoy your stay in Tejada Springs!"

They watched Swannie turn and walk off. Lumbering past tall spindly ocotillos. Gina put her hand on Luke's shoulder. Thinking her first impression of the man had been right: He was insane.

He stood on the terrace. Drinking a scotch despite his churning stomach. Staring at the statuary but not seeing it.

It was cold. Too cold for Smitty who'd abandoned him ten minutes ago. A wetness was in the air but it wasn't quite rain. More of a swirly mist that wrapped itself around you like a clammy gauze.

Somebody once had told him *todt* meant "death" in Dutch. Death Hill. He was living atop Death Hill.

He had never felt so isolated. So bone lonely.

He'd been up to see Millie. Her and her crooked vacant smile. Things were so complicated and seemed to be maybe falling apart and he longed so to talk things over with her. She would cut through the bullshit. Help him see the obvious. Do what he had to inevitably do. Sometimes he had the fantasy that when he passed through her door she would be as she had been forty years ago and so would he. A magic door. Like in some old black-and-white wistful bittersweet *Twilight Zone* episode.

The door opened behind him and he heard Eliana: "Mr. Pat? *Telefono* for you! It is your son!"

"Bring me the phone."

"No, Mr. Pat. You come inside. It is raining. You gonna get sick!"

He turned around and glared at her.

"Bring me the fucking phone!"

"*No!*" she said. All but stamping her foot in defiance.

He walked toward her. Shaking his head and grumbling: "Christ, Eliana. You're forgetting that I'm your boss."

She stepped out of the doorway and into the mist and pressed herself against him.

"No, Mr. Pat. *This* is my boss." And she rubbed her hand against the front of his pants.

He made a sound that was half growl half laugh then he kissed her and went in the kitchen.

"Where's the fucking phone?"

"On the table, Mr. Pat."

He sat down at the oak table. Put his glass of scotch down and picked the phone up.

"Joey. How you doing?"

"What the fuck's going on, Pop? How come you hadn't called?"

"I was going to. You beat me to it. I still haven't bought the new car."

"Jesus Christ! You're saying that bitch is still alive?! And where's my *son?!*"

Cicala was appalled. Because all calls into and out of prison were recorded or listened in on.

"Joey—I don't know what you mean—"

"Relax, Pop. I'm on a cell phone."

"Where'd you get a cell phone?"

"I bought it. From a guard. You know how much I'm paying that prick?"

"You still gotta be careful, Joey. Don't talk so fucking loud. Somebody might be listening."

"Come on, Pop. Just tell me what's going on!"

And so Cicala sipping scotch under the bug in the chandelier told his son everything.

"Mom's crying," said Luke. The dog standing behind him. As if he too had come to bear the news.

"Why?" said Gray.

"I don't know. She wouldn't tell me."

"Where is she?"

"She ran outside."

Gray was lying on his bed. Where he had been reading *Wanderer*. Now he got up and followed Luke and the dog out.

The last faint flush of light was leaving the sky and stars were taking over. She was standing by the swimming pool. Bare-armed and hugging herself like she was cold and perhaps she was because there was a chill in the air. She glanced around at him and he saw she indeed was crying. She made a quick swipe with the back of her hand at her runny nose.

"What's wrong?" he said.

"I went on Norman's computer—"

"Yeah?"

"I wanted to see what was happening back in Oklahoma. Gray, there's been more murders! On Sunday night."

"What happened?"

"A cop was killed in our apartment. Stabbed. And another cop was killed in front of the building. He was shot. And another guy was shot. Just down the street. He was out walking his dog."

"Do they know who did it?"

"No. But we do!"

The blond guy and the dark guy, he guessed. The cop had surprised them in Gina's apartment. The second cop had been his backup. The guy with the dog. Wrong place wrong time.

But it was strange. Why were those guys looking for Gina in Oklahoma when terHorst had already followed her to California? It was like they hadn't been working together then. But now they were.

"The one that was killed in our apartment?" said Gina. "I knew him. His name was Duane. He used to come in the restaurant. Where I was a waitress. He hadn't been a cop long. He was really just a kid. He was sweet. Kinda shy. He kept calling me ma'am till I made him stop. He was married. His wife had just had a baby. He loved apple pie à la mode. And now he's dead. Because of me."

"It's not your fault. It's the killers' fault. But—maybe it's time."

"Time for what?"

"To call the police. The FBI. Whoever."

"I told you. I can't trust them."

"Most of them are good guys, Gina. They're not like Frank."

"All it takes is one. One that's not a good guy."

She gazed down into the pool. Which was filled up to the brink with darkness.

"Luke told me you took it out. The snake. Thanks."

He nodded. She was still hugging herself. He put his hand on her shoulder.

"Come on, you're shivering. Let's go in."

They turned. They saw Luke and the dog. Standing at the glass wall of the club room watching them.

"Don't tell Luke," she said. "About what happened in Oklahoma."

"I won't," said Gray.

A commercial came on the TV. For Jack LaLanne's Power Juicer, Jack LaLanne looking ancient and decrepit in a blue jumpsuit.

"Good lord," said terHorst. "Is Jack LaLanne still alive?"

They were in his motel room. Eating Macho Nachos and curly fries and drinking tall creamy-yellow cans of Coors. Outside the smoky wind was blowing but not as hard as it had been. The Santa Anas were beginning to die away.

"Wonder what your buddies are up to tonight," said Lingo. "Jack and Jill."

"I got no idea," said terHorst. "They don't confide in me."

"I don't know what we're taking orders from *them* for. They don't know their hole from a butt in the ground."

"Let's whack 'em," said Ronnie.

"Ronnie, I keep telling you," terHorst said. "We can't whack 'em. They'd kill my daughter if we did that."

"Your fat daughter," said Ronnie. Stuffing a wad of curly fries in his greasy glistening mouth. His snaggly tooth sticking up. TerHorst could hardly stand to look at him.

"You know," said terHorst, "if it wasn't for you we'd probably be on our way home now. And my daughter would be free."

"What are you talking about?"

"You had an easy shot yesterday in the parking lot. And you missed."

"It wasn't so easy. The car was moving."

"Hell Ronnie, you never could shoot. You couldn't hit a cow's butt with a banjo."

TerHorst and Lingo both laughed. Ronnie's face turned red. He stood up and hurled his container of curly fries against a wall.

"Fuck you!"

"Ronnie," said Lingo sternly. "You better learn how to take a fucking joke. Now pick up them curly fries."

Reluctantly Ronnie went over and picked up the scattered fries.

"This is serious bi'ness, son. When you get up in the morning you better put your big-girl panties on. We got us some killing to do."

Ronnie nodded. Threw the curly fries in a trash basket.

"I'm sorry, Daddy."

"That's okay."

"I'm going to bed."

"All right."

Ronnie left. Went down a few doors to his room. Sat on the side of his bed smoking a Camel. Thinking about Steve. Out there all alone in the dark in the desert under the twisted tree. He hoped the coyotes didn't dig him up.

When he finished the Camel he got up and went over to his bag and took his Pocket Pussy out. Went back to the bed and pleasured himself with it. Thinking as he did so about what he was going to do to Gina when they caught her.

———

She shed the grungy clothes she'd been wearing the last two days and took a long hot shower. Then she toweled off and walked out naked into the bedroom. She opened the door of the closet. There were women's clothes in there. Norman's wife's she supposed. She browsed through them then pulled out a pale-yellow dress.

She slipped it on. Stood in front of the dresser mirror. Turned this way and that. It fit more or less. She was not a dress sort of a girl but she liked it. It seemed fresh and pretty.

She felt the nibbling of her sweet tooth. They had had some tasty strawberry ice cream for dessert tonight.

She headed down the hallway for the kitchen. The tiles cool on her bare feet.

He did not want to do this.

He wanted to go walking around trees in peaceful parks and go running on the beach with his dog. He did not want to kill anymore and he certainly did not want to be killed. He had been lucky two years ago to get out of Kangari alive but now it seemed like the whole world had become Kangari. Yesterday in Santa Monica adrenaline had kicked in and carried him through. But what about tomorrow? And the day after? Gina and Luke were counting on him to keep them safe. But Bangura and his wife had done that and look how they had ended up.

"Gray?"

He opened his eyes and looked up.

Gina was standing above him. In the semidark. In the yellow dress. Holding a bowl of ice cream.

"Are you all right?" she said.

He nodded. He was shirtless. In his blue jeans. He was sitting in an armchair facing the fireplace in the club room. His legs were pulled up and his arms were wrapped around them. The dog was sitting beside him.

"Were you sleepwalking again?" she said.

"No."

She put the bowl of ice cream down on the coffee table.

"Get up," she said. Reaching down and taking his hand.

They began to walk slowly out of the room. She was still holding his hand. She glanced at his face. Saw something there she hadn't seen before. Not even on that night she had found him out on the parking lot of the Sea Breeze Motel. It was a sort of desolation. A wintry absence of warmth and light.

"Don't worry," she said. "It's gonna be okay."

The dog watched them walking away. He seemed torn between following and staying where he was. With the ice cream. He opted for the ice cream.

They went in Gray's room.

"Just lie down," she said. "Get some sleep."

He lay down on the bed and looked up at her.

"I'll be right down the hall if you need me."

"I like that dress," he said then reached up and pulled her and her dress down on top of him. They looked at each other, their faces inches apart, then kissed. His hands went in her hair then went sliding over her dress. He could tell she was naked underneath.

"I love you," she said.

He left the motel and went for a walk. It was about eleven thirty and there was barely any traffic. It could have been that little town in Oklahoma for all the nightlife there was.

Palm fronds made a dry rustling above him in a surge of warm wind. No stars were visible. He could smell the smoke.

The more he thought about it the realer it became. Himself and Luke on the jewel-like little island. Nearly as off the beaten track as Pitcairn Island. Where the mutineers from the *Bounty* went to hide.

It would definitely be in the boy's best interest. Mother dead. Father in prison. All but an orphan. And they would walk on white beaches and swim in the turquoise sea.

He hoped he wouldn't have to kill Dima. Although he was a brute he had become quite fond of him. But in the end he would do whatever was necessary to save Luke.

He thought it was a dog at first. Trotting rapidly down the middle of Washington Boulevard. But then he saw it was a coyote. It had been caught in one of the fires. Its brown and white fur was mottled with burnt patches. It gave him a brief look as it moved by. Its eyes were crazed and frightened.

He stopped and turned and watched it. As it headed ever deeper into the gigantic city. Poor creature, he thought. Where did it think it was going?

She lay in Gray's arms. Not thinking about anything. Aware only of his heartbeat. The rise and fall of his chest as he breathed.

"You asleep?" he whispered.

"No."

He kissed her hair and she nestled in against him. As if she could get any closer. It would be nice to stay like this from now on. For her and him like insects in amber to be kept endlessly in this moment.

But then it started up. The barking, yelping, howling, and yipping. As it had done last night.

"God," she said. "I hate that."

"What?"

"The coyotes."

"Why?"

"'Cause that's a fucking horrible noise."

"Not if you're a coyote."

Luke went to the window. Hoping to see the coyotes. But all he saw was the flat still desert. The black humps of mountains. The sky and all its stars.

He thought of his friends back in Massapequa Park. Dylan and

Jeff and Frank and Aaron. He had always envied them their settled lives yet he wished they could see him now. Out in the middle of the desert. With a wild pack of coyotes howling outside his window. He had done and seen things they knew about only from TV and the movies. Someday he would go back there and tell them all about it.

He went back to his bed. Where the gun was.

This afternoon while his mother and Gray had been talking and talking out on the patio he had explored the house. He had found the gun in Norman's office in a drawer in his desk. A snub-nosed .32 revolver. Along with a box of ammunition. Although the gun was already loaded.

He sat down cross-legged on the bed. Picked the gun up and pushed out the cylinder and shook the cartridges out on the bedspread. Then he proceeded to reload them. He found this fun.

He had fired a gun before. His dad had taken him out to a wooded area once and they had shot at some cans. And his dad had banged away at some birds but hadn't hit any. So he knew there was nothing to it. Just point the gun and pull the trigger.

Now he would be able to help Gray. If and when the need arose.

And that night they dreamed.

Gina dreamed she was back in high school. And she was late for class and couldn't find her locker and she walked through long hallways lined with lockers that had no numbers on them. Markus Groh had a happy dream where he was sitting in the sunshine in a boisterous beer garden watching a troupe of acrobats performing amazing feats. While Bulgakov had a grim dream where he was a soldier again and on patrol in the destroyed city of Grozny. Norman's dead wife came to him in his dreams as she did on most nights. Latreece dreamed of her grandparents' farm in Jamaica. She had grown up there and been so happy there and was so happy in her dream. Mac Lingo dreamed he was driving a tractor across a dead dusty rutty field and then a huge dark flock of crows passed overhead blocking out the sun and Ronnie dreamed he was eating a big white cake. Eliana dreamed she was a singer in a sinister nightclub built next to a fetid river that ran through a jungle. The customers stared at her and listened closely but never applauded. DeWitt dreamed of Dee and Dee of DeWitt. Bobby the Hump dreamed Cicala was yelling at him and then to his own great surprise and chagrin Bobby broke down and began to weep. The dog, growling in his sleep, dreamed of a big pit bull named King. And he fought King and King was biting his ear. Gray in his dream was back on the Santa Monica Pier riding the Ferris wheel. Except it wasn't Gina and Luke with him but the Buddhist monk in the wraparound shades. And the monk didn't speak but just gazed at Gray with an amused smile. Joey Cicala dreamed he was getting drunk in a strip joint and getting a blow job from one of the dancers. Duane Butterfield's wife dreamed that she was wandering around a nightmarish theme park in Branson, Missouri, with her baby in her arms. Looking for Duane but not finding him. TerHorst dreamed that strange lights appeared in the night sky and they were alien spaceships and they started shooting death rays and he ran and ran, gasping for air, heart pounding as people burst into flames all around him. Jamie dreamed the ducks were living in the cell with him. Sitting all in a row on the bottom bunk. Quex, still in the hospital in LA, dreamed he was being held prisoner in an underground circular chamber and being tortured by hollow-eyed lunatics. Pat the Cat had one of his banal exasperating looking-for-a-clean-men's-room-so-he-could-take-a-leak dreams. While down the hall Millie dreamed she was lying in bed and began to shrink till she became so small she slipped through the molecules that made up her mattress which were glowing beautiful as stars all around her. Mr. Li, nodding off in his chair on his boat a little before dawn, dreamed he was on a jet plane and looking down at the ocean. And Luke dreamed of the white horse. It walked up to him and pawed the ground and snorted. It wanted him to climb on its back. And Luke did so and they rode away.

Friday

TerHorst smiled at Quetzalli. Who was pushing along her housekeeping cart past the blue and pink units.

"How you doing this morning?"

She smiled back. Showing her missing teeth. He walked across the parking lot in his gold ostrich cowboy boots. He was feeling a lot better today. Ready to kick some butt. He entered the office.

No one was there.

"Hello?" he called. "Yoo-hoo! Lucy, I'm home!"

Pete appeared. From a back room. Bringing with him a whiff of weed. "Morning," he said.

"Morning."

"Need a room?"

"Nope."

TerHorst badged him. Pete looked impressed.

"Wow. A marshal."

"Yup."

"I never met a marshal before."

"Well I'm pleased to be your first. I wonder if you can give me a little help." He put Gina and Luke's photos down on the counter. "You know them?"

"Sure. They been staying here."

"But they're gone now."

"Yeah. They left I guess it was yesterday."

"Know where they went?"

"No. In fact I didn't even know they were gone. They never officially checked out. The maid went in to clean the room and it was empty."

"So I guess she must've filled out some kind of registration form."

He nodded. "Wanna see it?"

"What's your name?"

"Pete."

"Pete, I'd love to see it."

Pete began looking through a stack of forms. "She seemed awful nice. Her and her son."

TerHorst made a noncommittal noise in his throat.

"She in some kinda trouble?"

"She's wanted for questioning. In connection with some murders. In Oklahoma."

"Murders. Shit. Here it is."

TerHorst looked the form over. Saw nothing of use. Phony name: Gina Blumenthal. Phony address in Oklahoma City. No phone number. Make and model and license plate number of the car that was shot to shit on Wednesday.

"Did she use a credit card?"

Pete shook his head. "Cash."

TerHorst put down the sepia wanted dead or alive photos on the counter. Tapped Gray. "Know him?"

"Yeah."

TerHorst perked up. "You do?"

"Yeah. He stayed here too. In room eighteen. He was here about a week I guess. But then I had to ask him to leave."

"Why?"

"He got a dog. No dogs allowed."

"What kinda dog?"

"I don't know. This big ugly brown dog. Looked like it'd been tore up in a fight."

"When did you ask him to leave?"

"I think it was on Monday."

"Any idea where he went?"

"No."

"Have you seen him since?"

"No."

"What kind of a fella was he?"

Pete shrugged. "He was just a nice regular kinda guy." He'd been looking through his stack of forms and now put one in front of ter-Horst. "There you go."

Printed with extreme neatness were a name and a street address in a town called Hubbard, Iowa. No phone number. No car info.

"Did he have a car?"

"No. Seemed to be on foot all the time."

"Credit card?"

"Cash."

TerHorst looked at the name again. "Eugene Gray," he said softly. Then he beamed at Pete. "Well thank you kindly."

They were walking round and round a prickly pear cactus. In the gliding way Gray had walked around the tree in the park in King Beach.

"When you're walking like this you build the energy up."

"The qi?" said Luke.

"Right. The qi. It's all about developing qi then using it efficiently." Now he stopped and lifted his arms up. Luke doing the same. "You can pull the energy down from the sky." Now he and Luke lowered their hands toward the ground. "And you can pull it up from the earth. There's an infinite amount of energy available to you. To *you*. To *Luke*."

"Could I do what you did? To that guy in the park?"

"Eventually, yeah. But remember what I told you. Fighting's just one form of qigong."

"I know. But it's the one I wanna learn."

"You need to learn it for the right reasons. To defend yourself. Not to be a bully."

"I know."

Gray gave him a long look. Then nodded. "Okay. To begin with it's not a matter of brute force or muscular strength. It wouldn't be fair if somebody big always beat up somebody small. Right?"

"Right."

"Now listen. This is the most important thing. You have to train your mind to *never leave your center*. No matter what's happening."

"Where's your center?"

He touched Luke's abdomen. Just below his belly button.

"There. When you find your center you're able to adapt to change in a balanced way. The best fighters are those that can change the fastest."

Gina watched them from a distance. Arms folded. Smiling a little. Her two guys.

She looked around for the dog. He was never too far away from either Gray or Luke. Then she saw him. Soaking up the morning sun and working on his Nylabone. He was hers too, she guessed. She now had a son, a guy, and a gigantic dog. How could life get any stranger?

She walked back to the house. Aware a vast chasm had opened up between today and yesterday. She felt qualitatively different. Lighter. And filled with light. All because of what had happened last night. The only nagging negative was when she had told him she loved him he hadn't reciprocated. For whatever reason. But maybe that would come today.

She wandered into his bedroom. She stood by his bed. No sign it had been the scene of some tumultuous doings a few hours before. He had made it up perfectly. Not a wrinkle anywhere.

As she turned to go out his billfold caught her eye.

It was lying on the dresser. Next to his sunglasses and the keys to the car and house.

She looked at it. Tempted.

She walked over to it. Picked it up.

It was made out of worn and creased black leather. It wasn't too thick. Didn't seem to be much in it.

She opened it. Pulled out his driver's license. Examined a photo of a slightly younger him. The license was issued by Washington state. It showed an address in Seattle. And his name.

Richard Charles Garber.

There were a couple of credit cards and a health insurance card. All for Richard Garber.

She put the billfold back down on the dresser. Trying to position it exactly as she had found it.

She looked at herself in the dresser mirror.

Another lie. Not Gray. But Richard Garber.

She turned and left the room.

"Where is fucking Iowa?" said Bulgakov.

"Middle part of the country," said terHorst. "Right next to Nebraska."

"They grow a lot of corn there," said Groh. "Yes?"

"Sure do," said terHorst. "Lotta fucking corn."

They were standing on the sidewalk near Gordon's Market. Ter-Horst was eating a Blue Bunny Caramel Chocolate Nut ice cream cone. Pleased with himself.

"They could be there right now," he said. "At 229 East Chestnut Street. For all we know."

"I doubt it," said Groh. "But we'll check it out. Perhaps it will lead to something."

"Well at least we know his name now. Eugene Gray."

Groh shrugged. "Men like him—they've been known not to use their real names."

"You mean your name might not really be Jack?"

Groh was quiet a moment. Thinking. "I wonder if she knew him beforehand. And that's why she went to the motel. Because he was waiting for her there. Or if they just met at the motel accidentally."

"You know what?" said terHorst. "When we see Gina we'll ask her to clear up that very point."

An American Airlines jet rose up out of the hills. Bulgakov lit a cigarette. Using a Paradise Motel matchbook.

"Maybe we go there," he said. "To fucking Ohio."

"Iowa," said Groh. "We mustn't go chasing off after phantoms. We should focus our attention here."

"I'm with Jack," said terHorst. "In fact I feel like this might just be our lucky day."

"That would be ironic," said Groh.

"Why?"

"It's Friday."

"So?"

"The thirteenth."

"Shit."

Nothing like that first beer of the day. To get the cobwebs out.

Stitch was sitting at the bar in the Prince o' Whales. It hadn't been open long. The only people around were himself and the bartender and a big guy sitting at a table by the wall.

He looked at the guy. The guy stared back. His mouth hanging open a little. A gnarly tooth visible. A dull sullen look in his eyes.

Stitch held the stare for several seconds. But the guy didn't turn away or even blink.

He took another drink of his beer. Looked at the TV. *SportsCenter* was on. Then he looked back at the guy.

Who was still staring at him.

He started to get mad.

"Dude, what's your fucking problem?"

The guy didn't answer. Stitch got off his stool and began to walk toward him. His combat boots clomping over the wooden floor.

"What are you looking at, asshole?"

Mac Lingo came out of the restroom. Saw Stitch standing over Ronnie.

"Dude, I'm talking to *you*!"

"What's going on?" said Lingo.

Stitch took in the brooding vulturine visage of Lingo. Losing confidence.

"He keeps looking at me. And he won't say nothing."

Lingo laughed. "Aw he ain't looking at you. He's sleeping!"

Stitch looked back at Ronnie. Who now seemed to be gazing at Stitch's stomach.

"Sleeping?"

"He sleeps with his eyes open. Ever since he was a tyke." He leaned down and shook Ronnie's shoulder. "Wake up, Ronnie! Wake up!"

Ronnie moved his big head around. He seemed confused.

"Whatsamatter, Daddy? What's going on?"

"Ain't nothing the matter. You was sleeping and this feller thought you was eyeballing him. That's all."

Ronnie looked at Stitch. "Yeah?"

"It was just a mistake," said Stitch. Eager to get away.

"Crazy white boy," said Lingo. Reading his tattoo. "That mean you hate niggers?"

"Maybe."

"We do too. Don't we, Ronnie?"

Ronnie yawned. "Yeah. Fucking niggers."

"Sit down," said Lingo. "We'll buy you a beer."

"Well—"

"Hey buddy!" Lingo yelled at the bartender. "'Nuther round over here!"

Stitch reluctantly scraped a chair back and sat down. Lingo sat down too.

Sighing and shaking his head.

"That was a sad day."

"What was?" said Stitch.

"The day they had the inniggeration of Barack Hussein Obama."

Stitch smiled. "Inniggeration. That's pretty good."

"Tell him about Gator, Daddy."

"Had me a old dog. Named Gator. And I taught him a trick. I'd say, 'Gator, would you rather be a nigger or a dead dog?' And old Gator he'd just roll over on his back and play dead."

They all laughed. The bartender brought their beers over.

"It ain't just the niggers," ventured Stitch. "It's the Jews. And the Mexicans."

"And the fucking ragheads," said Ronnie.

"We oughta nuke the whole fucking Middle East," said Stitch. Starting to warm up to the Lingos. "Let 'em all die for Allah."

"Amen to that," said Lingo. Who then reached into his shirt pocket. "Do me a favor, pardner. Take a look and see if you recognize either of them two."

He put one of the wanted photos of Gray and Gina down on the table in front of Stitch. Who said: "Shit."

The Lingos exchanged a look.

"You know 'em?" said Lingo.

"This motherfucker put my buddy in the fucking hospital!"

"Is that a fact."

"How come you're looking for him?"

"Let's put it thisaway. There ain't no love lost between us and him. You know where he's at?"

"No. But I seen him just a couple days ago."

"Now where might that've been?"

"At the coffee shop. Across the street. He was with *her*."

"But you don't know where either of 'em's at now huh?"

"No. But there was this other guy with 'em. This old dude. Maybe he knows."

"What's his name?"

"I don't know what his name is. But I see him around all the fucking time. He hangs out a lot at the Harbor Room. And the Sea Horse. And he drives around in this big old red Chrysler convertible."

"What's he look like?"

Stitch shrugged. "He's just this old fucker. Wears a baseball cap. And it's like there's something wrong with his neck. He moves like this." And Stitch gave a good imitation of Norman moving his whole torso as he looked this way and that.

He was taking a walk through the marina. Past white boats and blue water and a somnolent brown pelican. He took his cell out and called a number. An answering machine picked up and then he heard his own voice: "You've reached Stormin' Norman. How the hell did you get this number? You better have a damn good explanation."

"Hey it's Norman. Anybody there? Hello?"

"Norman." It was Gray.

"How's it going?"

"Fine. How are you?"

"Lonely. I miss you guys."

"We miss you too."

"Everything okay? Anything new?"

"Nothing's changed. We're just hanging out here. Laying low."

"Making friends with the coyotes?"

"Oh yeah. I'm the pack leader now. So what are you up to?"

"It's just another dynamic day in the life of Norman Hopkins. Thought I'd go over to the Sea Horse and grab some lunch. Have a drink or three. Flirt with whatever buxom fresh-faced waitress young enough to be my granddaughter happens to be on duty. Come back home and pass out. Then wake up in time for the six o'clock news!"

"Sounds like a plan."

"Have you and Gina gotten married yet?"

"Not yet."

"Good. 'Cause I wanna be best man. Give my best to her and Luke."

"I will. Hey I forgot to tell you. I got a bunch of rubber bands for you."

"Yeah?"

"You were right. They're all over the place. Once you start looking for them. I'll give them to you next time I see you."

"I can't wait. And congratulations. You're striking a real blow against entropy."

"Thanks."

"Take care."

"You too."

Gray was in the club room. Now, accompanied by the dog, he went in the kitchen.

Luke was sitting in a chair, towels draped around his neck and over his shoulders as Gina gave him a haircut. Quite a bit of hair was already on the floor.

"Looks good," said Gray.

"She's cutting off too much," said Luke. "Like always," and then he said: "Hey stop that!" To the dog.

"What's he doing?" said Gina.

"Eating my hair."

"Ugh."

"He'll eat anything."

Gray watched Gina skillfully wielding comb and scissors. "You're good at that."

"Thanks. My sister's a hairdresser. At one point I was thinking about being one too. We were gonna open a shop together."

"Why didn't you?"

"Oh I don't know."

"'Cause Dad wouldn't let you. Right, Mom?"

"Right. Your dad wouldn't let me. Okay," she said. Whipping off the towels. "You're done."

"Am I really done? Or do you just wanna get rid of me 'cause I mentioned Dad?"

"Both."

"My neck itches."

"Tough."

"Can I take the dog for a walk?" he asked Gray.

"Sure."

"Don't go far," said Gina.

"We're just going out on the golf course. He likes to chase rabbits out there. Come on, boy."

Luke and the dog walked toward the door.

"Farewell, Luke Dogwalker," said Gray solemnly.

Luke laughed. "Farewell."

Gina grabbed a broom and a dustpan and began to sweep up the hair.

"Need any help?" said Gray.

"No thanks."

They felt a little shy with each other. Despite or because of all that had happened last night.

"Norman called," said Gray. "He said to tell you hi."

"How's he doing?"

"Okay." And then he said: "Gina?"

Something in his voice caused her to stop sweeping and look at him.

"Yeah?"

"Did you go through my billfold?"

"Oh. How'd you know?"

"It looked like it'd been moved."

"Jeez. It's hard to get anything past you." She returned to her sweeping. "I suppose I oughta apologize."

"I'm not expecting an apology."

"It's just—you have so many secrets. I don't know what's real with you and what's not." She dumped the hair out of the dustpan and into the trash. And then turned to face him. "I mean who the fuck are you? Some guy named Gray? Or some guy named Richard Garber? And why do you keep saying you're a sailor?"

He grew up in Ansley, Kansas. Southwest of Dodge City. His father was Terry Garber. Terry had two brothers. Clay and Kenneth. The three brothers owned a farm-equipment rental company. And they and their families lived on small adjoining farms a few miles outside town.

Everybody in Ansley knew the Garber brothers. They were violent alcoholics. They loved to fight. Considering it a sport. They had no friends except for one another. To run afoul of one Garber brother was to incur the wrath of all. They would drive drunk, hunt out of season, cheat their customers and refuse to pay their bills, shoot their neighbors' pets and trespass on their property, beat up their wives and girlfriends in public and the local cops, not willing to tangle with them, would look the other way. The hideout of the Dalton gang had been only about fifteen miles from Ansley and now with the Garbers it was like the town had a gang of modern-day desperados in their midst.

Richard had a brother two years older named Mason. And two sisters, Sharon and Marsha. Their mother was a thin tense woman who chain-smoked Winstons and was obsessed with keeping her husband happy. The children were never touched except in anger. Never spoken to except to be rebuked or ordered to do something. The brunt of the brutality fell on the two boys. Their father beat them for being too loud and for leaving their toys lying around and for crying because he was beating them and most often and terrifyingly they couldn't figure out why they were being beaten. Sometimes punishment took other forms. Food would be withheld. For a couple of days. Or they would have to stand outside for hours in bad weather or the summer sun. Or once Richard knocked over his glass of Kool-Aid at supper and Terry jumped up and grabbed his shotgun and went out in the backyard where Richard's little dog Zipper was tied to a tree and shot him repeatedly, literally blowing him to pieces, and made Richard gather up what was left of him and bury him.

Terry was brutal and stupid and he did his best to teach his boys to be brutal and stupid. When Mason was in the fourth grade he was bested in a playground fight. His father heard about it and whipped him and promised to keep whipping him till he got even. The next day Mason came up behind the boy holding a brick and knocked him cold. The boys' parents, when they found out who the culprit was, begged the school authorities not to take any action lest their whole family become the target of the Garber brothers and the following day Mason (though not his victim) was back at school as though nothing had happened.

In 1983 when Richard was eight he was awakened one night by screaming. He ran in the living room to find his mother on the floor on her back with Terry astraddle her and strangling her. Mason and their sisters watched as Richard flung himself on his father's back and wrapped his arms around his neck. Terry, who was six two and 220 pounds, stood up with the little boy still hanging on and stumbled around drunkenly till he threw him off. Then he grabbed Richard by the wrist and ankle and swung him through the air and flung him through a window. Richard crashing through the glass and metal mesh of the screen and landing on the front porch. Covered with blood and unconscious he was taken to the hospital with a cooked-up story that everyone was too frightened not to pretend to believe. They treated him for a concussion and a dislocated shoulder and closed up his cuts with over a hundred stitches.

Two weeks later Richard and Mason went to the county fair. They were dropped off by their father who then went with Clay and Kenneth to their favorite bar. Richard and his brother walked around in the sawdust looked at the penned-up prizewinning cows and bulls and gigantic hogs and chickens in cages then went to the more exciting carnival part of the fair. They rode the Tilt-a-Whirl and Octopus and Bombshell. They threw darts at balloons and baseballs at wooden milk bottles. They ate hot dogs and drank soda pop. Then Mason ran into a couple of his friends from school. Richard tagged along with them awhile but they ignored him and he finally wandered off on his own.

It was a warm humid late-spring night. He didn't mind being alone. He bought a candied apple. He liked the colored lights and the corny music and the happy screams of the citizens of Ansley as they rode the scary rides. He was fascinated by the carnies. They seemed dirty and sinister. He wished he was one of them. He thought it would be cool to travel from town to town to town. As long as they never came back to this town.

He stopped in front of a tent. Looked at a lurid poster showing a gorgeous girl with eight limbs. Ariadne. The Amazing Spider Girl.

"Forget it, kid. It's a rip-off."

He looked around. A young man was standing there. A duffel bag over his shoulder.

"I already been in there. It's just a regular girl. With four plastic legs. And she's not even pretty. In fact she's a dog. I wouldn't waste my money if I was you."

He was short and stocky. Reddish-brown hair in a crew cut. A pug nose and some pale freckles. A loudly patterned short-sleeve shirt and khaki pants. "I'm Gray," he said. Sticking out his hand.

Richard hesitated then took it. He'd rarely been called upon to shake hands with anybody.

"What's your name?"

"Richard," he said. His voice barely audible.

"Richard. Now that's a good name. I got a stupid first name. Eugene. I hate it. So I just use my last name. Gray."

Richard was silent.

"You here by yourself?"

He shook his head.

"Who you here with?"

"My brother."

"Where is he?"

Richard looked around. Shrugged.

"So Richard. What the hell happened to you?"

His left arm was in a sling. Because of the dislocated shoulder. And there were all the cuts on his arms and head. Healing but still ugly.

"I had—an accident."

"What kinda accident?"

"Car."

"You poor kid. Was anybody else hurt?"

He shook his head.

"That apple looks good. Where'd you get it?"

He looked around. But the place he got it wasn't in sight.

"Why don't you just show me? 'Cause I definitely want me one."

"Okay."

They began to walk.

"So what's it like living in—what's the name of this place?"

"Ansley."

"What's it like living in Ansley?"

He shrugged.

"I only been here a couple hours. I'm from Iowa. Little town called Hubbard. Ever heard of it?"

He shook his head.

"I'm gonna tell you exactly where it's at. It's not far from Banger. Which is pretty close to Eldora. Which is down the road a piece from Grundy Center. You know where it's at now?"

Richard smiled a little. "No."

They reached the stand that sold the candied apples.

"Want another apple?" said Gray. "Or how about some cotton candy?"

"No thanks."

Gray bought an apple then they started walking again.

"See that brother of yours anywhere?"

"No."

"What's his name?"

"Mason."

"Betcha a dollar to a dog turd Mason's up to no good. What do you think?"

Richard laughed. And then he shyly said: "How come you're here?"

"In Ansley? I'm just passing through. I'm hitchhiking. I been home and now I'm on my way back to San Diego. To the naval base. I'm a sailor."

Richard looked at him. "A sailor?"

"Yeah."

"How come you're not wearing a uniform?"

"It's in here," he said. Indicating his duffel bag. "I'm enjoying being a civilian again. But don't get me wrong. I love the navy. Ever since I was a little kid I've wanted to be a sailor. I don't really know why. I never even saw the ocean till I was seventeen. When I enlisted."

"You live on a ship?"

"Yeah. The *Thomaston*. It's a landing ship. It carries landing craft. So like when we're invading an island or something we come up pretty close to the beach and then we launch our landing craft. The landing craft are filled up with soldiers and equipment and stuff and they land on the beach. It's called an amphibious operation."

Richard nodded. Eating his apple. He'd never had a conversation like this before. With a grown-up. It was fun. Exciting.

"I got a great job," said Gray. "In the engine room. I think it's the most important job there is. 'Cause it's like us guys down there, we're in the heart of the ship. It's like the ship would die if we didn't keep it going."

Richard saw Mason and his friends walk by. He was glad Mason didn't see him.

"Have you got any brothers and sisters?" he asked Gray.

"Nope. Not that I know of. See, I was raised by my grandparents. I don't even know where my parents are now."

"Are your grandparents nice?"

"Oh yeah, they're great. What about your parents? They cool?"

Richard nodded.

"What's your favorite ride?" said Gray.

"Mm . . . the Tilt-a-Whirl."

"Wanna ride it?"

"I already rode it."

"How about the Ferris wheel?" Which they happened to be standing right in front of.

"Okay."

At the ticket booth Richard dug in his pocket for some money.

"Naw," said Gray, "it's on me."

He left his duffel bag with a carny with a handlebar moustache then they climbed in one of the seats. Richard got a giddy feeling in his stomach as they were borne aloft. Rising above the trees that surrounded the fairground. They could see the lights of the town and beyond that a lot of dark nothingness.

Richard felt exhilarated as the wheel made its revolutions. It was a lot more fun riding rides with Gray than Mason.

Gray taught him a song. About the navy. *Bell-bottom trousers seaman second-class, you can take the Navy and shove it up your bell-bottom trousers seaman second-class . . .* It was neat because it didn't have an ending. You could sing it forever.

There was a flash of lightning off in the distance. Revealing the presence of tall black clouds. And then came thunder.

"Looks like a storm," said Gray.

"You think the lightning'll hit us?"

"Nah. It's still too far away." And then he said: "So how'd it happen? The car wreck?"

Richard shrugged.

"Who was driving?"

"My dad."

"Was there another car involved? Or just your dad's car?"

"Just my dad's car."

"But your dad wasn't hurt."

Richard shook his head. The ride ended. Gray got his duffel bag from the carny and they moved off through the milling crowd.

There was a gust of cool wind. As the storm closed in.

They came to a tent. A poster said: MADAME LISA FORTUNE-TELLER. And it showed a beautiful young Gypsy woman peering into a crystal ball.

"How about it?" said Gray. "Wanna give Madame Lisa a chance to cheat us out of our hard-earned dough?"

"Okay."

They pushed through a portiere of rattling black beads.

Three candles illumed the inside of the tent. Madame Lisa was sitting at a small table. She was quite pretty. Greatly resembling her poster, unlike the homely spider girl.

"Hello," she said.

"Hey," Gray said. "How much to get my fortune told?"

"Ten dollars."

"Hm. Any wiggle room in there? I'm kind of on a budget."

"Okay. Seven fifty."

"You got a deal."

He put down his duffel bag and sat down in a chair across the table from her.

"You seem kinda young for this," he said. Handing over the money.

"I'm old enough."

"Been at it awhile?"

"Since I was twelve."

"So where's your crystal ball?"

"I don't use a crystal ball. I use cards."

Now she put a deck of cards in front of Gray.

"Shuffle. Then cut into three stacks."

"Yes ma'am."

As Gray shuffled the cards Madame Lisa looked at Richard. Clearly curious about him. She had big eyes and dark irises and her pupils were big and black. And she glittered in the candlelight with rings and bracelets and bangles and spangles.

"Do you want to sit down, little one? I'll find you a chair."

"No thanks."

Gray cut the cards then Madame Lisa gathered up the stacks.

"I will tell you whatever I see in the cards. Good I will tell you. Bad I will tell you. Okay?"

"That's what I'm here for. The truth and nothing but the truth."

She began to slowly turn the cards face up on the table. Laying them down in a particular pattern. They weren't like any cards Richard had ever seen. They had colorful fantastical pictures on them. A ferryman carrying passengers across a dark river. A woman bound and blindfolded and surrounded by eight swords. A dog and a wolf baying at the moon. A naked child mounted on a white horse.

She turned up ten cards in all. She was quiet for a moment. Studying them. Thunder boomed. Much closer than before. And one side of the tent rumpled as it was hit by the wind.

"You don't live here," she said. "You are traveling."

Gray glanced at the duffel bag and then at Richard. Smiling a little.

"You see that in the cards?"

"Yes."

"What else you see?"

"Your soul is strong. People are drawn to you. You are a leader. You will go far in life."

"Think I'll be elected president?"

"Maybe you won't go that far. But your life will be very happy. And you will live to be very old. Over ninety. Do you have any questions?"

"Yeah. What about chicks?"

"Chicks?"

"Girls. You know."

"I see many girls. Many romances. One girl in particular."

"Blond or brunette? Or redhead?"

"Very dark hair. Almost black."

It thundered so loud it was like an artillery shell had landed next to the tent. There was a rattle of rain on the canvas roof. The storm, the strange cards, the flickering candles, Madame Lisa's bottomless dark eyes—all were beginning to make Richard more and more anxious.

"You're gonna be rich someday," said Madame Lisa.

Gray laughed. "Me? Rich? Come on."

"I see a treasure. A glittering treasure."

"I gotta go," said Richard.

The fortune-teller and the sailor looked at him.

"My brother. He's probably looking for me."

Then he turned and ran out. Bursting through the strings of black beads. Into the wind and rain.

"Hey Richard! Wait up, man!"

Gray was running after him. His duffel bag under his arm. "You okay?" he said as he caught up with him.

Richard nodded.

"Why'd you freak out like that?"

"I don't know."

"Listen. I'm worried about you."

"Why?"

"I don't think you got hurt in a car wreck."

Richard stared up at him. As they both were soaked by the rain. As the carnies took cover and the crowds around them broke up and hurried for their cars.

"Your father did it. Right?"

Richard was amazed. How did he know?

"How'd you get cut up like that?"

"He threw me through a window."

"Christ."

Gray bent down. Getting on eye level with Richard. Putting a hand on his shoulder.

"Look. My old man. Before he split? He was like that. So I know what you're going through."

Richard didn't know what to say. He wanted to run away again.

"Is there anybody that can help you? What about your mother?"

"What the *fuck* is going on?"

Richard looked around. It was his father. And his uncles. And Mason. Walking toward them through the rain.

"Get your hands offa him!"

Gray straightened up. His hand dropping off Richard's shoulder.

"You all right?" said Terry to his son.

"He's fine," said Gray.

"Shut up!" said Kenneth. "He wasn't talking to you."

"I'm okay," said Richard.

"What's he been doing with you?"

"Nothing."

"Did he put his hand down your britches?"

Richard shook his head. *"No."*

"You're sick, man," said Gray to Terry.

"Gray, no," said Richard. His voice trembling. *"Please. Don't make him mad."*

The Garber brothers moved in a little closer around Gray. Swaying a little. Eyes aglint with drunkenness and malice.

"Gray huh?" said Terry. His face inches away from Gray's.

"That's my name."

"I ain't seen you around before."

"That's 'cause I never been here before."

Clay snatched Gray's duffel bag away from him. "What's in here?"

"Hey come on, man," said Gray reaching for his bag but Clay knocked his hand away. He unzipped the bag and started pulling clothes out and throwing them on the muddy ground. He came to Gray's white uniform.

"Well lookie here!"

He put on Gray's white cap.

"I think we got us a sailor boy!"

"Is that what you are?" said Terry. "A sailor boy?"

"I'm in the navy. Yeah."

"I was in the army," said Clay. "And sailor's just another word for queer."

"What you doing in Ansley?" said Terry.

"Just passing through. If it's any of your business."

"Oh it's my bi'ness, smartass. That's for damn sure. Where you headed?"

"San Diego."

"How'd you get here? In a car?"

"I hitchhiked."

Kenneth grinned. "You know how hitchhikers get rides? They give blow jobs!"

"Yeah?" said Gray. "How would you know?"

Kenneth punched Gray in the stomach. He gasped and fell to his knees.

The Garber brothers loomed over Gray. Gazed down upon him. He looked up at them. Waiting for the beating. But then Richard came in and grabbed his father's hand and pulled at it.

"Dad, come on! Let's go home!" Terry looked at him. "He didn't do anything! I promise. We just rode the Ferris wheel."

Terry looked back at Gray.

"Get the fuck outa Ansley. You hear me?"

Gray nodded. Terry and his brothers turned and started to walk away.

Gray came to his feet. Began stuffing his muddy clothes back in his bag.

Mason had been hanging back. Fearfully watching. Now as Terry walked by him he grabbed his arm and gave it a jerk. "Come on, boy. I'll deal with you later."

"What are you gonna do?" said Gray. "Throw *him* through a window too?"

Terry stopped. Gave Richard a searing look. Then turned around and headed back toward Gray.

Gray watched Terry coming. Probably regretting he had opened his mouth. But then he threw down his duffel bag and said: "Okay, asshole! Let's go! Come on!"

He took a clumsy swing at Terry. His fist glancing off his cheek then Terry hit him in the face, knocking him on his back and sending him skidding a foot or two in the mud.

"Let's take him in the woods," Terry said to his brothers.

Terry and Kenneth grabbed Gray and hauled him to his feet. Woozy from the punch he stumbled along as they walked him out of the carnival. Clay following with the duffel bag and Richard and Mason bringing up the rear.

The storm in its full force was now on top of the fairground. Lightning and thunder flashed and crashed nearly continuously. They walked by the Ferris wheel where so shortly before Richard had had such a rapturous ride. By the stark light of the lightning he could see its empty seats rocking a little in the wind.

They went through a field. Cars had been parked there and now they were all leaving. Rain sparkled in their headlights. A red pickup was stuck in the mud, its tires spinning and groaning.

"Where we going?" said Gray. "Where you taking me?"

"Shut up!" said Clay. Hitting him from behind hard in a kidney. Gray let out a yell. They dragged him into a stand of trees. Richard and Mason could see what was happening only in the lightning flashes. Clay and Kenneth held Gray up as Terry hit him. In the face and chest and stomach and groin. Then he was on the ground. The three brothers surrounding him and kicking him. He curled up and tried to cover his head with his arms. Richard screamed at his father and his uncles *Stop! Stop! Don't! Don't!* and then ran over to them. He tried to pull and push them away from Gray with his one good arm but then either Clay or Kenneth, he couldn't tell who, was dragging him back. There was a lull in the lightning and he couldn't see anything in the windy roaring blackness under the trees and then came such a brilliance it was like a giant light had been switched on. He saw Gray lying facedown with Terry on his back. In a shallow puddle of rain. Gray's arms and legs were thrashing about. As Terry, both hands on Gray's head, was forcing his face into the puddle.

"So Dad drowned him," he said. "In about two inches of water."

Gina looked stunned. "I can't believe it."

She was sitting at the kitchen table. He was leaning against a counter.

"We had a big Buick. They put him in the trunk and we carried him back to our farm. Buried him and his stuff about a half-mile from our house. By a fence. Near a tree. Nobody ever talked about him. Nobody ever came looking for him."

"But don't you think somebody must've seen what happened?"

"Maybe. But people in that town were used to seeing the Garber brothers beating up people. And nobody asked any questions."

"And you never told anybody."

"Not till now."

"Are they still alive? Your father and your uncles?"

He shook his head. "None of them made it out of their fifties. I think they basically all drank and smoked themselves to death. Dad died of lung cancer. Kenneth died of cirrhosis of the liver. Clay had a stroke. Mother's dead too. She had cancer. And Mason was killed in a car wreck. When I was in the army. Ran his car into a tree. It was the only tree on that whole stretch of road."

"You think he did it on purpose?"

"Who knows? Maybe even Mason didn't really know what he was doing. Anyway. I just tried never to think about that night. But after I got out of the hospital a couple years ago I started thinking about it a lot. I went to Hubbard, Iowa. I was hoping his grandparents were still alive. But it turned out they died a long time ago. I couldn't find anybody that was related to him or even remembered him. And it started to seem so sad to me. So terrible. He was just this guy. He's got his whole life ahead of him. He just happens to come to this little town. And he tries to help this little boy he's never even met before and he gets himself killed over it. And now it was like he'd never existed. And so I—I just decided I'd live my life as him. It's been my way of thanking him. For what he tried to do for me."

He went in his pocket. Pulled out an oval metal tag.

"I found this on the ground. Close to where they buried him. It's one of his dog tags."

He walked over to the table and handed it to Gina.

"I know Dad burned his billfold so there wouldn't be any ID. But he missed this."

Gina looked at it. It said: GRAY EUGENE W. Followed by his Social Security number and his blood type. O.

She stood up from the table and went into his arms. Wanting to comfort him but not sure if he needed comforting. She couldn't tell how he felt. He'd told her the story in such a matter-of-fact unemotional way. The same as when he had told her about Kangari.

"So what should I call you now?" she said. "Gray? Or Richard?"

He thought about it a moment.

"Gray, I guess. I've gotten used to Gray."

His waitress's name was Lorrie. She came back with his credit card and check.

"Yes or no," he said.

"Yes or no what?"

"Have I been terribly wronged by *People* magazine?"

"Hm. In what way?"

"Because they've never put me on the cover as the Sexiest Man Alive."

"Yes, Norman. You've definitely been wronged."

"Ah Lorrie," he sighed. "If I were only eight years and three months younger."

She laughed and left. He wrote her out a hefty tip. Ah Lorrie.

When he came out of the Sea Horse he was met with a nice sea breeze. Thank god that ridiculous weather seemed to be over. Though the fires would continue to burn awhile. But at least the smoke was getting blown off the coast and he could breathe again.

He walked toward his BMW which was parked down the street a bit. He was feeling pleasantly virtuous. His doctor had told him to cut down on the drinking and lose twenty pounds and he had had grilled salmon and rice and just two glasses of white wine.

He became aware two men were walking along with him. One on each side. He hadn't heard them come up. They were just there. He turned his head and shoulders one way and saw a man wearing a baseball cap that had a bandage peeking out from under it. And then turned the other way and saw a handsome blond man. Who was smiling.

"Don't make a scene," said Groh, "or we will kill you. Right here. On the street. Do you understand?"

Norman nodded.

"Where are you going?"

"To my car. The Beamer."

They were there. They stopped.

"Get your keys," said Groh. "Unlock the door. We will all get in. Okay?"

"Okay."

Norman hit the unlock button and his car beeped and flashed. He went to the driver's door and opened it.

"Put your hands on the steering wheel and keep them there," said Groh.

Norman got in. Shut the door and put his hands on the steering wheel as Groh slid in beside him and Bulgakov got in the back. Now he noticed Groh was holding a pistol.

"What's this about? Are you robbing me?"

Groh didn't answer. He quickly patted Norman down. Taking his billfold and his cell phone. Then he reached and searched under his seat and then opened the glove compartment. He pulled out a .44 revolver.

"Why do you have this?"

"For self-defense."

"What business are you in?"

"I'm retired."

"From what?"

"Real estate."

Groh handed the revolver back to Bulgakov. "All right. Let's go."

Norman started up the motor. "Where are we going?"

"Just drive."

Norman checked his rearview then pulled out onto Alejo.

"We're looking for three people," said Groh. "A young woman named Gina, a boy named Luke, and a young man named Eugene Gray."

Norman pretended to think about it. He shook his head. "Names don't ring a bell."

"Turn right."

Norman turned. Onto a side street.

"Pull over."

Norman did so. Groh showed him the photos of Gina, Gray, and Luke.

"Where are they?"

"Can I put my glasses on?"

"Yes."

Norman took his glasses out of his shirt pocket. Put them on and peered at the pictures. He shook his head again. "Don't know 'em."

"You were seen with them on Wednesday morning. At Tanner's Coffee Shop."

"Wasn't me. Somebody made a mistake."

Groh suddenly grabbed Norman's testicles and squeezed hard. Norman screamed.

"Stop! Please! Stop it!"

Groh let go. Leaving Norman red-faced and panting.

"This time the truth."

"Okay. I know them. Not well. I just met them. I saw them Wednesday morning. I haven't seen them since. I have no idea where they are."

"He is fucking liar," said Bulgakov.

"My associate," said Groh. "In the backseat. He's skeptical."

"Give him to me," said Bulgakov. "I will get fucking truth."

"Drive," said Groh.

Norman pulled back out. They were on the street that went by the park. He saw a young girl wearing pink sneakers gliding by on her bike. Two little white kids on the playground seesaw. With their brown-skinned nanny looking on. Ducks on the lagoon. Girl, kids, nanny, and ducks—part of a world Norman had left about three minutes ago. The safe sane regular world. Whereas he had entered a free-floating realm where extraordinary things were possible: Torture. The betrayal of friends. Death.

Groh had pulled Norman's driver's license out of his billfold and was studying it.

"You have a red Chrysler convertible, Norman. Why aren't you driving it today?"

"It's in the shop. The radiator's cracked."

"What shop?"

"It's in Venice. On Lincoln."

"Let's go there."

"Why?"

"I want to see it."

"All right."

They reached the end of the lagoon. Where the elegant white bird was stalking the shallows. Where the street made a loop and turned into Vista del Mar. They drove by the bungalow where he and his wife had lived forty years ago. Or had it been yesterday? Time was a trickster. Now four minutes ago seemed like forty years ago. It was amazing how clearly he had begun to think. He saw he still had a slight chance of surviving this and knew just what he needed to do.

"The car's not in the shop," he said. "I gave it to them."

Groh glanced back at Bulgakov.

"Good. We're making progress. Now where are they?"

"I don't know. They called me Wednesday afternoon and said they needed a car. They were at Clover Park. So I drove over there and gave them the car and they took off. They didn't tell me where they were going. I don't think *they* knew. And I haven't heard from them since."

"You just *gave* them your car. People you barely knew."

"That's right. I liked them a lot. I knew they were in trouble and I wanted to help them."

"They left you in the park?"

"Yes."

"How did you get home?"

"I called a taxi."

Groh was looking again at the driver's license.

"You live at 4316 Admiralty Way? In Marina del Rey?"

"Yes."

"How do I know they're not there?"

"Who?"

"Our mutual friends."

"They're not there. They're long gone. They wouldn't still be hanging around LA."

"And we should take your word for this?"

"Absolutely."

Groh smiled a little. They had come to a stoplight. They were back at Alejo Avenue. Sitting directly in front of the Harbor Room.

Groh took his cell out and called a number.

"Look out the window," he said into the phone.

At the window of the tiny bar appeared the bald head and the moustache of terHorst. Groh waved.

"Get your friends, Frank. Follow us."

They had lunch at the café with the sly foxes on the wall.

Gray chewed on a grilled-cheese sandwich and gazed out the window. At the gulls again. Making slow dreamy circles on the other side of the highway.

"Wonder what the deal is," he said. Half to himself.

"What are you talking about?" said Gina.

"Those gulls. What are they doing in the desert?"

"Those are herring gulls."

They all looked at the man at the next table. A lanky Brit with a beakish face and longish graying hair.

"Sorry. Didn't mean to eavesdrop."

"That's okay," said Gray.

"They fly here from the Salton Sea. To dumpster-dive and so forth."

"The Salton Sea. I've heard of that. So it's near here?"

"About twenty miles to the east."

"A sea in the desert?" said Luke. Likewise eating a grilled-cheese sandwich. "Cool."

"It's just a colossal accident really," said the Brit. "It's over two hundred feet below sea level. Almost as low as Death Valley. About a hundred years ago some poorly constructed levees broke on the Colorado River and the flood waters poured into the basin. And so there it sits. A giant pathetic puddle we call a sea."

"Are there fish in it?" said Luke.

"Oh yes. But fewer with each passing year. It's becoming saltier and saltier. And more and more polluted with wastewater from irrigation and sewage and toxic chemicals from Mexico. The saddest thing is the birds. The migratory fowl. We've destroyed most of their ancient stopping-off places so now they flock there by the millions because they have nowhere else to go. They swim in the poisoned water and eat the poisoned fish. With predictable consequences."

"Can we go see it?" said Luke.

"I don't know if I want to," said Gina.

"Is it worth a trip?" Gray said to the Brit.

"Oh very much so. If you like strange putrid perishing places."

North on Lincoln. West on Fiji Way.

"What's he like?" Groh said. "Eugene Gray."

"Didn't know his name was Eugene," said Norman. "But he's smart. Easygoing. Good sense of humor."

He had adopted a policy of telling the truth as much as possible. Which hopefully would add a sheen of believability to his lies.

"But who is he?" said Groh. "What does he do?"

"He says he was in the navy. He just got out recently."

"Was he a SEAL?"

"No. Just a regular sailor, I think."

North on Admiralty. Groh looked back. Making sure the Lingos and terHorst in the silver Suburban were still behind them.

"How long has he known Gina?" said Groh.

"They just met. Last week."

"How?"

"Gina's car had a flat tire. Gray fixed it for her."

"Did you hear that?" said Groh. Swiveling around to look at Bulgakov. "It was all an accident. A flat tire! Isn't fate a funny thing!"

Bulgakov shrugged and said: "Da yebat mne soodeboo." Fuck fate.

Norman saw approaching from the other side of Mindanao a sheriff's department cruiser. What if he floored it? Rammed the cruiser? Maybe he could open the door and dive out at the last moment. Maybe the blond guy would be knocked out and—

"Norman?" said Groh. Tapping his knee with the barrel of his gun.

"Yeah?"

"Whatever you're thinking? Don't."

"I wasn't thinking anything. Except that you guys are wasting your time. They're not at my place and they're not gonna be there."

"You seem very eager for us not to go there. Which makes me all the more eager to see it."

"Okay. But you guys are gonna be disappointed."

"We'll deal with it, Norman. Don't worry."

Friday the thirteenth. Unbefuckinglievable. He had broken his leg playing football in high school on Friday the thirteenth. Of course it was Friday the thirteenth for them too. Gina and Luke and this Gray asshole. Bad luck for them would be good luck for him.

The Lingos' usual BO was especially powerful today. To the point of making him nauseous. He lowered the window and let some air in. Mac in the front seat looked back at him.

"How you feeling, Frank?"

"Hanging in there."

"Well we'll be getting this wrapped up soon. And we can all go home."

"'Cept Steve," said Ronnie. Who was driving. And drinking a can of Shark. "He can't go home."

"We'll be taking him home," said Lingo soothingly. "And we'll put him in the ground again. In a proper way. With a preacher. Don't you worry none."

No matter how old he got death had always seemed distant. Even when he cracked up his motorcycle on the PCH he didn't really think he was about to die. But now Norman wondered if he was in the final minutes of his life.

He slowed down and hit the blinker.

"This is it," he said.

He waited for the traffic to clear then turned into the entrance. Went down a short drive into the parking lot. He pulled into a space then turned off the motor.

Now the Suburban eased into the space beside them. Norman looked over and saw the unsettling sight of the faces of the Lingos and terHorst.

"What sort of security do you have?" said Groh.

"A guard in the lobby."

"Armed?"

"Yeah."

"Security cameras?"

"Yeah."

The back door opened and terHorst came in.

"What's the plan?" he said.

"Bill and I are going with Norman up to his apartment. You and your friends stay here. Keep an eye out for the red Chrysler. If it shows up call me. Don't do anything on your own."

"Okay. But I'm going with you."

"That's really not necessary—"

"Shoot, Jack, I don't mind a bit. I'm glad to do it."

"All right," Groh said. "Let's go."

They all got out. TerHorst went over to talk to the Lingos. Bulgakov spat three times over his left shoulder. Groh looked at Norman.

"What's the guard's name?"

"Luther."

"Do you like Luther? Do you want him to live?"

"Yes."

"Then don't do or say anything to make him think something's wrong. I'll be watching his face closely. If I see a hint of surprise, a quizzical look—I'll have to kill him. Do you understand?"

"Yes."

The four men walked across the parking lot. TerHorst craning his neck back to take a look at the high-rise.

"Where's yours?" he said to Norman.

"Twenty-eighth floor. The one on the top."

"That's the place to be."

Luther was sitting behind his desk at his computer updating his Facebook page. He looked up as they entered.

"Hey there, Luther," said Norman.

"Hey Mr. Hopkins. How's it going?"

"Great."

They walked toward the elevator. As Luther looked them over. Then he returned to his computer.

Norman pushed the up button.

"How'd I do?" he said.

Groh nodded. The elevator opened and they all stepped in.

Norman pushed twenty-eight. TerHorst was looking at his cap.

"Chargers huh? That your team?"

"Yeah."

The doors closed and they began to rise.

"I always liked the Chargers," said terHorst. " 'Member Hadl to Alworth? Lance Alworth?"

"Sure. Bambi."

TerHorst smiled. "Bambi, yeah. I'd forgot they used to call him that."

Norman had wanted to go back to his condo because of the guns. One in each room. Except the living room which had two. He knew he was an amateur and they were pros so his chances against them were slim but he didn't think they were nonexistent. He had spent two years in the army and he went out to a firing range every week or two and was a pretty good shot. Anyway he had nothing to lose. He knew they would kill him when they decided they had no more use for him. And he did not want to be tortured. For obvious reasons and because he knew eventually he would tell them about Tejada Springs. So this was the best solution. Kill them or make them kill him.

The elevator made a rapid ascent. No stop-offs at other floors. As if fate wanted to bring things to a quick conclusion. The elevator opened and they walked out into the hallway then stopped in front of Norman's door. He watched as all three men took their weapons out.

Groh grabbed him by the scruff of his polo shirt, put his gun to the back of his head and said: "Unlock it."

Norman unlocked it.

"Now open it. Slowly."

"This is all unnecessary. You'll see."

"Shut up."

Norman opened the door and he and Groh went through it. Groh using him as a shield. Bulgakov followed and then came terHorst.

Groh let go of him and said to terHorst: "Watch him." Then he and Bulgakov, guns held out in front of them, moved through the condo. Clearing it room by room.

"Now that's a view," said terHorst. Looking out through the tall wide windows filled with ocean and sky.

"Thanks."

TerHorst walked over to an antique escritoire. A jade sculpture of a beautiful woman with a beatific face was sitting on it. He picked it up.

"This supposed to be somebody in particular?"

"Kwan Yin. Chinese goddess of mercy and healing."

"How much it cost you?"

"Around twenty."

"Twenty bucks? What a deal."

"Twenty thousand."

TerHorst laughed. "I know. I was just joking."

He set the sculpture back down. Practically right on top of Norman's .357 Colt Trooper. In a drawer in the escritoire. His other living room gun, the .38 Police Special, was at the far end of the room. Secreted under the thick seat cushion of an armchair. He saw getting to one of his guns wasn't going to be easy.

Groh and Bulgakov came back.

"Now don't you guys feel silly?" Norman said then Groh slapped him across the face.

"Where are they?"

"I don't know."

He slapped him again.

"Where are they, Norman? Tell us."

"You can slap me all you want to. I can't tell you something I don't know. They just got in my car and took off. Who knows where the hell they are now?"

"You've been in touch with them. They've called you. You've called them. What's their cell phone number?"

"They haven't called me. I don't know what their number is."

Bulgakov bent down and took his knife out of his boot. He pressed its blade against the loose wrinkled skin at Norman's throat.

"You tell us fucking truth," he said and then he pressed harder.

"Okay," said Norman. "Maybe I do know something."

TerHorst smiled. "Now we're getting somewhere."

"But if I tell you—how do I know you won't kill me?"

"We have no reason to kill you," said Groh. "Not if you tell us the truth."

"That's right, Norman," said terHorst. "We like you. The last thing we wanna do is hurt you."

"Would you please take the knife away?"

Groh gave a nod to Bulgakov. Who lowered the knife.

"I'm not feeling well," said Norman. "I need to sit down."

"You need to begin to talk," said Groh.

"I'm diabetic. My blood sugar's going crazy. I need my insulin shot."

"Quit stalling," said terHorst.

"I'm not stalling."

He closed his eyes and put his hand to the side of his face and rubbed it.

"Where is your insulin?" said Groh.

"In the kitchen. In the refrigerator."

"The refrigerator?"

"I have to keep it cold."

"He talks first," said Bulgakov. "Then gets fucking insulin."

Norman was swaying a little. As if he might be about to keel over.

"If I go into a diabetic coma it won't be doing anybody any good. It'll take twenty seconds, for god's sake. Come on."

"All right," said Groh.

They walked toward the kitchen.

"Did you know Jesus Christ is coming back to earth again?" said terHorst.

"No," said Norman. "That's bullshit."

"You'll think bullshit. When you wake up screaming your head off in hell."

They entered the kitchen. Norman's shakiness as he pulled out a chair and sat down heavily at the farm table was real. For he was overwhelmed with the momentousness of what he was about to do.

There was a pistol under the table. A Walther P5 semi-auto. It was in a holster he had affixed to the underside of the table. It bore a chambered round. Which meant all he had to do was slide it out of its holster and point and fire. If he could do so quickly and accurately three times he had a chance to live.

"Would somebody get it for me please?"

Groh nodded to Bulgakov.

Norman leaned forward. His forearms on the table. He was waiting for the moment when the least amount of attention was being paid to him. Groh was standing across the table from him. Bulgakov was moving toward the stainless-steel Liebherr refrigerator. Ter-Horst had wandered over to a counter and was opening a cupboard.

"Where are they, Norman?" said Groh.

"Last I heard they were in Nevada." It was difficult to get the words out. It was like they were dry bits of wood that he had to expel from his mouth one by one.

"Where in Nevada?"

Bulgakov opened the refrigerator and peered in.

"Elko," said Norman. As the realization rose in him like a mighty sun that as lonely and broken as in many ways he felt, he did not want to die. He wanted to live and live and live and live.

"Why Elko?" said terHorst. He had taken a tumbler from the cupboard and had moved to the sink.

"Gray has friends there."

"I don't see fucking insulin," said Bulgakov. Bent over the fridge. Poking around in it.

"Look in the door," said Norman. "In the butter compartment."

Norman lifted his hand off the table and coughed into it and then his hand dropped to his lap. As terHorst at the sink filled his glass with water. As Bulgakov lifted the door of the butter compartment. As Groh's eyes moved to Bulgakov.

"I don't fucking see—" Bulgakov began and then Norman pulled the gun out and pointing it over the table shot Groh. Groh dropped out of sight as Norman swung the gun toward the refrigerator and fired twice. Bulgakov had ducked behind the steel door and the bullets hit it and then Norman felt a pain in his leg. He realized Groh had shot him beneath the table and then it was as if some titanic baseball player had swung his enormous bat and knocked Norman right off his chair. He saw the tiles of the floor coming up to meet him. He had always been worried about the passage of time but now he had plenty of time. The tiles were floating up. So slowly. He remembered the morning when he and his wife had gone to the tile store on Fourth Street in Santa Monica and had picked out this particular tile and then the tiles seemed to scatter and float right past him. He wasn't in the kitchen any longer. Door-ways led to doorways which led to more doorways and then—whether it was the last fitful flickerings of a hypoxic brain or objectively existing phenomena—Norman saw his big fat yellow cat, Mr. Jones, waiting for him and then his wife. And then Nor-man Hopkins was absorbed into boundlessness.

They headed east in Norman's car. Down a lightly traveled state road. Through the brown and gray and buff and dun badlands. A tortuous terrain of mud hills and mazelike canyons and arroyos and fissures and boulders and washes. You could see in the sand-stone cliffs layers of sediment laid down millions of years ago by a vast vanished sea.

The top was down. The sun shared the sky with just a few blurry-looking grayish clouds. Gina began to root around in her purse for sunblock.

"I know it's in here somewhere," she said.

"It must be," said Gray. "'Cause you got everything else in there."

"She left a tuna fish sandwich in there one time. For like two weeks!" said Luke.

"It was more like two days. And it was in a ziplock bag. It wasn't like it was gross or anything."

"Was too two weeks."

"Here it is." She handed the tube of sunblock back to Luke. "Really slather it on."

"You know what else she's got in there?" Luke said to Gray. "Diamonds!"

Gina gave him a sharp look.

"Diamonds?" said Gray.

"Just a few," said Gina.

"Oh come on, Mom. You got a whole bagful."

"Really?" said Gray.

"Yeah. I guess."

"Can I see them?"

She shrugged. Went back in her purse and pulled out a leather bag. It looked like a bag of marbles. Till she loosened the drawstring and tipped some of its contents out into her palm. The sun struck them and it was startling the brightness with which they glittered.

"Wow," said Gray.

They were big stones. Mostly in the three- to five-carat range.

"Where'd you get them?"

"Joey gave them to me. Not all at once. Over a period of years. One here, a couple there."

"Where'd he get them?"

"You better watch out," Luke said to Gray. "She starts getting real mad when you ask her questions like that."

"*You* better watch out," said Gina. "You're really getting a big mouth."

"See what I mean?" said Luke.

"Does anyone else know about these?" said Gray.

She didn't answer. She put the diamonds back in the bag and the bag back in her purse.

"Gina?"

"Frank, I guess. The marshal."

"How does he know?"

"One day I left work early. I wasn't feeling well. When I drove up to my apartment building I saw Frank's car parked outside. Then when I went up to my apartment the door was unlocked. Then I walk in and Frank comes walking out of my bedroom with this shit-eating grin on his face. I ask him how he got in and what's he doing here. He says he has his own key and he's conducting a routine search for drugs. He says it's all just part of his job. I told him to get the fuck out. And then he said, 'Where'd you get the diamonds?' I'd hid them in a drawer in my bedroom. My underwear drawer. I wasn't surprised he was looking in there. He was always hitting on me. Saying disgusting things to me. Anyway. I told him it was none of his business where I got them. He said they were probably illegal contraband and he had a good mind to seize them.

I said if he didn't leave immediately I was going to call the police and then I picked up the phone and started dialing and he left. And then I had the lock changed."

"You think that's why he's after you?" said Gray. "'Cause he wants the diamonds?"

"Well I'm sure my father-in-law paid him off. But maybe the diamonds are part of it. I don't know."

Gray became silent. Staring straight ahead at the road. Gina wanted to say something else but couldn't think of anything and she became silent too.

Luke in the backseat started putting on the sunblock. But then he said: "Hey, stop that!" and giggled. For the dog was licking it off as fast as he could put it on.

Wherefore take unto you the whole armour of God, that ye may be able to withstand in the evil day . . .

He was lying on his bed. Smoking a cigar and reading the Gideon Bible he had found in the night table drawer. Or more exactly the Bible had found him. In the darkest and wretchedest hours of his life it always had found him. This indeed was the evil day. His heart failing. His daughter kidnapped. Gina continuing to elude his grasp in the most exasperating way. And ever since they had left the old man's condo he had heard the unmistakable sound— now louder, now softer, but ever present—of the beating of angels' wings. Had they come to help him or to carry him off? Well as the Injuns used to say it was a good day to die. If it came to that. Or to smite his enemies and free his daughter and get his diamonds and go off to live his wonderful life in Thailand. If the good Lord willed.

He put down the Bible and got up. Walked over to the dresser. Where the heathen idol he had taken from Norman's condo was sitting. He stood there admiring it. He didn't know anything about art but he could tell she was a beaut. What a face. He rubbed her head. For luck.

Dr. Pol-Lim was finishing up patching up Markus Groh. The bullet had passed through the fleshy part of his right side. Nicking a rib but missing anything important.

"Today is your day to be lucky," said Pol-Lim. "Like your friend on Wednesday."

"If we were really lucky," said Groh, "we would not have been shot to begin with."

Pol-Lim shrugged. Going into his black medical bag for bandages. Like an old-time country doctor. "I suppose it's all in how you look at it. I tend to be an optimist. Like my brother. He's in the doughnut business. He says the important things are the doughnuts. Not the doughnut holes."

"What I really was was stupid. Incredibly stupid."

He had underestimated the old man. Who had turned out to be a wily old fox who had almost done him in. He was used to success but everything so far about this assignment had been botched, messy, frustrating, unexpected. Was it possible he already had begun to lose a step? Maybe assassins were like athletes and by the time they reached their thirties their best years were behind them. Yes, it was time to get out. To rescue Luke and retire to paradise.

Bulgakov was sitting at the desk. He was going through piles of files and bills and unopened mail they had taken from Norman's condo. He had already discovered something potentially valuable: the license plate number of Norman's Chrysler. And now he announced: "He has other fucking house."

"Where?" said Groh.

"Tejada Springs."

"Hm. Wonder where that is."

"Oh I know," said Dr. Pol-Lim. Happy to be of help. "It's east of San Diego. In the desert."

Bulgakov brought over to the bed electric and phone bills.

"Here is address. And phone number."

Groh looked the bills over. "One hundred Desert Club Drive."

And then he said to Bulgakov: "Would you get me Norman's cell phone? It's on the dresser."

Bulgakov brought it over. It was a cheap Nokia. Groh hit the send button. Which brought up in the display window the last number called. He checked it against the number on the phone bill.

"Norman called his house in Tejada Springs today. At 11:26 a.m."

"I wonder who he was calling," said Pol-Lim. Who had no idea who Norman was or what was at stake but as usual was enjoying thoroughly his walk on the wild side.

"I wonder that too, doctor. Am I fit to travel?"

"No. Of course not. You are fit for the hospital."

"Too bad."

Groh winced as he straightened up and swung his legs off the bed.

"Dima? Would you get me some clean clothes?"

They drove around Salton City. Which made Tejada Springs look like a vibrant metropolis. Dilapidated houses and abandoned or half-built buildings. Houseless streets lined with telephone poles and fire hydrants. Lots of optimistic signs for lots or houses for sale. The Sidewinder Golf Course. Looking about as verdant and inviting as Norman's golf course. They saw hardly any people. A toothless old lady scooting by on a golf cart. Some black kids playing soccer in the middle of a dusty street. But they did encounter several mean-looking black dogs. Barked at by the malamute and barking in return. All and all it seemed like the post-apocalyptic town of a science fiction movie. The street they were on ended at a flat shimmering miragelike sheet of water. You could see across it but lengthwise water and sky melted together in the dreamy distance just like a real sea. Rusting shopping carts were scattered along a bleak beach. A skinny man stood at the edge of the sea fishing. He turned around and glared at them. He was wearing sunglasses that had one blue lens and one red.

Gray turned the car around and they went back to the highway. They turned north. The sea was to their right and to the left were emerald fields sealike in their magnitude. Shabby bent-over figures toiled in the fields. They were wearing gloves and long-sleeved shirts and hats and scarves against the sun. You couldn't actually see the people, only their clothes. It was as if the fields belonged to some dark magician who had cast a spell to get rid of the people and have all his work done by these empty sets of clothes.

The orange ferry slid across the green water. Cicala was sitting outside. Hands stuck in the pockets of his overcoat. A scarf around his neck. The wind whipping his sparse hair. He had been riding the ferry back and forth between Staten Island and Manhattan all afternoon. He had always liked to ride the ferry. Ever since he was a kid. It had been a nickel then. Now it was free. How could you beat that?

Grinning tourists were standing at the railing. Posing for a picture with the Statue of Liberty in the background. Pretty soon it would be too dark for pictures. Night was about to descend on the city. Day night day night day night day night. What was the fucking point?

He could feel the vibrations of the engine. Coming up through the metal bench. He needed to pee as usual and his butt was numb but he didn't feel like getting up. What was the point? You got up and went to the men's room then ten minutes later you'd feel like you needed to get up and go to the men's room.

He was waiting for news. From the west. The good thing about cell phones was you could ride the ferry all day and still not be out of touch. Which was also the bad thing about cell phones.

Gina had been a lousy wife and was even a worse mother for putting Luke in danger like she had. She richly deserved what she was about to get. He only wished he could do it himself. Though it was funny. He'd ordered many killings but he had never personally killed anybody. Not that he hadn't been a tough guy coming up. He'd busted plenty of lips and broken lots of bones and noses. But he'd never done the ultimate deed. He had been a delegator of death. Like the president. If you were a president you were called the commander-in-chief. If you were a private citizen you were called a gangster or a mafioso.

Bobby came out on the deck. Holding two Styrofoam cups of coffee. He handed one to Cicala.

"It's fucking freezing out here," said Bobby. "Ain't you cold?"

Sure. But he wanted to be cold. They said the dead were cold but they were wrong. The dead weren't anything. Only the living were cold.

In his immaculate white jacket Okafor advanced. Bearing with self-conscious dignity a silver tray. On which rested a sandwich and a cup of tea.

He set the tray down on the desk at Mr. Li's elbow.

"Thank you, General Okafor."

Okafor actually no longer was a general but had been one in Nigeria. Before the fortunes or rather misfortunes of war had forced him to seek a new line of work. Now he was happy to be a steward on the *Invictus*. It was a good entry-level job if you wanted to be in the System. And who wouldn't want to be in the System?

Okafor bowed and left.

It had been a long day. Mr. Li had forgotten to eat until now. He took a sip of the tea and examined his sandwich. A grilled-shrimp panini. His favorite.

He took a bite and chewed and took another bite and then his Mac made an underwater *bloop* sort of sound. Indicating an e-mail had just come in. At an address reserved only for the most urgent communications.

It was from Groh. Again. He hoped it was better than the last one. Which had contained the disturbing information that Groh had been wounded in some kind of wild shootout.

On way to Tejada Springs. Hope to have good news soon.
Feeling fine. Dont worry.
Sent from my iPhone

If he ever permitted himself regret he would be feeling fervently sorry he had ever agreed to see Cicala on Saturday night. But since he dealt only in the here and now all he did was sigh, put down the panini and Google Tejada Springs.

The two-car caravan was nearing Lake Elsinore. Where fires were still burning in the hills.

Groh had lied in his e-mail. About feeling fine. He was sprawled across the backseat in a lot of pain. It hurt to breathe. Pol-Lim had given him Vicodin but he didn't want to take it. Didn't want to do anything that might dull his mind or slow him down. Not till the job was done. And it needed to be done fast. Before they found out what had happened to Norman. Because once they did and assuming they really were in Tejada Springs they would immediately take off and the best chance to catch them would be lost. Also he was concerned about the surveillance cameras at Norman's building. Their images might be on TV on the news. He had to kill Gina and Gray and grab Luke and get the hell out of America.

"Hey Bill," said terHorst. In the front seat. To Bulgakov who was driving. "I got one for you. What did the termite say when he walked into the bar?"

Bulgakov stared straight ahead at I-15.

"Don't wanna take a wild guess? Okay. He said: 'Is the bar *tender* here?'"

Silence from Bulgakov. TerHorst grinned and shook his head.

"I'm gonna get a laugh outa you one of these days, Bill. You just wait and see. I'm gonna tickle your fucking funny bone."

He took out a nitro tablet and let it dissolve in his mouth. His chest was hurting again. They were quite a crew, the three of them.

Jack and Bill both had been shot. And he seemed to be on the verge of another heart attack.

A Beach Boys album was going on his iPod. It was great traveling music. Sunny and cheerful. But now a line in the song that was presently playing made him laugh out loud: *This is the worst trip I've ever been on . . .*

They drove around the north end of the sea then circled south. Moving along at a pokey pace as they looked at things. It was less developed on this side. Not many buildings or people or irrigated fields. Lots of birds though.

Train tracks ran parallel to Highway 111. A freight train came toward them. A guy was sitting on top of one of the boxcars. He waved at them and they waved back as the train rumbled by. Gray once had ridden a train like that. It had been great. He watched it in his sideview till it disappeared.

They were looking for a good place to pull over and walk by the sea.

"What about here?" said Gina.

A little dirt road ran down to an inviting-looking white beach. Gray drove down it and they parked. The dog couldn't wait to get out. To take a crack at all those birds. He bounded across the beach and birds beat their wings and scattered.

"No!" hollered Gray. "Leave those birds alone! Get back here! Now!"

The dog came loping back. Looking absolutely delighted with himself.

"It's pretty here," said Gina.

"It stinks," said Luke.

A rancid fishy smell wafted in off the water. Gray saw on the beach a rotting tilapia. A dead dried-out grebe. The beach crunched under their feet as they walked slowly forward. And then "Jesus Christ!" screamed Gina. "It's bones!"

What they had thought was white sand was millions or maybe billions of bits of bone. Fish bones mostly. Mixed in with the feathers and bones of birds and shattered barnacle shells. All up and down the shore.

"I'm outa here!" said Gina. "I'll wait in the car."

Gina turned around and hastily crunched off over the bones. The dog picked up the dead grebe in his mouth and trotted off with it. Luke running after him and yelling at him to drop it. Gray was left with the bones and the birds. He had never seen so many birds. Ducks and grebes and gulls and coots and terns and geese. And boobies and cormorants and white pelicans. They sat on the beach or waded through the shallows or swam across the water or dived underneath it or flapped and floated and circled above it. Yes, the Salton Sea was an exceedingly strange place like the man in the café had said. Seething with energy, entropy, feathers, and fins. Like some yeasty primordial matrix of death and life.

And then there was the dream. About the dead lake in the desert. And the shoreline littered with bones. And the implacable menace that was drawing near to him.

Gray gazed across the water. To the west.

DeWitt and Dee. Had a certain ring to it. Sounded like a real couple. You could imagine at a party people saying, *Where's DeWitt and Dee? They here yet? Oh yeah, I seen 'em outside. By the swimming pool.* Walking around with a girl like Dee on his arm. At a party. Man, think about that.

But what if he had to kill her?

Maybe they wouldn't make him do it. Maybe they'd send somebody else. What if Smith-Jones and Jones-Smith were to come back for her? She had told him what that asshole had done to her. And how he'd been fixing to rape her till the other guy stopped him. How could he just turn her over to them? But what was he supposed to do? Pull out his gun and start shooting? Guns and shooting weren't his deal and even if they were he'd worked hard to escape Ratliff and rise in the System and how could he just throw all that away?

The dryer stopped. He opened the door and pulled out the clothes. They were hot and fragrant. Mostly his but some hers. Her blouse, pants, and underwear. It gave him a strange feeling seeing their clothes mixed together. It seemed as intimate almost as sex. He had this daydream. Everything worked out with her dad and he was able to let her go. And she went back to her life and he went back to his. But he found a new dermatologist who cleared his complexion up or maybe he went to a plastic surgeon who gave him a whole new face. And he arranged to run into her and they started dating and fell in love and she didn't ever know the truth. Or maybe she would look at him and his blue eyes and suspect it but she wouldn't know for sure and they would go to parties and people would say *Where's DeWitt and Dee? Oh I seen 'em out by the pool.*

He left the laundry room and went upstairs. Unlocked the door of his apartment then quickly slipped his ski mask on and went in.

She was tied up on the burnt-orange sofa. Glaring at him over her gag. She always got mad when he had to leave her alone and tie her up but what did she expect him to do? Not tie her up and let her just mosey out the door? Call the cops and have him arrested? Girls just didn't think rationally.

He set down the basket of laundry and ungagged and unbound her.

"You don't know what it's like," she said. Rubbing her wrists. "It's so fucking humiliating."

He picked up his notebook and pen and wrote: *sory*.

"No you're not. You enjoy it."

dont b sily.

She stood up and started walking around. To get the circulation going. She was wearing a maroon bathrobe his mother had given him. The color looked great on her.

"Well at least I got some clean clothes," she said. Going over to the laundry basket. She rummaged through it pulling her own clothes out and then to his astonishment she undid the sash of her robe and pulled it off her shoulders and let it drop and stood before him completely naked. He looked at her breasts. Her big pink nipples. The crenulated bruises left by the pliers. Her carefully trimmed pubic hair. Then she was stepping into her panties and slipping on her bra.

"You don't like me do you?" she said. " 'Cause I'm fat."

She put on the rest of her clothes. As he wrote something in his notebook.

"What you writing?" she said. Walking over to him.

He showed her.

yur not fat. yur purfit.

"No," she said. Nearly in a whisper. "*You're* perfect."

She pressed herself up against him. And she had just taken a shower and washed her hair and she smelled of shampoo and soap, smelled so clean and her body was so soft.

"I want you so much," she said. "And you want me too, I can tell."

Her face was coming up toward his face, her mouth was only inches from the mask and then her hand was reaching toward it.

"Take this off," she said but he grabbed her wrist and shook his head.

"Why not? I wanna kiss you. I wanna *see* you."

And she reached for his mask with her other hand and now De-Witt nearly spoke. Making a gruntlike sound that was kind of like *No!* as he shoved her away.

She stumbled back and smacked into the coffee table and almost fell over it. He hurried over and tried to help her but she pushed him away.

"Leave me alone! Don't touch me!"

Suddenly she leaned down and picked his cow skull up from the table by one horn and flung it against the wall. Then she moaned and crawled into a corner of the sofa and curled up and began to cry.

"They're gonna kill me. I know it. They're gonna come back and they're gonna kill me. They're gonna kill me."

DeWitt sat down beside her. He wanted to take her in his arms and assure her everything would be fine but instead he just looked at her.

She sat up a little and sniffled and wiped at her nose.

"Let me go. Please. I promise I won't tell anybody about you."

He shook his head.

"Why not? Please. Please. Let me go. Please."

He picked up his pen and notebook.

i cant. thaid kill me if i dun that.

They drove up into the high mountains. The Suburban behind the Land Cruiser. The sun setting behind them and filling the juniper forest with golden light.

"Purty country," said Mac Lingo. Looking at it and nodding. Like he was the proud owner.

Ronnie behind the wheel didn't seem to care about the country.

"You got a cigarette, Daddy?"

"Sure."

He gave Ronnie a Marlboro then lit up one for himself.

The past had been crowding around him in a strange way all day. For instance he had an intense hankering for muscadine jelly. His mother used to make it. From the muscadines they'd collected in the woods. And they'd eat it on hoe cake hot out of the pan. That was dripping with butter. Nothing in the world could beat hot hoe cake. And he remembered going duck hunting with his daddy. And this old black retriever they had named Racer. And Racer swimming along in the freezing water with a dead duck in his mouth. And Joe Keith's farm. He worked on it when he was a teenager. God it was hot putting hay up in July and dodging those old red wasps in the top of the barn.

His cell phone rang. He could see terHorst up ahead. Looking back at him. Holding his phone on his ear.

"Hey Frank."

"We'll be there before long," said terHorst. "Y'all ready?"

Lingo looked over at Ronnie. "Frank wants to know if we're ready."

"Yup," said Ronnie.

"Ronnie said yup," said Lingo.

The shadows of the mountains advanced across the desert till it was all shadows and simply dusk. Gray turned the headlights on. He had already put the top up because it was getting chilly. Nobody had said anything for a while. He looked over at Gina to see if maybe she was asleep. But she wasn't. She smiled at him.

"It's gotten awful quiet back there," he said.

She looked in the backseat.

"They're both conked out," she said.

Luke was sitting up but his head had fallen forward. The dog's massive head was lying on his lap. Luke's arm was resting on the dog's shoulder.

"He really loves that dog," she said.

"He's never had one?"

She shook her head. "Joey didn't like dogs. He didn't like any kind of animals. He wouldn't even let Luke have like a goldfish. Or a turtle."

"How'd you ever wind up with him?"

"I was eighteen. I was working at this seafood restaurant. In Freeport. Down by the water. And Joey would come in with his friends. He was cute and funny and left big tips. And everybody knew who he was. Pat Cicala's son. He was older than me and he just seemed kind of . . . I don't know . . . exciting. Anyway. To answer your question. I was young and stupid so we got married. But Luke came out of it. So I guess in a way it was worth it."

He nodded. As the big car glided through the last of the light. As a couple of stars began to shine.

"You're mad at me aren't you?" said Gina.

Gray was puzzled. "No. Why?"

"'Cause of the diamonds. 'Cause I didn't tell you about them."

He thought about it. "I'm willing to put my butt on the line for you and Luke. But not for a bunch of stolen diamonds."

"You're just like Luke. Judging me. You don't know what I've had to do to keep it all together."

They lapsed into silence. They reached Tejada Springs. Turned right on Tejada Springs Road. It was rush hour. Which meant there were two or three other cars on the road. The headlights of which could be seen by Groh, Bulgakov, terHorst, and the Lingos. Who had just topped the San Ysidro Mountains and were beginning the long zigzaggy descent to the scattered lights of the little town.

The coyotes eyed them as they came down Desert Club Drive. Pulled up in front of Norman's house and got out of Norman's car. The dog sat down and started licking his balls. Then suddenly as though sensing the coyotes' presence looked out toward the desert and barked gruffly. But the coyotes already had slipped away.

Gray unlocked the door then disarmed the alarm. They walked through the house.

"Well we've seen the Salton Sea," said Gina. "Now I'm gonna take a shower. Try to get this fucking dead-fish smell off of me."

"You really do smell terrible," said Luke.

"Thanks. So what's the dinner plans?"

"What do you say me and you do the cooking tonight?" said Gray to Luke.

"Okay. What'll we make?"

"How about a tofu scramble?"

"Yummy," said Gina. Heading down the hallway. "I'll have to shower real fast. I can't wait to eat that."

They drove by the gas station/grocery store and the souvenir shop and the bleak motel and the Tejada Springs Café. Where the foxes were playing tricks on the dull fat people. In the Suburban Ronnie finished a can of Shark. He lowered the window and threw it out and it bounced and clattered on the pavement as Mac reached into the backseat and got his Protecta shotgun. He checked the drum magazine. It was fully loaded. With twelve rounds. In the Land Cruiser Bulgakov behind the steering wheel sneezed and sniffled. The Astra C losing in its battle against the cold virus. Groh gritted his teeth as a wave of pain went through him. He put his hand in his jacket pocket. Luke's sock was there. It was comforting to touch it. This was all about Luke. Protecting Luke. For there was about to be much danger and death and he must be as it were Luke's guardian angel. And terHorst took another nitro. As pain radiated out from behind his breastbone and the wings of the angels rustled around him. At times he thought he felt invisible feathers brushing his face.

They passed the Lucky Horseshoe Trailer Park. Bulgakov glanced at the GPS map on the dashboard. On which the Land Cruiser was represented by a red dot crawling up Tejada Springs Boulevard. They had put in 100 Desert Club Drive as their destination and now a robotic female voice commanded: "Turn right on Rango Road in three hundred feet."

Gina came in the kitchen. Wearing another dress, a light-green one this time, from Norman's wife's closet.

"Need any help?" she said.

"Nah," said Gray, "we got it covered."

He was at the stove stirring around stuff in a pan. Luke was at a counter cutting a cucumber up for a salad. The dog was wandering around with a happy grin. A small TV on the counter was tuned into the six o'clock news on a San Diego station. They were showing a story about a wildfire still burning out of control east of San Diego near El Cajon.

Gina walked over to a cabinet and took out a wineglass.

"Want some wine?" she said.

"Sure," said Luke.

"I was talking to Gray."

"Sure," said Gray.

She poured red wine into two glasses. Went to the stove and gave Gray one.

"Cheers," she said.

"Cheers."

They touched glasses and drank. Looking at each other. Then Gina took a look at the pan.

"Smells good. What's in it?"

"Onions. Tomatoes. Celery. Black olives. Garlic. And of course tofu."

"Wow. I feel healthier just looking at it—"

"Norman Hopkins, a wealthy real estate developer and philanthropist, and a native of San Diego, was murdered today in Los Angeles."

Gray, Gina, and Luke turned simultaneously and looked at the square-jawed anchor on the TV.

"Hopkins was shot to death in his beachfront condominium in Marina del Rey."

"Oh my god," said Gina. Putting her hand over her mouth.

"Also killed was a security guard who was shot to death in the lobby of the building. Police say they are looking for three suspects who were seen exiting the building near the time of the slayings."

Gray turned the flame off under the pan.

"We're leaving. Get your stuff. Now! Go!"

He had hid them under his mattress. The .32 revolver. And the box of ammunition. He shook some cartridges out of the box into his hand and put them in his pocket and stuck the gun in the waist of his pants on the left side. So his shirt would cover it. Which is what Gray did. And then he ran out of the room and almost collided with his mother who was running down the hallway clutching her purse.

"Come on, baby!" she said pushing him along and they saw Gray at the end of the hallway with his rucksack waiting for them.

"You think they know we're here?" said Gina and Gray said: "Maybe. Let's go!"

They hurried out of the house. Gray pulled the front door shut behind them and they ran toward the Chrysler.

"Where's the dog?" said Luke.

They looked around. No dog.

"Forget the dog!" said Gina.

"No!" said Luke and he ran back to the house and opened the door and the dog came bounding out his Nylabone held fast in his jaws.

They piled in the car. Gray and Gina in the front seat and Luke and the dog in the back. Gray started the engine and turned on the headlights and they took off.

They went up Desert Club Drive. Past the DESERT CLUB OF TE-JADA SPRINGS sign and the fat fan palms and the thin fan palms and then Gray saw them. The headlights of the two SUVs moving fast in their direction down Rango Road.

"That's them, amigos!" said terHorst.

They watched the Chrysler suddenly veer off the road and head off into the desert.

"Stay with them, Dima," said Groh.

Bulgakov floored it. The Land Cruiser accelerated down Rango Road then at the point it intersected with Desert Club Drive went airborne over the shoulder and made a bone-rattling landing in the desert.

The Lingos were right behind them. Ronnie cut loose with a joyous yell.

"It's payback time, Daddy!"

"You got that right, boy!" said Mac Lingo.

———

Gray looked in his rearview at the pursuing pairs of headlights. Which weaved and bounced just as the Chrysler weaved and bounced. Dodging ocotillos and smoke trees and big rocks and clumps of brush and jolting across dry creek beds. He saw Luke and the dog's heads pop up as they looked through the back window.

"Luke! I told you to stay down!"

"Get down, Luke!" said Gina. "Now!"

Luke and the dog disappeared. Gray reached over and grabbed Gina by the back of the neck and shoved her down on the seat.

"You too. Down!"

"Ow! Okay!"

He saw the headlights were gaining on them. The Chrysler couldn't compete off-road with the SUVs.

He reached under his shirt and pulled out the Glock.

TerHorst heard bushes thumping against the front bumper and scraping along the bottom of his Land Cruiser. He could see ahead the red glow of the taillights but it was impossible to care about them much. Sweat ran into his eyes and stung them and he hastily unscrewed the top off the bottle of nitro tablets. He shook several out into his palm and clapped them into his mouth. It had happened twice before and so he knew: he was slap-bang in the middle of a full-blown heart attack.

"Get me to a hospital," he croaked.

Bulgakov looked over at him and gave a harsh laugh.

"Dima, where are they?"

Groh was leaning forward between the seats. His eyes wide and glistening in the dim light from the dashboard.

"I don't see them!" he said.

Lingo scanned the landscape. Beyond the throw of their headlights the desert was inky black.

"Musta turned his lights off. But don't you worry none. We'll get him."

"I ain't worried, Daddy," said Ronnie. "I'm just worried one of them other fellers'll kill him first. 'Fore I get the chance."

The SUVs eased forward. East into the desert. The sky above them filled with stars but moonless. The landscape becoming more broken and littered with rocks and boulders.

Groh's side was throbbing and blood was seeping through his shirt. He felt odd. Light-headed. And aware of a growing sense of dread. As if they had made a calamitous mistake in leaving the road. As if they had been tricked into traveling into a malignant dark immensity which they would never be able to make their way back out of.

Bulgakov was silent as usual. What went through his mind? Anything? And terHorst was annoyingly noisy. Moaning and babbling about heart attacks and angels. And then he noticed he could no longer see the headlights of the Suburban. He loathed the Lingos, they were brutal idiots but it was disconcerting and deepened the dread that they too seemed to have vanished.

It was basic military tactics. If you were being followed or thought you were you circled back. Laid up and waited. Prepared an ambush for your enemy.

They were north of the golf course and south of the rough hills. In a dry wash. Near the ravine where he had practiced shooting the Glock.

The lights were out on the Chrysler but the motor was running. Gray, Gina, Luke, and the dog were all sitting silently. Staring into the dark. They would arrive soon and since he knew this area and they didn't he thought it might give him an edge. But he had no plan. He believed in preparation but not in plans. The moment when it came would tell him what to do.

In the backseat the dog, sensing the strangeness and tension, whimpered. He heard Luke whispering, "Shh, it's okay." He knew Luke and Gina must be terrified but he did not allow himself to care. Only by not caring about them could he save them. He needed to be empty. Like a cup. Only an empty cup could be filled. No future or past. No desire or fear. No love. Just the desert in the faint starlight. The desert in the starlight. Just the desert. The desert.

Beams of light flared past throwing long shadows and then he heard the crunch of tires rolling over the crusty ground. He raised his pistol to the window and then the Land Cruiser was going by. He saw three shadowy shapes inside. Two in the front. One in the back.

"That's Frank's car," whispered Luke.

It reached the edge of the ravine and stopped. Its engine idling. Its headlights shooting across nothingness and illuminating the far side.

Gray didn't like not knowing where the other SUV was but there was nothing to be done about it.

"Lean down," he said. "Cover your heads."

They contemplated the void.

"What should we do?" said Groh. "Go back? Or find a way around it?"

"Fucking fly over it," gasped terHorst. Holding his chest with both hands. And then Bulgakov, eyes on his rearview, shouted: "Fuck!"

Groh turned around. He could see the cold gleam of chrome as the Chrysler came speeding toward them out of the night and then they were all rocked violently as the car slammed into them. The SUV was knocked forward to within a foot of the ravine. Groh pointed his pistol at the back window and fired. The glass shattered and fell and Groh shot into the windshield of the Chrysler. Gray hunkered down and kept his foot on the gas. Bulgakov's foot was jammed down on the brake but the Chrysler's roaring

V-8 engine was enough to send the Land Cruiser over the edge. It
went bouncing down the steep side of the ravine and then one tire
caught on an outcropping of rock sending the vehicle torquing out
into space. Groh and Bulgakov cursed and terHorst hollered as
they saw the bottom of the ravine rushing up to meet them.

"Everybody okay?" said Gray.

"Yeah," said Luke.

"Let's go!" said Gina. "Hurry!"

Gray began backing the car up. Sending the end swinging
around. But then the engine died.

He put it in park and turned the key. Which produced an un-
promising stuttering grinding noise.

"Gray, come on!" said Luke.

Steam was rising up from the ruptured radiator. The grinding
noise continued.

"I think it's finished," Gray said and then windows broke and
lead pelted metal as the darkness boomed and banged and flashed
with orange light.

Gina screamed and Gray yelled: "Get down!"

The gunfire continued. Coming from Gray's side of the car.

"Get out!" he said. "Keep your heads down!"

Gina opened her door and crawled out and Luke and the dog
came out of the back and Gray scrambled over the seat and he was
out too. They crouched against the side of the car. Gray had iden-
tified two shooters. One had a shotgun. Some kind of semi-auto
judging from the rate of fire. The other had a large-caliber hand-
gun. Maybe a .45.

A cut over Groh's eyebrow was pulsing out blood and making it
hard to see.

"All right, Dima. You're almost out."

The Land Cruiser had come to rest upside down, its roof

smashed among some rocks. Groh was helping Bulgakov squeeze out of the squashed driver's-side window.

"We're almost there!" said Groh and he gave a hard pull and Bulgakov came slithering out. He lay on the rocks. Bleeding and panting. Like some terrible baby Groh had helped deliver.

Above them they heard gunshots. Groh looked up the craggly side of the ravine. It was about sixty feet to the top.

"We must get up there, Dima."

Bulgakov nodded. They had not become the top assassins for the System by being easily daunted. Groh helped Bulgakov to his feet. And then he pulled a fresh mag out of his pocket and popped it in his gun.

"Hey!" they heard. "Hey!"

They bent down and looked in the Land Cruiser. Saw terHorst dangling from his seat belt and shoulder strap. Clawing at them like an animal caught in a trap but unable to get loose.

"Smell that? It's gasoline. I'm soaked to the tits with it. Get me outa here!"

They stood back up. Looked at each other.

TerHorst hung there in the darkness. The gasoline dripping off him. Puddling below him on the roof. And agony in his chest from his ongoing heart attack. He laughed. What was that Laurel and Hardy line? This is another fine mess you've gotten me into!

He heard a faint scraping noise then outside there was a puff of light.

A hand appeared at the window. Holding a flaming Paradise Motel matchbook. Which was tossed inside.

It landed below him. At the edge of the pool of gasoline.

He reached for it. His hand came up a couple of inches short.

He laughed again.

Gray heard wild screaming and looked over his shoulder. Golden light was coming up out of the ravine. As if the earth had cracked open and exposed its fiery core. The screams subsided. So at least one person had survived the plunge. For a minute or two anyway.

The shooting stopped and then they heard: "You kilt my brother, asshole! You're fixing to die! Y'all are!"

Gray assumed the speaker was the large ogrish man he had attempted to run down in the parking lot. He had not fired back yet. There wasn't any point. He needed to get closer. He did not think he'd have much trouble with them. After all if they were any good he wouldn't be thinking anything at all right now. He'd be dead. After he dealt with them he'd go down in the ravine. Make sure nobody was left alive down there. And then they would get the hell out. Find a fast freeway that took them far away.

More shots were fired. Gina was holding on to Luke who was holding on to the dog. The dog was agitated by the gunfire. Shaking and whimpering as Luke tried to calm him.

"Stay here," Gray whispered. "Don't move. I'm gonna go take care of those guys. Okay?"

"Be careful," said Gina.

He started to move off.

"Gray?" said Luke.

He looked back.

"Don't worry about Mom. I'll protect her."

Gray nodded.

He came out from behind the Chrysler on his belly. So his shape couldn't be picked up against the glow of the fire behind him. He could move quick for a man on his belly. He had watched iguanas in Guatemala and had admired the way they would seem on their short legs to be flying just inches over the ground and it was something he had practiced. Hour after hour. Moving like an iguana.

The shooters were behind some big boulders seventy-five or eighty feet away. He intended to flank them and kill them before they knew he was even there.

———

Lingo slipped into the rotary mag of his Protecta a dozen red shells.

"How come they ain't shooting back?" said Ronnie. Peering over the rocks toward the car.

"I don't know," said Lingo.

"Maybe they're dead already. Maybe we done kilt 'em."

"Maybe. Or they could be playing possum."

"You think that was Frank that was screaming?"

"Kindly sounded like him didn't it?"

And then Lingo rose over the rocks and began to blast away. The empty shell casings jumping out of his shotgun. Ronnie joined in with his revolver.

Buckshot rattled against the car. The dog squirmed and bucked in Luke's arms and then broke loose and bolted.

"No," yelled Luke, "come back!"

The dog yelped as he was struck in the haunch by some pellets. He stumbled but kept running. Luke darted out after him before Gina could stop him.

"What are you doing," she screamed, "are you crazy?"

Ronnie saw Luke running. Silhouetted against a backdrop of flickering light.

"There's the kid!" he said and began banging away at him.

"Knock him down, Ronnie!" said Lingo. "Put his dick in the dirt!"

But the bullets all missed and Luke disappeared into the tangle of brush and the jumble of rocks into which the dog had run.

Below him the Land Cruiser burned and sent up a twisting cloud of black smoke. It drifted across him and he struggled not to cough. He had nearly reached the top. Bulgakov had taken a different route. The idea being to trap Gray between them. Now he looked for Bulgakov but didn't see him. He must already be out of the ravine. Waiting for him. It was tough going. He hurt and he bled and he was dizzy and being choked by the smoke. But this was not the first time he had been challenged to the utmost on an assignment. He had always succeeded before and he would succeed now.

And then he heard just above him: "Here, boy. Come here, boy. Where are you?"

It was Luke! Calling out softly for the dog. The brave boy. Hearing all the shooting Groh had been so worried about him but what luck to have come upon him this way. In the chaotic dark. In the smoke- and flame-filled night.

Luke gave a low whistle. "Come on out, boy. It's okay."

He heard a noise and turned around and saw a man crawling out of the ravine. His faced was covered with blood and smoke was floating around him like he was a visitor from some infernal realm.

"Luke," he said. "Don't be afraid."

He began to move toward Luke. He had a gun in one hand but it wasn't pointed at him and the other hand was being held out to him.

"My name is Markus."

The blood on his face looked black in the darkness. Luke could see in the blood the gleam of the man's white teeth as he smiled.

"I've come to help you."

Luke pulled Norman's gun out from under his shirt and shot the man in the chest. The man stopped and stood there. Luke shot him again and then the third bullet sent him stumbling backward and into the ravine.

Groh did two backward somersaults down the upper face of the slope and then he was falling free and fast. Not dead yet. Still conscious. Aware of what was happening. He knew when he hit the bottom it would kill him. But amazingly he didn't hit the bottom. He had a recurring dream of falling from a great height, of falling miles and miles knowing he was certain to die but of course he never did die in his dream and this was like that.

He was like a spark from a fire. Falling and fading. Fading and falling. And finally just fading away.

———

Gina found him there. At the ravine's edge. She had heard the three shots and saw now the gun in his hand.

"Luke," she said, grabbing him. "What happened?"

He just looked at her. Something blank in his eyes. She took the gun from him.

"We gotta hide, honey. We gotta hide!"

The Lingos' most recent fusillade had punctured the gas tank of the Chrysler and set it ablaze. The Lingos watched it burning. How Ronnie loved to watch things burn.

They too had heard the shots. And were puzzling over their meaning. To the extent their brains were capable of puzzling over anything.

"That musta been him shooting, Daddy," said Ronnie. "The feller that kilt Steve."

"But who was he shooting at?"

"Us?"

"Naw. Wasn't nobody shooting at us."

"Anyhow. I'm tired of waiting. Let's go get him."

"All right."

They left their hiding place. Advanced toward the rocks where Luke had disappeared and the shots had come from.

About fifteen feet to their right Gray rose up to a crouching position and put a bullet into Lingo's ear. Lingo pitched forward without making a sound.

"Daddy!" hollered Ronnie and then Gray shot him. He put four rounds into the center of his humongous mass and Ronnie shook and juddered but didn't go down and the fifth time Gray pulled the trigger nothing happened. Ronnie lifted up his gun and pointed it at Gray and Gray dived as Ronnie fired and then as Ronnie's arm swung and he fired again Gray dived again and then Ronnie's eyes rolled up in his head. He began turning around on his stubby legs.

Taking little mincing steps in a strangely dainty way like a dancing hippopotamus in a cartoon and then he went down. Falling heavily not far from his father.

Gray got to his feet. Looked at the Lingos and then examined the jammed Glock. It was a feedway stoppage. He grabbed the slide, locked it back, pressed the mag eject—

He wasn't sure whether he heard something or saw something peripherally or maybe it was some psychic sense of presence. But he knew he wasn't alone.

He turned and saw Bulgakov. About twenty feet away.

His gun was pointed at him. He seemed amused. He said: "Zastrial pistolet? Eto khuyovo."

Gun jammed? That's fucked.

It was like Kangari. When he had driven between the two buildings and seen the hog wallow and the mud wall. He knew he was without a doubt dead. And in a flash he saw Gina dead too and Luke in the hands of vicious criminals and then the malamute came hurtling out of the dark. Colliding with Bulgakov just as the gun went off. Gray heard the bullet ripping past and then he was running. Toward Bulgakov and the dog. The dog savagely snarling was after Bulgakov's throat and Bulgakov was trying to fend him off. Gray saw a spurt of light and heard a shot. The dog yelped and jerked and fell and Bulgakov moved his gun toward Gray. Gray kicked it out of his hand and it went flying and he gave Bulgakov a double palm strike to the chest. Which should have fractured his ribs and put him on the ground where Gray could finish him off but it was like Gray had hit something as solid and hard as an iron stove. Bulgakov staggered back but kept his feet.

They faced each other. Feinting and weaving. The burning car creating shadows that weaved and feinted too. Bulgakov threw a right hand and Gray caught the punch. Put him in an elbow lock and threw him face first into a cactus. He screamed as the needles punctured his skin then Gray went after him. Bulgakov turned and bent down and pulled his knife out of his boot. Gray almost right on top of him didn't have time to stop as Bulgakov thrust the knife up toward his ribs. Gray spun and trapped the arm with the knife. Grasped the thumb and broke it and took the knife and continuing to spin in a corkscrewing motion stabbed Bulgakov in the back of the leg. Then he unwound from his coil. Spinning back the other way. Twisting Bulgakov's body around and his head snapped back exposing his throat and Gray with a quick slash severed the carotid artery.

His face was sprayed with Bulgakov's blood. Bulgakov grabbed his throat and sank to his knees. He made gurgling choking noises as the blood spurted out between his fingers. He looked up at Gray. Who lifted his leg, put his foot on his shoulder and shoved him over. Then he tossed down the knife. Into the blood pooling around Bulgakov's head.

Gray looked at the dog. He wasn't moving and wasn't going to move. He had been shot in the head. But Gray didn't have time to care about that now. He had to find Gina and Luke.

But they had found him. They were walking toward them. He went to meet them. He saw Gina was holding a gun.

She stared at his bloody face.

"Gray, oh my god!"

"I'm fine. It's not my blood."

"What happened to him? What's the matter with him?" Luke. Looking at the dog.

Gray didn't say anything. Luke ran over to the dog.

"He's hurt. We have to get him to a vet."

"Luke," said Gray. "A vet can't help him."

It reminded him of Bulgakov. The way Luke went to his knees.

"No-o-o-o-o!" he wailed.

"We have to go," said Gray. "Now. There might be more men coming. They might already be on their way."

Luke was petting the dog's neck. He had begun to cry.

"But we can't just leave him."

"We have to, honey," said Gina. Going over to him. "You heard Gray."

———

They walked off. Leaving behind the dog and Bulgakov and the Lingos and Norman's burning Chrysler and the burning SUV with the stolen jade sculpture and what was left of terHorst in it and Groh's crumpled body at the bottom of the ravine. They found the Lingos' Chevy Suburban nearby. Key in the ignition. Gray started it up and they drove away.

Luke sat in the front. With Gina's arms wrapped around him. Nobody said anything. Luke kept crying for a while then stopped. And it was silent except for the sounds the vehicle made as it bumped over the desert. Then they reached Rango Road and the ride was smooth.

Saturday

They saw the moon rising in front of them around two a.m. A slender white crescent. They were driving east for the same reason eleven days earlier Gina and Luke had driven west. Not to reach something in front of them but to escape what lay behind.

They had stopped at a gas station in Indio. Where Gray had gone in the men's room to clean himself up so he wouldn't look like he'd just got off the night shift at a slaughterhouse. And Gina had done her best to clean up the Suburban. Getting rid of the Lingos' cigarette butts and empty cans of Bud and Coke and Shark and fast-food wrappers and half-eaten candy bars and lengths of beef jerky and porno and gun mags. She couldn't do anything though about the stains from Steve's blood or about the smell. They tried driving with the windows down but it got too cold for that. But after a while their noses got used to it and they could barely smell the Lingos anymore.

The hours passed and a total of maybe a couple dozen words were said. It was hard for them to speak. Hard to do anything. All three felt as though all their bones had been broken. As though the fragments of their bones were rattling around in a thin sack of skin that was all that was left of them.

Luke finally crawled into the backseat. Curled up and went to sleep. But it was a fitful sleep broken up by moans and mutterings. And then once they could tell he had woken up because they heard him sniffling and crying again. Gina asked him what was wrong.

"The dog," he said. "We never even gave him a name."

Gray was assailed with unbearable thoughts. He felt as if he had botched everything and the only reason they had survived the night was luck. If he had done his job properly Luke would never have been forced to face alone in the desert in the night a professional killer. Wouldn't have had to cross that terrible line and take the life of another. And Luke would be forever changed by what he had done. As Gray had been changed by the killing of the three soldiers in Haiti. And he thought about all the men he had killed and how good he had become at killing and what did that say about his soul. And he thought about Kangari. The children he had shot down. As they had run through the rain across the grass. It was not their fault they had been born into a nightmare world that put guns in their hands. And for all the killing he had done that day he had not saved the president and his wife. They had trusted him and he had failed them.

And what ultimately was it with him? He had gone to King Beach with nothing more on his mind than enjoying the sunshine and reading a book in a pink and blue motel by the sea. Within days he had beaten somebody up in the park. Besmirched the pretty town with blood. And that had been just the beginning. Why had his days been so filled with violence? Did he seek it or did it seek him?

And then there was Norman.

Poor Norman were two of the two dozen words they had said. Murmured by Gina a little after midnight. Gray hoped they hadn't made him suffer before they murdered him. He need never have become implicated in all this. He had generously offered them his car and his house in the desert but considering the power and evil of the forces that were after them Gray should have turned down his help. Found other means to effect their escape. Norman's death was his fault too.

Somewhere in the middle of Arizona Gray began to nod off a bit. Gina touched his elbow and told him either let her drive for a while or they should stop at a motel. Neither wanted to stop so

Gray pulled off on the shoulder of the interstate. They got out and a truck thundered past and they were whipped by its wind and they changed places and went on.

Gray was soon asleep. He dreamed about the dog. No longer was he scarred and skinny and mottled and one-eyed but he was strong and handsome. With bright brown eyes. He thanked Gray for rescuing him in the park. He told him he shouldn't feel bad about not giving him a name. He said that in the past they had shared many lives together and Gray had given him many different names and then Gray woke up.

He looked over at Gina. She was driving with her hands at exactly ten and two on the steering wheel. Like an earnest driver's-ed student.

He looked into the backseat at Luke. Who was now sleeping quietly. Breathing deep and long.

He couldn't lose sight of one thing. Gina and Luke were still here. Alive on this planet. And so was he.

He took a long drink from a bottle of water. Gazed through the windshield at the moon.

He had wings too. Though his were scaly and reptilian. While hers were feathery and white. They flew side by side high over the earth. She saw forests beneath them and mountains and seas. She had never understood before how incredibly beautiful the world was. She would look over at him from time to time and he would look back at her. His eyes so blue in his black mask. She loved him but the mask frightened her. If only he would take it off. But then all at once she realized she was wearing a black mask too. And she was happy. Because that meant she didn't have to be afraid anymore.

She woke up. Saw sunlight seeping around the edges of the curtains.

She felt her usual sense on waking up of disbelief. That she really had been kidnapped. And then she felt her usual indignation that she was tied up. Plus she badly needed to pee.

"Hey!" she yelled. "What's-your-name! Get in here!"

The bedroom door opened so quickly it was as if he had been standing just outside it waiting for her to yell. He came over and pulled the bedclothes back and unbound her.

"You sleep good?" she said. "'Cause I didn't. I slept like shit."

He stepped back. She swung her legs out of bed. Sat there rubbing her face with her hands. Groggy and yawning.

"I'm sorry. I guess I'm kind of cranky in the morning. Before I get my coffee."

She looked up at him. He was staring at her.

"What's wrong?"

He just kept looking at her.

"You're scaring me."

There was something truly disturbing about his eyes.

"What's the matter? Tell me!"

He handed her the notebook. In which he'd already written a note.

git redy 2 go. im turning u loos.

They were grateful to see the sun rise. Because it had been a long long night.

They stopped at a truck stop in Santa Rosa, New Mexico, for breakfast. Their waitress's name was Fernanda. She was plump, cheerful, and efficient. She brought Gina and Luke omelettes and Gray pancakes.

He put pat after pat of butter on his pancakes and soaked them in syrup. As Gina watched.

"Looks good," she said.

"My favorite meal."

"I thought tofu and seaweed was your favorite meal."

"That's good too."

They each smiled a little. Their first smiles since yesterday. Luke looked at them. Not smiling.

"Where are we going?" he said.

Gina sighed. "I don't know, Luke. Where do you wanna go?"

"I don't know."

Gray tucked into the pancakes. It really was his favorite meal. Ever since he was a kid. Impossible to put too much butter and syrup on a pancake. He hardly ever had them anymore. Except when he felt the need for a bit of pure uncomplicated pleasure. And he felt that need now not only because of what had happened last night but because gradually over the last few hours it had dawned on him they were headed someplace in particular after all.

Bobby the Hump was on the phone to Chuck. The Chinaman.

"Well how long's this fucking meeting supposed to last?" said Bobby.

"Tell him I'm getting impatient," said Cicala.

"The boss is getting impatient."

Bobby listened a moment then said: "Okay, Chuck," and put the phone down.

"Chuck said Mr. Li's in a real important meeting and he don't know when it's gonna be over. But he'll call you when it's over."

"Who is he to keep *me* waiting?"

They were sitting at the oak table in the kitchen. Under the chandelier. Cicala took a drink of his coffee. Shook his head grimly. "I hate all of 'em. Slant-eyed dog-eating little-dicked bastards."

"Yeah," said Bobby, "me too. I hate fucking chinks. But Chuck's okay."

"Bobby, just 'cause he likes the fucking Jets that doesn't make him okay. You can't trust a slant. They're treacherous. Sneaky. You never know what they're thinking about. They smile and nod at everything then they cut your fucking throat."

Latreece came in. Wearing a coat and carrying her purse.

"You going somewhere?" said Cicala.

She laughed. "Oh I just tell you, Mr. Cicala, you forgot. I'm going to get my hair done. Make it byooootiful! At the beauty shop!"

Cicala was embarrassed. She *had* told him. Not half an hour ago. Was he going fucking senile?

"What about Millie?" he said.

"Eliana. She'll take care of Miss Millie. They like each other."

His wife and his mistress. How cozy. They liked each other. He got up from the table.

"Call Joey," he said to Bobby. "Tell him we still don't know anything. Come on, Smitty. Let's go outside."

Cicala and the dog walked out into the garden.

The waiting was killing him. Yesterday had turned exciting. The Russians were heading out into the desert. Following some hot new lead. Maybe moving in for the kill. And they could have fallen off the face of the fucking earth for all the news he'd had since then.

The weather was better. The sun was out and it was much warmer. White clouds were being blown across the blue face of the sky.

Cicala and Smitty walked slowly over the grass and the fallen leaves. Among the statues of saints and angels. It was true what they said. A man's best friend was his dog. Dogs really had it good when you thought about it. Better than people. Dogs with good masters anyway. Smitty had everything taken care of for him. Plenty of food and water and toys. Lived in a fucking mansion. Got the best medical treatment money could buy. It was true he didn't have his balls anymore but balls were a mixed blessing. His life was a lot more peaceful because he didn't have to spend his time chasing around after cooz. And the main thing was, Smitty never worried. About anything. He had no idea that someday he was going to get old and sick and then die. As far as he was concerned he was going to be walking around like this in the fucking garden forever.

He sniffed around on the grass then squatted and shat. Cicala leaned down to inspect the results. Smitty's digestion was off sometimes but now he had produced three firm well-shaped turds. That glistened in the sunlight.

"Good boy!" said Cicala. "Good Smitty!"

———

She rode in darkness. Eyes taped up and sunglasses over them. Like on the day she was kidnapped.

He had written her a note that said he was going to take her somewhere and drop her off and she was not to take off her blindfold till she heard him honk his horn three times. The vehicle he had led her out to seemed like an SUV. Still pretty new judging from the clean leathery smell of it. She could tell they were driving on city streets for a while, stopping and going at stop signs and traffic lights, then they picked up speed and were moving fast and she knew they were on a highway.

He wouldn't be wearing the mask now. That seemed strange. Him sitting right next to her without the mask. And she still couldn't see his face.

She had gotten used to their way of communicating. Her talking and him writing notes. They had been getting downright chatty with each other and now it seemed weird and uncomfortable just riding along in silence.

"Can we listen to some music or something?" she said.

The radio was turned on. To KRXO. A local rock station.

"Thank you," she said. Her voice sounded thin and quavery to her. She was racked with conflicting emotions. Exhilaration because she was about to be freed and terror because what if she wasn't? What if he was taking her off to be killed?

She couldn't bring herself to believe that he personally would ever hurt her. She could look in his eyes and tell he was smitten with her. Though why a guy like him would ever go for a girl like her she didn't get. Him so cool and powerful and sexy and her just a fat little nothing. But maybe those two guys had come back and he was going to turn her over to them. Because after all she knew what they looked like. She could ID them. And maybe she would be raped and tortured before being buried in the woods or thrown in a farm pond.

They slowed down and she could hear the ticking of the turn

signal and then they turned right and they were on another road. She couldn't hear the rumble and swish of traffic anymore. Their speed dropped from maybe sixty or seventy to thirty or forty.

Her heart was beating fast and she could barely breathe. Something unbelievably wonderful or incredibly horrible was just about to happen to her.

"You're not going to hurt me are you?" she said.

There was no answer.

"Well are you?"

She felt his hand take hers. Give it a reassuring squeeze. He started to pull his hand away but she wouldn't let go of it. And so they drove holding hands for a while. Like romantic teenagers then she could feel the vehicle slowing down again. He took away his hand and they were turning left. Onto another road. It seemed to be unpaved. They bumped slowly along it for a minute or two then she could feel the car swinging out and around then he put it in reverse and back into forward then when it was pointing in the direction they had just come from he turned the motor off. She heard his door opening and his footsteps crunching around and then her door opened. He took her arm and helped her out. Shut the door behind her and led her away a few feet then stopped.

The air was a little chilly. She could hear the songs of birds. She could tell he was standing right in front of her. She could hear him breathing. What was he doing?

She felt under the tape and cotton tears coming into her eyes. Her eyes burned.

Was he just standing there? Was he just looking at her? What was he doing?

Suddenly something was pressed into her hand. She heard his footsteps moving away quickly and the car door opening and slamming and the motor starting up. Then she heard the SUV moving off. Then after a few moments: *Honk! Honk! Honk!*

She took off the sunglasses. Pulled the tape and cotton away from her eyes.

She was standing by a narrow dirt road. In the woods.

She looked up the road toward where she'd heard the honks. The road was empty. Bending around and disappearing into the trees.

She looked at what was in her hand. A folded-up piece of paper. She unfolded it. It was a note from him.

im reel sory. yur dady is ded.

They left I-40 near Tucumcari and took US 54 east. An hour and a half later, not long after they had crossed into the panhandle of Texas, Gina began to cry.

"Mom?" said Luke. Anxiously from the backseat. "What's wrong?"

She didn't answer. Just shook her head and went in her purse. Pulled out a packet of Kleenexes and dabbed with one at her nose and eyes.

"Gina?" said Gray. "You okay?"

"No, I'm not okay. And you're not okay. And Luke's not. None of us are."

"What are you talking about?" said Gray.

"Yeah, Mom," said Luke. "We *are* okay. We got away."

"We got away last night. You think we'll get away today? And if we get away today you think we'll get away tomorrow? They're not ever gonna stop looking for us. Never!"

"That's why we need help," said Gray. "The FBI. Or somebody. We have to tell 'em what happened. With the marshal and your husband and—"

"But Gray, you don't get it. We don't have any *proof.* Sure Joey's a fucking idiot. But Pat's really smart. Why do you think he's been a gangster his whole life and he's never spent one single night in the joint? He's careful. He covers his tracks. Nobody's ever been able to touch him."

Gray could see her point. He thought it over.

"I know you don't want to," he said. "But you and Luke probably need to go back in the protection program."

"And then we'll be right back where we were two weeks ago.

Living in some crappy place where we don't know anybody. And waiting for some asshole with a gun to show up."

"Gray'll protect us," said Luke.

"And who'll protect Gray? It's not fair to keep asking him to risk his life for us."

"Look," said Gray. "I love you. And I love Luke. And I'll do whatever I can to keep you guys safe."

For whatever reason this provoked more crying in Gina. She went through a couple more Kleenexes. As Gray and Luke waited it out. Finally she gave a shaky sigh.

"It's just no way to live. Like a fucking hunted animal."

The three of them were silent awhile. As the Lingos' Suburban cruised across the flatness of Texas.

"The joint just ain't the same since the fucking War on Drugs," said Lippy D'Alessio. "It's all filled up with nigger crackheads and pot-smoking hillbilly sons of bitches. Us real cons we're like the fucking Last of the Moheegans."

They didn't call him Lippy for nothing. Always moving his lips. And saying the same shit over and over. If Joey had heard that Last of the Moheegans line one time he'd heard it fucking fifty times.

"Last of the Moheegans," Lippy repeated.

They were sitting in the bleachers by the softball field. It was a sunny day and Joey was enjoying the warmth. Although he couldn't stop thinking about Gina and Luke.

"Yeah," said Lippy, "it just ain't like the old days."

"You mean when you was working for Capone?"

Lippy laughed. "I'm old, Joey. But I ain't *that* old."

Lippy loved to read supermarket tabloids and he had one in his spotted trembling hands now. He peered at a headline through heavy black-framed glasses.

"'Woman Gives Birth In McDonald's Restroom, Tries To Flush Baby Down Toilet.' What kinda shit is that huh? What kinda country are we becoming?"

"I dunno, Lippy."

"I tell you one thing. Any country that'll elect a nigger for president is going to the fucking dogs."

"I'm with you on that."

Fucking cunt. It was all her fault he was gonna be stuck in here for years having to listen to Lippy D'Alessio.

"He sure loves them ducks don't he?"

Lippy was looking down the first-base line at Jamie. Who was tossing out pieces of bread to his five ducks.

"Yeah. Fucking moron."

"Aw he ain't a moron. I 'member doing a ten-year bit in Terre Haute. They had all these fucking chipmunks. Cutest little motherfuckers you ever saw. Lotsa guys used to feed 'em. They was like pets, Joey, you know what I mean?"

Joey snorted. "Pets. Never understood the fucking point."

He stood up and went down the bleachers and headed toward Jamie. Not that he had anything in particular he wanted to say to him. It was just something to do.

He saw Glaspers. The guard. Moving his index finger around on the screen of his smartphone.

"Hey Glaspers. How much would it cost me to get me one of them?"

"A lot, Joey."

"Can you get fuck movies on it?"

"Sure. Anything you want."

"Well get me one."

"I'll see what I can do."

He moved past Glaspers. Jamie saw him coming and waved. Like he was real happy to see him. Like it'd been days since they'd seen each other. Instead of ten minutes. He must've been dropped on his head when he was a fucking baby or something.

And then he saw two guys. They'd been ambling along near Jamie. But now suddenly they were running right at him.

Jamie turned to meet them. Dropping the bread. As the ducks took wing.

Jamie tried to fight them off. They were flailing their arms wildly then Joey saw a spurt of blood and saw they were holding shanks.

He looked over his shoulder for Glaspers. But Glaspers was gone.

When he looked back at Jamie he saw he was on his back. The two guys above him and stabbing him quickly and methodically in the chest. Like they had ice picks and they were chipping away at a block of ice.

"Ima cut yo dick off!"

Joey turned. It was Little Willie. His eyes wide and showing their whites. Another black guy was with him. He was big and ripped. He looked like that football player. The one with the big mouth. Terrell Owens.

Joey ran. But he felt a blade entering his back and fell. Then he was being stabbed in the back in the same way as Jamie. *That cunt* he thought. As the ducks wheeled above the yard then disappeared over the wall.

She knew somehow. That her son was dead. She had started to know a lot of things she had no way of knowing. The boundaries between herself and everything else had been growing increasingly permeable. So the bird outside her window was a snowstorm in the Arctic was Millie sitting in this chair was a comet looping around the sun was her son lying dead in Pennsylvania. Thus it was not an occasion for grief. There was only the joy the joy the joy the joy.

Cicala shook his head. Looking at her.

"Ah Millie," he sighed.

"Don't be sad, Mr. Pat," said Eliana. "She is happy. Can't you see?"

"You shoulda seen her. Twenty years ago. *Ten* years ago. You shoulda seen her."

"She is hungry."

"Yeah? How can you tell?"

Eliana shrugged. "I don't know. I make something for her to eat. Maybe you too?"

"No. I'm not hungry." He put his hand on his stomach and his face looked sour. "My stomach."

Eliana laughed. "Oh Mr. Pat. You and your estomach!"

They left Millie's bedroom. Went down the hallway and started down the wide staircase. *Why hasn't he fucking called me?* he thought, half aware she had dropped behind him. *What's this prick trying to hide?* then something made him turn and he saw the gun. A small revolver she was moving toward his head. He grabbed at it with his closest hand which was the left and there was a *bang* and blood spurted as a bullet passed through his palm. He yelled and threw a right hand that really clocked her. Breaking her nose and sending her slamming back into the wall. She dropped the gun and it clattered down the marble stairs. She started after it but he grabbed her and then punched her again and she took a spectacular tumble down the stairs past the gun and ended up on the landing. Cicala, blood dripping off his fingers, hurried down the stairs and picked the gun up and pointed it at her. She came to her feet and looked up at him. Blood pouring out of her nose.

"You cunt!" he screamed.

He was astonished that he had just been shot and by his fucking maid and his hand was hurting like hell but there was another feeling. Exultation. He was an old sick man and sure she was just a broad but she was healthy and strong and a third his age and look who had come out on top. Ever since he was a kid this one or that one had been coming after him but he was the one who was still standing. That was why they called him Pat the Cat. He had nine or ninety or nine hundred lives!

Bobby came running. Holding his gun. He came up a few of the steps and then stopped and looked with his mouth hanging open at Eliana and Cicala.

"What the fuck's going on?" he said.

"That cunt tried to kill me!"

"She did?"

"Shoot her!"

"Here?"

"Yeah! Fucking here!"

Eliana, hand over her bleeding nose, looked at Bobby. Smiling a little.

"Yes, Bobby," she said. "Shoot."

Bobby lifted his gun and shot Cicala in the face. He crumpled and dropped. Rolled down a couple of steps then stopped face up. Blood was streaming out of his shattered cheek. His eyes were closed but he was still raspily breathing.

"Otra vez!" said Eliana.

Bobby's face was twisted up and he was crying.

"Jesus, Pat. Jesus."

Then he shot Cicala through the forehead.

Eliana retrieved her gun. She looked down at Cicala. Then spat on him.

"Asqueroso repugnante viejo!"

She grabbed Bobby's arm.

"Come, Bobby. Let's go!"

Chuck's cell rang. He checked the caller ID then said: "Hi, Bobby."

He listened a moment.

"Okay. Great. I'll be in touch."

He was in a long limousine. In front with the driver. They were on the West Side Highway in Manhattan. Nearing the Lincoln Tunnel. He speed-dialed and then: "Yes," said Mr. Li. In the back of the limo.

A panel of dark glass separated him from the driver's compartment and there was dark glass in the windows all around. "That's good to hear," he said. "Thank you," then he put his phone down beside him on the seat.

He felt a sense of relief. The Cicalas had become more trouble than they were worth. Colorful anachronisms. And they had cost the System two of its best men. In futile pursuit of a frivolous goal. Which really was the final straw.

He did feel a touch of sadness for the elder Cicala though. There was something nearly Shakespearean in his tragic destiny. He didn't realize how alone at the end he actually was. Forsaken even by his faithful retainer, the charmingly named Bobby the Hump. Mr. Li had always liked Cicala. Even though ever since the Venezuelan woman had put the listening device in his kitchen he had known exactly what Cicala thought of him. But in a way his unfortunate attitudes were not his fault. He was trapped by his past. Like most men. Those who would thrive in the brave new world that was aborning would be pure creatures of the present moment. Hovering and flitting about like dragonflies on a bright summer morning as they sought out and captured everything of value on the earth.

He was on his way to Teterboro Airport in New Jersey. Where a private jet was waiting for him. His first destination: Montreal. After that: Aruba, São Paulo, Shanghai, Mumbai, Kuwait City, Belgrade, London. And then probably New York again. He was looking forward to the flight because he had set aside a little time for reading. He had a well-thumbed volume of the poems of Tennyson. His great-grandfather Aldersey had been working on a book on Tennyson when he died. He had a sort of stuffy reputation as the pompous poet laureate of Victorian England but his way with the English language was really wonderful. *"I am half sick of shadows," said the Lady of Shalott.* Mr. Li could say that line a thousand times and never tire of it.

They crossed the panhandles of Texas and Oklahoma then entered Kansas. Passing over prairie grasslands under an enormous sky. It wasn't long before Highway 54 took them right into Ansley.

Hard times had hit these parts. Downtown was just the dried-up husk of what it used to be. There were lots of old redbrick buildings with big empty windows. Western Auto, J.C. Penney, Clevenger's Drugstore, Scottie's Men's Wear, the jewelry store and the dime store and the barbershop—all were gone. And they had turned the movie theater where he had been so entranced by *E.T.* and *Beverly Hills Cop* into a multiplex then that had died too.

Gray looked at the handful of people he saw on the sidewalks and unsuccessfully tried to recognize somebody.

"You used to *live* here?" said Luke.

"Yeah. You look horrified."

"What was there to *do* here?"

"Actually quite a bit. We'd watch grass grow. We'd watch paint dry. Then sometimes we'd race our pet turtles."

Luke laughed.

"So you're gonna show us where you lived?" said Gina.

"Yep. The Grand Tour."

They passed through Ansley pretty fast. Just outside the city limits was a Walmart. Which to judge by the number of cars in the parking lot was doing a whole lot better than downtown. Then they drove by the fairgrounds and the skating rink which had closed down and a small used-car lot with red, white, and blue pennants which had once been the site of the Garber brothers' farm-equipment business.

They continued down the highway about four miles then Gray said: "Almost there." He turned off onto a small road with heavily patched pavement. They went by fences and fields and some cows and horses and occasional trees and a house here and a barn there.

Gina looked over at Gray. To see how he was doing. Because she knew coming home had to be a big deal for him. He looked tired and he hadn't shaved so there was a stubble of beard but beyond that he seemed like he always did.

He looked at her and smiled and she smiled back. She had felt a kindling of happiness in herself. Ever since he had said he loved her.

"When was the last time you were here?" she said.

"In 1996. For my brother's funeral."

"Do your sisters still live here?"

"No. They moved away a long time ago. This is it."

He turned left onto a bumpy dirt drive that led up to a house. A FOR SALE sign was stuck up out front. The house was obviously empty. No curtains hung in the windows. One windowpane was broken. The paint was peeling off. Two crows stood on the roof over the sagging porch. Watching with their bright dark eyes as they got out of the SUV.

"Does your family still own the house?" said Gina.

"No. The bank owns it."

Gray went to the back of the SUV and opened it. Took out the shovel the Lingos had used to bury Steve. Gina and Luke looked at each other.

"What's that for?" said Luke.

"I've got something I've gotta do," said Gray and then he looked at Gina. "Get your purse."

"Why?"

"Just get it. Okay?"

Continuing to be puzzled Gina shrugged. Went back in the Suburban and got her purse. Then she and Luke followed Gray as, shovel over shoulder, he walked off around the house.

They went by the ramshackle barn. Where Gray and Mason used to have corncob fights. With dusty sunlight shooting through the cracks in the plank wall.

The crows cawing stridently flew overhead. As if keeping an eye on them.

They reached a fenced field. Filled with weeds and tall brown grass that blew in what wind there was. A deeply rutted road if you could call it that ran next to the field and they walked up it.

"Mom," said Luke after a while, "I'm thirsty."

She went in her purse and pulled out a bottle of water. Luke drank from it then so did she. She was about to offer it to Gray when she saw he had stopped and was looking toward a tall cottonwood tree that was growing near the fence.

"Is that where he's buried?" she said.

Gray nodded.

Luke was staring at them. "Is that where *who's* buried?"

"When I was a kid," said Gray, "my father and my uncles killed somebody. Murdered him. They buried him right here."

Luke, who had seen a lot, seemed to take this information in stride.

"Why'd they kill him?"

"Because he was trying to help me. He was in the navy. He was a sailor," and he reached in his pocket. "Here's one of his dog tags."

He handed it to Luke. Who looked at the name embossed on it.

"He's got the same name as you."

Gray nodded.

"Was he related to you?"

"No. He was a stranger."

Luke eyed the shovel.

"And you're gonna dig him up?"

"No." He took the dog tag back from Luke. "I'm gonna give this back to him. As a way to—I don't know—honor him." Because it seemed too dramatic he didn't say what he was really thinking: *As a way to give his bones a name.*

Gina and Luke moved away a bit. Into the shade of the tree. As Gray began to dig.

The sun was a little past its meridian. It shined down on him and it was a warm day for November in Kansas and pretty soon he was sweating.

Gina sat with Luke in her arms. His eyes began to droop and then he fell asleep. From time to time Gray would look over at them and see Gina watching him. She would smile and Gray would feel very glad they were there.

It was quiet except for the sounds the shovel made in the dirt and the chirps and cheeps of birds and the cawing crows. There were several of them now. Flying or hopping about or landing briefly in the tree or on the fence before flapping away. It was clear they thought the farm belonged to them now.

"Are you sure you've got the right spot?" said Gina after a while.

"I'm sure," said Gray then a minute or two later the shovel blade struck something. He put the shovel aside and leaned down and, like a careful archaeologist uncovering some ancient artifact, brushed the dirt away. A long slender brownish bone was revealed. Whether it was from an arm or a leg he wasn't sure. Sometimes that night seemed like a dream but this hard piece of bone was no dream. He took the dog tag out of his pocket and placed it by the bone. And then he stood up and turned toward the tree.

"Gina? Bring me the diamonds."

She stared at him. "What?"

"You heard me."

"No. You're crazy."

Luke was waking up.

"Mom. What's going on?"

"Luke and me, we need them," said Gina. "We won't have anything without them. Nothing! Just the clothes on our backs!"

"Gina," said Gray, "I'm not going another mile with you. As long as you have those diamonds."

"Mom, please!" said Luke.

Reluctantly she opened her purse. Took out the leather bag. Then she walked over to Gray and handed it to him. He emptied it. The diamonds tumbling out in a glittering heap. Beside the dog tag. Then he stepped out of the hole and grabbed his shovel.

The filling in went much faster than the digging out. He leaned on his shovel in front of the low mound of fresh earth. Sweating and a little out of breath.

"Well. I guess that's it."

But he just kept standing there. A change stole slowly over his face. Gina and Luke were looking at him.

"Gray?" said Gina. "Are you all right?"

And then an anguished sound escaped from Gray. Letting the shovel fall he sank to his knees. He was breathing hard and tears were running down his face.

"*I'm sorry,*" he said. "*I'm sorry. I'm so sorry. I'm sorry.*"

Luke in a panic looked from Gray to his mother.

"Mom, what do we do?!"

They held on to Gray. Till he was done with his weeping. And then the three of them stood up and they walked away.